WELCOME T
THE FAMOU

DUKE The owner. He built it and made it the celebrity showplace of the world.

PETER The heir. He refined his father's easy style into hatred and used it to destroy.

BRETTE Married to Peter, loyal to Duke . . . and in love with the one man she could never have.

NICK The manager. Every woman in New York wanted to go to bed with him. And most did.

SAYDEE Duke should have married her, but he did the next best thing. He loved her all his life . . .

Plus: The Countess, the Star, the TV Critic . . . you'll meet them all at

THE BEST TABLE

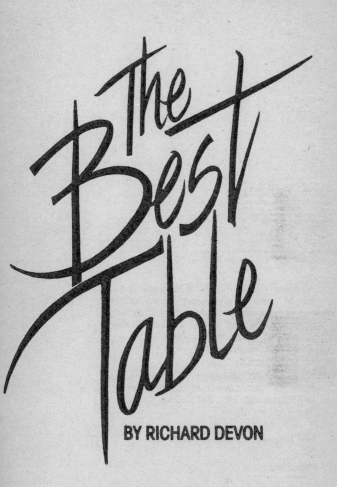

The Best Table

BY RICHARD DEVON

A JOVE BOOK

First Jove edition published October 1981

First printing

Printed in the United States of America

Jove books are published by Jove Publications, Inc., 200 Madison Avenue, New York, NY 10016

For Bill Grose,
who came up with the idea
in the first place.

A life of pleasure requires an aristocratic setting to make it interesting or really conceivable.

—*The Life of Reason*, George Santayana

PROLOGUE

Chapter One

MARION DE PETRIE is a good-looking, rather ordinary woman in her late forties about whom an extraordinary anecdote—perfectly true—is told. Marion once refused the first table on the left at Duke's 44 Club.

It occurred during Morty Landau's short and terrible reign over Universal Studios. Marion was married to Morty at the time and was in New York on a sweltering August Saturday afternoon attempting to decide on the most advantageous method for becoming unmarried.

She had grown up in Chicago and spent her early adult life in Beverly Hills and knew, at the time, little about the high life as lived in Manhattan. Besides that basic ignorance, Marion asserts that she had good reason to refuse that damned first table on the left. She had a thing about round tables and it was all jammed up against the banquette and she could tell just by looking at it that it was the sort of table that was continually jostled by waiters. "I'd have had to spend the entire meal waiting for a spilled Bloody Mary to come cascading down my back." And then everyone who went into the dining room from the bar had to pass by. "All I needed was for one of Morty's spies to tell him I was lunching at 44 with the lawyers Cohen."

And there was the incontrovertible fact that the only really good view from the table was directly into the Club Room where the bar was ridiculously crowded for two o'clock on an August Saturday in Manhattan.

What Marion required from 44 was seclusion, the sort of quiet, refined meal that passes for elegant dining in Beverly Hills and Chicago.

"They couldn't have known who I was," she said when she first told the story to her best friend in the more comfortable atmosphere of the Beverly Hills Hotel's Polo Lounge. "But I told them straight off that I was Mrs. Morton Landau and that table wouldn't do at all. The maître d' did a complete turnaround. Couldn't have been more apologetic. Immediately showed us up to the most elegant dining room. Sublime, exactly the sort of meal I envisioned having at 44."

Marion's friend, a whey-faced ICM agent named Nancy, who knows her New York as well as she knows her Beverly Hills, let out a yelp and then burst into what was for her a fit of hysterical laughter. After carefully blotting her eyes, Nancy explained to Marion that what she had given up was the one item in the world—well, in their world—that only a subtle and perfectly balanced combination of money, power, social standing, background, blue blood, and beauty could buy: the best table at 44.

Though Marion has tried, she has never been offered the best table again. Once, with Rose Kennedy and Mary Lindsay in tow, she was seated at table seven, the Kennedys' usual luncheon spot. And, small blessings, she has never again had to be seated in the cool, upholstered elegance of the upstairs J. J. Walker Room where the forever unknown and unknowing are directed.

But though she has pleaded and cajoled, bribed and flirted, and, on occasion, demanded, Marion Landau de Petrie has had to learn to live with the fact that the best table at 44 is never to be hers. As Nancy, now a senior vice-president in the production wing of Metro, likes to remind her: "You had your chance, Marion, and you muffed it."

For half a century the first table on the left at 44 has been a barometer for Wall Street and City Hall, for Broadway and Park Avenue, for Washington and Hollywood, indicating who is in favor and who is not. The best table at 44 can never be reserved. Nor do 44's regulars often get the opportunity to dine at it. They have their own zealously guarded tables. Early on it was established that if 44 were to be the closest one could get to a public private eating club, then there had to be a place reserved for honorary members, for visiting aristocracy who find themselves in Manhattan and require a perfect situation in which to dine.

That situation is, of course, the best table at 44. Morty Landau's ex-wife notwithstanding, a great many precautions have been taken over the years to insure that the wrong people do not get shown to the first table on the left in the main dining room. The most elaborate safeguard against some unknowing neophyte headwaiter repeating the Landau fiasco is 44's card system. Assiduously developed over the years, it contains three kinds of cards in its wooden cabinet located in the manager's office: pink, denoting those barred from any table at 44 for real or imagined misconduct; blue, indicating a certain amount of cordiality is to be displayed, but nothing as ostentatious as a trip to the best table; and white, symbolizing those dear friends of the house who have a crack at the first table on the left if they call early enough and if their celebrity is stronger than other white cards calling on the same day.

Lawrence, 44's erstwhile maître d', is an unabashed snob, taking his cue from 44's cofounders. Preference is always given to European aristocracy. If Princess Elizabeth of Yugoslavia and Joan Mondale arrive at the same moment, Joan gets shown to table three while Elizabeth is taken to the best table.

Those media men and women who are allowed entry into 44 and who usually wind up at the bar keep a wary eye on the best table to observe which senator with presidential aspirations gets seated there and which senatorial presidential aspirant is taken to table four or into the Club Room, an indication of another sort of favorite son at 44.

Five weeks after Chappaquiddick broke in *The New York Times,* Ted Kennedy and a shaky Joan were taken directly to the first table on the left by the Duke himself, thus illustrating 44's abiding faith in the Kennedy clan and vice versa.

When Barbara Walters and Harry Reasoner appeared simultaneously during the height of their jockeying-for-position feud at ABC, Miss Walters was taken into the Club Room. Reasoner accepted the first table on the left with his usual offhand graciousness. Duke's 44 is loyal, too.

It has often been said that if the best table shouldn't, logically be New York's best table, then 44 shouldn't be numbered among New York's best restaurants. It has three rooms set aside for dining in the old brownstone in which it is located. The Club Room is to the right, off the foyer when you enter and where the bar hides the entrances to the ladies' and men's rooms. To the left off the foyer is the main dining room, which is low ceilinged and dark, paneled in mahogany and not unlike a dining room in a London club. The J. J. Walker Room, reached by a stairway at the end of the main dining room, is the largest and most comfortable of the dining rooms and, as indicated, the least desirable.

The food at Duke's 44 Club is well prepared by half a dozen chefs under the direction of their chief, a thin, perpetually ailing man named Maurice Gotlib. The menu emphasizes American cuisine with such specialties as Duke's chili at lunch, steaks at dinner.

It is always noisy and usually smoky (the low ceilings on the first floor trap the smoke) and rarely uncrowded. It is intensely intimidating for the uninitiated.

Duke's 44 Club is a New York institution, despite all of its shortcomings. For members of the highest international social, financial, political, and artistic circles, being in New York and not dining at 44 is akin to visiting Rome and not breaking bread with the Pope. Bob Benchley, that archtypical man about New York of the thirties, called 44 his "home away from home." George Kauffman, who had wooed and won Mary Astor at the Club Room's table three, called it his bachelor digs, while such men as J. Edgar Hoover, Laurence Olivier and David Eisenhower have all, at one time or another, referred to 44 as their New York club.

The men and women—Princess Grace, Margaret Truman, Mary McCarthy when Lillian Hellman isn't on the premises—who make 44 their New York headquarters treat it with the sort of awe usually associated with religious institutions.

And indeed there is a sort of icon that presides over the diners in the Club Room. It is the famous Chamberlain portrait which hangs next to the bar. A full-length painting, slightly larger than life, it shows a man with slicked-back dark hair and large black eyes. He is smoothly handsome with high cheekbones, a strong nose, and a cleft chin. He seems remarkably comfortable in his white tie and tails. One hand holds a cigar while the other rests casually in a trouser pocket. He looks as if he is about to ask a beautiful young woman to dance or, perhaps, to make love. Beneath the tailored clothes and the civilized patina, the artist has managed to capture the easy animal grace, the consumate style that was the trademark of the man five decades of notables called Duke.

Chapter Two

DUKE GREENE pushed the Scotty away but the black dog, Hector, insisted on climbing up onto the red leather sofa. "You're a lousy dog," Duke said, giving way, allowing Hector to bury himself under the sable throw one of his ex-wives—he supposed it was Irene in her extravagant period—had insisted upon having. "If you slobber all over me . . .," Duke started to say to the dog who had already closed his eyes and seemed to be sleeping. He's not above feigning sleep, Duke thought, giving in and petting Hector behind the ears, allowing his own head to rest against the pillow his manservant had placed there for him. He refused, categorically, to call Robert a valet, no matter what Robert chose to call himself.

He remembered, quite vividly, the place where he had first met Robert. All of his memories, lately, seemed especially documentary like, full of Technicolor set pieces and verbatim dialogue. If Chris Isherwood is a camera, Duke thought, then I'm a goddamned video-tape machine. He closed his eyes and he could see Robert quite clearly, at the German prison camp at Tubize. It had been 1943. Robert had been seventeen and thin as a metal hanger. Duke had been thirty-three and ill with some unspecified disease. Together they had escaped and gotten themselves to the coast and then to England where Robert was "rehabilitated" and sent back to the front lines and Duke was sent down to the hotel turned into a hospital in Torquay.

It turned out that his lung had been punctured by shrapnel though Duke couldn't be certain just when that had happened. "You're going to take a long time to heal," the doctor had said. That was certainly the truth. He never did see battle again, but he had written to Robert offering him a job in New York if and when the war ever ended.

Robert had turned up at 44 a year after the war to take him up on his offer. Thirty-some-odd years later, he remained as thin as a wire hanger and not much more talkative. Duke still wondered what Robert did for sex. For all he knew, there might be a Mrs. Robert tucked away in Long Island City.

He shook his head. He didn't want to think of the taciturn Robert. He wanted to remember the hospital. He had had a small, selfish triumph there, and he still enjoyed thinking about it.

When he arrived at the hospital, there had been a huge parcel waiting for him. He and his fellow officers and the nurses with their bad teeth and good-humored starchy smell had unwrapped the monstrous package. It was filled with tinned turkeys and hams, pounds of Russian caviar, and the pure butter cakes Duke had doted on. There was no note, but it was obvious to Duke that there was only one person in the world besides Churchill who could have put those ill-gotten goods together in the midst of a war that was leaving millions starving. That was, of course, his best friend and partner, Cecil Townsend.

Even the nurses let themselves be cajoled into taking part in the feast that followed, wheeling him out onto the sun-warmed terrace of the former Hotel Imperial, allowing his fellow patients to partake of the unexpected picnic. The usually grim English coast looked cheerful in the light of this holiday from privation and war.

It was then that a thin and pale Charles Lindbergh, surrounded by a cortege of fancifully uniformed men and women, strode across the terrace toward him. Before the war, in '39, Duke himself had politely asked Lindbergh not to return to 44; his political views were unacceptable.

"I never did care for Jewish hors d'oeuvres," Lindbergh had said, leaving.

But then, in 1943, he seemed not nearly so certain. Without registering surprise at finding the wounded flier eating caviar with a thin silver spoon, he presented Duke with a gold watch on behalf of some obscure aviation society.

There had never been such a society, Duke thought, putting his hand in his dressing-gown pocket, coming out with the gold watch, opening it, laughing again at the inscription which had used his given name, Jacob Louis Greeneberg.

Not that he blamed Lindbergh. It had been the sort of publicity stunt Lindbergh himself would have been incapable of. He may have been an anti-Semite and a Nazi partisan, but it was naïveté and innocence, not cynicism, that had made him so.

Lindbergh's friends had set up the watch presentation, arranged for it to be carefully recorded by Pathé cameras, by CBS and NBC radio correspondents, by the local AP photographer. It had been his friends who had worried that any part Lindbergh might come to play in postwar American politics had been whittled away, until it had disappeared, by his pro-Nazi pronouncements.

Even in 1943, it had been too late to win back popular sympathy. Or private for that matter. Though Duke had accepted the watch and even allowed himself to shake Lindbergh's strong, thin hand for the cameras, there was never to be a table for Lindbergh at 44, no matter how many days or weeks in advance a reservation was made.

"But, Duke," his second wife, Irene, objected in that British voice which he had found so seductive. "Lindy is a dope. He didn't act out of malice. You can't bar a man because he's a dope."

"Best goddamned reason I ever heard," he had told her, and she had given him that cool, appraising look of hers which was supposed to reduce him to, if not jelly, at least a very fine aspic. He had picked up too many things in London, he thought, putting the watch back in his pocket.

Things. He liked to hold on to things. He had closets and closets filled with things. Most worthless, some invaluable. But things. His son, Peter, had called him an anal retentive, and he had told Peter to watch who he was calling an asshole; but still, he had to admit, he loved his things.

He had gotten that trick of holding on to his possessions from his mother, that rock-hard lady who had loved him so much. He tried to summon up her image, but all he could envision was a cool day in Warm Springs, Georgia, and Eleanor Roosevelt coming at him with a cup of tea.

I wonder why, he asked himself, I'm suddenly so caught up in the war years. He had a moment of pain and was about to call Robert or SayDee but it passed and he suddenly knew. So many of those years had been spent in fear and bravado. Fear of dying. False bravery defying small people and ideas, like Lindbergh and his anti-Semitism.

I'm not so brave now, he thought. In the war there was a fifty-fifty chance he would die. Now the odds were a hundred to one he would. "And I'm still afraid," he said out loud. "I'm still so goddamned afraid of dying." He could smell the fear, and he hated it.

He threw the fur rug aside, causing Hector to whimper, and with a certain amount of effort managed to get himself off the red leather sofa. He secured the blue and white polka-dot silk robe SayDee had bought him at Sulka with that unerring terrible taste of hers and went to the tiny padded elevator in the foyer that rode between his duplex and his restaurant.

He emerged in the Club Room and, allowing his eyes to become used to the dim night lights, made his way behind the bar and poured himself a glass of Drambuie. He liked the glass with its odd facets and narrow stem. He remembered the day Cecil had taken him to the old Baccarat showroom on Fifth Avenue and tried to convince him to stock 44 with "really fine crystal."

"Hey, Cecil, we got maybe two grand left in the bank. Mookie Goldstein can fill the joint with glasses for a couple of hundred bucks and you want me to spend half of our bankroll?"

"Perhaps if I leave you alone," the saleswoman—French, with pockmarked skin and furious eyes—said, going to the door, looking around as if to inventory each piece of crystal in the event, in the likelihood, one should be stolen.

Cecil waited until she had shut the door behind her before he uncoiled himself from the upholstered chair he had been lounging in and walked to the counter where he picked up a brandy glass with exquisitely cut facets and held it in front of

Duke's eyes. The sunlight streaming in through the high window caused it to turn into a rainbow of colors. "Poor Dukey. I've taken you out of Delancey Street but I can't seem to take Delancey Street out of you." He twirled the glass around. "You want, in your very own words, a hotsy-totsy club, do you not? You want the crème de la crème to drink your bootleg booze, to rub knees under your tables, to spread the word throughout the land what a superior speak Duke Greene and his pal, Cecil Townsend, are running? Well, the club will neither be hotsy-totsy nor talked about when there's inferior glassware on the tables. You can get away with commercial linen, not quite first-rate cutlery, even—perhaps, especially—mediocre cuisine. But the gentle folk of the world know when you're trying to do the cheap with lightweight, undistinguished glassware. Believe me, my dear, they will turn up their snub noses and take their custom elsewhere." He placed the glass on Duke's head and turned for support to the girl standing at the window, looking out at what traffic there was on Fifth Avenue on a winter's morning in the early 1930's. "Tell him, Phebe."

She had dark hair which fitted her like a cap and violet eyes of such intensity that they nearly obliterated her other features, all of a particular cleanness of line which spelled money, a good deal of money.

"I don't know what I'm doing with you two, wasting my time," she said, turning, walking around Cecil, taking the glass from Duke's head and placing it back on the display counter. "I should be down at the settlement house helping old lady Harkness sort clothing for the jumble or at home studying for my finals . . ."

"I thought Vassar girls were too finished to take finals," Cecil interrupted.

"Instead," Phebe said, ignoring him, "I'm at Baccarat looking at crystal that costs what most men today earn in a week, if they earn anything." She sat down in the chair Cecil had vacated. "I could understand it if you two wanted to open a school for the blind or even a restaurant for the needy. The world is in a terrible depression and you two lounge lizards are talking about establishing what no one needs or wants now: another fancy speakeasy."

"That's what I adore about you, Phebe," Cecil said. "Your

bleeding heart. If you once gave me any encouragement, I'd open a soup kitchen."

"That's just what you don't need, encouragement. Duke, what *are* you doing now?"

He had pressed the button which summoned back the saleswoman. "I'm going to order the glassware. Cecil's right, as usual. Baccarat has a nice feel to it."

It still did. Duke sipped at the Drambuie and laughed, remembering how much in love Cecil had been with Phebe, how involved he himself had been with his speakeasy.

He looked up at his portrait, painted a few years after 44 had opened. He wished Cecil had allowed himself to be painted, too. But he had refused. "Modest little bastard," Duke said, pouring himself another finger, laughing to himself, thinking what a fuss SayDee and the doctor and maybe even Robert would kick up if they knew he was downstairs in the middle of the morning, drinking Drambuie out of a Baccarat glass.

He turned up the light on the far wall behind the bar where the photographs were hung, looking for one of Cecil. Each picture was framed in black ebony. Nick had complained about the cost of framing new photographs, suggesting they switch to plastic.

Not bloody likely. Plastic frames were like cheap glass. They weren't nice to look at, they weren't nice to touch. Close up, he couldn't see the pictures as clearly as he wished. His eyes had gone tricky on him in his old age. He could only see sharply when he was far away. He walked across the Club Room into the main dining room and stopped for a moment, waiting for his strength to return. Then he carefully righted the two chairs that had been placed on the best table, put down his drink, and slid onto the leather banquette. The thought came to him that he didn't mind the dying as much as he minded the physical discomfort, the exhaustion, the pain.

He sipped at his drink again and stared across the entrance foyer into the Club Room at the wall photographs. He caught sight of Bea Lillie, with a peacock's feather in her hair and a grin on her wonderfully expressive face and thought that perhaps it would have been better to have gone as she had, her brain first and then her body.

"I have a thirty-year-old mind in a seventy-year-old body,"

he said aloud. "It's not fair." He started to finish his drink and then stopped, putting his glass down. He didn't know if he would have the strength to get himself back upstairs.

He didn't try to summon it. He had plenty of time to get upstairs. Months. Or weeks. Or surely, at the least, days. He had never lived in the past until recently, when he found there was no future and too little present.

Though he knew he was afraid of death, he also knew that he didn't mind dying. He couldn't do so many of the things he had once gotten such pleasure from. Eating. Loving. Even that remote pleasure, polo, which he had taken up because Cecil had told him it was a gentleman's sport. He missed the horses he had kept in Connecticut. In the dim light, with his new long-distance vision, he could make out a photo of the last of his horses, and perhaps the most beloved, Bloomers, standing straight and tall in front of her stable.

Laura, his first wife, had called him a spendthrift. She had wanted him to live in pristine Protestant penury, practicing her own family's form of inverse prestige, burying money in banks and blue chip stocks and old masters.

He preferred his Bloomers. Below her were Al Jolson, Eddie Cantor and Fanny Brice, mugging, flanked by separate photos of Ike in his uniform and Mamie in one of those terrible dresses she affected.

Next to Mamie was a studio portrait of Willie Maugham, for once without Gerald.

He closed his eyes, reveling in the momory of an evening in the mid-1930's, a special birthday supper Gerald had arranged for Maugham. In those days Maugham was a fairly courageous homosexual though he very rightly kept a certain facade of heterosexuality for the public. He didn't want to go to prison, and he wanted his books to be read. Consequently there were two women at the table, lesser members of the British aristocracy, "beards," disguising the virtually undisguisable fact that Maugham and Gerald were lovers.

Just before the dessert was to be served—some sort of flaming ice cream, Duke remembered—Cole Porter, Cecil Beaton, and Noel Coward burst into the restaurant, all three wearing white tie and white tails, looking like naughty chorus boys. They grouped themselves around Maugham's table, the best table, and, hats in hand, sang a song Beaton took credit for because the other two wouldn't. Though he remembered the title—"Willie, Won't You Come Out Tonight?"—Duke couldn't remember much more except that everyone in the restaurant had clapped heartily, even Maugham, though Gerald had pretended to be shocked. Then the three men had kissed Maugham on the cheek and ran out to the waiting limousine which had been, of course, an all-white Daimler.

Duke had laughed but he had to ban them from his club for six weeks. He wasn't going to have his guests embarrassed and even though Noel called him and said he would rather die than live without Duke 44's chili, Duke was adamant. But twice a week, for the entire six weeks, he sent Coward double portions of the chili, free of charge, in large Statforshire containers.

He tried to see who was standing in the photo just below Maugham's and as he leaned forward for a better view, the glass fell out of his hands and onto the carpeted floor. The glass hadn't broken but the sticky liquor had spilled, causing an ugly reddish-brown stain to appear on the gray carpet. Duke looked around for a napkin, but the soiled ones had been collected and the fresh ones not yet put out.

He took the silk handkerchief from the breast pocket of his robe and began to dab ineffectually at the stain when he realized the elevator doors had opened and closed. He looked up. SayDee was coming toward him, her hands clasped together in front of her in a characteristic gesture indicating she was worrying about him.

He sat up, still holding the handkerchief. He expected a lecture and supposed he deserved one.

"Duke," she said, standing over him, putting her hands on his head, drawing him close to those once famous hips in much the way his mother used to console him as a child. After a moment she got down on her knees and put her head next to his and her arms around his shoulders and he could smell that delicious aroma of Joy, cleaning fluid, and SayDee's own special chorus-girl scent that always seemed to envelope her. "Baby," she said in her whiskey voice. "Baby, what are you crying about?"

He pushed her away and sat back, putting his hands to his face. It was true, he had been crying. He allowed her to dry his tears with the hem of her robe. "I'm crying," he said, not altogether truthfully, "because I'm a weak old man who can't hold a glass in his hands. Look at that carpet."

"Lawrence will get that out in two seconds. He may be your maître d' but he can give any housewife a run for her money in the stain department." She took his hand and kissed it.

"I'm also crying," Duke said, "because all my functions are going fast. All I seem to have left is my mind which is like a once beautiful room filled with old flowers and yellowed photographs. I'm crying," Duke said, standing up, putting one hand on SayDee's shoulder, allowing her to support him, "because I'm dying, SayDee, and I'm not at all certain I want to. Part of me wants to go to sleep. I'm exhausted. The other part wants to stick around, to see what happens to Peter, to Brette, and yes, goddamn it, to Nick and my club."

They had reached the elevator where Robert was waiting with the wheelchair. Duke sunk into it gratefully. "Now stop it," SayDee said, taking his hand as they rode up to the duplex, allowing her free hand to wander up to her bright pink curls, curls which hadn't changed color or shape since Duke had kissed her twenty-five years before and forever changed her life. "I want you to stop it, Duke. You should be in bed, resting up for Friday. It's not every day 44 has a fiftieth anniversary."

He looked up and realized it was she who was crying now, and he began patting her hand, comforting her.

Later, after SayDee had gotten him into the enormous canopied and mirrored bed they shared, Duke found his mind, so much more remarkable in its tenacity than his hands or his heart or his eyes, still working, still remembering. Now, as he looked up at his reflection in the Art Deco canopy's blue mirror (what a dreadful piece of work that bed was), he found that he could recall the photograph under Maugham's and he wondered why he hadn't immediately recognized its subject.

He remembered exactly when it had been taken.

Chapter Three

In September of 1930, the newly appointed dean of men for the University of Pennsylvania was faced with his first seemingly insoluble problem: what to do with the sudden surplus of freshman dormitory rooms. The preceeding year's stock-market crash had caused many parents to change their minds about sending their child to an expensive Ivy League school like Penn, and the dean suddenly had all those empty rooms on his hands.

He solved the problem by closing nearly half of the dormitories and doubling up boys of widely disparate backgrounds in the rooms that remained. Usually boys from similar backgrounds were roomed together (preppies with preppies, Jews with Jews) but these were, as Dean Hackett liked to say, extraordinary times.

Thus Jacob Louis "Duke" Greeneberg and Cecil Barnett Townsend found themselves sharing one of the lesser suites facing the large quad in Harrington "A." Dean Hackett hadn't acted solely on whimsy when he put the two boys together. There were similarities. They were both twenty years old (far too old to be freshmen). And they both stood about as much chance, from the dean's point of view, of lasting through the semester as the demented janitor in Harrington "B."

It had taken the combined efforts of Duke and his mother, Etta, to earn the money to send Duke to Penn. Etta worked for two decades for Macy's head accountant, taking care of the books, putting her money under the mattress in the Henry Street apartment in which she and her son lived, waited for the day when he would go to college and become a "genuine Yankee."

Etta, who had arrived in New York early in 1910, widowed (she said) and pregnant, surviving the journey from Poland to England to the United States without doing any real damage to her health, lived only for her son. It was she who nicknamed him Duke (after the hero in the first nickelodeon film she had seen, the *Duke of Barret Street)* and filled him with dreams of becomming a merchant prince on the lines of a Straus or a Gimbel.

And it was Etta who had found Duke an after-school job running booze for Mookie Goldstein who had, as he liked to say, the carriage trade in the palm of his hand. It was while he was delivering boxes and crates of genuine imported champagne and Scotch to houses and penthouses and merely lavish apartments on Fifth Avenue and Central Park South that Duke became enamored of the good life, the life of pleasure. He quietly discarded Etta's dream for him and began to create one for himself. He liked the way the blond women who occasionally could be glimpsed over servants' shoulders spoke and moved. He liked the way their husbands and protectors said "cahn't" and "ahnt" rather than "can't" and "aunt." He began to say "cahn't" and "ahnt" which resulted in a certain amount of difficulty at the Thomas Alva Edison High School down on Pitt Street, but Duke could and did take care of himself in the fisticuff department and what was a black eye, after all, compared to that life of pleasure he dreamed about?

By the time he reached the University of Pennsylvania, where every budding merchant prince, Etta had ascertained, started out, he knew he didn't want to be there. He wanted to be in New York wearing a black tie and a wing collar, sitting in an exclusive speak, drinking pink gin and listening to the vibrato voice of his glorious blond companion.

When Etta died from what was diagnosed as pneumonia immediately after midterms, ecstatically happy with her son's grades, Duke was plunged into heart-wrenching despair. But just below the sorrow and the regret he knew he felt a new emotion, and that was relief.

After the funeral, after he collected the money Etta had stuffed her mattress with ("And wasn't I right?" she had asked after the Harmonia Bank on East Broadway had closed its doors), he returned to Philadelphia and the university, mostly because there was no other place for him to go. And also because he was still in a state of shocked sorrow and wanted solace, which he knew he would get from Cecil.

Cecil Barnett Townsend, well known by armies of undergraduates at Princeton, Dartmouth, and Brown—the three schools he had attended prior to Penn—was descended from a family that had come over if not on the Mayflower, at least on the very next boat.

His father, a monocled, bearded, angry man, had died during the Great War at Flanders, leaving his wife with Cecil, family pride, and little money. Emma Townsend, a frail, brown-haired woman, soon rectified that by bleaching her hair and marrying Sven Stieber, a sort of Norwegian Ivar Kreuger.

Four years after that marriage, in 1922, Emma disappeared from the town house Stieber had bought for her on Forty-fourth Street just east of Fifth Avenue in Manhattan. It had been Christmas Eve.

She left Stieber without a chauffeur and with her thirteen-year-old son. Stieber developed a disheartening case of what he called "der blues" and a genuine affection for his wife's son.

When Cecil found that his roommate at Penn was going to be a fellow named Duke Greeneberg, he shook his head and then the roommate's oversized hand and immediately went out to look for the friends he had known at boarding schools and the other universities he had been asked to leave. He had learned, he thought, the valuable lesson that opposites may attract, but not for much longer than a half hour. Cecil liked the comfort of what he called his own kind.

Duke stayed in the bedroom off the living room he was to share with Cecil, attempting to commit to memory whole passages of Grollier's *Freshman English Handbook*. He felt isolated, and not a little frightened. All the other freshmen, even those several years younger than he, seemed to possess enormous reservoirs of poise and social savvy. To a man they all said ''ahnt'' when talking about their fathers' illustrious sisters.

It was not until the end of September that the roommates became friends. It was after Dean Hackett decided it was time to interview the two candidates he had already chosen for E. P. D. (Earliest Possible Dismissal).

He hadn't been introduced to either Duke or Cecil, but he had studied their records and had developed what he decided was a fairly accurate mental picture of the two men. He knocked on the door of their living room politely and stepped in, announcing who he was, sitting himself on the brown sofa that stood in the center of the room, crossing his legs, laying down the rules of freshman behavior.

The Jew, the dean thought, looked and acted exactly as he had known he would. He wore thick, rimless glasses, was pale and small and became increasingly insolent as the dean continued to speak. Whereas the young man with decent blood in his veins was tall with shiny black hair and deep blue eyes and the sort of profile the dean admired most in young men. He looked and acted like an heir to a great American tradition.

''My dear Townsend,'' the dean began, addressing Duke Greeneberg. Duke began to correct him, but Cecil, twisted up in the usual contortion he liked to get himself into, signaled Duke to be quiet. ''There's the question of what the women who make your beds should be tipped,'' the dean continued, looking at Duke. ''I don't suppose I have go to into that with you, Townsend,'' the fat man continued, then turned his attention for the first time to Cecil. ''But perhaps, Greeneberg, you should be made aware that the bed makers must get at least a dollar a month if we're to keep them happy.'' He smiled what he thought of as his ''least patronizing but still superior'' smile and turned back to the more presentable youth, prepared to speak to him about his uncle, who had been at Yale with the dean.

But the thin, sickly looking young man had stood up and was pointing at him—*pointing* at him—with his index finger. ''Has anyone ever told you, dear Dean Hackett, that you're a flaming asshole? No? Perhaps you simply weren't listening. I want you to listen now, dear Dean Hackett, and listen carefully. Get out of our rooms, Hackett. And never, ever return or I'll personally see to it that Penn never gets another penny of my family's money and I'll make certain that the powers that be know it was because of you." The dean stood up with some care, his face an apopleptic red.

"You're Townsend?"

"Marvelous, Hackett. Next time round you'll be dean of logic. Now get out. And one more caution, dear Dean: don't ever presume to instruct me or anyone else on how to disperse one's gratuities." Cecil walked across the room and opened the door, waiting until the fat man had walked through. "Gentlemen never do," he called after the departing dean.

"Jesus," Duke said.

"Cecil will do," Cecil said, polishing his glasses with a tired handkerchief, smiling up at Duke. "I don't suppose you'd like to come into my bedroom. No, no homosexual romp, so you can take that look off your handsome visage. I merely want you to sample a drop of the grape, homemade. You see," he said, taking Duke's arm, "I've set up a little still . . ."

For the three months they were to spend at the University of Pennsylvania, they were never out of one another's sight.

Cecil found Duke's lack of collegiate sophistication charming, and he enjoyed playing mentor. Duke was startled by Cecil's knowledge, by his ability to milk pleasure out of almost every situation, even subsequent run-ins with Dean Hackett.

Cecil took Duke to his tailor on Chestnut Street and directed the little man as he measured Duke for his first dinner jacket. When it was finished, he took Duke with him on the rounds of Main Line debutante parties, shortening his name to Greene because everyone, he said, was so fearfully anti-Semitic.

When they weren't at deb parties where Duke Greene was rather too much of an instant success for some mothers, they were perfecting the gin Cecil continued to make in his bathtub, occasionally selling it to undergraduates for three dollars a pint.

"It costs nearly that much to make it," Duke complained.

"Think of yourself, dear Duke, as a modern Carpathian

monk, bringing the pleasures of the vine to those who otherwise would go without,'' Cecil advised him. ''Though I must say, I've never seen anyone who looked less monklike. Helen Whitney virtually had her hands down your trousers the other night at the Warwick. What did you do with her in the back of that Packard?''

''What do you think?'' Duke asked.

''Dear God! I've been trying to get into her pants since we were both seven, attending Miss Martha's dancing school for upper-class tots, bumping our back seats together during the Mexican hat dance.''

When Duke returned from his mother's funeral, he told Cecil he was leaving Penn.

''Leaving me all alone to fend off dear Dean Hackett, you coward.''

''I only came back to say good-bye. My mother had five grand stuffed in her mattress. I figure there's no reason to spend it here.''

''Too true. As it happens, I am also leaving these hallowed grounds. Coincidently there's been a death in my family.'' He handed Duke a copy of that morning's *Inquirer*. ''Sven Stieber Takes Life'' was the headline. ''Financial empire in ruins'' was the subhead.

''You're broke?'' Duke asked.

''More or less,'' Cecil said, putting his arm around his friend's shoulder, which was a little awkward but he managed. ''Except for the house. Years ago Sven put it in my name. He wasn't all bad, you know.'' Cecil turned toward his bedroom and kicked open the door. A half-packed steamer trunk stood in the middle of the room. ''Let's go to New York, Duke, and live in my town house on your five grand and see what we can see. Shall we?''

What they saw when they arrived at 44 East Forty-fourth Street were the moving men repossessing Sven Stieber's handmade reproduction antiques.

Cecil sat on his steamer trunk while Duke paced as the men brought what seemed like an inexhaustible supply of fake Louis XIV consoles out of the house. It was a large town house, some fifty feet wide, a hundred feet deep, and when they were finally allowed entry, they found themselves in a handsome marble-floored foyer facing an enormous Victorian staircase. To their right was a paneled smoking room where Sven had had a bar installed to serve his Wall Street friends. To their left was another paneled room that ran the full length of the house.

"Sven thought paneling was the epitome of masculine good taste," Cecil said, standing in the middle of the room. "And perhaps he wasn't all that wrong."

All that the repossessors had left them were Sven's extensive wardrobe which providentially fitted Duke ("My dear, you'll be able to go anywhere," Cecil said as he got his friend into his late stepfather's tails), the mahagony bar in the smoking room, and, just inside the drawing room, up against the three windows that looked out on Forty-fourth Street, a round mahagony table and two chairs.

Cecil went into the smoking room where his trunk stood and began removing from it his home-brew apparatus, taking it with him into the bathroom off the smoking room. "Sven was always clever about where he put his baths," Cecil called out as Duke sat down at the table in the drawing room and lit a cigar he had found in Sven's closet.

"My mother left me five grand," Duke called out.

"Yes, so you said," Cecil shouted back.

"You know, Cecil, I've always wanted to open my own speak," Duke went on, running his hand over the smooth wood of the table.

"There are easier ways to throw away money," Cecil said, giving up on the bathtub for the moment, joining his friend in the empty drawing room. He took a silver flask from his jacket pocket and offered it to Duke. "Baby, it's cold outside. Not to mention inside."

"I figure," Duke said, standing up, ignoring the flask, "that it will cost us three grand to square the cops." He began to walk up and down the length of the room. "And the rest for some more tables, glasses, hootch."

"There's always Cecil's Home Remedy."

"We'll get better and cheaper from Mookie Goldstein."

"You're serious, aren't you?" Cecil asked.

"Sure I am. Listen, we got the place, we got a little dough . . ."

"Oh, you don't have to convince me, Duke. I'm all for it.

Can't think of anything I'd rather be than a speak owner. Drive my family mad.'' He took a long pull on the flask. ''What are we going to call this sparkling new addition to New York speakeasies?''

''Duke's 44 Club.'' Duke smiled and held out his hands. ''Who would come to a joint named Cecil's?''

''People who want their hair cut.'' Cecil stood up and faced his friend. ''You've had this all thought out, haven't you? Right down to the name?''

Duke nodded.

''You're not as dumb as I thought, my dear Duke. I have this terrible feeling that from now on, I'm going to be taking orders from you.'' He laughed. ''And who is going to come to Duke's 44 Club? Have you thought of that?''

''Sure,'' the Duke said, putting Sven Stieber's top hat on the back of his head. ''All of your fancy friends.''

On October 31, 1930, a group of young society people made their way up the steps at 44 East Forty-fourth Street. It was a warm evening. The young women wore diaphanous gowns that touched their ankles, and they carried satin and silk evening purses. The young men, in their Brooks Brothers' custom-made dinner jackets, were mostly blond with clean-cut profiles and patent-leather lace-ups. Virtually all of them had belonged, at one time or another, to such bastions of social-register manhood as the Knickerbocker Greys and the Fence Club at Yale.

A speakeasy on East Forty-fourth Street was not their usual destination.

''You don't suppose this is some elaborate rag of Cecil's, do you?'' a beautiful young van der Velde daughter, Laura, asked her escort.

Before she received an answer, the town house doors were thrown open. Standing on the threshold were Duke Greene and Cecil Townsend, resplendent in white tie and tails. Cecil was already a little drunk but Duke's high came from within. It showed in the gleam of his eyes, in the hundred-watt glow of his smile. The beautiful young van der Velde fell immediately, irredeemably in love with the tall, dark man as the neon light over the door was switched on and Cecil shouted, in his high, cheery voice, ''Welcome to Duke's 44 Club, kiddies.

Every time you introduce a friend, you earn yourself a free drink."

"I thought tonight was on the house," Freddie Thornton said as he brushed past Cecil on his way to the bar where a nervous black man in a white jacket was waiting to mix his first cocktail.

"At the time the invitations were issued, so did the house," Cecil said, joining him at the bar. Which was true. But at the last moment Mookie Goldstein had called a conference. Yes, the three thousand dollars had taken care of the police but there were still the federal agents to be considered. And then of course there were rival speaks managed by not always gentle gangsters and perhaps, Mookie wanted to know, he might offer a suggestion? Duke and Cecil had said certainly he might offer a suggestion. He indicated that they might solve their protection problems by hiring a young man he knew, an ex-member of the New York City police department who had been cashiered for a mere indiscretion and who had no heart for gangland politics. He wanted a nice quiet job in a respectable speakeasy.

Victor Reo was hired that afternoon at four hundred per month. He was to be a combination maître d'hôtel/bouncer/ambassador to the police and other protectionist organizations. He was only a few years older than Duke and Cecil but decades more mature. He looked not unlike a rough-hewn version of Duke, though he was two inches taller and a great deal broader.

That first evening on the job, he succeeded in winnowing out the two federal agents who had tried to crash the "private party." "How'd you know?" Duke asked him.

Victor, a man of few words, pointed to his face. "I got a nose," he said. "I can smell those fuckers two blocks away."

It was Victor who insisted upon a lock with keys for members. It was Cecil who thought the keys should be gold and Duke who came up with the idea of numbering them.

"And we shan't give them out to just anyone," Cecil said. "We'll have to make absolutely certain they can pay their bar bills before we give them a gold key."

Victor Reo looked down at the runty Cecil and shook his head. Half the time he didn't understand what the little man was talking about. He couldn't decide whether or not he was a ponce; but he did know that Cecil had a kind heart, and for Victor that was all that mattered.

Looking exactly what he was in his new and ill-fitting tuxedo—which Duke had insisted upon—Victor Reo stood at the door that first night and for the next forty-three years, separating those who belonged from those who didn't by the sheer instinct which he claimed was lodged in that handsome Roman protuberance of his, which came to be known as "Victor's Nose."

On that first night, as Victor was explaining in his careful English to a man in a blue suit that "djs is a private party, buddy," and as Cecil entertained Phebe Hamilton and other old friends at the mahogany bar, Duke led those guests who wanted to dine into the former drawing room where rented tables had been set up.

Cecil left Phebe in charge of the Club Room at one point and made his way to the drawing room. He wanted to know who Duke was putting at the table his stepfather had left for them, the first and best table because it was the most stable. The rented ones were apt to collapse at odd moments. He was surprised to find the young Mellon heir and his beautiful van der Velde date at what was already being called the best table. He hadn't told Duke who the Mellon kid was and what his future patronage might mean to them.

Duke, too, it turned out, had a nose.

Cecil turned and went back to Phebe at the bar. At that moment the photographer Cecil had hired took a picture of him. It appeared in the next issue of *Town and Country* and showed a fair young man with thick, rimless glasses in white tie and tails, a glass of champagne in his hand, a smile on his plain, childlike face, saved from cynicism by virtue of its obvious sincerity.

It was the way Cecil always looked when he caught sight of Phebe, and it was the way Duke always chose to remember Cecil. That was the photograph he hadn't been able to recognize in the Club Room when SayDee had come to his rescue.

Duke closed his eyes as he lay in the canopied bed, listening to the harmonious sounds of SayDee's and Hector's snoring. He thought that perhaps now he was ready to fall asleep.

But again sleep eluded him. The vision of Phebe Hamilton standing at the bar in the Club Room, her violet eyes lighting up with affection at the sight of Cecil, cropped up as it had every day since he had met her.

Chapter Four

DUKE'S 44 Club did very well during the first week it was open. "We cleared nearly five hundred bucks," Duke told Cecil.

"A veritable gold mine. What shall we do with it?"

"Buy tables that don't fall down. Have a few more gold keys made. Pay Victor. Get the men's room painted. Buy some . . ."

"All right, Duke. Enough. I had this sudden attack of whimsy in which it occurred to me that we might just go out and spend it."

Duke's 44 Club didn't do nearly as well in its second week. "We're eight hundred bucks in the hole," Duke announced as Cecil poured himself a drink in the empty Club Room. "Where the hell did everyone go?"

"Back to college," Cecil said, topping off his glass with imported Scotch. "I'm afraid we made a tactical error, dear Dukey: we only courted college students. Their Thanksgiving vacation is over. They're all back in Boston and New Haven and New Jersey. We'll do marvelously well after June, when they all graduate."

"By then it will be too late. We can't hold out until June. We got to get ourselves some new customers. Why don't you invite the parents? You know them all."

"They wouldn't come. I'm not respectable, alas."

"Then we got to make you respectable. Quick."

"And how, dear chap, do you propose to do that?"

Duke opened up the *The New York Times* to the society page. "We're going to get you married, Cecil. We'll have the reception right here. Next to each guest's plate, we'll put a little gold key. We'll expand our patronage among the people that count." He hit the society page with his flat, muscular hand. "They'll come, won't they?"

"Oh, they'll come," Cecil said, looking up admiringly at Duke in his stepfather's custom-made pin-striped suit. "They'll all come to a Townsend wedding. The big question is: whom am I going to marry?"

"Phebe, who else? You get all goopy every time you see her. She's not only a good looker, she's got money, too. Maybe we can get her to invest a little in the club."

"Duke, the problem is that Phebe doesn't get all goopy over me."

"Horse balls. You should see the light switch on in those violet eyes whenever you come into a room. All she wants to do is put your head against her breast and mother you."

"Do you really think so, Duke?" Suddenly Cecil lost that fey facade he protected himself with and looked as nakedly ingenuous as any boy his age, hopelessly in love.

"Are you kidding? You mean to tell me you didn't know? Cecil, you need new glasses. Now get on the phone and call her at that castle on Fifth Avenue her mother calls 'the little town place.' She didn't go back to Vassar, did she?"

"No. She's taken a semester off to work at the settlement."

"You called it when you told her she was a bleeding heart. Now you can be her own private charity case. Take her to dinner somewhere quiet, tell her how lonely you are, and then pop the question."

"I don't suppose you'd like to do it for me, dear boy," Cecil said, putting his Scotch down on the bar, reaching for the telephone.

"Nope," Duke said, and Cecil always wondered if he was serious. "Phebe'd never marry me."

The following morning Duke kicked Cecil's door open and went into the bedroom where Cecil's stepfather once held business conferences. He walked across the marble floor and sat on the edge of the severely modern chrome bed someone had lent Cecil and shook him.

"So what did she say?"

"Dear chap, do you have any idea what time it is?" Cecil asked, reaching for his glasses, suppressing a yawn.

"Never mind the time. What did she say?"

"She said she'd let me know by Friday. She had to think it over."

"What do *you* think?"

"She said she loved me," Cecil said, hooking the metal frames of his glasses over his ears.

"That's something."

"But she said she wasn't certain love was enough."

"Jesus. What more does she want?"

"I think she's afraid I'm not going to be very good in the bed department.

"So why didn't you take her to the nearest hotel and prove that you would be?"

Cecil smiled. "We're all not so sure of our masculinity as you, Duke. I, too, am afraid I'm not going to be so good in the bed department."

"Have you ever been laid?" Duke asked, looking at his friend. "Don't answer that. Of course you haven't. So how do you know you won't be any good until you try it?" He stood up and began to pace and the room seemed smaller and Cecil began to feel a bit better. "I'd take you over to Polly's," Duke said, thinking as he paced, "but that would probably be terrible. You're the type that's got to be in love." He sat back down on the bed. "I think you'd better get married, first, Cecil, and believe me, it will all work out. Maybe not the first time but the second, you'll be fine. It's the kind of thing that once you learn, you never forget." He started to get up when another thought occurred to him.

"You do like girls, don't you, Cecil? I mean you think about them and all that, don't you?"

"All the time."

"You ever, uhm, jerk off?'

"All the time."

"Well, stop it. Pretty soon you're going to have the real thing."

"Anyone ever tell you, Duke, that you'd make a divine father?"

"Did you tell her you wanted the party here?"

"She hasn't said yes, yet, Duke."

"She will."

Victor took the call when it came, and he didn't get a chance to tell Duke about it until late that night. An eating club Cecil had once belonged to during his short stay at Princeton had decided to drive in to the city and had ended up at 44 where Cecil was entertaining them.

"She said," Victor told Duke, "you should call her back no matter what time. She sounded like she really wanted to talk to you."

Duke looked in at the Club Room where Cecil was leading the Princeton men in chorus after chorus of naughty song and then he went down to the telephone in the Nedicks on the corner and called her.

"I have to see you," she said.

"I don't think that's such a good idea, Phebe."

"Why not?"

"I just don't think . . ."

"There's no one here. The servants have the night off and my parents are in Palm Beach with my sister Alice." She waited for a moment and then continued in her clear, soft voice. "If I don't see you, Duke, I'm not going to marry Cecil. And I know how very much you want me to."

"It's not just the money or the club," he said to her as she let him into the Beaux Arts limestone facade house on Fifth Avenue and Seventy-fifth Street. "Cecil needs you."

"It just happens to be convenient that he needs me now."

He couldn't see her. The lights in the marble entry foyer were dim and she stood in the shadow of one of the columns which dominated the space.

"Phebe . . ."

She stepped into the light. She was wearing a flannel housecoat, the sort that buttoned up the front, the sort that had been designed for virgins. "Come with me," she said and turned, and Duke, not knowing what else to do, followed her up the marble staircase to the bedroom which was shirred in a soft pink material and as girlish, as innocent, as the rest of the house was cold and sophisticated and governmental.

She undid the flannel housecoat and stood in front of the canopied bed. She was perfectly nude. Her soft skin glowed in the light from the fireplace. Her breasts were high and her nipples were hard and her violet eyes seemed to bore right through him.

She put her hands on the curve of her hips. "I want you to make love to me, Duke. There'll be no consequences for you, believe me. I need . . ."

"Phebe, Cecil's my best friend. I couldn't . . ."

"Don't you see, Duke, you'll be doing both of us a favor." She came to him and put her arms around him and pressed her body up against him. "He'll never be wonderful in bed. He's not built that way. He'll be just okay. You, you're meant to be a lover. I have to find out if it's worth it. I have to find out how important it is to me. Before I ruin Cecil's life." She brought his head down to hers and began to kiss him. "Oh, Duke, make love to me. Please."

He picked her up and put her on the bed. He took off his clothes. And, as gently as he could, he spent the night making love to Phebe Hamilton.

It was Cecil's turn to kick open Duke's door. "Go away," Duke said, turning over. "I didn't get to bed until . . ."

"She's going to do it, you genius."

"She's going to do what?" Duke asked, and suddenly he was wide awake.

"She's going to do everything. Everything, dear chap. She's going to marry me. She's going to give us money to run the club until it's a going proposition, she's even going to let us have the reception—though not the ceremony, she made that very clear—here. She's going to make me a man, dear Duke. She's going to be the mother of my babies. And I owe it all to you. No one else but you. I want you to be my best man, Duke. Oh, the family will cluck but they always cluck at everything I do and it won't hurt your reputation to be the best man at the wedding, if not of the year, then of the hour.

"Phebe's being marvelous. She adores you. She told me to tell you that she adores you. She knows what this place means to you and she wants to help. She's even going to let the newsreel people film part of the reception, and if you think that's a Hamilton tradition, you got another thing coming.

"Get up, Duke. Come. We've got to go buy morning coats and striped trousers and pearl stickpins. I've got to hit up some of my lesser aunts to give me some of the family jewels. I can't have my bride strolling about ringless. Will you please get up? At the very least you must congratulate me."

"Congratuations, Cecil," Duke said, holding out his hand.

Cecil took it and sat down on the bed, next to his friend. "On my wedding night, promise me you'll stick by the phone in case I have to call you to get any of the mechanics straight."

Duke sat up and put his big arms around Cecil's thin body and held him for a minute. "I promise, kid. But believe me, you're not going to have any trouble."

Cecil Townsend and Phebe Hamilton were married at St. Bartholomew's on Park Avenue on January 1, 1931, in one of the more lavish weddings of the year. People who knew Phebe were surprised. She was famous for her social conscience; an expensive wedding in the middle of the Depression didn't seem her style.

Nor was it her style to apologize. She wanted a big wedding because Cecil wanted one, she said. What she didn't say was that Duke had wanted it most.

He sat at the best table with the bride and the groom and the beautiful Laura van der Velde and only very occasionally did he allow his eyes to seek out Phebe's.

She was happy, radiant, exactly the way a bride was supposed to be. It was obvious, even to Duke, that she had made the right choice. He stayed by his telephone that night but it never rang.

Not long after there appeared a discreet announcement in the *Times* society page. Laura van der Velde and Duke Greene had been married in Justice Brand van der Velde's study. Only the immediate family and Mr. and Mrs. Cecil Townsend were present.

Chapter Five

DUKE SLEPT for an hour when a noise from his dressing room woke him. SayDee was in that fifteen foot square room, surveying for perhaps the ten-thousandth time his wardrobe. In all the years they had been together, she had never stopped treating it as if it were a museum filled with invaluable works of art.

"Did you ever see so many clothes?" he heard her marvel at Hector who trotted around after her as she went from the fitted shelves to the cedar-lined closets to the lacquered cabinets to the ebony trunks. "And doesn't Robert keep Duke's shoes nice?"

Shaking his head, trying to get the ghosts of the past to leave him alone, Duke reflected that Robert did indeed keep his shoes nice. There were dozens of pairs of them, all handmade by Lobb. After he wore a pair, Robert would take them up to the counter in the service pantry behind the kitchen and polish them until the leather shone like new metal. Then he would replace the hand-carved shoe trees with their silver plaques with Duke's name engraved on them and he'd carry the shoes down to the dressing room as if they were a priceless pair of Ming vases.

Each day Robert set aside one hour for the wardrobe, even

though Duke no longer wore any of the clothes in it. He had shrunk; nothing remotely fit. Still Robert would realign each perfectly aligned row of shirts—all white, all silk, all from Sulka who embroidered "Duke" in blue thread on the shirttail—making certain each individual plastic container was dust tight. He refolded the dozens of pairs of black silk socks which had a tendency to unfold themselves and busied himself with the huge, embroidered Irish linen handkerchiefs, the custom-made silk underwear, the jewelry closet where the cuff links and the watches and the gold collar stays were stored. He even aired the white tie and tails that had been Duke's trademark until the war and the half-dozen tuxedoes and forty-odd suits and the starched piqué evening shirts and the silk scarves and the collection of hats, ties, and bathrobes, at-home robes, smoking jackets.

But before Robert began his ministrations, SayDee liked to go into the dressing room with Hector and simply look, her huge, powder-blue eyes never ceasing to be amazed at the enormity of it all.

He heard the door open and watched her from half-closed lids as she came into the bedroom and moved about, Hector following, now examining the leather-tooled books which took up one wall of the bedroom. "Real books," she had said the first night she had stayed over. "How do you like that?"

He didn't want to talk as she touched the leather bindings. He wanted to savor the pleasure of watching her. She moved so nicely, with an exquisite, show-girl grace that never, not even now, lost its appeal for him.

He remembered the day he had walked into 44, coming back from some long vacation with a woman he hadn't liked very much, to find SayDee behind the glass cigar case.

He had stormed over to the new building to find Cecil in his office. "What're you trying to do?" he had demanded, "take over where Lou Walters leaves off? Putting a chorus girl in that black uniform with that orange-pink hair and those tits behind that counter . . . Do you think that's class, Cecil?"

"My dear Mr. Duke," Cecil had said, looking up with his thick glasses, "when will you learn that people come to 44 precisely because it isn't classy." He smiled his annoying, endearing smile and said, "At any rate, the lady ain't no chorus girl."

"Yeah? She looks like a professional of some sort. You bedding her?"

"Why, I should like to know, does he always sound like something out of Victorian England when he gets onto the subject of fucking?" Cecil asked the ceiling above him. "No," he said, turning to Duke, "I am not 'bedding' the lady though she seems eminently bedable. I am as faithful to my Phebe as on the day we wed. I interviewed sixteen dozen or so prospective hat checkers while you were having it off with Lady Sommerville in Cap Ferrat—a damned silly place to go with a married woman; Winchell reported it twice and Harry Sommerville is ready to shoot you. SayDee Roth was the only interviewee who had one penny's worth of chic, one centime of *chien*, one drachma of style. I'll tell you what. *You* interview her, Duke. You give her ten minutes of your valuable time and if you don't like her, you find a replacement. Now run upstairs. Phebe and the baby are dying to see you, though heaven knows why. Comic relief is what they need, I expect."

SayDee Roth wasn't at all nervous when Duke called her up to his drawing room and sat her down on the red leather sofa in front of the baronial fireplace and proceeded to interview her.

"That's a peculiar way to spell your name," he said.

"I didn't want to change it when I went on the stage—they all said Sadie would never play, so I figured it wouldn't help if I spelled it a little different. P.S.: it didn't."

"You act?"

"Not exactly. I tried to act. Nobody ever said I succeeded."

"But you were in all these plays." Duke held up the glossy black and white photo on the back of which were listed her credits.

"I got a talent for being able to stand still for a long time and look good." She opened her generous mouth and laughed, and Duke found himself laughing along with her. He hadn't laughed for a long time.

She had had a husband named Dave who was killed in the war and she didn't have any boyfriends because most men her age were too "immature" and sure, she'd love to have a drink, if he ever had the time.

For the next month or two every time he passed the glass

cigar case, he found himself smiling and then, around November, when the onset of the holidays and his divorced, only partially familied state began to hit him with their first sadistic thrust, he said what the hell and asked if he could buy her that drink.

She was as good and as caring in bed as she had let on she would be, and after only a dozen or so sessions under the canopy he asked her to move in and told Cecil they were going to need a new hatcheck girl.

"This time, dear Duke," Cecil had said, "you interview."

"This time, dear Cecil," SayDee had said, "I'll interview."

SayDee Roth. She was close to sixty, Duke reflected as he watched her pull a book from the shelf, but she still held onto her talent for looking good. Her hair was the same improbable pink, her body was still molded into that ultimate 1950's female outline, as if she were always wearing a sequinned evening gown with a fishtail hemline and a Faye Emerson cleavage.

I never loved her, he thought. Not the crazy, all-enveloping way I loved Laura and Irene and even little Rose. Not the way I loved Phebe. But I like her more than I liked any of them. I should have married her and now I want to marry her but the lady isn't willing. "What's wrong with common law, anyway?" she had asked whenever he brought up the subject. "If it was good enough for Ingrid Bergman, it's good enough for yours truly."

He realized, as she put the book back into its place, as she let Robert in so he could begin his wardrobe fetish, as she folded sheets and straightened vials wrapped with doctors' prescriptions, as she shushed Hector who was inclined to go into uncontrolled, unprovoked fits of barking as he grew older, that SayDee was acting as a sort of midwife-in-reverse. She could have agreed with the doctors and he would have understood. She could have allowed him to stay in the hospital where it would have been easier on everyone.

But SayDee had insisted he come home. She was going to help him go out of life with all the care others gave to the miracle of birth. What about the miracle of death? she wanted to know.

He drifted off and was just aware that Nick was in the room, looking down at him, and then had left without speaking. It was odd, Duke thought, but Nick did look like Victor. He had that same Roman centurion's nose. That nose. Even Lawrence didn't have it. He had once kept Jean-Paul Belmondo waiting half an hour for a J. J. Walker Room table because he didn't recognize the face and didn't like the man's shoes and couldn't find his name in the card file.

Victor hadn't needed the cards. He had that nose. He always knew who the princess was even when she came disguised as the maid. Victor somehow always knew, instinctively, who deserved the best table.

He had known from the start that Rose was a princess. He had gladly accepted the story, the marriage, the arrangements Cecil had come up with. And when Rose had died in childbirth, Victor had brought up the boy he named Nick, giving him the sort of love few boys knew from their fathers.

It was love, Duke knew, that had rescued Nick from the drugs and the depression he had returned with from Vietnam. It was love that had given Nick the strength to start over, first working with Victor, then taking his place as 44's manager when Victor had died, as quietly as he had lived, in the bedroom of his own town house a block away on West Forty-fourth Street.

He spent too much money on that goddamned town house, Duke thought, wishing Victor hadn't died, wishing he was there at that moment. Victor had become a rich man but he gave too much money away and then he bought the vacant town house five years after the war because he wanted, he said, to make certain his son always had a decent place to live.

Victor hadn't been smart with the money he had earned from 44. Most of it had gone to educate Nick—because Victor would never take a penny for that—and to maintain his town house, that absurd white elephant on the wrong block of Forty-fourth Street.

Nick, Duke thought, had turned out to be a real person, a *mensch,* as Duke's mother would have said. He wished Peter had turned out more like Nick. But Peter was like his mother, more British than American, spending his youth and his resources social climbing in London society, of all the damned foolish occupations.

And as he thought of his son, Peter, he naturally thought of his son's wife, Brette. More than anything else, he longed to see her, to hold her in his arms.

Chapter Six

WHEN DUKE left for England in 1939 to join the RAF, his wife left for Reno. That was one of the few things Laura and Duke had ever agreed upon.

What Duke found hardest to leave was his club. Though Laura had been a disappointment, Duke's 44 Club had fulfilled every one of its promises. In its eight years of existence, it had become what George Jean Nathan called "the last bastion of aristocratic dining in Manhattan. Not," he added, "that the food's all that good. It's the setting."

But after Laura, after other disappointments with various women, what Duke decided he needed was a new setting, a new challenge. What better one could there be than England's war with Germany?

"And the club?" Cecil asked, longing, in his own way, to go with Duke, knowing that he'd never pass the physical, that he could never leave Phebe.

"You'll manage it just fine," Duke reassured him. "As you do everything else. You've got Victor and you've got Phebe and you've got a million and one contacts. All you have to do is stand at the door and flash that idiot grin at the people who come in. If the truth were known, Cecil, you're a much better restaurant man than I."

"How delighted my erstwhile relatives would be to hear that, especially the Boston branch. You must remember to put that on my tombstone, Duke."

They gave him a going-away party. Everyone from Dewey to Brenda Frazier to Gary Cooper was there. Just before he left, as he kissed Phebe—on the cheek—good-bye, Duke wondered if he was ever coming back.

He did come back and with Irene on his arm. She had been an actress, a Mayfair darling, with a father who was an earl. She had a gift for lending drawing-room comedies an air of absurdity that made it all right to laugh, even during the grim days of war.

He had met her at a house party in Norfolk and then again at the hospital in Torquay where she was visiting a wounded cousin. Sparks, as Irene said, were ignited almost immediately. When he asked her to marry him, to return to New York with him, she said yes. The idea of postwar London was almost more depressing than mid-war London.

Duke immediately took over the management of 44 while Irene did a play, a drawing-room comedy, for David Murray, and had parties in the duplex over the club.

During the war Cecil and Phebe had bought the two town houses adjacent to 44, had broken down the connecting walls, and fitted out the new double house with the appointments appropriate to Phebe's fortune.

It took Duke almost half a year to realize something was wrong with Cecil and then Phebe had to tell him. "You romanticize us both too much, Duke," she said, sitting in the red leather sofa in his drawing room, sipping at the tea Robert had brought her. "You still think we're the super gentiles with all sorts of strength 'neath our thin Yankee frames. You're the strong one, Duke."

She did look thin. Far thinner than Irene, whose seamless blond body was, at that moment, walking across the stage at the Ziegfeld. Though her black hair was as lustrous as ever and the defiant light in her violet eyes still shone bright and strong.

"Do you want more tea?" he asked.

"Why are you always so nice to me?" she asked, holding out her cup, allowing Duke to pour more tea into it. "I was so terrible to you."

"In what way?" He liked sitting in that room with the enormous windows and the huge fireplace, with Phebe drinking tea, looking a little shabby in an old sweater but still extraordinarily alluring. He couldn't remember having been alone with her since before she married Cecil.

"What's the feminine of cad? That's how I acted. I seduced you, I used you, and then I turned you loose. It didn't occur to me until my wedding day, when we were sitting downstairs at the best table, that you might have had some feelings for me, that you weren't so simple a stud as I had tried to make you out, that you hadn't made love to me simply to help me make up my mind to marry your best friend.

"I want to say I'm sorry, Duke. And I want you to know that the reason I married Cecil was because I was frightened. I was scared of so much ecstacy. I'm too Protestant. I didn't see how any good could come of it."

"Phebe . . ."

"Not that I'm sorry I married Cecil. I love Cecil. We don't have children and it's not because we haven't tried . . . but we do have one another and that's why I'm here, Duke. It's very difficult for me, but I want to ask you another favor." She turned her head away. "Duke, I'm asking you to help me find some way to stop Cecil from drinking. He's almost a confirmed alcoholic, you know."

"I didn't know."

"He does it very well. While you were away, he had a reason not to drink. There was the club. Now you're back and there's nothing to stop him."

"Oh, yes there is," Duke said, standing up. "I didn't come through that war to come home to that little bastard poisoning himself with booze. I'll stop him."

He did. He went down to the Club Room, took Cecil by the arm, and put him in the front seat of his Packard convertible and drove him up to Silver's in Connecticut where only the very rich and the very far gone go.

Then he drove right back to New York and cornered Phebe in her house. "He's got to have something to do. You've got your settlement house and I've got my club but Cecil's got nothing and with nothing he feels like nothing. If you had kids it would be different, but you don't. I don't suppose you want to adopt . . ."

"I've begged him. Cecil says he doesn't want anybody's rejects."

"Then I have another idea. All through the war I've been wondering: where has Cecil been able to put his hands on the Scotch and the salmon and the caviar and the vodka to keep both 44 and all of his friends supplied? I'll never forget that basket of goodies he sent me in Torquay. Every general who ever hit Europe would open up his suitcase and bring out a bottle of gen-u-ine Scotch, courtesy of 44 and Cecil Townsend. How'd he do it?"

"That's Cecil. He knows everyone and when he makes up his mind that he wants something, he always has a very good idea who to ask for it."

"I think you and Cecil are going to start a new business, Phebe."

"And that is?"

"Importing liquor and fancy foods. You've already got one big customer: 44."

Thus, when Cecil came down from Dr. Silver's in Connecticut in Duke's Packard, with the top down, his hands steady and his eyes clear, he found that he was president and managing director of 44 Industries, a position he was particularly well equipped to handle.

Cecil had begun importing "44" Scotch early in the war for the club and for important friends who were having trouble finding their favorite drink. Somehow, even during the two-year war prohibition, he had managed one way or another to keep both the bar and the friends well supplied.

He and Phebe were to be the sole shareholders of the new company. Their offices were established on the first floor of their town house.

"You know how to get the booze and you know where to get it and the club needs it and you know how it is when it comes to the club. I'm buying you out of 44, Cecil. You take the money and you use it to rent warehouses, to bribe whoever has to be bribed at the customs house. Now you got your headaches and I got mind so get out of my office and go see how many cases of 44 scotch you can get me, by next week, the latest."

Cecil stood up. He was a little shaky but he didn't seem a moment older than he had on that first day when he shook Duke's hand in the dormitory at the University of Pennsylvania.

"I ever tell you I love you, Duke?"

"Get out of here, kid. You got work to do. So do I."

"I love you, Duke."

By the early 1950's, 44 Industries was a company that, share for share, was far and away more valuable than the original Duke's 44 Club.

By the early 1950's, Duke had gone through his own depression laced with alcohol. Irene had a baby, Peter, several years after their marriage, but it was too late.

She had divorced him with the agreement that their son, Peter, was to grow up in England with his mother, to spend his vacations with his father in New York. In addition to the generous alimony settlement, Duke had agreed to leave his son either the sum of two million dollars or the controlling shares of Duke's 44 Club.

On Peter's fifth birthday, which Peter was celebrating with his mother in a large London flat, Cecil found Duke in 44's Club Room, drinking by himself.

"Dear boy," Cecil said, "don't tell me *you're* becoming a lush?"

"I'm feeling sorry for myself," Duke said, looking up. "I should have never let her take him back to England. I don't have a son anymore."

"Well, you've a share in one, maybe. I wonder if you're well enough to hear this bit of news?"

"Let's have it," Duke said, putting down his drink.

"After all these years, at the ridiculous age of forty-three, our Phebe has what is popularly called a bun in the oven. She's pregnant, dear boy, and though I may end up being the oldest father in the playground, I can assure you I will also be the proudest. You are to be godfather, godparent, guardian, advisor, et cetera. We intend to name him Duke, of course."

The baby was born on September 4, 1955, and she was named Brette, after Phebe's mother because, as Cecil said, even Duke could understand that they couldn't saddle a child with the name of Duchess Townsend. Not and feel good about it, they couldn't.

Duke held her in his arms not too long after she was born.

She already had a cap of black hair, exactly like Phebe's, and eyes of the same intense violet. "When she grows up," Duke said, holding her very carefully in his huge hands, "she's going to marry Peter and be very, very happy."

"That gives us several years to amass the dowry," Cecil said.

Phebe, looking up at Duke holding her child, said she thought that was a very good idea and then Cecil wanted to know why she had tears in her eyes and she said something about it being an aged mother's prerogative, and they were tears of joy which wasn't, strictly speaking, true.

They had five years of happiness with their child and then, for no satisfactory reason any religion or philosophy was ever able to come up with, Cecil and Phebe were killed in a plane that was scheduled to land at the Palm Springs airport and instead crashed into the desert killing everyone aboard.

If there had been no Brette, Duke didn't think he would have been able to bear the pain of losing both Cecil and Phebe. She had been staying with Phebe's sister, her Aunt Helen, at the family compound in Katonah. The family was appalled, once again, by Cecil's and Phebe's behavior when they found Duke had been left in sole charge of the child.

Only Helen, who had none of her dead sister's beauty but a great deal of her common sense, liked the idea. She allowed Duke to move her and Brette into Manhattan into the town house next door to 44, over the offices of 44 Industries, as it was called. Brette had inherited all shares of 44 Industries, but they were to be under Duke's management until she reached the age of twenty-one.

In the meanwhile Duke relied on Helen to make certain that Brette went to the right schools and had the right friends. He spent as much time with the child as he could. She was a permanent fixture at 44 and more than one visitor changed his impression of Duke after watching him sit for hours on end with the beautiful little girl on his knee, greeting friends, but reserving the heart of his attention for his adored Brette.

During all her years of growing up, he never once missed a dancing recital or a gymnastic exhibition or a school play. Unlike some of the other adults in the audience, he enjoyed himself. He liked to watch the children as they went through their paces, though he felt sad when he recognized the frightened ones, the ones who were afraid to perform.

Not that his Brette seemed afraid of anything. As long as Duke was in the audience, she was fearless, the prima ballerina in the pink tutu, the trapeze artist doing half flips on the school trampoline, the remarkably good-natured witch in *Hansel and Gretel*. Duke, she knew, would never let her down.

Duke dreamed of her now, those ebullient eyes and those soft arms reaching up for him when the covers were suddenly pulled away and his reverie was ended. "SayDee," he said, "what the hell are you doing? I'm chilled."

She took off the robe that was made of some fabric by Du Pont and got into the ridiculous bed, pulling the satin quilt over them, planting her still firm body against his sadly aged one.

"I knew you were cold, your highness. I only thought you could use a little animal warmth." She put her arms around him, and Duke Greene gave himself up to the absolute comfort that remarkable woman was able to give him, even now.

"Oh, yeah," she said, kissing his cheek, holding him. "I got a surprise for you. Peter called while you were on cloud nine. He's in New York for the anniversary party. He's going to come over and see you later."

"And Brette?" he asked, realizing his voice sounded like a child's, an eager child's, and not caring. "Is she here, too?"

"Yes, *mamele,*" SayDee said, holding him tightly. "Brette's here, too."

He closed his eyes and fell asleep again. He needed an awful lot of sleep lately.

BOOK 1

MONDAY

Chapter One

DINAH SHERIDAN, twenty-eight years old with blond streaks in her thick, dark hair, and light blue smudges under her plaintive brown eyes from too many sleepless nights, sighed. She had full breasts and high cheekbones and lips seemingly poised in a perpetual pout. An admirer had suggested that those lips were a permanent invitation for fellatio.

Dinah was aware that he, along with most of the other men she knew, thought of her as "hot." "Hot" was the word of the year. She would have preferred to have lived in another time when she might have been described as "smoldering."

Gloria Grahame, she decided, was smoldering. Suzanne Somers was hot. The world progresses, she thought as she allowed her eyes to open. Cautiously she lifted her head and allowed herself a glimpse in the mirror which covered the wall opposite her bed. She closed her eyes quickly, allowing her head to fall back on to the silk-covered pillow. She hadn't liked what she had seen; she tried to turn over, away from the mirror, but realized she couldn't.

I'd sell what little soul I have for a cigarette, she thought, avoiding the mirror, looking at the Camel-filled gold cigarette case that sat, tantalizingly, less than twelve inches away on the Lucite night table. I wonder if I could reach it with my mouth, she asked herself, click it open with my teeth, hook a cigarette with my tongue, and operate the goddamned lighter with my chin? Perhaps I was a parapalegic in another life.

She decided not and tried to focus her attention on the silver-leafed ceiling, wondering what her mind would come up with next to help screen what was evidently the most crucial issue of the morning: how dangerous, on a scale of one to infinity, was the man sleeping so soundlessly next to her?

Usually it didn't matter but usually she didn't let them sleep over. Usually, after the fun and games, she managed to get rid of them. But this one hadn't been so easy to get rid of, and she hadn't been at all certain that she wanted him to go.

Now she wished he would evaporate. With his belt, Dinah thought, looking down at her wrists which he had expertly tied together with the black leather belt he had used on her so inventively during the night. She desperately didn't want to think of what had gone on during the night.

She suddenly remembered a girl in her class in finishing school in Switzerland who, it was said, had gone too far. If Linda Randsteddter went too far, Dinah thought, then after last night, I've dropped off the edge.

She moved her fingers experimentally, to see if there was circulation. There was, and she tried, unsuccessfully, to work the belt's latch.

A vision of one of the sexual acts he had performed upon her came into her mind. They had been in the bathroom. Her hands had already been tied. She was on her knees and he stood over her, his black trousers below his knees, his hands gripping her head when he . . . No. She forced herself not to think of that.

She latched onto something someone had told her at lunch on the previous day: Brette Townsend Stewart-Greene was coming to New York to celebrate 44's fiftieth anniversary.

Dinah had always liked Brette, ever since they were children. She had always been, under that upper-class, violet-eyed beauty of hers, a tough little cookie. Though Dinah had never understood her. Or vice versa. They were two women who operated on different levels, different synchronizations.

She remembered when she was a child, not quite seven, and her father had brought her to New York for what was to be his last formal concert at Carnegie Hall. He had sprung on her mother, at the last moment, that Duke was giving a birthday party for Cecil's little girl and that Dinah was invited.

"And where am I supposed to get her a party dress at this hour?" her mother had asked, her uncertain mind grasping the one fact she could cope with. Within a very short time Dinah had found herself encased in yards of baby blue satin with high white stockings and dark blue Mary Janes and—the pièce de résistance—an enormous blue satin bow in her hair.

"She looks like Shirley Temple," her father had complained as he went off to the rehearsal hall.

"Fat lot you care," her mother had said. "If you had your way, she'd look like Marilyn Monroe."

Brette's birthday party had been scheduled for a Sunday afternoon when 44 was closed. "Aren't you coming in with me, Mommy?" Dinah had asked as her mother deposited her at the door.

"Don't be absurd, darling. What would Mommy do at a party for children? Have a good time. I'll have the car call for you at three so be certain to be outside."

Little Mike, 44's doorman-bouncer, opened the door for her. The first person she saw was Duke. He was wearing a black cowboy suit which seemed odd.

"Ah, the little Hollywood princess," he said and came to her, kissed her, and took her up in his arms. He carried her into the main dining room where each of the tables was occupied by children. Children in cowboy and cowgirl costumes. There were rotating rodeos on each table and the Club Room had been cleared for square dancing.

"I didn't know," Dinah said, feeling ridiculous in her satin dress with her satin bow, looking at the New York kids in their Saks Fifth Avenue cowboy clothes staring at her, all of them suddenly silent.

"It doesn't matter," Brette assured her from her place at the best table, with Duke's son, Peter, on her right and the manager's boy, Nick, on her left. "You're to sit at my table and you're going to have a wonderful time. It's my party and whatever I say goes. Right, Duke?"

"Right, darling," Duke said.

Dinah gave Brette her present—a tiny pearl bracelet from

Tiffany's—and feeling self-conscious and unhappy, allowed herself to be seated at the best table in her satin dress.

All through the party no one, except Brette, said one word to her. She refused to dance any of the square dances even though the caller—prompted by Duke—asked for her by name. She sat in her seat at the best table until Peter, older and more assured than the other children, reached over and, with his forefinger and thumb, undid the big satin bow.

Dinah ran crying from the room into Duke's arms, but she could hear little Brette telling Peter she would never have him at another party again. "I don't care if you are half English. You have no manners," Brette had said and turned away to go and say good-bye to Dinah. Little Mike was taking her home in a taxi.

Dinah had stopped crying long before they reached the hotel, long before—ruined ribbon in hand—she had to walk across the long gold and pink lobby with her tall escort and ask the concierge to ring her room. When her father opened the door of their suite, she forgot all about the party, all about her embarrassment.

"I thought you were rehearsing," she said to him.

"That's what I told Mommy," he said, upending the glass he held in his hand, then taking her in his arms. "I didn't say rehearsing for what, did I?"

He laughed and held her and she laughed and kissed him and it wasn't until later, when she was in her bed in the hotel suite that she remembered the party and the ribbon and Brette. She wasn't confused about why the other children had been so mean to her. In their place, she knew, she would have acted in the same way. What perplexed her was Brette's behavior. Why had Brette taken up her cause when it would have been so much easier to ignore the Hollywood child in the ridiculous dress? She still didn't understand.

The man next to her suddenly made a sound, bringing Dinah back to the present. She had to admit to herself that she was thoroughly scared, a feeling not unlike the one she had experienced when she had been pushed into 44 when she was seven to face a bunch of New York kids in cowboy clothes.

Only I'm not seven, she told herself, and Daddy isn't waiting to comfort me when I come home crying. A brutal stranger is lying next to me and God knows what he's capable of doing to me when he wakes up.

She brought her bound hands up to her neck and touched the gold key which hung there. She remembered how fascinated he had been when she had taken off her dress and he had first seen the key. He had handled it with all the awe of Lancelot touching the grail.

She herself felt quasi-religious about the key. She was never without it and hadn't been since her father had given it to her on the night before he died. It seemed a part of her and it was odd that this stranger should so instantly recognize it as something more than a decoration.

She turned toward him and, for the first time, studied him. He lay unnaturally still, flat on his back as if he had been laid out for interment. She thought he was younger than she by about five years though she couldn't be certain.

He smiled in his sleep. She wondered what on earth he could be smiling about. Men like him, she thought, shouldn't smile. He had huge hands. They were too big for his body and his nails were too carefully shaped. They rested, protectively, on his penis.

Not that even those hands fully covered that oversized organ. It was both long and thick, its head a darker color than its trunk, almost purple. Though she didn't like herself for still wanting him, it, she knew herself well enough not to deny the thrill the thought of it plunging into her gave her.

She had a moment's fantasy, instantly rejected, in which she had an ongoing relationship with him. But of course that wasn't even remotely possible. He wasn't the kind of man with whom she could ever be seen in public. He was short and clearly working class with a hairless body made nearly grotesque by weight lifting. His muscles had no angles. They were round and hard and had the fascination of the unnatural.

She looked at his face with its blank, slightly undeveloped features and then, frightened once more, looked away, at the digital clock that was part of the miracle of electronics—Dinah's very own home entertainment center—that made up the wall to her right.

"You'd better get up," she said loudly. "I'm late."

Instantly he was awake. He opened his eyes which he called blue but were, in reality, no particular color. He stared at her for a moment, without recognizing who she was. Immediately Dinah lost the sense of ridiculous that had seen her through so many of these situations. She realized he possessed a dimension of danger she hadn't had to deal with before.

She held out her hands. He gave her a half smile, hesitated, and then easily undid the belt. He wrapped it around his fist as if he were about to hit her, and she instinctively edged away. He shook his head. Then he stood up and went down the glass-paneled hall to the shower. From the bedroom she could see him. In the distilled light coming through the glass brick of the shower stall, he seemed like some atavistic being, with the body of a man and the single-directed mind of an animal.

For a moment she wanted to follow him but instead she turned and, rubbing her wrists, went to the guest bathroom and thanked God there was Valium in the medicine chest.

He found her in the room she called her office a quarter of an hour later. He was dressed in black trousers, white shirt. He looks like a waiter, she thought. She turned and stared out at Central Park. She had showered and had done something to her hair and put on a robe. She wished she were going to be ill, genuinely ill. That she would have to stay in bed for days, under the covers, eating baked potatoes, watching old movies on television.

"I'm going to need some money," he said in that soft voice.

She handed him her purse. He took all of the cash that was in her wallet, stuffing it into his trouser pocket without counting it. It was clear he wasn't in it for the money; the money was part of the ritual.

He stood in the doorway until she turned and looked at him. "Next time," he said, "we'll get into something a little more serious."

"There won't be a next time," Dinah said, opening the gold cigarette case, taking some consolation in the fact that her hands were not shaking, busying herself with lighting a Camel.

"I didn't have my equipment on me," he said, apologetic.

"Next time, Miss Sheridan, we'll really get it on. Next time I'll bring my stuff."

"There won't be a next time," Dinah Sheridan said again, but he had already closed the front door.

The telephone blessedly rang before she had to think.

"Honey," the cigarette-hoarse voice of her producer, Meagin, said. "Where in God's name are you?"

"I'm not in God's name, I'm in my apartment, trying to recover from . . ."

"Honey, we got seventy people in Studio B, each and every one of them waiting for little old you. We're *supposed* to be going over the live section of Friday night's special."

"I forgot," Dinah said, cradling the receiver between her neck and her chin, playing with the key that never came off. "I honestly forgot, Meagin. I swear it."

"Honey, you are the only food critic in history to get prime time. Honey, you are the only . . ."

"I've heard this before, Meagin."

". . . television personality anyone could remotely imagine handling 44's fiftieth. Honey, three point two million people are going to be tuning in Friday night to watch you conduct the only genuinely glamorous event to hit commerical television since Edward R. Murrow went into Dietrich's living room. Honey, get your ass down here in the next half hour."

Meagin hung up and Dinah sat down at her desk. The important thing, she knew, was to keep herself from thinking. If she let herself think, she would go back to the medicine cabinet and swallow every pill she could find. She would draw a warm bath in the Jacuzzi and slowly sink into it, slicing the veins in her wrist exactly as her father had done fourteen years before.

She picked up the photograph of that brilliant, twisted man and stared at his dimpled, youthful, joyous good looks. It was a studio glossy but even its artificiality couldn't disguise that ebullience that was such a part of him. Nor could it show the other side of his nature, that constant need of his for instant gratification.

When she was sixteen, her mother had suddenly packed her off to Tahoe where he was introducing a new act. "*He* called and *he* wants you and God knows I could use a little freedom so off you go. If *he's* ready to act like a father, you'd better take advantage of it. It won't last long."

He had met her at the airport in a great big heliotrope Cadillac convertable which they had laughed about and then he had taken her back to his suite and they had had dinner, just the two of them, and he had kept her laughing all of the time.

Then he went downstairs to do his act which he said he really liked; he said he really didn't mind. But he had crashed into her bedroom at five in the morning, high on speed, she guessed, and raped her so thoroughly, so expertly, giving her such incredible ecstacy, that she still dreamed nightly of what it had been like.

And in the morning he had bought her a huge American breakfast with a dozen red roses and specially grilled French toast, because he knew she adored French toast, and he had looked at her so ruefully, so like a bad boy, and said, "Sorry baby. I don't know what got into me."

And she, being after all a Beverly Hills brat and terribly sophisticated, had said, "Ditto," making a smart joke of it, making *him* laugh, for once, allowing him to brush the event—the major event of her life—aside as one more peccadillo in the career of an artist. "So I play piano in Tahoe and they give me fifteen grand to be funny at the keyboard. Does that stop be from being an artist?" he had asked, avoiding the bloody sheet Dinah had kicked into a corner, avoiding his daughter's dark eyes.

And that night, after his act, when he came to her—because, after all, he had to come to someone—she had been ready for him, even wanting him. But he wasn't able to perform that act, and he started smacking her around because he was angry at everyone; everyone was a goddamned audience—and she tried not to scream because she didn't want to embarrass him and what was a little pain suffered for the man one loved?

He had broken three of her ribs and her left arm was fractured, but they didn't discover that until later. Because in the morning when she had gone into his bathroom and seen the pale red water in the tub and his blue nude body looking pathetic under the water, she had known immediately and definitively, that it was her fault, that she had killed her father, that she had failed him, that she was responsible, that she would be punished.

So she lived with the pain in her arm and in her chest for weeks because that was one way to keep her father, to have him with her. And she bitterly cursed the soppy nurse at Miss Ryan's School for Young Ladies for discovering the injuries, for taking her pain away.

Over the next few years she learned that she didn't like "straight" sex, that there were men who would do the punishing, who would bring the exquisite pain. Usually no one had to say very much. There was a worldwide fraternity of punishers and those who sought punishment, instantly recognizable to one another by mutual chemistry. She had met her punishers in hotel elevators in foreign countries and not had to say one word, give one direction. They had known what would satisfy her.

And each time she had promised herself that it was the last time. It was sick and debasing and why did she need it when she was young and rich and good looking with a great future, an enviable career?

And each time, when she had met that glance, that look in a man's eyes, she had asked for it, begged for it. It hadn't mattered what he looked like; as long as he was willing to debase her.

A kind of miracle had happened when the television thing had panned out. She had stopped looking for it, stopped thinking about it. Sex, straight, twisted, or upside down, had stopped being important to her. All she thought about was food and scripts and camera angles.

That had lasted for some six months until she began to prepare for the live coverage of 44's fiftieth anniversary. The tension made her nervous and difficult to work with. She wasn't used to live TV. She preferred tape where everything, if need be, could be reshot.

And then she had met him and she had thought that she would indulge herself, ease the tension. They would have sex and then she would send him on his way.

She stood up and stopped twisting the key on the chain around her neck. "There won't be a next time," she said, going to her bedroom, to her closet, wondering why the hell the maid was an hour late and thanking God that she was; wondering what the hell she was going to wear; wondering why the hell she couldn't stop thinking about her father, suddenly, and why the hell she couldn't stop playing with that key.

Just before she left for the television studio, she called her secretary and told her to make a reservation for two for the following night at 44.

"You ate there last night," her secretary said.

"Joyce, when I want frequency data on my dining habits, I'll ask for it. And besides," she went on, because she liked Joyce, "I'm trying to get a feel for the atmosphere."

She had avoided 44 in recent years. It had been her father's favorite restaurant in the world. Duke had been her father's only genuine friend. Her father, she thought, as she let herself out of her apartment, would have enjoyed celebrating 44's fiftieth.

Chapter Two

PETER STEWART-GREENE sat in the back of the maroon Lincoln limousine, waiting for the chauffeur UNITAS had thoughtfully provided with the car to get out and open the door for him. Peter didn't like the car—he would have preferred a black Caddy without such accoutrements as stereo systems and moon roofs. And he didn't like the chauffeur who was taking an insolent amount of time in getting to the door. But he had long ago learned that one didn't let servants affect one's emotions.

So unlike his father, that self-proclaimed Duke, who knew every busboy's sordid biography, who was aware that the second chief's wife had a brain tumor, who had long and stormy political arguments with the bar captain.

The chauffeur finally opened the maroon door. He would be replaced, Peter said to himself, in the morning. In the meanwhile he smiled and said thank you. He was in no particular rush to see his father. He stood on the sidewalk in front of the brownstone that housed 44, taking a last inhalation of the thin, sweet-smelling cigarette the little shop in the Burlington Arcade made up for him from Egyptian tobacco.

"I shan't be more than an hour," he said to the driver who was in the process of lighting his own cigarette. "Quite possibly less. Please wait."

He dropped the cigarette into the gutter and took a deep breath, thinking that New York's poor air quality was greatly overexaggerated, thankful for the late October sun which gave a warm, comforting tone to the brownstone in front of him. Still he knew it would be cool inside. It always had been. The single most memorable sensation left over from his summers spent in New York was the chill that the over air-conditioned 44 invariably afflicted him with.

I wonder why I'm having such trouble going up those steps, he asked himself. It's not as if I'm frightened. He has no power over me now. Quite the reverse. It's all the old ghosts, the old associations, the fear I felt during those endless summers.

He reached into his vest pocket for the gold key. He wondered if he would have qualified for a gold key if he weren't Duke's son and knew that of course he wouldn't have. He was as different from Duke as night from day and he had always been proud of that fact. Except perhaps during those summers when he would watch his father greet movie stars and politicians and society leaders with that ever open glad hand of his, that remarkable open embrace of his, that positive need of his to say what he felt. "Get it off your chest," he would tell his son, who had retreated into that rigid British reserve which was the hallmark of Winchester, the public school he attended in England.

"We don't get it 'off our chest' at school," Peter had instructed him.

"You poor kid," Duke had said and tried to embrace him, but that was another indulgence gentlemen didn't allow themselves. He had stood stiffly, his arms at his side, until Duke had let him go. "What the hell is she doing to you?" Duke had asked, studying his fifteen-year-old son. Embarrassingly there were tears in his eyes. "I'd just like to know what the hell she's doing to you?" And he had left that ridiculous room on the second floor of 44 with its butter-yellow leather-bound books and its red leather sofas, left his son standing on the turquoise Chinese carpet, the apparent victor in a battle that never seemed to end.

Peter forced himself to walk up the steps, remembering that there were just fifteen of them. More inconsequential memories. He recalled a Sunday morning when he was seven or eight, playing tag with Nick Reo on those stairs and being told by Nick's father to play somewhere else.

"What're the customers going to think, two wild Indians playing grab ass on the steps?" Victor wanted to know, going back inside the restaurant. Nick, who had been irrepressible, began the game again and this time Victor came out with the porter's broom, half serious about hitting them.

"You'd best consult my father," Peter had said in his carefully controlled accent, "before you do some irreversible harm with that broom."

Victor had looked at him and shook his head and then went inside to return with Duke. His own punishment had been a half hour's lecture on the sacrosanctity of 44's steps. Nick had been taken down to the kitchen and given a whipping with Victor's belt. Nick had emerged from the kitchen with a sugar cookie in each hand, crocodile tears in his deceptively sleepy eyes, Victor's protective arm around him. Peter had never understood that easy relationship between Nick and his father. He had never understood why, deep down, he would have preferred the licking to the lecture, the sugar cookie and the protective arm to the dinner with Henry Cabot Lodge at table three in the Club Room.

As he attempted to fit the gold key into the intricate lock on 44's massive door—it was hidden in a cast iron rose to deceive the old federal agents hunting for illegal liquor—he found that his hand was shaking, that his stomach had turned sour.

He blamed it on the ill-prepared breakfast the borrowed cook had prepared, but he knew better than that. His father's death had been an event he had long hoped for and now, when it seemed as if it were about to happen, he was feeling guilty, as if he were responsible for it.

It hadn't taken that charlatan analyst to tell him that his was a classic case of arrested Oedipal complex. It was a minor miracle that he wasn't living in a walk-up flat in Chelsea, worrying about the flocked wallpaper in the tiny loo, politely asking someone with suspicious hair to please pass the lemon pepper.

Not that his mother wasn't responsible. As each summer approached, she would drive down to school in the old green

Rolls Riley kept polished so perfectly and put him through his catechism, her anti-Duke Greene indoctrination.

She had felt she was doing her duty, protecting her son against the man who supported them both. "Darling," she would say, putting one long, elegant white arm round his shoulder, drawing him close to her in the secure cocoon that was the back of the green Rolls. "Your father is a very interesting man but not a very nice one. I shouldn't want him to influence you overly much. He's a Jew which is not his fault but which explains a great deal. And he's a restaurateur which tells the rest of the story. He makes his living pleasing people. That's a very low way to earn money, don't you agree?"

She would drive him up to London for long weekends, supervise Kaplan, the tailor on Savile Row, as to the cut of his blazers and his flannel trousers. She would take him to tea with Royalty and to country weekends with Gentry, always in the spring, always just before his dreaded departure for New York.

She had taught him exactly the correct note of amused condescension to strive for when anyone made mention of Duke's 44 Club. "In British society your father, odd as it may seem, can be an asset if you use him correctly, if you never let on you're ashamed. You must pretend that the accident of your birth is a charming, mysterious prank. You must pretend that you adore Duke but from a distance. You must always be perfectly correct in your own behavior. Your first slip and they will all say, 'Ah, that's the father coming out.' "

Ten years after the divorce, she had married an old friend, a discreetly homosexual minor baronet who providentially died six months later, allowing Irene to be called Lady Carston and to stay on in her Mayfair flat where she gave charming dinner parties, mixing members of the theater with members of Parliament.

It was Lady Carston's hope that her son would devote himself to the classical theater, that he would act as a gentleman producer of England's great plays, that he would eventually win his own knighthood.

To that end, he had taken the money his father had given him on his twenty-first birthday and bought a West End theater where Vanessa Redgrave and Irene Worth and, on very special occasions, Lady Carston herself, would give new meaning to old plays. They were well received and both the queen and Prince Charles made a conscientious effort to attend each new offering. Certainly Peter would eventually be knighted. Even Mrs. Thatcher—not a great classics lover—had been seen in a box recently.

The only ingredient Peter needed to keep it going was money. The Stewart, his theater, was a great success with the critics, even with Society, but not with the general public.

"I'm not so certain I would much like it if it were," his mother had decided. During a long, trans-Atlantic telephone call his father had said he could not lend Peter any more money, that he was having his own problems with 44.

"And of course 44 comes first," Peter had said bitterly.

"First, last, and always," Duke had returned, wondering why his son always brought out the worst in him.

As he entered 44 on that late October morning, Peter tried to put both his parents out of his mind. He could hear the various noises the staff invariably made in the morning—it was close to ten thirty, he decided—emanating from the huge kitchen in the former basement. He stood in the foyer and listened for a moment. Then he looked at the dim restaurant and wondered why natural light was anathema to four-star restaurants.

The foyer itself looked very much as it must have when Duke's 44 Club had first opened its door nearly fifty years before. The paneling had been painted a soft and creamy white while the cloakroom had been enlarged to hold hundreds of coats. There was a glass counter in front of the cloakroom containing Jamaican cigars in glass tubes which sold for two dollars each. Next to the cigars were books about 44 or by 44's house authors, O'Hara and Hemmingway, Auchincloss and Mailer.

The pure white marble floor was still intact, and the octagonal ceiling still boasted its original chandelier, a crystal confection which looked like a greatly enlarged Edwardian lady's earring.

I wonder if they'll change it, Peter thought, looking into the main dining room which seemed smaller and more charming than he had remembered. He laughed aloud when he saw the best table, still in its awkward place. Though the other tables still wore overturned chairs, the first table was graced by only a perfect Baccarat brandy glass.

Peter remembered sliding into its leather banquette on one of his earliest trips back to New York. It had been a late June Monday afternoon when the dining room was relatively empty. He and his father were going to dine alone, a rare occasion.

"We never sit there, son," Duke had said, taking his hand.

"Why not?" Peter wanted to know.

"That's the best table. It's reserved for visitors who are very important. You and I have our own table, number nine." Table nine was at the far end of the dining room, too close to the kitchen, too close to the stairway that led to the J. J. Walker Room, a place it was reputed that Duke had never been. Because of the mirrors that surrounded it, table nine commanded a clear view of every table in the room but it was evident that it was the least desirable seating place on the first floor: *no one* could see who was dining at table nine.

They took most of their meals there, more often than not, during those summers, with Nick, the manager's son. And more often than not, at six—an hour in England when Peter would usually just be finishing his tea. But Duke liked to be free after seven when his friends would began to arrive.

"Peter," a voice said and Peter turned and looked into the Club Room but it was too dark to see. But suddenly, like a special effect in a conjuring act, the lights went up and there, looking very much like a magician, stood Nick under the Chamberlain portrait of Duke.

He was a few years younger than Peter, perhaps thirty, and he hadn't changed that much in the years since they had last met. His hair was still black and curly and barely tamed, his dark eyes still glowed with some private joke, and his lean, hard body still seemed inappropriate for the dark suit he was wearing. Peter looked up at the portrait of Duke and thought that Nick would be able to carry off the white tie and tails. He had that sort of theatrical grace.

"Is there anything more desolate than an empty restaurant?" Peter asked as he walked across the foyer and shook Nick's hand. "Even on an empty stage one feels the presence of past plays. But fifty years of prodigious meals? The thought of the gluttony and the waste is anything but comforting."

Nick smiled. "Welcome home, Peter. You've become a talker. Come on in and I'll buy you a cup of coffee." Nick moved behind the bar and said something into a microphone.

"All very up to date, aren't we?" Peter asked, sitting at the bar.

"Oh, yes. We have electric lights and central heating."

"All I can remember is the central air conditioning," Peter said, looking at Nick as a boy brought in a tray with cups and a pot of coffee and placed it on the bar. "You seem very fit, Nick. Even happy."

"I guess I am. And you, Peter?"

"Not much to complain about. How is Duke?"

"You're here. I suppose you already know."

"You always were so bloody direct. One would have thought as executive director—that is what they call you these days, is it not?—of Duke's 44, you might have learned tact." Peter sipped at his coffee. "Officially I'm here for the half century. Between us, I've spoken to that doctor—what was his name?—at Sloan-Kettering. I wanted to see Duke before he died."

"Admirable."

Peter continued to sip at his coffee. "Not every day a man's father dies. One likes to be around for the crucial moment no matter how ill one got along with him. You must have felt something like that when Victor had his stroke. Though I was told you were right here at your place the following day, in your nice blue suit and the black tie and that carnation-in-your-lapel trick you borrowed from Duke."

The lights in the dining room and the chandelier in the foyer were illuminated and a young boy in white shirt and black trousers began taking down chairs, placing them upright, diplomatically ignoring the two men in the Club Room.

"It was a good place to be at the time," Nick said. "And it was certainly where Victor would have wanted me to be. He was a gent from the old school."

"So are you, Nick. You're a romantic. You still see 44 as the last bastion of fine club dining and yourself as its protector. Do you remember Cecil's phrase when someone showed up at the door who didn't pass muster and he wanted to alert one of the staff to that fact?"

"D.N.O.K.D. Definitely Not Our Kind, Dear."

"Very good, Nick. There's less and less of 'our kind' out there nowadays. I've been talking to the men who know. Duke's 44 has been operating in the red for years. It can't go on as it has and I've told Duke that half a dozen times. He's been financing 44 out of his own pocket."

"And what do you plan to do about it, Peter?"

He looked at Nick and thought that he had never seen a more finely made man. Every detail of Nick's face, from his Roman nose to his long black lashes seemed as if it had been painted by one of the old neoclassicists. Peter suddenly realized he hated him in much the way he hated his father. "As soon as Duke dies, I'm going to sell every single share of 44 and 44 Industries I own."

"I thought Brette had the controlling shares of the Industry."

"She did. But she's my wife, the mother of my children. Like the good little women she is, she signed everything over to me."

"Whose buying?" Nick wanted to know.

"UNITAS. They're most interested in acquiring the Industry. Seems they and their computer believe 44 liquors and fancy foods can be turned into a profitable business. Naturally they must have the restaurant. It adds sex appeal to the Industry. I shouldn't worry about your job, old chap. They'll probably want to keep you on. Familiar face at the door and all that."

Peter put down his coffee cup. "And now I suppose it's time to see my father. It's been a pleasure talking to you, Nick." He stood up and went toward the elevator.

"Don't tell Duke about your plans for 44, Peter."

Peter stepped into the elevator and put his index finger on the hold button. "If you think the old devil doesn't already know, you're a greater fool than I thought you were. One more thing, Nick. Brette wants to come to lunch. Put her down for the best table, like a good chap."

Nick put the coffee cups back on the tray and picked it up. "You know the rules, *old chap*. The best table is always held in reserve. For important people."

Peter took his finger from the hold button, allowing the doors to close. "I imagine," he said, "that all that will soon change."

• • •

Peter's interview with his father lasted less than a half hour. SayDee, in Peter's view an asburd, impossible person, had greeted him at the elevator with the news that it was not one of Duke's good days.

"I'm so happy you could come for the fiftieth," Duke said, and Peter couldn't believe that that vibrant, virile man had turned into this thin, gray shade, this almost indistinguishable ghost of himself. His valet had tarted him up in a red velvet smoking jacket, an ascot to hide his pathetic neck, but there was no mistaking the fact that Duke was dying.

When he left, Peter promised he would return the next day. He allowed himself to be kissed. "I'll be better tomorrow," Duke had promised, holding onto him. "It's been too long, Peter. Too long."

Peter hadn't said anything. He couldn't wait to escape from that place, from that dying man who was his father. He didn't take the elevator. He didn't want to see the restaurant or Duke's portrait in the Club Room. He went down the stairs that led directly to Forty-fourth Street. He didn't even bother to wait for the chauffeur to open the Lincoln's rear door. He got himself into the limousine, told the driver to take him to his appointment at UNITAS headquarters on Lower Broadway, lit a sweet Egyptian cigarette, and used his old school discipline to force himself not to think of what he had just seen.

Chapter Three

"WHAT'S THE matter with you?" Nick asked Lawrence, as he led the way into his office which was situated behind the Club Room, down the same hall that led to the ladies' and men's room and to the public telephones. Victor had never used it ("I'm going to sit behind the ladies' room?"); but Nick found it was useful, a quiet place to think. At that moment he would have liked to think over what Peter had told him, to see if he could come up with a solution. If 44 went, he had a feeling he would go, too. Back to the drugs and the drink and the other escape hatches he had tried to slide down after Nam. Duke's 44 was his continuing therapy, his glue, and he knew it.

But it was too close to lunch and there were too many easier, quicker problems to solve. Lawrence, 44's maître d'hôtel, looked like an egg with a fringe of hair on the top of his head. He was a fastidious, mercurial gourmet who loved food almost as much as he loved the reflected glory he was able to garner from the celebrities who went out of their way to be nice to him.

"What's the matter with you?" Nick asked again, looking away from Lawrence's face which wore his most pained expression. "The caviar tainted?" Each morning Lawrence performed the ritual of the caviar, taught to him by Cecil, which consisted of minutely inspecting each open tin and then painstakingly tasting each of the samples to make absolutely certain they were up to 44's standards.

"Nearly as bad," Lawrence answered, folding his hands in front of him, putting the tips of his fingers to his lips, always a sign of distress. "Georgio was late again today." Punctuality, in Lawrence's book of behavior, was on a par with cleanliness and motherhood.

"Fire him," Nick said, reaching for the reservation book, which was the first step in another daily ritual, the assignment of tables.

"He's the best busboy I've ever worked with," Lawrence, who was given to overstatement, said. "He's unobtrusive looking. He's very strong. He doesn't roll his eyes and mutter '*Yo no se*' when a diner mistakes him for a waiter. He's quick on his feet, he's unerringly polite, and he didn't beat up the sous chef when he made a pass at him. I couldn't possibly fire him."

"Take him off the best table. Make him think it's a demotion."

"I'll give him one more chance, I think. I love people with obsessions."

"What is his?" Nick asked, seduced once again into a time-wasting conversation with Lawrence.

"I don't know yet and I'm not at all sure I ever want to. But obsessed he is, that's perfectly clear. Sometimes his eyes are like the tiny pinpoints of madness, not unlike Rasputin, whom, I'm told . . ."

"What was all that screaming about in the kitchen this morning?"

Maurice Gotlib, the chef, Lawrence told him, was shouting at his third assistant for some minor change in the order of the cutting boards. "You know our Maurice. Now don't you feel it's time to get down to the reservations?" Lawrence asked as if it had been Nick who had been wasting his time. They applied themselves to the book where each reservation was entered with the time that it had been taken and the name of the person answering the call. Neither Nick nor Lawrence had to resort to the white, blue, and pink cards to ascertain the desirability of those who had reservations for the day.

When all the tables were alloted for both the luncheon and the evening meals, Nick closed the book, but Lawrence made no movement to leave. "I understand Peter's in New York."

"Yes."

"If I may be so bold to ask, for what purpose?"

"The anniversary."

"I may look like a naïf, Nick, but I assure you I . . ."

"He's here to see his father die and then to sell 44 to UNITAS so they can make a cafeteria out of it."

"It's that bad?" Lawrence asked.

"I'm not sure. I have to talk to Duke."

"I'm sorry I asked. I'm going to put what you've just seen fit to burden me with, Nick, out of my mind. I'm not going to let it ruin my day. I'm going to see to my guests." He went to the door and turned back. "And if there's anything at all I can do, Nick . . ."

"Thanks, Lawrence," Nick said, looking up from his desk and smiling. "I know."

Lawrence, who was not able to put Nick's information out of his mind, who tended—as his mother, who lived with him high on Central Park West enjoyed pointing out—to dwell on unhappy thoughts, arrived in the foyer just as Valida Rand was being allowed into the foyer by Little Mike.

"Mr. Lawrence," she said in that familiar whiskey voice that had been thrilling theatergoers and movie fanatics through a career that had weathered thirty years, three marriages, innumerable love affairs, and more than one announcement of retirement. "Mr. Lawrence. How are you?"

"Very well, thank you, Miss Rand," Lawrence said. "What may I do for you today?"

"I wanted to know," she said, letting her voice descend slowly into a confidential whisper, "who has the best table for lunch?"

Lawrence's mouth shut closed disapprovingly. "I'm not at liberty to say, Miss Rand. Perhaps you should talk to Mr. Reo . . ."

"And there he is now," she said, spotting Nick entering the Club Room. "The boy always had perfect timing."

Nick had posted himself at the tail end of the bar, under the portrait of Duke, his usual position during the luncheon hours. From there he could greet customers, keep an eye on business and on the comings and goings of the staff members who worked the bar.

Valida Rand moved toward him with that effortless grace she was so well known for, and kissed him on the cheek, lightly. "You always remind me of your father when I see you," she said, taking his hand in her gloved one. "Though I can't think why. You don't look at all alike. Perhaps it's the way you stand, as if at any moment you're going to take out a gun and shoot someone. If you ever give up the restaurant game, darling, you can always be a gangster."

Nick took her arm and walked her away from the bar. He had been in love with her when he was a teen-ager. But he knew when he was getting her razzle-dazzle treatment and he wanted to know why.

"I never could fool you, darling. Actually I don't think I could ever fool anyone. Listen, Nick. I need the best table. I've never asked for it before and so when I've gotten it, it was always marvelous, like receiving an unexpected gift the day after Christmas. And I will understand, Nick, if the queen of Rumania is visiting, but if she's not, Nick, for the next week or so, when I come, do try."

She put her face very near to his and though she was at least fifty and in close-ups her features were too large and it turned out she wasn't pretty at all, still he could feel the heat of the magnetism that had gone into making her a great actress and, in his book, a great woman. She was so relentlessly a lady and yet, at the same time, so indelibly sexy. That thin European accent and those slightly slanted, Slavic eyes.

And again, that deep, whiskey voice. "You know, darling, that I don't usually care. There were nights when your father put me upstairs at a table next to a radiator and I didn't care. But it's important that they think I'm still bankable, that they believe Valida Rand still makes movies that make money . . . that 44 is behind me.

"Am I talking too much? I always do when I'm feeling nervous and old. Well, I am nervous and old. In the old days Duke and Cecil would have . . . how is Duke? No, don't tell me. I don't want to know. I'm as superstitious as a peasant and if you tell me he's ill or dying, I'll start thinking I'm ill and dying and that sort of business always shows in my face.

"I know. I am being terribly selfish, terribly movie star, but Nick, this is so important to me, I swear to you."

He put his arm around the sable throw she had worn, hugged her, and took her to the place where Lawrence stood, disapprovingly tapping a silver pencil. "Lawrence, show Miss Rand to the first table on the left, won't you?"

She gave him that radiant, ear-to-ear smile that had won her two Oscars and said, "I won't forget, Nick. I promise."

And Nick hadn't forgotten his sixteenth birthday. Victor, of course, had to work, but Duke had given him a special dinner and made a fuss and Valida Rand had been at the bar and had followed the cake into the room and sat down with Nick when Duke had to leave to talk to the then governor of Pennsylvania. She had said she was sorry she hadn't brought a present for him. And then she had said he seemed old for sixteen, fully grown, just like a man. And he had said that Duke had told him he *was* a man today. Oddly she volunteered to walk him home to the big empty town house that Victor poured all his money into on West Forty-fourth. She had asked if she could come in and then she had asked if she could see his room and finally, when she was in his room, she had said to him, "And now that you're a man, Nicky, what are you going to do about it?"

He came before he managed to get his trousers off, but there were to be a half-dozen more orgasms during the night. Just before she left him in the morning, tiptoeing out with her heels in her hand so as not to waken Victor, she had bent over him and whispered in that unforgettable voice, "You're a marvelous lover, Nicky. And you're going to get better. I envy all of the women who will have the pleasure of your body."

He reached up for her but she was gone.

He knew even then that he had been extraordinarily lucky to have his first lovemaking experience with that patient, generous, wonderfully giving woman, Valida Rand.

"Who'd I displace?" he asked Lawrence, who lowered his eyelids and pursed his somewhat thick lips in disapproval. "Only your President's wife. But Ma Kennedy canceled so I'll switch her to table two. If we're lucky, she'll think it's a sign of something or other."

Nick turned back to the Club Room as Valida's agent,

Saunders, came through the door guarded by Scotty and Little Mike and joined Valida at the best table. Nick watched them for a moment, wondering what the crisis was, and then his attention was taken by other customers, further requests.

"You look radiant, Valida," Saunders said as he slid into the banquette so that he sat next to her. "But all black? Isn't that a touch too severe for the occasion?"

She allowed him to kiss her cheek. "Saunders, darling, you will move to the outside seat if and when he shows, won't you? I don't want him to be able to look directly at me. I didn't have a good night. Of course it shows. Don't bother contradicting me, darling . . ."

"You're nervous," he said, taking her hand, kissing it.

She looked at him and smiled. He was tall, broad shouldered, white haired, with a hawklike profile and enough charm to seduce Bess Truman, and she wondered why she didn't chuck the project and marry him. Saunders, too, wondered why she wouldn't marry him, aloud.

"We would be very right together, you know. We've reached that point, Valida."

"Hush, darling. I'm nervous enough without going over all that. I'm doing everything I can not to wring my hands." She smiled at Henry Fonda and his son, Peter, as they were taken to a banquette along the mirrored wall. "This is the most thoughtfully lit restaurant in New York, don't you think? Duke is always the gentleman, even when it comes to supplying peach-colored lights for his aging clientelle. Dear me, who is that with Burt Reynolds and what are they doing on this coast? I didn't know Hollywood moguls dined at 44. Well, I did but . . ."

Saunders put his wide, manicured hand over Valida's small, still youthful one and said, "Sssh. Be quiet for a moment. Sip your gin. You'll never get what you want from him this way."

She closed her eyes, opened them and drank half of the glass of Bombay gin which had been placed in front of her automatically. "You're right, of course," she said after a moment. She finished off the drink. "You always are, damn you."

"You never could drink like a lady," Saunders said, still

holding her hand. "Do you remember how crazy you made Quintero during the Philadelphia tryouts of *Seventy Cents?* You were supposed to be a lady and for the life of you, you could not hold your pinky out while you were supposed to be nipping politely at your sherry. You kept swilling it like a stevedore with his first beer of the day."

"It's a brilliant screenplay, Saunders, isn't it?" she non-sequitured. "Frank put everything he had—which was considerable—into its writing."

"It is a brilliant screenplay," Saunders said, "and Frank was a genius but it would be nice to have a conversation with you in which neither the screenplay nor Frank's genius was brought up. Just once."

Charles, the best table's waiter, placed another Bombay gin in front of Valida. She took a long pull at it. "Darling Saunders, you must understand. After the years and the men, I finally thought—no, strike that—I knew that I had found what all my films and matinee plays had been promising all those women all those years: love. God knows I felt silly enough, a woman in her forties falling head over heels in love with a short, squat Italian the same age but there it was.

"Everyone gave us ten minutes and we had nearly ten lovely years. Now he's dead and I accept that because there's not much else I can do short of devoting my life to God. But he has left the screenplay, Saunders, and if Frank were alive, I know he would have gotten it made, somehow. So I've got to try as hard as I can to get it made for him."

"You will, Valida."

"I'm not at all certain. They don't like me in Hollywood. They never did. Once, all my films made tons of money and that was enough. Now they think I'm no longer bankrollable. Perhaps I'm not. I'm old and my last three films barely crawled into the black and that was only because of Europe and they're not interested in talent but in how firm or large or small one's breasts photograph . . ."

"Shut up, Valida. They're all interested. I've been to every studio, every major independent, even Canada. There's all the backing in the world. *If* you can get a bankable male star. The screenplay is currently with Dusty Hoffman, Robert de Niro, Al Pacino, Robert Redford. I only left out Woody Allen because he's too short for the gestures required and you're not fond of him.'

"If any one of them says yes—and Hoffman just might, if he can get out of his *Moon Man* commitment—then we have a package and a film. But if we can get Laddy Wister to say yes, then we have a package and a film they'll put everything into. If we can get Laddy Wister, we'll have to beat the backers away."

"Laddy Wister! God has a terrible sense of irony, making Laddy Wister the Star of the Moment. My dim-witted, adorable ex-child groom. I like to think I married him while I was playing Vegas. Only I never played Vegas. What do they see in him, Saunders?"

"*Presumably* the same thing you saw in him."

"I thought he was poetic under all that cloudy blond beauty. I thought he would make me young again. It turned out he was as poetic as Patricia Nixon and a veritable fountain of youth in reverse. Six months with Laddy and I aged a decade. And now he's not going to show. Do you believe the colossal nerve . . . yes, Lawrence?"

"There's a call for you, Miss Rand. Shall I bring the phone to the table."

"Please."

She and Saunders exchanged glances as Lawrence brought the white telephone to the table and connected it to an outlet, rather as if he were presenting the papal crown.

"Thank you, Lawrence," Valida said, grimacing at Saunders, removing her right earring, a golden wing, placing the receiver to her ear. "Of course," she said after a moment. "Darling, Laddy, don't be absurd. No, Saunders and I went right ahead. At this very moment we're knee deep in salmon mousse. Yes, well, I used to prefer lox but one's taste gets refined. No, tomorrow's fine. Same place. Same time. Of course; I understand. I am, too." She replaced the receiver on its cradle, signaled Lawrence to remove the phone and Charles to refill her drink.

"His little wife," she said, replacing the earring, "the charming American Indian apologist, Daisy, came down with a sudden and terrible flu. Laddy feels he can't leave her. One only hopes and prays it leaves the both of them permanently disfigured."

"You were very good with him on the phone."

"I have a terrible premonition about this, Saunders. I think he's enjoying this. I think he's playing with me. He was always slightly sadistic in bed . . ."

"Spare me the details."

". . . the only place he had any power over me. I want to make this film, Saunders. Like no other film I've ever been involved with. I want to make it for Frank and let's face it, I want to make it for me. I want to make one last great film before I start playing John Belushi's mother and Goldie Hawn's dotty aunt. I want one last genuine, brilliant success."

Charles appeared to take their order.

"Chili, darling," she said, getting up. "I'm going to the ladies' and have my breakdown."

As she passed through the Club Room, she managed to smile at Nick who returned it. But his eyes were looking beyond her, to the foyer where Brette Townsend Stewart-Greene was throwing her arms around Little Mike, the six foot two doorkeeper.

Chapter Four

"WAS THAT Valida Rand you kissed on the cheek?" Mary Jane Hammacher asked. She was a young plump woman in an ill-fitting black velvet suit which she hoped, vainly, would make her appear svelte. Mary Jane took the napkin from the gold-rimmed white plate in front of her and wondered if the napkin would leave little white threads all over her skirt. She pulled it from her lap after a moment and saw that it had. She and her companion, a slim, dark-haired woman about her age, had been seated at table six, which was at the far end of the dining room, facing the best table.

"Yes. We see her in London every now and again at garden parties for the queen's fag and other such notables."

"Who is the queen's fag?"

"It used to be Tony Blunt but now that he's a Russian spy, it's anyone's guess. Would you like a drink?"

"I'm not sure I should. I was so nervous about meeting you—here—that I took half a tranquilizer an hour ago. You don't suppose I'll start hallucinating if I have a glass of wine?"

Brette Townsend Stewart-Greene ordered a bottle of Verdicchio and sat back, watching the room.

"Brette, are you all right?"

"Yes, of course," she said, smiling. "Combination of deep despair and mild jet lag. Don't you loathe and despise airplanes?"

"I rarely get to go on them." They were silent for a moment. "Brette," Mary Jane said after the wine arrived and had been poured, after they had toasted the future, "the youngish, fatish matron, with a note of real concern in her voice, asked tremulously: don't you want to talk about it?"

Brette smiled. "I do and I don't. But now I suppose I'll have to. As that pig of a Latin teacher—that one who always wore the huge gold cross on her pink sweater set? . . ."

"Mary Murphy."

"Yes. As Mary Murphy used to say, I'll give it to you in a nutshell: I don't like my life."

"Oh, I know it must be terribly difficult," Mary Jane said, drinking the Verdicchio. "With that tiny fifteen-room flat in Mayfair and that damp little rose-covered cottage in the Cotswalds and those rented villas on the Riviera. It must be an awful strain keeping up with the Snowdons and Lady Diana Cooper and the Douglas Fairbanks, Juniors at those interminable house parties. There was a picture of you in the *Times* dancing with Prince Charles at a party Baron Guy de Rothschild gave in Paris and my heart just went out to you. Your dress alone must have cost . . ."

"To start with, there's absolutely no cash. The dress was lent to me by Halston because he thought it would be clever to have an American designer's dress at the Bal de Nuit and the jewels belong to Peter's mother and aren't really very good. Lots of setting, few stones."

"I thought you owned, singlehandedly, 44 Industry," Mary Jane said.

"I did. I handed it over to Peter when we were married. The money that comes in goes for basic maintenance and to support his theater. But money is not the real problem. The real problem is Peter."

"Oh." Mary Jane put down her glass and took a rueful glance at her lap where it seemed to have snowed. "I'm sorry," she said. "I was being brittle—such a super word, brittle—because it's hard to believe Brette Townsend could ever be unhappy. I envy you just about everything and always have. You were the most beautiful girl at Brearly and you were the most beautiful girl at Vassar and you not only had 44 and Duke Greene behind you, but you were an orphaned Townsend, to boot. You had everything and all I had was family—which maybe three people cared about—and my friendship with you.

"I used to be scared shitless that one morning I'd wake up and you wouldn't be my friend. And beneath the genuine love I feel for you is a layer of pure anger."

"Anger?"

"Dyed-in-the-wool anger. Brette, when we were seventeen and Mummie forced me to have a deb party at the Waldorf (can you imagine anything more embarrassing than the Waldorf?), my date was poor Willie Hammacher. You came with the president of Mexico's son and left with that Brazilian hockey player—Bebe what's-his-name?—who was so sexy, every time he came into a room, I had to go out of it."

"Mary Jane, you married poor Willie Hammacher."

"Yes, and you married Peter Stewart-Greene and got to live in London and mix with the posh international set while I sit in New York on half a dozen benefit committees and have Willie's porky babies. In the summer we go to Willie's mama's house in Newport because she still thinks East Hampton and the Maidstone Club are a rifle fast.

"In the winter we get to visit the family manse at Lyford Key where the bugs eat me alive and dear Mama Hammacher says, twice a day, in that voice that makes me want to grind my teeth into little piles of powder, 'And Someday, Mary Jane, This Will All Be Yours.'

"Brette, I do love you but you must understand why it's not a pure and unadulterated love. Besides, no man could look like Peter and be all bad."

"He's not a man, Mary Jane. Here, let me get another bottle of wine."

"No, Brette, I beg you. I can't get blotto today. I have a Lexington House meeting this afternoon . . ."

Another bottle of Verdicchio was brought and Mary Jane allowed her glass to be filled. "Where was I?" Brette asked. "Oh, Peter. He's not a man. He's a boy. An aging boy. Nobody loves an old boy."

"For me, Peter Stewart-Greene will always be an oh boy. Would you like to complain about your sex life?"

"With Peter? It barely exists and hasn't since the second girl was born. He thinks it's my fault we didn't have a son and now he claims we can't afford a third child. He spends half his time in that bloody theater, fooling with moldy productions of Marlowe, and the other half social climbing. I tell him there's nothing more virulently anti-Semitic than English society and he looks at me with that you-poor-dummy expression of his and tells me that I'll never understand, that the well-born English are a race apart.

"He wouldn't mind unloading me and marrying some simpering English deb—there's half a dozen at his heels—but I am, in my own way, a social asset and it wouldn't be inexpensive to divorce me. Not unless he had something on me and he doesn't."

"Brette, sweet, do you think we might just order? I'm drunk and famished."

"Not until I've finished. You asked me for this lunch. You cast yourself in the role of faithful old friend. I'm picking up the tab; you're going to pay by listening.

"Do you know why we're in New York, Mary Jane?"

"Of course. To celebrate 44's fiftieth."

"Not even close. Peter could care less about 44. Actually he hates it. We're here because he found out that Duke is dying. The moment he does, Peters' selling 44 and 44 Industry to an international consortium that's going to turn this place into a super McDonald's and 'equalize' the flavor of all 44 products. The Scotch is going to taste like iodine and the caviar like pigeon turds."

"Really, Brette . . ."

"I married Peter because I thought he was Duke. Don't forget my parents both died when I was a child. Duke was, is, my family. He brought me up, with Aunt Helen's not very estimable help and I wanted to do what I thought he wanted me to do.

"It was very clear that he liked the idea of my marrying Peter. Peter, of course, took great delight in separating me from Duke, in taking me off to live in England.

"Peter had a nervous breakdown a couple of years ago—some viscount snubbed him at a party—and went to one of those shortcut analysts. He came out of it claiming that I had married him because in reality I wanted to be Duke, I wanted to be a man. When he's pissed and talking to me, he calls me Miss Penis Envy of 1976."

"Do you hate him?" Mary Jane asked, eating her tenth breadstick.

"Oh, I got over hating him."

"Do you take lovers?"

"I'm discreet. I was having a mad, sort of silly affair with a rock star but before I would get in bed with him, I insisted he lease the flat above ours so I could sneak up the back stairs."

"Which rock star?"

"Mary Jane," Brette asked and looked away. "What the hell am I going to do?"

"If it was either Mick Jagger or Rod Stewart, I'm going to stab you with this butter knife."

"Mary Jane . . ."

"You're not going to do anything. There's no reason to. When you fall irrevocably in love, then you can leave him. And you will. You're the sort that does. Only do try and make him an American, Brette. Preferably a New Yorker. If you knew the sort of conversations I usually have with women at lunch. We don't even talk about clothes any more. We're all too fat and everything's so damned expensive. It's schools and benefit parties and . . ."

"Hello, Brette."

"Nick. I didn't think you were going to recognize me. You look wonderful." She stood up, took his hand, and introduced Mary Jane. "I saw Duke before lunch," she told him and there was a moment of silence.

"He's not so healthy," Nick said.

"No." She looked up at him. He smiled, then Lawrence motioned to him from the door, he said good-bye to the both of them and moved away.

"If I were ever going to have an affair with a man," Mary Jane said, finishing her wine, hesitating. "No. Let me rephrase that. If a man were ever going to have an affair with me, I should like him to be that one. Even if the affair only lasted fifteen minutes in the back seat of a taxicab, I should like him to be that one. He's notorious, you know."

"In what way?"

"You see all these gorgeous, rich, and desirable women

sprinkled about this room? Rumor has reached even my sanctified ears that he has had each one. But only once, no matter how smitten the lucky girl is. He has one genuine passion, it is said, and that is Duke's 44 Club. He only makes dates in the mornings so he can devote the rest of his energy to 44."

"For a person who lives such a sheltered, old New York Hammacher life, Mary Jane, you seem to know a great deal about restaurant society."

"I live life vicariously. I watch Rona Barrett every morning and Dinah Sheridan every night." Nick walked by their table on his way up to the J. J. Walker Room. "God, he is a sulky beauty, isn't he?"

Brette laughed. "He always was. You know, we more or less grew up here together. I lived next door with Aunt Helen and he was here everyday with his father. I was a terrible little snob, very much the upstairs brat while Nick was lurking about in corners, since Victor didn't want him to make a nuisance of himself.

"I was always being shown off by Duke, getting called out to be introduced to visiting movie stars and royalty. I remember Peter visiting during the summer. Naturally I was in love with him, he was several years older and spoke with that delightful accent and seemed so terribly remote. Once he condescended to tease me about something or other—my pigtails, I suspect—and I burst out crying. The next moment Nick had sprung from nowhere and was at Peter's throat. Though he was four inches shorter and ten pounds lighter, he gave Peter a terrible beating. Victor banned Nick from 44 for a month which was like taking candy away from other children."

Mary Jane stood up. "Brette, I have reached the point where I invariably pass out. I have two requests: push me toward the ladies' room and order something for me. Anything that's quick and filling. Now where do I go?"

"The ladies' room is behind the elevator in the Club Room. I'll get you a steak sandwich and piles of home fries."

She watched her friend teeter off toward the Club Room and then she looked up across the room. Nick was talking to Nancy Kissinger, saying something which made her smile. As he left her, he looked down the length of the room at the table where Brette was sitting. They looked at one another for several moments until Mary Jane resumed her seat.

Nick left the dining room with a quiet smile but in the few seconds it took him to cross the foyer, to reach the place at the far end of the bar in the Club Room where he habitually stood, all traces of affability had left him.

He told Mickey to fix him a double Johnny Walker Black, on the rocks. Mickey, an actor at heart like many a bartender, restrained himself from commenting. He only raised his eyebrows a fraction and made the drink. When Nick Reo ordered a double Black, and in that tone of voice, Mickey knew it wouldn't do him any good whatsoever to comment. He didn't even ask, as he was tempted to do, whether Nick wanted crushed ice or lemon. In past dealings with Nick Reo, Mickey had learned restraint.

Even Lawrence, who had been known not only to stand up to Nick, but to question him, at first contented himself with a sweeping gaze around the bar, a few seconds emphasis on the glass in Nick's hand, and then a studied, military pivotal turn of his oval body. Lawrence, who held definite ideas on the subject, figuratively as well as literally, turned his back on the spectacle of 44's manager drinking, in public, during the day, at the bar.

Nick turned, too, but away from the restaurant, away from the crowds. He faced the wall of photographs behind the bar. He wasn't looking at the celebrity snapshots. All he could see were the violet eyes of Brette Townsend Stewart-Greene and the steady, not unsympathetic gaze those eyes had leveled at him.

When she had married Peter, he had hoped he wouldn't have to think of her again. He had vowed that he wouldn't. But her name kept cropping up, often when he least expected it. In Duke's increasingly reminiscent conversations. In queries from her friends who dined at 44. "We saw Brette in London," Mary Emmerline told him. "When on earth is she going to give New York a chance?"

Well, Nick thought, now she's giving New York a chance. He had thought he had developed an immunity to her, that after so many years and so much pain, that that volatile mixture of feelings—love and hate and desire and something else—would have lost its kick. Lost its kick? he asked himself. Not for a moment. I feel as if a terrorist's bomb just exploded in the pit of my stomach.

He swallowed half his drink when he felt a hand on his shoulder. He swung round, expecting Brette, getting Lawrence. "If I may interrupt this little midafternoon debauch, SayDee is on the house phone. She wants to talk to you, if you're in any condition to talk."

"Lawrence . . ."

"Dear Nick, don't say what you're going to say. Bite your tongue. Think lovely thoughts. You know you'll regret it. You might just be able to bring off the anniversary celebration without me. But it won't be easy or even pretty."

"Lawrence, go fuck yourself. And tell SayDee I'll call her back in a few minutes."

Lawrence's voice went softer and lower. "Nick, if there's . . ."

"There's nothing you can do, Lawrence," Nick said, touched by the concern in his friend's face. "Not now, anyway. Look, there's C. Z. Guest waiting to be shown to her table. Go take care of her. I'll be okay in a minute."

Nick finished his drink and left the Club Room with another, going to his office, telling his secretary—who was deep into the November issue of *Vogue*—that he didn't want to be disturbed.

He sat down at the desk, put his drink on the glass that protected the old red leather inlay, and closed his eyes. He rested his head on the desk on one arm and with his free hand felt the old wooden sides of the desk. It made him think of his father, Victor.

"What're you moping around here for?" he remembered Victor asking him on a dark blue summer evening in the late 1960's. Nick had been in the same position, his head down, as he was now. "Why don't you go and play ball in the park?"

"It's too hot."

"That college expects a good athlete in September, not some skinny runt who's afraid of the heat. Duke didn't get you a draft exemption so you can lay around my office."

"Cornell could care less about my athletic ability and Duke

got me a draft exemption so I wouldn't get all shot up in Vietnam, Victor."

"Don't call me Victor."

"I'm sorry. *Mister* Reo."

"You got a mouth on you, Nick, and I don't like it. I was too easy on you when you was a kid because you didn't have a mother, and now . . ."

"I'm sorry, Dad. I'm sorry." He got out of his father's chair and stood up, not knowing what to do with himself.

Victor put his arm around him and held him for a moment. He smelled of Dutch Masters' cigars and Old Spice after shave. "Listen, Nick, you got a bad case of puppy love."

"It's not puppy love, Dad," Nick said, freeing himself gently.

"All right, it's the real McCoy. What good's it going to do you? She's not for you, Nick. Duke's had one idea ever since Cecil and Phebe died and that's for Brette to grow up and marry Peter. You're not in the picture, Nick."

"I know, Dad."

He picked up his light summer jacket and went out into the hall. Duke was just coming up the stairs from the kitchen. "How you doing, kid?" He put his arm around Nick's shoulder, leading him out into the Club Room.

"Hey, Duke, my father's going to have a cow if he finds me in 44 without a tie."

"It's all my fault," Duke said, holding onto him, taking him with him into the elevator. "The worst that can happen is he'll fire me." Duke looked at him as they stepped into the elevator. "You're not laughing? Well, it wasn't that funny. I shouldn't be undermining Victor but tonight I'm so proud, I'm popping. I want you to come upstairs. I want you to see something."

Duke hadn't been all that sensitive to Nick and his pain. When he wanted to show off one of his possessions—whether it was a new horse or a new car or even a new woman—nothing could get in his way.

That night he wanted to show off his son, Peter, in a new incarnation: the Oxford man.

Peter traditionally spent long, painful summer vacations with Duke. Duke continually tried to win his son's favor while Peter remained as relentlessly immune to Duke's charm as only his mother's son could be.

But this summer Peter was to be in New York for a short ten-day visit. He was at Oxford, at Balliol, and had signed up for a summer term.

As Duke and Nick, in his chino trousers and Windbreaker jacket, entered the air-conditioned atmosphere of Duke's duplex, Peter turned from a contemplation of Forty-fourth Street. He wore a white dinner jacket. His hair was combed back and slicked down. He held a drink in one hand, a cigarette in the other. He looked like a refined Duke, thinner, finer, both less robust and less vital.

In the space of a year he had become set in his own personality. He had become a man.

"Look who I found in Victor's office?" Duke said, leading Nick into the drawing room, which never failed to awe him.

"Hello, Nicky," Peter said, putting his cigarette in his mouth, his drink on a glass table, walking across the room as if it were his. "How are you, old chap?"

Nick shook the outstretched hand and said he was fine.

"Would you like a drink? Robert, get young Mr. Reo a drink," Peter said, and Duke just stood there, a bemused smile on his tanned face. One could see how proud he was of this aristocratic son, of this young heir of his who could give David Niven a run for his money in the sophisticated nonchalance department.

Nick said he didn't want a drink and then he said maybe he would have a beer. Robert brought him a Miller's on a tray with a glass but Nick didn't take the glass.

"I hope you don't try to choke me tonight if I tease Brette," Peter said, referring to an occasion when they were younger. "I think you did permanent damage to my windpipe. Do you remember, Father, when Nick . . ."

That reminiscence was cut off when SayDee entered the room in a pink and white ensemble that fought with the graceful colors in the room and lost. "Nicky," she said and smiled as Brette followed her, and Nick held his breath.

No one noticed. They all turned to look at her. She was seventeen and not unlike her mother at that age, with black hair and very fair skin and a face dominated by violet eyes. She was wearing a black evening dress, cut low in the back.

It exposed her lovely shoulders and made her seem both very young and very sophisticated at the same time.

"Peter's taking Brette to a party at the British consulate," Duke said, and Nick wanted to hit him. He wanted to hit them all.

"Hi, Nick," Brette said, coming up to him, giving him a little kiss on the cheek, putting one hand on his chest. She wore Real Ritz Red nail polish and a gardenia perfume that cut through the air as if it had seeped into the room through the air-conditioning ducts.

"You've got too much perfume on," Nick said.

"Mr. Charm. Such a way with the ladies," Brette said, turning toward Peter. "Hadn't we better go?" she asked, hurt. "We're already late."

Peter smiled condescendingly. "One should be half an hour late for cocktails, no more than fifteen for dinner; at least forty-seven minutes are allowed for consulate balls."

SayDee put a white mink wrap around Brette's shoulders, Peter took her arm, and they left.

SayDee and Duke stood about the drawing room, smiling at one another, like proud parents. Nick went to the window and watched as Brette and Peter got into the car Duke had hired for them for the evening. They looked as if they belonged to a world filled with consulate parties, with chauffeured cars.

Nick knew he didn't.

In the morning he went to the building on lower Broadway where he was told he could begin the process of making himself an officer in the United States Marines. "We Need A Few Good Men," the marines' poster said. Nick wanted to prove that he was one.

In the fall he didn't go to Cornell. He went, instead, to Da Nang, where he prepared to lead an elite squadron of experts in armed combat into that peculiar country and conflict known as Vietnam.

Chapter Five

"DID YOU talk to Duke?" Lawrence asked, his hands folded together and held in front of him like a friar in a monastery.

"No," Nick answered, entering the foyer, which was very much Lawrence's domain. "SayDee says he didn't sleep all night, that he barely recognized Peter. It's one of his bad days."

"Did you tell her it's absolutely critical that you speak with him? Sometimes our SayDee can be a bit overprotective.

Nick looked at his maître d'hôtel. "What do you know from critical?"

"My dear boy, as Cecil used to say, I was standing just inside the main dining room, supervising the morning setup, when you and Peter had your little tête-à-tête. It's amazing how voices carry, especially in the A.M.

"My lips are sealed." He pantomimed, locking his lips and throwing away an imaginary key. "What are you going to do, Nick?" the oversized, egg-shaped man asked, becoming serious.

"I won't know that until I talk to Duke. Is everything all right here?"

"Is there ever a time when everything is all right? New

York's dining habits seem to have undergone an overnight revolution. I have more customers waiting for tables now, at half past two, than I did an hour ago. Suddenly everyone's eating their midday meal in the middle of the late afternoon. You don't suppose it's the Arab influence?"

Nick looked into the main dining room which was indeed especially crowded for that hour. Mrs. Robert Wagner was sitting where Brette had been.

"She left fifteen minutes ago," Lawrence said.

"Who asked you and how come you know so much about my personal business?"

"I'm a maître d', Nick. Maître d's are supposed to know everything."

"So who has the best table for cocktails?"

"La Hull," Lawrence said, moving his head back slightly to register distaste. "And the papists."

A lapsed Catholic, Lawrence was vehemently anti-Church though he remained as courteous as was appropriate when he was dealing with Joan Hull and the stream of monsignors, cardinals, bishops, and other Vatican-blessed dignitaries who accompanied her to 44 on the rare occasions when she was in residence in New York. Her town house, one of the last of Fifth Avenue's private residences, looked like a great nineteenth-century men's club and was much coveted by real-estate developers.

"I'll burn it to the ground first," Joan Hull was reputed to have said, "before I let Harry Helmsley and that wife of his get their hands on it."

Were it left to Lawrence, Joan Hull and her spiritual advisors would have been given a lesser table. But Joan Hull's father, P. Palmer Hull, had been a classmate of Cecil's at Choate, one of the original guests at 44's opening night, and he had left his daughter his own father's money—one of America's great fortunes—in tact, based on railroads and coal and canned soup.

Joan Hull had little interest in the money save for what influence it could buy her within the hierarchy of the Church. She had found religion early and would have been a nun had P. Palmer allowed her, had he not forced her into a marriage at eighteen from which she emerged at twenty, hating temporal men with a fervor that rivaled her religious dedication.

She sent her husband, a man who enjoyed sex and alcohol and his own brand of muddy Catholicism, more or less in that order, to the wrong side of Barbados where she kept him in adequate luxury with the proviso that he never return to the United States, that he never leave the island.

When both he and her father died within a year of one another—one from a heart attack, the other from kidney failure—Joan Hull was able to be even more supportive to the sort of men she found it comforting to be with: those of the cloth.

Joan Hull, a lean, tawny, rather sere woman who might have been any age but happened to be in her early fifties, had one other interest besides the Church. Or perhaps it should be said that Joan Hull had an interest that was firmly entwined with the Church. That was her nephew, the young and brilliant Monsignor Paul McGuigan.

On that Monday afternoon he was due to have cocktails with his aunt and, as he talked with his elderly guest in the small, exquisite office that had been loaned to him in the building behind Saint Patrick's Cathedral, he felt a decided thrill of anticipation. One of his secret affections was for movie stars, and there was always one or two to be glimpsed at 44.

Paul Palmer McGuigan was very nearly named D'Arcy by his mother, a foolish, lovable fluff of a New York society woman, Catholic branch, built much on the lines of the late Billie Burke. Her father could deny her nothing, not even the McGuigan—as he was known by friends around the world—as a husband. Her elder sister, Joan, however, could and did deny her a great deal.

It was Joan who chose the baby's name, their father's, after discarding D'Arcy as a "piece of Jane Austen whimsy." And it was Joan who took on the baby, who offered to bring him up, when the child's mother died.

Paul's father, a man who felt only genuinely at home despoiling the jungles of South America, Asia, and Africa, causing huge and usually unworkable factories to be built for local governments intent on modernization, breathed a rueful sigh of relief when the formidable Joan Hull stepped in, took over, and allowed the McGuigan to return to the Amazon.

An aunt of Joan's, Mrs. Angell, had left her a huge, unpleasantly Victorian estate in King of Prussia, Pennsylvania, where Joan Hull held court to a constant stream of church plenipotentiaries. From the beginning she knew what she wanted from, of, and for the child Providence had seen fit to put into her strong, ugly, capable hands.

There was certainly never to be any doubt in either her mind or in that of her advisors as to what Paul's vocation would be. From the start he was surrounded, nearly suffocated, by men in black. "I was brought up in a house filled with skirts," Paul once said to the one priest he trusted above all others, Father Heart. "Black skirts with men in them."

He read Latin when he was six and could converse fluently in that language and in Italian by the time he was eight. He was privately educated by a series of tutors who would arrive for six months at a time at Joan Hull's Pennsylvania manor house. He would virtually live with his priest-tutor, receiving a cram course in whatever the priest's specialty was. "Sort of like thirteen years of Catholic Berlitz," was the way he described his early education to Father Heart.

"The Jesuits are the best teachers," Joan Hull had decided early on, "but I don't want them getting control of him." Thus she had devised the six months rotation period. "They can't do too much damage in a half year and naturally I'll be certain there are other influences at work on him." Father Heart, an athletic priest from nearby Villanova University, had been engaged to instruct Paul in the arts of swimming and boxing and riding a bicycle around the grounds of the estate.

"You sound," said Cardinal Zoltan, a man Joan Hull exchanged confidences with, "as if you're grooming the first American pope."

"And why not?" she had asked, raising her thick, dark eyebrows in what another man might have construed as a flirtatious gesture. "And why not?"

Cardinal Zoltan, who held an influential if unpublicized post within the Vatican, forebore to tell her. "Why not, indeed?" he asked after a moment, formulating his own plans. His thin-faced, pale good looks caused him to resemble an idealized early ascetic.

"Then I can count on your support?" Joan Hull asked.

"Definitely," the cardinal answered without hesitation. "I

can't think of anything I should like better than to have my own king at court."

Paul, who was anything but asectic looking, was nearly six feet tall with broad shoulders, bright red hair, and dark gray eyes. He was, as the cardinal noted soon after Paul's fourteenth birthday, "a bit too attractive. He's going to need more strenuous exercise. Get Father Heart to arrange for him to take gym glasses at Villanova. He should go to bed each night too exhausted to indulge in secret vices."

"You're as interested in his future as I am," Joan Hull said, looking at the cardinal with an eye that her enemies said cried out for an appraiser's loop.

"Well, why not an American pope?" Cardinal Zoltan wanted to know.

Over the years Paul somehow managed to develop a sense of humor. He was sent to Rome when he was sixteen and that time spent away from his aunt made him less serious and taciturn, more willing to allow that a priest could enjoy life, too.

As he paced the office behind Saint Patrick's, a month after his thirtieth birthday, he seemed to his visitor to be a very youthful thirty, as if his protected, scholarly life had kept him from aging the way an ordinary man might.

Paul had that ability to carry on a conversation and think, privately, at the same time, and he wondered what celebrities would be found at 44. At the same time he chastised himself for being so frivolous, when he thought of the decision he had to make.

"There's probably some psychological label for my state of mind," he said, in English, to the man seated across from him.

"Free-floating euphoria," the older man offered. "You know, Paul," he continued after a moment, studying the handsome young monsignor's face, "perhaps you should give some thought to seeing your confessor."

"*You* should see my confessor, Father Heart. He's eighty-four and still hungry for sin. I can't appease his appetite." He looked at the treasured, battered watch on his wrist, once his father's, and stood up. "I'm afraid I shall have to go. I'm late as it is, and you remember Aunt Joan."

"Far too well. She has a magnificently righteous way of

depriving those around her of the most innocent of pleasures."

"She may have changed, Father. She's invited me to 44 for cocktails and, even better, she's asked me to accompany her to 44's fiftieth anniversary on Friday."

"I wonder how your advisor will respond to that."

"Cardinal Zoltan? I have every reason to believe he will be there with us."

"The modernity of the new Church," Father Heart said, getting slowly to his feet, "often appalls but occasionally makes me feel I was born too soon." He held out his hand and then he embraced the younger man. "I'm glad we've had these talks, Paul. Whatever their outcome, it's good for my soul to be so honest outside the guidelines of Mother Church. But I can't help but wonder if I've genuinely been of help."

"Immeasurably. Now why don't you finish your tea? You have an hour or so until your train. I'll see that my secretary makes certain you get to Penn Station on time."

The two men embraced once more and Paul went out onto Madison Avenue, decided it wasn't quite cool enough to warrant a taxi, and walked to Fifth where he succumbed to a large Checker, which seemed to be waiting for him, its door open, its driver involved in a racing form. "Temptation all about me," Paul said, getting in, giving 44's address.

Joan Hull was already seated at the first table on the left, wearing a dull, gray dress, her dark blond hair arranged in its usual severe style. She wore no makeup and her only jewelry were two diamond earrings set in gold which had belonged to her sister. She allowed Paul to kiss her dry cheek and cut short his apologies.

"I've heard from Zoltan," she said after Charles took Paul's order for a glass of red wine. "They're going to offer you a bishopric." She looked off into the Club Room without seeing it. She was watching, in her mind, some inner vision that consumed all of her attention. "Then you're returning to Rome for a year. You'll be Stephano's secretary which should be tricky but you know how to walk a careful line by this time. Then they're going to send you to someplace troublesome like Asia or even the Mideast where you can prove your mettle." She took a sip from the martini Charles had brought for her.

"It's all going according to plan and I couldn't be prouder

of you.'' She put the glass down and looked at him, finally. ''Of course there's a fly in the ointment. There always is. They're appointing—or Lord knows, they may already have—a special investigator to make what Zolton charmingly calls 'inquiries.' They're worse than the FBI, the CIA, and the KGB all rolled into one. Even Zoltan won't know who the investigator is until he makes himself known and his findings are published or announced. Then we're supposed to be overcome with surprise that there was an inquiry to begin with.

''Naturally Zoltan's fuming under that oiled glass exterior of his. He feels, rightly so, that his word and judgment are being made suspect with this inquiry. I think we're going to have to disassociate ourselves from Zoltan after a time. He's getting rather obsessive but men of his age without sexual outlets often do. What on earth are you staring at?''

''Jackie Kennedy.''

''It's Onassis now, at least for the time being.''

''She's far prettier than she is in her photographs.''

''Paul, there is no reason to worry about this investigator, is there?''

''Depends upon what he's investigating.''

''Purity of heart and purpose, adherence to the correct party line, obedience to current dogma, et cetera. I do wish Zoltan had gotten the name of the man heading the inquiry. It could be anyone. Of course you know better than most how they work.''

''Do you think I might have another glass of wine?''

She signaled Charles to bring him another.

''Zoltan is coming to New York on Thursday,'' she went on. ''He doesn't want to miss 44's anniversary party though he'd go to the stake rather than admit it. At any rate I imagine he'll make you the offer once he gets the all clear. He says it should come in by Friday at the latest. Your secret life won't exactly fill volumes.'' She looked at her nephew once again. She wished he didn't have that red hair or those dark gray eyes or that cleft in his chin. All very attractive to lady parishioners but not exactly the vision she had in mind. The eyes would fade and perhaps the hair would go white. ''There isn't anything that could turn up, is there, Paul?''

''There's that weekend with Ali MacGraw.''

"If you shouldn't go as high in the Church as you might, Paul, I think we will be able to blame it on your ill-timed humor." She stood up, adjusting her skirt. "You'll let me know if anything out of the ordinary occurs?"

"Certainly," he said, standing, kissing her dry cheek once again.

"Then good afternoon, 'Bishop.' "

Paul finished his wine, watched Jackie Kennedy Onassis leave on the arm of a man who looked like an expensive publisher, tried to pay the check but was told it had been taken care of, and then, looking at the battered wristwatch, made his way to the telephone booth behind the Club Room. He wasn't surprised to find that his hand was shaking as he searched for a dime.

Chapter Six

IT WAS a few minutes past eight P.M. when SayDee Roth emerged from the elevator into the Club Room, feeling nearly as ill at ease as she had on that historic day when Duke had forced her to come downstairs to the restaurant with him, which was tantamount to announcing to the world that she was his mistress.

The Duke's mistress. Maybe someday her life would be serialized on public television. "From a lonely cigar girl to the favored consort of his royal majesty, Duke Greene, this is the tale of . . ." The tale of what? she asked herself. Some thought she was a hooker who struck it rich and others thought she was a dumb Dora with blind luck but only she knew how deep and how genuine her love was for the man who lay dying in that whore's bed two stories above.

She looked around. No one seemed to notice her. She liked the sounds, the clink of the glasses and the silverware, the low hum of voices made rich by too much smoke and wine. She saw Lawrence looking at her as if she were a street urchin who had just wandered into Kensington Palace Gardens and she told him that she wanted to see Nick. The maître d'hôtel walked off huffily into the main dining room while SayDee stood in the foyer, looking at the really beautiful portrait of Duke, wondering where the hell that fat fucker, Lawrence, got the *chutzpah* to be so high and mighty.

While she waited, she looked into the main dining room. She wondered what Liza Minnelli was doing having dinner when she was supposed to be on a stage and then realized it was a Monday night when most theaters were dark. Maggie Smith was sitting at an adjoining table with the Hovings and Hal Prince. How the hell can so much business make so little money, she asked herself as she spotted Nick talking to Margot Hemmingway. There was something about celebs, SayDee thought, watching them, that was delightfully unreal. Maybe it was the transition from photograph to actual life that created that aura that seemed to hang around, protectively, even at their worst moments.

"What's wrong?" Nick asked as Lawrence took over, escorting Margot and her friends to a table in the Club Room.

"Nothing. Duke's not coming down tonight, and he wanted me to tell you in person."

"The Duke is missing a night at 44?"

"What's so terrible? A man's sick. He doesn't feel like a drink."

"It's just that it's the first time."

"I found him sitting over there at four this morning, reminiscing. He's tired, Nick. After all these years the man deserves a night off, doesn't he?"

"Sure he does."

"He wanted me to to tell you that he was sorry he didn't get to see you, that he wants you to come up first thing tomorrow morning."

"You want a handkerchief, SayDee?"

"I'm not crying."

"Yes you are." He handed her his handkerchief, and she turned away, carefully blotting her eyes, telling him she'd have Robert launder it, that she had gotten mascara all over it. And then she walked very quickly to the elevator and stepped into it. The doors closed on her before she turned around.

Nick stood for a moment in the foyer and whistled softly. The Duke is in residence and he's not coming down for his nightly drink? He's saving himself for Friday, Nick told himself, wanting to believe that. When those sensors every good restaurant man possesses went into action, he felt rather than knew something was very wrong. He turned toward the front entrance where trouble usually appeared first.

Little Mike had his butcher's hand on the arm of a young man dressed in a rough tweed suit. Little Mike never put his hands on anyone unless he thought there was a chance of violence or untold commotion. Scotty, who never put his hands on anyone without leaving a serious memory of the moment, stood holding the door open.

"Can I help?" Nick asked, coming up on the far side of the young man with all that dark hair, so that if there were trouble, he and Mike and Scotty would be able to effectively contain it in the foyer.

"This gentleman says he's meeting someone here but he don't want to say who it is," Mike said, his hand still firmly holding the other's arm.

"It is a private matter," he said. Nick categorized him as European, probably Eastern and most likely not Real Trouble but maybe Minor Trouble.

"Perhaps if you told me what name the reservation is in," Nick said, smiling, signaling Little Mike to let him go, turning, walking into the Club Room toward the bar so that the young man had no choice but to follow.

"Countess Vera," he said, looking at the bar as if it were surrounded by alien enemies, acting as if he had just imparted a state secret, his accent especially pronounced on the 'V.'

"Would you like to wait at the countess's table?" He was nervous and angry and Nick thought if he could get some alcohol into him, that would help. He led him to the first table on the left, amused to catch Little Mike's incredulous expression. A suit like that hadn't sat at the best table since Tennessee Williams had brought the young Marlon Brando to lunch after *A Streetcar Named Desire* opened.

Nick had Charles bring the young man a double vodka and went back into the Club Room. Nick wondered what the countess was doing with that refugee from the Baader Meinhoff gang. Usually she wouldn't be seen in public with anyone below the rank of Vanderbilt.

Countess Vera sat in the back of her yellow Rolls-Royce looking at the yellow roses that were placed, each morning, in the crystal vases on either side of the rear compartment. She had seen Ivan enter and she was going to give him time to get used to 44, to have a drink, to relax. She was dressed in yards of red and yellow organdy with diamond clips holding down the bodice, her neck recklessly free of jewelry or other camouflage. She wore her famous yellow diamond bracelets and her blond hair was combed straight back, set as if for life. One of her dearest enemies, Charles Revson, had said of her, not long before he died, that Vera Nickleson had learned, finally, the secret of the Gabor sisters: how to look forever middle-aged.

She had not been born Vera Nickleson, countess. She had been born Iris Levy, pharmacist's daughter, in 1923 in the Bronx when there were still vacant lots and a couple of small farms there. By 1940, she had already developed and marketed the fragrance known as Fontanna di Jeunesse—based on a scent her father had made in his drugstore in the Bronx—and which middle-class women all over the world immediately began spraying under their arms and pouring into their bathtubs and secreting little pads soaked with the scent in all the bureau drawers of their houses.

Never mind that Helena Rubenstein (Princess Gourielli) referred to it as Youth Pew or that Elizabeth Arden claimed that it was distilled from the fats of martyred kosher chickens.

Vera (Iris) Nickleson (Levy) was a born marketing genius who knew her market target right down to its most arcane demographic. Because, as Vera knew, had she not had the guts or the genius or the belief in herself, she, too, would be someone's wife, playing bridge or Mah Jongg once a week, taking winter vacations in Miami Beach or the Virgin Islands, worrying about her daughter marrying a professional and her son becoming a dentist.

Vera Nickleson was, but for the grace of God, her own market target, and she knew it all too well. Her customers not only loved her fragrance, they loved her life. With her noble husband and her houses in Palm Beach, Paris, Rome, New York, and Cannes, with her picture in the papers on a regular basis, attending parties and openings and showings and events only the very rich and very highborn could ever hope to be invited to, Countess Vera fulfilled every American hausfrau's fantasy life. It was only fair that they bought her products.

She had built on that flair for marketing, and on that thin, cloying fragrance her father had invented, so that now she was head of a cosmetic empire rivaled only by Lauder and Revlon.

Though Bill, of course, had helped. He had been a young account executive, good looking in a wholesome sort of way, when she had met him, working in the first advertising agency she had hired. When she found that his father had been a noble German who still used his title and that Bill himself was a generous, more than satisfactory lover, she married him. She hadn't waited for Bill's father to die before she became Countess Vera. She hadn't waited for Bill to recognize the importance of publicity when he became the senior vice-president of her company. It was she who had made certain that her name and face appeared with such regularity in the gossip and society columns. And it was she who had recognized that the "perfume" her father had concocted for her in the back of his pharmacy on the Grand Concourse would sell lipstick as easily as it would toilet water.

Countess Vera Cosmetics, with its familiar Vera yellow logo, never failed to make Fortune's five hundred list of top American corporations.

"And don't you forget it," she said aloud to herself, as the chauffeur helped her from the Rolls, as she stepped up the familiar staircase that led to 44. No matter how many times she had been there, no matter how often the society doyennes and the international princesses invited her to tea and dinner and charity balls, she still always felt like Iris Levy from the Bronx, and that everyone knew and laughed.

She smiled at Nick who came and took her to her table. The best table. She had worked long and hard for the privilege of sitting there and had only once been denied it when Princess Margaret had been in town. With a great sense of noblesse oblige, she had told Duke that the princess might have the table. "She needs it more than I do," Countess Vera was widely quoted as saying.

"Chéri," she said as Lawrence held the chair for her, as the young man stood up awkwardly, his dark, roughly handsome face remaining unsmiling. "Have I kept you waiting terribly long?"

"I thought we were going to be someplace private," Ivan said.

"Chéri, this is the most private place in the city of New York." She smiled as Charles brought her her usual glass of dry white wine. "Is your hotel suite all right?"

"What are you playing now, Vera? Concierge? I do not care about the hotel or this food or your damned cosmetics. I care about you. I have come to New York . . ."

"Chéri, this may be the most private spot in New York but it's not absolutely soundproofed. Be quiet for a moment. I know it's difficult for you but for once in your sainted life, think of someone else; think of me. I'm going to tell Bill at the end of the week. I want to break it to him in exactly the right way. I want to remain on good terms with him. I want him to stay with the company."

Ivan laughed, and suddenly one could see the charm in his face. "What I adore about you, my Vera, is your incredible sentimentality. You would sacrifice all for love. Except the company. Well, I say bugger the company. I say . . ."

She let him go on without listening to his words. He had lowered his voice so there was not going to be a scene, though of course he was perfectly capable of standing up and having a shouting match in the middle of 44. But not tonight. He was too tired to play the role of irate lover with much conviction. She wondered—as he went on about her dedication to the capitalist golden rule, business first and foremost—whether he had showered. And suddenly she had a vision of his body and that thick mat of hair which descended from his chest to his penis and she felt a surge of overwhelming sexuality. It was a feeling, a desire, she had long ago ceased to expect, and she wasn't certain she liked it. She knew only one way to deal with it and that was to get into bed with Ivan.

She had met him at the Countess Vera plant outside Paris, near Orly. She had gone to France especially to talk with him. The Paris chief had told her that he was a brilliant young Yugoslavian chemist, that he had come up with a facial moisturizer that erased lines for as long as two weeks. It worked, as did several other products on the market, by filling in and inflating the skin under the lines. But where the others lasted for hours, Ivan's worked, effectively, for weeks at a time.

It had been a cool, gray September day and industrial France wasn't any more attractive than industrial America. The long metallic factory with its glass squares of windows had proven particularly depressing after the endless flight (she had gone to Washington to take the Concorde but it had had to circle for hours). The French version of Musak played throughout the factory and gave her a headache while the antiseptic white tile floors reverberated with the click-clack of the female technicians' high heels as they wandered in and out of laboratories.

Ivan's blunt masculinity cut through the sanitary bleakness like a knife through butter. He reminded her of her favorite film star, John Garfield. And he reminded her of the European exiles who had streamed through her father's apartment over the drugstore in the 1930's, refugees from Hitler and Stalin. He had an electric force that she found overwhelming, at the opposite pole from the neat appeal most of the men she knew projected.

Vera had had affairs over the years but they had been quiet romances, doomed almost from the moment they began. None of them had been consummated until hours of obligatory and often whispered phone calls had been gone through, notes and sly looks passed. There had always been a long prelude to Vera's sexual operettas. The third act had invariably found the lovers relievedly bidding one another adieu.

Ivan wasn't interested in subtle preliminaries. He was rough and direct and not overly clean and when, after they had worked late that first night at the factory outside Orly, he had taken her back to his apartment and made prolonged, violent love to her, she had found herself more than infatuated.

She had brought him to America, ostensibly to oversee the manufacture of the new moisturizer. But it was obvious that there were half a dozen chemists in the Long Island City plant who could have done that. She had brought him to America, she admitted to herself, because she couldn't be apart from him.

"If you have any idea of keeping me around like a pet bear, giving me pocket money and little cars, you had better think again, Vera," he was saying. "I want to marry you, Vera. And I do not wish to wait."

She watched as he sawed away at his steak and wondered how much time they might have together. He was in his early thirties and she might hold up for ten years at the outside, five definitely. It would be a nice way to step into old age, with Ivan in her bed. But when she had finally and firmly crossed that border, when that dark, natural smell of his no longer stirred her but faintly nauseated her, what was she going to do with him?

Her greatest fear was not that he didn't love her. He wasn't the sort of man capable of romantic love and she wasn't interested in investigating the peculiar pathology that was causing him to become so sexually aroused over a woman nearly a quarter of a century older than he.

It was all genuine. In the midst of his tirade, before the steak had been served and he had become totally involved in it, he had reached under the tablecloth, taken her hand, and placed it on his crotch. Feeling his thick erection through the rough tweed material of his trousers did nothing to make her more calm.

Still, what would happen if, after a few months, or a year, she suddenly found that she didn't want him, that this new and devastating sexuality of hers had vanished, leaving her a foolish old woman with a rude and uncaring husband? *That* was her greatest fear. That she would give up her comfortable life only to find that Ivan and his throbbing erections had become a kind of stale irritant.

And then of course there was Bill. She recognized that she needed him in the business, that he was the one man she could always count on. He had been content being Mister Countess Vera but she doubted that he would be content being Mister Ex-Countess Vera. He had had his own adventures during their married life and there was a woman in San Francisco who seemed to take up a great deal of his time. Were they to divorce, he might marry again. He might go to work for Revlon or Avon or Estée Lauder.

If only Ivan would allow her to support him for a while. She saw nothing wrong in it. Tons of other women in her position did and life went on. But in that thickheaded way of his, Ivan was both too bright and too greedy. It would be simple enough to make him rich if that's what he wanted. But it wasn't. Ivan made no bones about it. He wanted to be fabulously rich. He wanted to live in the houses in Paris, Cannes, Palm Beach; he wanted to have his own closets filled with his own clothes (presumably he would give up the rough tweeds) in the New York, London, and Rio residences. He wanted the cars and the clothes and the jewels.

Countess Vera laughed.

"What is so amusing?" Ivan wanted to know, looking at her suspiciously, pushing his empty plate to the side.

"You, my dear little decadent Slav. You're a male Lorelei Lee and you don't care who knows it."

"What is Lorelei Lee?"

"A literary gold digger of little note who manages, somehow, to live on."

He put his hand on her wrist. "Let's go. I do not want coffee. I want you."

She took her wrist from his hand. She had thought it would be a good idea to dine her new genius of a chemist at 44 in front of the world, that such bravado would destroy incipient suspicion. Now she wasn't so certain. Several pairs of familiar eyes were watching her, taking mental notes.

She laughed and signaled Charles for the check. As she signed it, she said, "As much as I want to, I am not coming with you tonight. The women who buy my products are not ready for my picture in the paper, above yours, with half a dozen lines of copy about our torrid love affair. Be quiet, Ivan. You will walk me to my car, you will kiss my hand and say good night. I will see you later in the week for another meal. In the meantime I will think, I will talk to my advisers and to myself. I will let you know my decision later."

"And what am I to do while you take this week to think?"

"Work. Work with Bill. He needs to know how the moisturizer is going to affect women's skins if he's going to market it." She smiled at him as she stood up. "And play. Take some young lady to the theater, to the museums. Take her to bed. I'm not a jealous sort, Ivan."

"That, I think, remains to be seen, Countess Vera."

He escorted her to the car and waited as the driver opened the rear door. "I will be waiting, in my hotel," he said, slamming the door shut.

The thought occurred to her—when she was halfway up Park Avenue and had told the driver to turn back, to take her to the side entrance of Ivan's hotel—that if she divorced Bill to marry Ivan, she would no longer be Countess Vera.

Chapter Seven

"THE DUKE'S not coming down tonight?" Little Mike, towering over Nick, asked as the last of the late supper crowd had been seated.

Nick said no, Duke wasn't coming down tonight. He, Nick, was tired. It had been an especially long Monday, never his favorite day. Mondays at 44 were like Saturdays at other restaurants. It was the smart night to dine there and all the tables in each of the dining rooms had been filled from noon on.

"You know that guy never missed a night here since I can remember. Not when he was in New York. Even on his wedding night, when he married that English broad, he came down at midnight for a champagne cocktail. Imagine the nerve of that guy, leaving his wife on their wedding night to have a drink at the bar with the boys." Mike shook his head in admiration.

Nick smiled an encouragement he didn't feel and moved on into the main dining room. A man who seemed to be taking virtually all of his meals at 44 for the past week or two was back. He always managed to come in with a well-known customer but Nick still hadn't found out who he was. Tonight he was sitting at Lee Radziwell's table, telling a story she and her guests seemed fascinated by.

Nick's father and predecessor, Victor, had told him from the day he started work, "The most important thing in this business, kid, is to know your New York. You don't know your New York, you're out of business."

Times had changed since Victor had managed 44, since Nick had come home from Vietnam and made a tenuous recovery from heroin addiction, looking for a safe, ritualistic place to land and to hide and had found it where he least expected, at Duke's 44 Club.

"I know who the gent at table eight is," Lawrence said, his portly Hitchcockian figure moving purposely out of the main dining room, leading the way toward the back of the Club Room where he and Nick habitually held their more private conferences. "His name is Morgan Brooks. I overheard the princess say, 'Morgan Brooks, if you mention that one more time, I'll strangle you.' You do know who he is?"

"UNITAS's acquisition man."

"He eats restaurants like ours, I am sorry to say, for breakfast."

"Lawrence, this is not our restaurant. It still belongs to Duke."

"And pretty soon," Lawrence said over his shoulder, sailing away, looking up at the portrait of the founder of what he called "the fifedom," "it won't belong to him."

"Hello, Nick," the pretty, young blonde said as she came from the ladies' room.

"Hi, Mrs. Boyd. Haven't seen you in a very long time."

"Hutch keeps me locked up in D.C. But I wasn't going to miss 44's fiftieth for anything. He's in a place called Bahrain, but I got the gold key, and I brought Pat Foreman along for company. I'll be able to bring her, won't I, Nick?"

"You can bring anyone you wish, Mrs. Boyd."

The gold keys were going to act as admission to the anniversary celebration. Anyone who had ever been given one—and that included a long list of celebrities, power brokers, and just plain good friends of 44—was invited.

Nick watched Honey Boyd go to the best table and thought, as she sat down with Pat Foreman and a swarthy man in a pin-striped suit who looked as if he were auditioning for the role of sultan's assassin, that she was keeping fast company.

Frances Roosevelt Wharton Tyor Boyd had been known as

Honey almost since the day her mother, Ruth Tyor (Rep., W. Va.) was scheduled to make an impassioned plea for the abortion bill and wound up, instead, giving birth to her daughter on the Senate floor.

Honey grew up in Washington, surrounded by senators and governors and presidents and lobbyists and somehow managed to remain totally innocent of the way the political system operates in this country.

It was said that her father, Nate Tyor, a surgeon descended from several political families, had had the part of his brain labeled politics deliberately lobotomized. He had had his fill of politicians, especially of lady politicians. He wanted a sweet young thing about the house and that was what he got when Honey came of age. She and her father meant a great deal to one another, rather in the way the only two Americans in a small foreign town might. When he died, Honey married, with her mother's enthusiastic approval, Hutchinson (Hutch) Boyd (Rep., Va.), who was some thirty years her senior and was himself tired, as he put it, of "politically savvy broads."

"Saiad and I are going to put our heads together and find you a job, Honey," Pat Foreman told her when she returned to the table.

Pat Foreman had lived through and survived the Kennedy, Nixon, Ford, and Carter administrations. She gave the best parties and knew the best people and though no one ever quite knew where her money came from or where her political or sexual sympathies lay, Pat Foreman always managed to come out with a respectable reputation.

Neither Hutch nor Honey's mother quite approved of Pat Foreman but she did seem to take a real interest in Honey and more important, gave Honey something to do in the way of luncheons and charity committees.

When she took an interest in Honey Boyd, when she first took Honey up, as it was said, most people in D.C. thought Pat Foreman was being typically kind; though a few wondered.

When she suggested taking Honey to New York, accompanying Honey to 44's fiftieth, Ruth Tyor heaved a figurative sigh of relief. Her daughter's husband had been called away on crucial business and she herself was feverishly involved in preparing new E.R.A. groundwork. Having Honey out of the way, in New York, under Pat Foreman's aegis, was a blessing not to be too carefully investigated.

At first Honey wasn't so pleased. She was a little frightened of Pat Foreman and privately thought of her as a kind of lizard. A very attractive lizard, but still she seemed to slither when she moved and there was something about the way she was constantly touching Honey that gave her, as she told her diary, "the willies."

On that first night, after they had arrived, Pat Foreman had volunteered to give Honey a massage but Honey had said no, a little too emphatically, and beaten a hasty retreat into her bedroom.

But now everything was much better. That evening, while they were standing in the lobby of the ANTA where they had seen a musical Honey never did get the name of, Pat Foreman had introduced her to Mr. Saiad. She had said he was a businessman, a lobbyist, which meant little enough to Honey. She had an image of a lobbyist as a man who sat around hotel lobbies, trying to buttonhole congressmen. When she once shared that image with her husband, Hutch had laughed and said she wasn't that far off.

She was excited to be in New York, away from her mother and Hutch, who both spoke a language she never fully understood.

She looked around, pleased to be able to nod to Andy Young and Hugh Carey who were being seated in the Club Room. Honey loved it at 44. She had always sat at the best table, ever since she first came to 44 as a baby with her mother. She was just naïve enough to think she was still being seated there because she was so peppy and cute.

"Now, Saiad," Pat Foreman said, drinking her Brandy Alexander as if it were an ice-cream soda, through thin straws, "I want you to put your thinking cap on. We have got to find a job for poor Honey."

"Do you need money, Mrs. Boyd?" Saiad asked, smiling, showing his very white teeth to Honey.

"Don't be ridiculous, Saiad. She's loaded. Honey needs something meaningful to do. She's going out of her mind with boredom in D.C. Hutch is either filerbustering for hours about cutting down oil imports or he's off, as he is at this very moment, in your part of the world, causing diplomatic rows.''

"Perhaps you should be a professional beauty, Mrs. Boyd. Devote your time to attending embassy teas. You're lovely enough to be very successful in that field.''

Honey didn't know how to respond so she smiled. Mr. Saiad was only a little more understandable than her husband. He shared the same air of quiet authority Hutch and her father had in such abundance and she found it easy to be with him. He seemed, unlike Hutch and her father, a man of infinite patience.

Also he was a good deal younger than Hutch. He looked, she decided, a little like Omar Sharif, only slimmer. He had what the novels she read often described as liquid eyes. She found him terribly attractive. She wondered that she had never seen him at embassy parties since Pat said he sometimes lived in D.C.

"I try to keep a low profile in Washington, Mrs. Boyd,'' he said. Honey wondered if he ever relaxed his smile and, almost simultaneously, she had a disturbing vision of herself in a bed with her firm white legs over Mr. Saiad's shoulders and Mr. Saiad's long, hard hands holding her buttocks and forcing himself into her. Hutch only took her from behind and that was early in the morning when he still had what she called "beagle's breath'' and wasn't in the least interested in anything else but having an orgasm. Hutch said it helped to wake him up, while Honey privately said it helped to put her back to sleep.

"She's far too bright to be a professional beauty and that, unfortunately, is what she's turning into. She's suffering from her husband's benign neglect. Now you know everyone in D.C., Saiad, though you pretend you don't. I want you to come up with something.''

"Agreed. How long shall you be in New York, Mrs. Boyd?''

"Just until Saturday. There's the anniversary party—Hutch gave me his key—and Pat and I decided, at the very last minute, to come on up and catch some shows and get away from stuffy old Washington while we could.''

"Would you like me to find you a job, Mrs. Boyd?''

Honey liked the way he spoke. The deep timbre of his

voice seemed to go right through her. "I sure would appreciate it, Mr. Saiad. I need something to keep me busy in D.C."

Saiad promised that he would come up with a job for her. He had something in mind, in fact, but he would have to do some further checking before he would feel free to talk about it.

Pat Foreman ate her chocolate parfait with a wolf's smile, and Nick, watching from the Club Room, wondered if he shouldn't call Ruth Tyor, Honey's mother, and tell her something unsavory was in the air. Then he decided it wasn't really his business, that he had too much to think about as it was, and that Pat Foreman would surely take care of Honey Boyd, if only from her own sense of survival.

Nick said good night to Lawrence, who enjoyed the chore of locking up, looked up at the portrait of Duke, jaunty as ever, and went home to the empty town house on the west side of Forty-fourth Street.

Monday was at long last over.

have seemed to go right through her. "I sure would appreciate it, Mr. Sand. I need something to keep me busy until—"

Sand promised that he would come up with a job for her. He had something in mind, in fact, but he would have to do some further checking before he would feel free to talk about it.

Pat Forman ate her chocolate parfait with a spoon and a smile. Neil, watching from the Club Room, wondered if he shouldn't call Keith Lyons, Honey's mother, and tell her some-[illegible] was in the air. Then he decided it wasn't really his business; that he had too much to think about as it was, and that Pat Forman would surely take care of Honey, if only from her own sense of survival.

Neil said good night to Lawrence, who enjoyed the ritual of locking up, moved to sit the doorman of Duke's jaunty over, and went home to the empty brick house on the west side of Forty-fourth Street.

Monday was a long, bad day.

BOOK 2

TUESDAY

Chapter One

"HOW IS HE?" Nick asked in a half whisper as Robert allowed him into the huge sunny drawing room on the third floor of 44. That room, with its stucco walls and beamed ceilings, a 1920's re-creation of a gothic common room, always made Nick feel both sad and comfortable. One wall was lined with books and photographs of 44's past. Three comfortable red leather sofas sat on an enormous turquoise Oriental rug around a baronial fireplace on which was affixed a crest Cecil had had made up for Duke. It consisted of a shield held by a lion on which were a fork, a knife, and a spoon.

"He's better," SayDee Roth said, answering the question for Robert as she swept into the room, placing her right hand with its long painted fingernails on the intricately carved swooping pink mass that was her hair. "He slept all night and he hasn't done that in a long time, let me tell you."

The terrier, Hector, came out of his hiding place under one of the sofas and she picked him up, holding him to her breast which was encased in a pink silk dressing robe. "He's got a lot of color today, Nick," she said, sitting down, patting the place next to her, indicating he was to join her and Hector. "Bring us some tea, Robert, will you, dear?" she asked the valet who nodded and disappeared. "I used to think Robert was so creepy, never saying a word. Well, he is creepy but, as Duke says, he's a perfect servant, and he's really rather sweet under all that creepiness. Though I do think that if he hadn't gotten a job with Duke, he might have ended up taking little girls into vacant lots."

She petted the dog absently; Robert came in with the tea. "You should have seen the breakfast Duke wolfed down this morning. Sausage *and* pancakes. He wouldn't even let Robert help him out of the bed. You don't suppose," she said, letting the dog scamper down to the floor, "that the doctors were wrong, do you, Nick? Yesterday I thought he was a goner and today . . ."

The door which led to the hallway which led to the room Cecil had dubbed Duke's seraglio opened, and Duke came in. He was wearing a blue quilted smoking jacket, dark silk trousers, the sort of black velvet slippers that cost one hundred and fifty-nine dollars and are embroidered in gold thread with a lion's head. He had expertly knotted a dark green and blue scarf around his neck but that was the one wrong note. The scarf only emphasized how inadequate his neck suddenly was, how thin he had become.

He sat on the arm of the sofa and put his hand on SayDee's cushiony shoulder. "Don't attempt to fool yourself, kid. The doctors weren't wrong. Like you said, I'm just having a good day."

She looked up at him with tears forming under and around the powder-blue eye shadow she resolutely applied every morning. "Oh, Duke."

"Don't 'Oh, Duke,' me. Go get dressed. I want you to take me for a walk. Let's see how many new porn shops they've opened on Forty-fourth Street in the past ten minutes."

"A walk?" Saydee asked, standing up, her face reading incredulous. "A walk? You really think, Duke . . . ?"

"We'll see how far we get. Go. Put on something snappy."

She left for the second-floor dressing room as Duke slid down on the red sofa, taking her place, holding out his left hand to Nick. He seemed, suddenly, drained. "You notice I always shake with my left hand," Duke asked, grasping Nick's hand, holding it. "Got it from David, the Duke of Windsor. He did it because when he was Prince of Wales, he had to shake so many hands, his right one got tired. I do it because of affectation. Smile, Nicky. Stop looking as if the Angel of Death were about to stroll in. He's coming, but he hasn't arrived yet. I'm counting on his waiting until after Friday. I don't care so much about the party as I do about the years. My Fifty Years Reign. I'm like an old miser who gets off on counting his dollars. Only I been counting my years.

"You want something besides the tea, Nick? What about a white-meat chicken sandwich, lightly brushed with mayo, the crusts cut off, a little pickle on the side?"

Nick grinned. It had been his favorite sandwich since the time he had heard General MacArthur order one.

"I'm not hungry, Duke. I don't want anything."

"That's always been your trouble, kid. You should want more. You're too much like your father, like SayDee. All SayDee ever wanted was me and now she's not even going to have that. I should have married a woman like her in the first place, but no, not me, not the grand Duke Greene. First I had to have someone from Cecil's world, a gentile princess with breeding, a pale blond beauty with the ethical standards of Eva Braun. You know how my first wife died, Nick?"

"Car crash."

"Yeah. A car crash. She was going down on the chauffeur and when he came, he lost control, pitched the whole shebang right over the lowest mountain in New Jersey. At the funeral I overheard Dorothy Parker say that Laura was the only van der Velde who deserved to go down in New Jersey history. You want to know something? I broke out laughing. They thought I was hysterical." He closed his eyes for a moment.

"And then," he said, opening his eyes, massaging the thick bridge of his still strong nose, "I had to have an English lady. Irene Bresson Stewart, daughter of an earl, maybe. She was so perfect playing the duke's wife, it was rumored that I got her from central casting.

"Look at that photograph, the one next to Scott Fitzgerald. Isn't she perfect?"

Nick went to the photograph and looked at it. The Duchess of Windsor was on the right, her dark hair parted dead center, her smile professional and unconvincing. Elsa Maxwell, looking like a very old pug dog, was in the center. A handsome blond woman with a broad face and laughing eyes, looking much like the Duchess of Windsor's matched set, only fair, was on the far left. Behind them was the familiar corner, indicating they were sitting at the best table.

"I could have forgiven Irene most anything except for the fact that she was so relentlessly aristocratic. I should have married a woman like SayDee and had a child by her and let her paint this place shocking pink and avocado green.

"Now it's too late. SayDee says she doesn't want to redecorate any more and she doesn't want to marry me any more. She says it would be a 'mercy marriage' and she's never been anybody's charity and doesn't intend to start now."

Duke reached out for Nick with his left hand and Nick took it. "You'll see that she's not lonely, won't you, Nick? She's always felt she didn't belong downstairs, with the gold-key members, and perhaps she's right. When she came to live with me, she gave up all her old girl friends, her family, the career on stage she never had. You'll make sure that she doesn't waste away up here, a bird in a gilded cage, won't you, Nick?"

"I will, Duke."

The older man turned away and looked toward the leaded-paned windows which ran from floor to ceiling, allowing in the pale warmth of the late October sunshine. "Peter will try and do her out of everything, but the lawyers tell me the will's airtight. Peter's inherited his mother's fine sense of benevolence. He'd put SayDee on the street if he could. Sometimes I think he'd put me on the street if he could."

He struggled to get out of the sofa and finally Nick had to help him up. He went to the windows and looked down on Forty-fourth Street, at the light morning traffic. "He's in New York, you know."

"I saw him yesterday," Nick said.

"He came for the anniversary party. He brought Brette along. She was such a beautiful baby. And what a woman she's turned out to be. Cecil would have loved her. Just his kind of broad. Sassy with shoulders and that kind of dark-haired, violet-eyed gentile beauty that always knocked that sucker for a loop.

"She came to visit yesterday, after Peter. I'm sorry that I pushed her to marry him. It was a mistake. I thought she would warm him up. He's got about as much warmth as an East River fish.

"You know what he plans, don't you Nick?"

"That's what I wanted to talk to you about."

"There's not much to say, kid. The minute I die, he's going to sell 44 and the Industry to UNITAS. You know why? Because he thinks that if he sinks a fortune into that theater of his in London, he'll earn himself a knighthood. I see his mother's hand in all this. I try not to think about it, but the truth is, it makes my heart sick."

"Don't leave him 44," Nick said, moving to the windows, standing next to Duke. "Leave him money. Leave him something else."

"There isn't any money. You know as well as I do 44's been in and out of the red for the last half-dozen years. And then there's Irene's divorce agreement. I either leave Peter 44 or two million bucks, and I haven't got two million bucks."

"Suppose I got the two million and bought 44 from you?" Nick asked.

"You have to get it before I die," Duke said, returning to the sofa, letting himself down onto it carefully. "There's not much time, kid."

"You okay?" Nick asked.

"A little pain. Robert," he called to the taciturn figure standing at the far end of the room, "you'd better get me back to my bed."

"Your walk?"

"Pipe dream."

"How much pain you in?" Nick asked.

"On a scale of one to ten? About a six. The pills will fix it. And the bed." He allowed Robert to help him up, to put him in the hated wheelchair. "Every bastard in the world has made fun of that bed but I love it. When I was a kid, I saw a bed like that in a Valentino film and I wanted it with all my heart and soul. First money I made, I got this set designer to come up and build it for me. Laura hated it and Irene laughed at it, but I always enjoyed just lying in it, surrounded by all that satin and mirror and luxury. I tell you something, Nick: I'm glad I'm going to die in that bed."

Robert wheeled him off, but Duke stopped him as they

reached the door to the hall. "You think you got a chance? For the money, I mean?"

"I'm going to talk to some people, Duke. I think I got a good chance."

As Duke was wheeled off to his bedroom, Nick could hear SayDee babying him, fussing over him, which—oddly enough—the Duke enjoyed. Nick thought that he didn't have such a good chance to get the money. He had a fair to poor chance. But he sure as hell was going to try.

He went to the elevator and descended to 44 where the luncheon crowd was just beginning to stream in.

Chapter Two

NICK EMERGED from the elevator, smiled at Gloria Vanderbilt who was at a table in the Club Room. He looked around and saw that Kurt Waldheim had been given the second table on the left, thus signifying that he was David Rockefeller's guest. He saw Tony Perkins, his wife, and his sister-in-law, Marisa Berenson, making their own way across the main dining room to the stairs which led to the J. J. Walker Room. Perkins preferred it up there, away from the noise and the smoke and the table-hopping.

Lawrence pursed his lips and folded his hands in front of him, letting Nick know that everything was as fine as it could be during a Tuesday lunch hour.

Mickey, the bar captain, Little Mike, and Scotty all seemed to be under no unusual strain. Nick wondered how the hell Duke's 44 Club could be losing money when it was filled from noon to two or three in the morning every day of the week. At the same time he knew. Beluga caviar, the good stuff, was going for nearly four hundred dollars an ounce and 44 was still selling it at pre-1975 prices. The same with the champagne and the beef and the salmon. Every other restaurant in town was cleaning up on private parties but long ago Duke and Cecil had declared that 44 was quasi-private anyway and if they had wanted to go into the catering business, they would have gone into the catering business.

Then there was the staff. Duke never liked firing anyone and up until he became ill he had insisted on hearing each case where a dismissal was involved. And who was going to argue with him? It was his restaurant, his realm. But still there were half a dozen men sitting in the kitchen with nothing to do. Who the hell, Nick asked himself, needs four sous chefs for an operation like this?

Nick looked at his watch. It was both too early and too late to get through to Blue Bowen, the head of Bowen Frères. He checked the reservation book and found that Blue was coming to lunch on Wednesday, but Wednesday might be too late. He would try to get Blue after two, though Blue was known for taking occasional afternoons off.

If Blue would lend him the money, if Blue would follow through on a promise he had made one night shortly after Duke went into Sloan-Kettering and it was fairly well known that Duke was going to die, Blue would have to work fast. Well, he was also known for working fast.

The crushing reality of Duke's imminent death suddenly hit Nick, as it often did, unexpectedly and with almost stultifying pain. He forced himself not to think of it, to occupy himself with restaurant business.

He caught Charles on the way to the kitchen and asked him how Georgio, the busboy was doing, if he had been late again. "No, Mr. Nick. He was early today. He's okay. A good busboy. But a strange boy. Looks like he's angry about something all of the time; but he's always polite, never says anything unless you say something to him. I don't know, Mr. Nick. I guess it takes all kinds."

He let Charles go about his business and went into the foyer to say hello to Marietta Tree. He noticed that Joan Hull, with that metallic aura she never seemed to be without, was back at the best table, sitting with a man who was either the power behind a South American autocracy or a king's minister without portfolio. The thin gray-haired man in the rich black suit radiated behind-the-scenes power.

"Zoltan," Joan Hull said, drawing in long and hard on her cigarette, "you've barely eaten. Of course you never do.

That's why you've stayed thin as a stick all these years."

"As have you, dear Joan."

"So I have. But it's odd. When I was a child, they all predicted I would be fat. And when I first met you, Zoltan, I thought to myself that when you got old, you would end up fat, a fat priest, running a monastery in upstate New York where the speciality was an acidulous wine served to tourists."

The cardinal smiled and took a careful sip from his glass of Perrier. "I don't think that was your image, Joan. If it had been, you wouldn't have gone to such lengths to have me on your side. Besides, neither you nor I are food people. We have other needs."

"I want you to tell me about your sex life, Zoltan."

The cardinal smiled and looked down at his plate where a portion of Dover sole lay uneaten.

"Shall I tell you about mine?"

"Have you had too many martinis, Joan? It's not often that you can't hold your liquor."

"I'm worried," she admitted, reaching for the glass ashtray, rubbing her cigarette out carefully, in a circular, angry gesture.

"About what?"

"I'm suspicious, Zoltan. Suddenly you're in New York, in mufti. You've become famous for never leaving the Vatican. It's said that you're afraid too. I can't think what you're doing here unless you feel someone's sabotaging one of your labrythinic plots and you have to be on the spot to keep it going."

"You have a way of making the Church sound like a structure dreamt up by Machiavelli."

"Wasn't it? There's only one scheme of yours that could get you out of Rome at a time like this and that's the one involving Paul. You're frightened yourself, Zoltan. You're afraid they're not going to give Paul the bishopric."

"I'm in New York solely because you invited me, Joan. I'm here to attend Duke's 44 Club's fiftieth anniversary. There are certain temporal events at which the Church feels it should be represented. Good PR, as they say."

"You're worried, Zoltan. You can't hide it from me. I know you too well. You've got a great deal at stake. You've put too much of your influence behind Paul not to suffer if we lose this. My guess is some other prince of the Church is after your ass. You're all such a bunch of old women with nothing to do but be venemous to one another.

"I know what you're afraid of. That my early prediction will come true. And it might. You could end up, like the dear departed Fulton Sheen, in Rochester. If they could do it to him . . ."

He smiled at her, revealing his small, even, very white teeth.

She smiled back. "Yes, I don't suppose you're getting along all that well with the peasant pope and his crowd. Too athletic for you. Too much the man of the people.

"You're too refined, Zoltan, that's your problem. Too cultured, too cultivated. You belong in another age, another time, when the Church had real power outside the Vatican and men like you stepped silently through the back corridors, white kittens at your feet and bloodred rubies on your fingers."

The cardinal laughed and put one of his thin, elegant hands on Joan Hull's arm. "You mustn't worry, my dear. It will all come right in the end."

"So there is something to worry about. What is it? Why have they started this investigation? Who's in charge of it?"

"It could be anyone," the cardinal said after a long pause. "Anyone. The new regime believes in closed investigations. It might be a twenty-three-year-old priest out of Brooklyn or a European prelate schooled in the finer nuances of pure and holy faith. It does not matter, Joan. Investigations are now pro forma. It would be extraordinary, even suspicious, if there were none, considering Paul's youth and the enormity of the post he's being considered for. I'm told I'll receive a report no later than Thursday. If it is positive—and I am certain it will be—I shall ask Paul to accompany me to Rome for his investiture. Certainly you would be most welcome if you chose to accompany us."

Joan Hull lit another cigarette. "Nothing could keep me away."

"Hey, Nick," a stout, bald-headed man hailed him from the bar. It took Nick a moment to recognize Buddy Samson, senior vice-president in charge of ABC-TV programming. "Let me buy you a drink."

"Never on working time."

"Who you fooling? I've seen you drinking with half a dozen people at all hours of the day and night. Say, you don't look too happy, Nick. Anything I can do, you say the word."

"I'm fine, Buddy."

"Hey, I have a piece of news for you that might bring a smile back to that pretty *punim* of yours, *yonkle*."

"You'd better go easy on the drinks, Buddy. Whenever you break into Yiddish, I know you've had three too many."

"You want to hear this or not? Listen, I'm going to tell you anyway. Dinah Sheridan's doing more than just covering 44's anniversary Friday night. She's going to do a two-hour special, most of it live. The taped part is going to start the program. She'll do a little history, profiles of Cecil and Duke and his wives, some clips of films made over the years. Then she's going to come on in living color and interview some of the gold-key celebs. She's going to wind up the festivities with a fifteen-minute considered opinion on—get this—the food, the wine, the prices, the service, the moistness of the toilet paper in the ladies' sand box. You want to know what kind of a rating La Sheridan is going to give 44?"

"Not especially."

"Sure you do or you would've moved off a long time ago. I'm going to tell you, Nick, 'cause I like you: nobody knows. Can you imagine the nerve of that little cunt, not letting anyone—and I mean anyone—know what she's going to say?

"She's got eighty million people out there listening to her mouth off nightly about what she knows about fancy restaurants and the people who eat in them and she's got herself into a position where she don't have to tell anybody anything. She can ruin this joint in fifteen words, Nick." Buddy Samson stopped to take a drink from his glass.

"Bullshit, Buddy. She could make a dent, that I admit. But the families who have been coming to Duke's for the last fifty years aren't going to stop because Dinah Sheridan doesn't like the steak tartar. And the odds are she does like it. Her father and mother were married and divorced here. Her first meal in a restaurant was right here. She's celebrated her sixteenth and twenty-first birthdays at the best table. When her father cut his wrists, Duke was on the first plane to Tahoe. I'm not all that worried, Buddy."

"You never know what that little cunt is going to say, believe me."

Nick turned away, realizing that he did believe Buddy, or he would have never gone into that defense he just gave. When he saw Little Mike, he said, "Next time Buddy Samson tries to come in, give him a hard time, will you?"

"He's barred?"

"Yes, he's barred."

Nick went into his office, had his secretary try Blue Bowen again. He was in. "Listen, Blue," Nick said, when their respective secretaries had gotten off the line, "I wonder if you could give me a few minutes. I could get down there in half an hour . . ."

"What about late this afternoon, Nick. I'm scheduled for a drink at 44. I'll come a few minutes early."

"Great, Blue," he said after a moment's hesitation. He had wanted to say that he *had* to see him right away, that it was goddamned urgent. But Duke had taught him early on that whether you're playing craps or poker or the market, you never let them see how scared you are.

But I'm plenty scared right now, he thought, as he went out of his office and into the restaurant where he put his host's smile back on his face. Cary Grant and his daughter were just entering, and they liked to have Nick take them to their table.

Chapter Three

IT WAS after two when Valida Rand came into 44, wrapped in an enormous white fox coat. Saunders carefully remained a few feet away from her, claiming that the coat was alive and molting, that it left his dark suit looking like a prop from an antidandruff commercial.

"It's too early to be wearing a heavy fur like that anyway," he said, allowing Nick to help her get it off.

"I look glamorous in it," she said, letting Nick take it away to the checkroom.

"You look more chic without it," Saunders said as Paulette Goddard and Andy Warhol, that unlikely pair, came out of the dining room and stopped to say hello. Over the silver-haired artist's shoulder, Valida could see that the first table on the left was still empty.

"He's not here yet. Do you think it's possible he's not going to show a second time?"

"Anything is possible with your ex-husbands, my dear."

"Saunders . . ."

"Don't say anything you'll regret, Valida."

She laughed. "How is it you always know when I'm about to be bitchy, Saunders?"

"You get a pinched look about your mouth and your eyes

become noticeably smaller. I'll order you a Bombay gin while you see to your makeup. It looks as if Amanda laid it on with a trowel."

"I did it myself this morning. Amanda has the week off. Today she's visiting her mother. Times like this when I wish *I* had a mother."

"Go do something about your face. If Laddy turns up, I'll hold his hand."

"Careful, darling. Laddy's been known to hold more than a man's hand in his time."

"There's that pinched look."

She laughed and walked across the Club Room, aware that a good many eyes were on her. She didn't feel fifty. She felt decades younger. She only wished she didn't look fifty. She wondered if she were going to succumb to the seduction of a face-lift. She thought not. No matter how expert the doctor, everyone always came out with that terrible surprised look.

She glanced up at the portrait of Duke and remembered a spring day when she was going through a divorce (she couldn't, for the life of her, remember who she had been divorcing) and Duke had been disconsolate about Irene and they had gone up to Connecticut to see a man about a horse and wound up in a motel that featured heart-shaped beds and fat couples in Bermuda shorts and ankle-length socks with little clocks on them.

She couldn't remember very much about their lovemaking but Duke had made her laugh, very much the way Saunders could, and she had returned from Connecticut in much better spirits than she had gone, ready to start all over again, though of course not with Duke, who had still been legally and emotionally tied to Irene.

She went into the ladies' room which was pink and black, with flattering lights over friendly mirrors and she thought, as she studied herself, that perhaps she didn't look fifty.

She wished she could relax. She wished she didn't care so much about the film she was trying to get made, so appropriately named, *Neon Lights*.

Why *do* I care so much? she wondered as she sat down at the vanity. But she knew. She cared because this film was going to be a justification of Frank's career, of his incredible ability to tap and display human emotion. And, she had to admit, it was going to be a justification of her own career, of her ability to enact human emotion.

"How are you, Miss Rand?"

"Fine, Sophie," she said, wishing it were so. "And you?"

"Quite well, Miss Rand. You need anything, you ask. So nice to see you back here at 44 again."

"Actually, Sophie, I only came in here to think. I've done some of my very best thinking in this ladies' room."

Sophie laughed and went back to contemplating her neat, beautifully manicured hands. She had been a 44 ladies'-room fixture for as long as anyone could remember, always crisply turned out in the pink and white outfit that Diana Vreeland claimed belonged in the Metropolitan Museum's haute couture collection. It was said that Adrian had designed it especially for Sophie when once he had mistakenly wandered into the ladies' room and thought she looked too grim "in solid black, head to toe."

Not that she was black. She was more of a mocha color with white hair and a spare body that remained strong and unaged. No one knew how old she was and she wasn't telling. "No mandatory retirement for this lady," she had told Nick. Valida Rand hoped that she would be as calm and attractive as Sophie when she got to wherever Sophie was at.

Valida thought about redoing her makeup and decided Saunders was wrong as she sat back in the high, upholstered chair that faced the vanity, thanking whatever god was responsible for preventing Duke from installing Muzak in the ladies' room, speculating about why there was almost a religious peace imbuing those ceramic tile walls. It's because there are no men in here, she decided when she realized that someone had come in and was sitting next to her.

She took her eyes off herself and, defenses in place, turned. She knew immediately who the short—well, petite—blond woman sitting next to her was. She was wearing the sort of little-girl dress Californians thought de rigueur for lunching in smart restaurants in Manhattan and the sort of "natural"-look makeup that had been popular the year before.

She's pretty, Valida thought. And she's young. But thank God she doesn't have bones and that stumpy little neck is cheering. She holds great promise for an early and complete fade-out.

"I'm Valida Rand," Valida said, holding out her hand, tossing her black mane of hair back in that affected, characteristic gesture that had become, after so many close-ups, part of her nature. "And you're Daisy Wister. There should be a phrase for our sort of relationship, don't you think, one perfect word that immediately sums up the connection between the ex-wife and the current wife? There probably is, in Hindustani or Sanskrit."

"How do you do, Valida," Daisy Wister said with—Valida had to admit it—a certain amount of sang froid. Well, her father, Harry Monaco, had a certain amount of sang froid. Anyone who was caught embezzling a hundred thousand dollars from one of his actors and then had the nerve to reemerge, a year later, as head of yet another movie company, had a certain amount of sang froid. It was said of Harry Monaco that he ran movie companies as a vocation and embezzled as a career.

Daisy was the fruit of his only marriage. She looked a bit as if she had been plucked too early, as if she had matured under an artificial-light machine instead of on the vine.

"I've always wanted to meet you, Valida," Daisy said, doing something with a powder puff to her button of a nose. She paused, young Daisy did, held the silence for a measured beat, and then came in with the clincher, perfectly timed and clearly expected, but nonetheless painful, like a telegraphed punch. "Ever since I was a little girl. Laddy's always talking about your old films and how helpful you've been to his career and all."

Like a lot of new Californians, she affected a Texas accent. Possibly because Houston was the city of the hour.

"Yes," Valida found herself saying. "He was going nowhere fast when I plucked him out of the steam room at that bathhouse." Valida stood up, trying to keep her hands at her side, trying to keep them from searching for Daisy Monaco Wister's neck.

"He confessed," Daisy said, outlining her thin lips with a bloodred lipstick, "that he always liked masculine types until he met me."

"Ah, what the hell," Valida said, putting down her purse and grabbing the tail end of Daisy's neo Punk hairdo, slapping her face three or four times until Daisy managed to get off the chair, free her hair, and aim a high-heeled kick at Valida's groin. Valida caught the younger woman's foot and lifted it high in the air, upending her.

"Round one to you, Grandma," Daisy said as she picked herself up. "We'll see who takes the match."

"I'm glad, for Laddy's sake, that there's more to you than meets the eye," Valida said, taking her purse, winking at Sophie who had remained somnambulant throughout, leaving the ladies' room, walking across the Club Room, sitting down at the best table between Saunders and Laddy Wister, swallowing half the Bombay gin that was at her place without one wasted gesture.

"Darling," she said, kissing Laddy on his forever smooth cheek. "You don't look a day over thirty-one. How are you? I've just run into your new little wife. Who would have thought Harry Monaco had all those peaches and cream in him?"

Saunders placed his knee gently against Valida's in warning. She chose to ignore it and drank the rest of her gin, asking Charles if she might have another, turning to Laddy. "Is she lunching with us, Laddy?"

He smiled a slow smile that had been practiced in thousands of mirrors around the world. "Nope. Daisy just dropped me off. We got the studio car. Then she decided to use the little girl's room."

"Pity she made a mistake and came into the little ladies' room. Tell me, Laddy, how have you been?"

"Bushed." He flashed his multidimpled smile again with more assurance. "Just wrapped *Toronto Express* up in Canada and let me tell you, it was no picnic. They had us up at four every morning to catch the goddamned sunrise . . ."

Laddy Wister talked on about the problems of being on an all-male shoot in Canada as Valida looked him over. He was so big. One forgot that. Everyone else these days—Pacino, Hoffman—was so short. She was always nonplussed by the sheer size of Laddy Wister. He was at least six foot four with Knute Rockne's shoulders, Kirk Douglas's cleft chin, Victor Mature's muscles, and Elizabeth Taylor's eyes.

If she didn't know what a terrible wimp he was, she would still, she had to admit, find him one of the most attractive men in he world. In the old days Cleopatra or Sheba would have had his tongue cut out and made perfect use of him. She dismissed that thought because his tongue had once played an important if not key role in their lovemaking. She tired to concentrate on what he was saying in his slow, self-styled laid-back drawl.

"Daisy wants me to take a nice, long rest," was what it was, delivered as promised in his best west Texas shoot-'em-up voice, though he never could quite cover the East Chicago slur under it.

"Laddy," Daisy said, materializing at their table, her hair back in place, her face a ring of smiles. Saunders stood up and both he and Valida were introduced.

"Valida and I already had the pleasure, Laddy. She's just as you said she was. The spit image. Now I mustn't interrupt. But I want to remind you, Laddy, not to make any promises you can't keep. He has such trouble saying no," she said, directing her pale blue eyes to Saunders. "He's going to take a nice long rest and then he's committed to Daddy's next project. Now I must run, but I do want to say it's been a real pleasure meeting you both."

She left, Saunders and Laddy sat down, and Laddy began to say something, but she cut him short. "So the little woman's read the script."

"Now, Val . . ."

"Valida to you, Laddy boy. Let's cut the crap and take it from the top. I haven't been waiting for two days to have lunch with you because of old time's sake, dearie. Or because I've missed your all-American bottomless charm. Frank's screenplay has been in your pigeonhole at the Plaza since last Friday. Was Little Mary Moonshine letting me know, in that adroit, adenoidal way of hers, that you've read it and you're not interested? Or was she being disarmingly indirect, waiting for an offer?"

"Neither of us have had a chance to read it yet, Val. We only arrived . . ."

"Then I want you to get your ass out of here and go back to your penthouse suite and read the goddamned movie. Laddy, Frankenheimer is set to move. He doesn't care who plays the part. You, Keith Carradine, or Sally Fields."

"Then why all this pressure?" Laddy wanted to know.

"Because Frank wrote it with you and me in mind. I want

this film to be his picture, the way he conceived it, the way he wrote it. It's important to me, Laddy. It's even more important to you. It's your one chance to make a film that means something. It's your one chance to be an actor. You appear in another one of Daddy Monaco's ah-shit productions and you'll be playing a butch Rock Hudson for the rest of your life. You've got your choice: you can do a Bert Reynolds and break out of category or you can swim along with Johnny Weissmuller and Lex Barker and the other unforgettable stars of the jungle. Now go back to the Plaza and read the goddamned screenplay."

Laddy Wister finished his bourbon and stood up, looking down at Valida. "I guess I can't lose nothing by reading it."

"If you don't get back to me in the next couple of days, Laddy, I'll assume you're not interested. I'm flying to the coast on Saturday to meet with Frankenheimer and Warner's." She held out her hand. Laddy took it and then, unexpectedly, raised it to his lips and kissed it.

"I'd like to work with you again, Val. I'd like to . . ."

"Laddy, dearest. Just read the script."

He gave her the rueful grin John Wayne had bequeathed to him and left.

"He can easily find out that Frankenheimer's not touching *Neon Lights* unless he or Dusty or Al or any of them are ready to sign on the dotted line," Saunders said, signaling Charles for menus. "All he has to do is make a phone call."

"Laddy hasn't mastered direct dialing as yet," Valida said, waving the menu away.

"Daisy has."

"Laddy's dumb but not dumb enough to let her know he's interested. He realizes that what I told him is, as they say out on the Hollywood ranches, 'the straight shit.' He needs a new dimension and he knows I can give it to him."

"The big question is whether his wife is going to let you."

Chapter Four

"I REMEMBER this room when Cecil and Duke were using it as an office," Blue Bowen said. "Most of the time we shot craps in here." He moved about the book-lined room, his hands clasped behind his back, his cornflower-blue eyes filled with a seeming innocence as he examined the books. For the most part they were autographed, presented to Duke by the authors who had made 44 their clubhouse over the years.

"I remember another time—oh, this was early on—when the feds were forced to raid the joint because the head of the New York Drys, a terrible old bag named Mrs. Millander, was putting all this pressure on them.

"Duke had had the bar fitted out with a lever so that when it was lifted, the shelves tipped backward, sending all the bottles of booze crashing down to the alley outside. They had a crazy bartender at the time, a little fellow called Harry. Harry loved booze the way other people love women. He used to sit around and admire the color of the bourbon. Anyway, one day the signal that meant the feds were at the door was rung and Duke goes for his magic lever. Harry went off the deep end—he didn't want all that beautiful booze destroyed—and he starts fighting with Duke, using every ounce of his strength to keep Duke from the lever. For a little guy he was pretty strong.

"Just as the feds were breaking through the door, Duke picked Harry up in his arms and Cecil pushed the both of them up against the lever. The booze went crashing down to the alley, making a terrible row.

"The feds wanted to know what the racket was all about. Cecil looked at Duke, holding a passed-out Harry in his arms, and then he looked at the commissioner. 'It was Duke,' Cecil said, 'lamenting the loss of his loved one.' That Cecil. He was something else."

Blue rested his rump on the edge of the red leather-covered partner's desk that took up so much of the room and laughed. He had a good laugh, infectious. He was a nice-looking man in his early sixties with thinning white hair parted on the left, a flat belly, and the sort of bland, aquiline features Nick associated with textbook illustrations of Confederate generals.

No one knew his real first name. It was said that he was called Blue because of his eyes; and because, as a child, he was famous for sulking alone in corners. The black woman who looked after him—according to this second version—threw up her hands one day and said, "My, that chile always is so blue, I'z gonna call him Blue."

Whatever the derivation of his name, he was a great favorite at 44 and an especial champion of Cecil's.

"Everyone talks about Duke but Cecil was a lalapalooza in his own way. Witty, that man could sit at the bar in the Club Room and keep a dozen of us entertained for hours." Blue Bowen played with the gold key Cecil had given him nearly forty years before. He wore it, he said, because one had to wear something on a watch chain and 44 was the only honor society he had ever belonged to.

"This was the first place I came to when I hit New York, fresh from being thrown out of Harvard. I had a few friends here and a couple of relatives and we were all out there, sitting at the bar, when someone asked me what I was going to do and I said I was going to be a stockbroker. Well, they all got so tickled, they could hardly stand up. We were in the middle of the Depression, you know, and the stockbrokers who hadn't jumped off the Empire State Building were digging ditches.

"Cecil and Duke could see that though I was laughing, I was hurt, so they each gave me a hundred bucks, right out of their pockets. 'See what you can do with this kid,' the Duke told me.

"I went right out the next morning and bought them three hundred shares each of a stock called Black Beauty Mines. Coal. Only they found out it was the sort of coal that didn't burn and Black Beauty went bust a couple of weeks later. I was ready to jump, too, but Cecil gave me a talking to. He said he could understand jumping over a couple of million bucks but not over a couple of hundred. It took me nearly a year to pay them back, but I did."

Blue Bowen had not only paid Cecil and Duke back, he had made millions for himself and everyone who invested with him in the years that followed. He established Bowen Frères ("Where's the brother?" he was asked; "there ain't none," he had answered. "Frères just sounds better, that's all."), Investment Brokers, in the late 1940's, putting together a financial empire that made his firm the most influential of the small houses on Wall Street.

"Speaking of two million bucks," Nick said, "that's exactly the amount I want to borrow."

Blue looked at him over his cigar but didn't say anything.

"Duke is dying, Blue."

"And his son, Peter, is selling. I know, Nick. We've been watching 44 Industry for a long time. It's a performance stock. But in terms of profitability, the Industry needs a new management organization. It's got all the potential but it's never lived up to its promise. It can't with the kind of absentee management it's been getting."

"And 44?"

Blue Bowen smoked on his cigar for a moment. "Never thought about it, Nick. Never occurred to me that the family would want to be out of it. I never thought of 44 in terms of profit and loss."

"Duke says I can buy it for two million bucks."

"While he's alive, right?" Blue asked, going to the bookcase, picking out a first edition of *You Can't Go Home Again*. "This man wrote the way I would have liked to. He used to come in here with that lady friend of his and they'd sit up front in the Club Room . . ." He shut the book and put it back on the shelf.

"I'm going to tell you a secret, Nick. I haven't got two million. Not in cash and not in anything I could turn in without having a lot of questions I can't answer at the moment asked. I'm going to have to do some fast work. I have to see the books. I have to get a few of the boys together. In the old days it would have taken ten minutes. They would've thought of it as a shelter, as a way to keep an institution alive.

"But the tax laws have changed and so have the people with the money. They're not looking for shelters anymore. They're looking to make more money. But there's a lot of sentiment going for 44, Nick. Like I say, first thing I have to look at is the books. You call the accountants—Wasserman, if I remember—tell them it's okay."

"Sure, Blue. Listen, I can't thank you . . ."

"Don't thank me yet, Nick. Not until I can get something going. You have to realize you're fighting Peter *and* UNITAS. UNITAS doesn't want the Industry without the club. The club's the prestige, the sex appeal." He ground out his cigar in the oversized glass ashtray on the desk, touched Nick on the shoulder, and went to the door. "I'll call you, one way or the other, soon as I find out if there's any action."

"You know Duke is . . ."

"I know. There's a rush on. I'll talk to you in two, three days tops."

"Thanks, Blue."

Dinah Sheridan found Lawrence and told him that if her dinner guest, Terry Winters, appeared, he should be seated and given a drink.

"Yes, Miss Sheridan," Lawrence said, indicating with an upraised eyebrow that he didn't need to be told what to do with waiting guests.

"Is Nick in his office?" she asked, putting her hands in the sheared beaver sport coat she was wearing and which Lawrence considered inappropriate for dining at 44. He told her Mr. Reo was not in his office at present but if she would care to wait there, he would see that Mr. Reo would appear within a very short time.

Dinah thanked him casually and walked across the Club

Room to Nick's office. As she did so, she caught a glimpse of Brette Stewart-Greene getting into the elevator which led to Duke's duplex.

She let herself into Nick's office, sat in the visitor's chair, and lit a Camel as she studied the books that lined one wall. But she wasn't seeing them. She was seeing Brette and she was honest enough to admit that she was still jealous. "There but for the curse of God," she said, drawing on her cigarette.

For no apparent reason she remembered a time when she was seventeen and Brette was sixteen. After a disastrous encounter with Duke which she steadfastly refused to think about, she had convinced her mother to send her to finishing school in England, Darlington Hall. She hadn't exactly had to twist her mother's arm. A young and burgeoning—that was the word her mother had used, burgeoning—girl was not an appendage a young and amiable Beverly Hills widow needed or wanted.

She had come back to the States for Christmas holidays. She was to spend them in New York with her mother. But there was a message and a car at the airport. Her mother had been delayed. The car took her to the St. Regis.

"Darling," her mother said when Dinah called. "What could I do? Lanny had the most terrible fever . . ."

"Who's Lanny?"

"Darling! Lanny Wilson. My fiancé. I could hardly leave him with one hundred and three . . ."

"What do you want me to do?" Dinah asked, sitting down on the bed in the hotel room, kicking off her heels.

"I thought that perhaps tomorrow you could fly out here on that perfectly lovely United afternoon flight. I got Miss Mapes to make you a reservation. Then we can all spend the holidays together."

"I'll see you tomorrow night, Mother."

"I'll have Miss Mapes meet you with the car."

There was a message that Duke expected her to lunch at 44 on the following day and she thought that perhaps he regretted the last time they had met.

She dressed carefully. A little Chanel black suit. (Her mother was very generous as long as Dinah kept her distance.) Patent-leather heels and purse. A bright purple silk blouse for color. Not much makeup. She didn't need the mirror to tell her she looked more twenty-five than seventeen.

Little Mike didn't recognize her until she told him who she was and he told her, again, the story of how he carried her to a taxi in her blue satin dress when she was seven.

Victor Reo took her hand and then led her to the best table. "The Duke isn't going to make it," Victor told her. "He's got business down in D.C. But he sent a replacement."

And then Brette had come racing in, handing her school books to Little Mike to check, wearing a green jumper over a cotton blouse and low-heeled shoes and looking more fifteen than sixteen.

"I'm sorry," she said, sitting down, putting her hand on Dinah's. "I know I'm dreadfully late but I'm editor of the yearbook and today was the final day to get our photographs in and at the last minute I realized I hadn't given them one of me. It wouldn't have been so terrible if I weren't editor." She looked across the table at Dinah. "God, you look gorgeous. That suit must have cost the earth. Aunt Helen wouldn't let me look at it much less own it. God, sometimes I wish they had sent me to boarding school someplace terrifically smart. Do you love it?"

"It's all right," Dinah said and then she looked at Brette with her pageboy haircut and pink lipstick and the perfect skin and said, "Actually I loathe it. All the girls are far too spoiled and rich. At Darlington Hall one is either hard and nasty or soft and soppy. I don't suppose I have to tell you—well, perhaps I do—that I'm hard and nasty."

"You look wonderful to me," Brette said, sighing. "Every girl in my class at Brearly would give her right eyetooth to look one tenth as sophisticated as you do."

Charles interrupted them at that moment and took their orders, wondering whether or not to give Dinah the glass of white wine she asked for and deciding he could.

Brette talked about going to Vassar in the fall and Dinah said she was staying on in Europe, that she had gotten herself an apprentice job at the Hôtel de la Poste in Beaune, France. That she wanted to learn about food and France was the place to do it.

"Do you ever see Peter?" Brette asked as dessert was being served.

"Duke's son? Yes, not too long ago at the Savoy. He

bowed and then he came over and said something earnest about my being out after curfew. Evidently he knew I was at Darlington Hall. I'm afraid everyone at my table laughed. Curfew at Darlington Hall is about as rigidly observed as Passover. No one pays the slightest bit of attention to it."

"Was Peter hurt?"

"I hope so. He's such a pompous stick despite his good looks."

"You must have tons of boyfriends," Brette said, abandoning Peter, eating her sundae.

"Boyfriends? You go out on dates with boyfriends?" Dinah asked.

"Not too often. Aunt Helen is very strict. Saturday nights and occasionally Fridays . . ."

"You mean you're still a virgin?" Dinah asked.

"You mean you're not?"

And then, for no special reason, they both laughed and Dinah found herself staying the night at Brette's house instead of at the St. Regis. They stayed up until six in the morning, Brette listening breathlessly as Dinah told her about her first lover (a ski instructor at Gstaad) and her last (a member of the Coldstream Guards). Dinah didn't tell Brette how she lost her virginity to her father or how, when the Coldstream Guard began to spank her during foreplay, she begged him to continue. She made it sound rosy and fun and romantic.

There was something so appealing, so innocent about the look in Brette's violet eyes. She didn't want to destroy it.

"I should lose my virginity," Brette said at one point.

"You will," Dinah assured her. "But there's no need to rush."

"No one's ever even tried."

"Right now you have the sort of looks that make men all soft inside. They want to cuddle and protect you. Wait. In a year or two you'll be chasing them away."

"Really?"

"I promise," Dinah said.

She also promised she would stop in New York on her way back to England for another "pajama party." In the morning she and Brette had breakfast with Duke who was very kind, who seemed to have forgotten what seemed like an unforgettable incident. He had Victor Reo's son, Nick, escort her back to the St. Regis to pick up her luggage.

Now if I wanted someone to save me from my nonexistent virginity, Dinah thought, looking at Nick's unruly black hair, his broad shoulders. She thought about inviting him up to her room but there was another message from her mother at the desk. She thanked Nick and sent him on his way and then called California.

Her mother was beside herself. "What do you think?" she asked Dinah. "I've caught the damn flu myself. And I'm wildly contagious. I'm afraid you mustn't come, darling. I wouldn't want you . . ."

Dinah said what she was supposed to say and then she hung up the phone only to pick it up a moment later to send a wire to the Coldstream Guard. She would be in London for the holidays, after all.

Nick entered his office, not looking happy.

"I wanted to talk to you, Nick, about Friday."

"Anything I can do to help," he said. She was wearing a bright red dress under the beaver coat, cut low in front. Hanging between her nearly exposed breasts was her father's gold key, suspended on a threadlike gold chain. Each of the keys had a number engraved on its head indicating in what order it had been issued. Dinah's father had been very proud that his gold key was number seven.

"I want to bring a crew over here in the early A.M. to interview Duke and of course you and perhaps Lawrence and I think the chef. We'll put it all on tape. What's 44's schedule like on Friday?"

"We're closed for the day in honor of the fiftieth but there'll be people in and out, coming to congratulate Duke . . ."

"That's okay. I like civilians in the background. Do you think he'll let us shoot upstairs?"

"Probably not. You know how he is about privacy."

"The club's colorful enough. We'll tape in the morning and come back at night for the live action. We'll set up in the foyer, interview the usuals, and then get out of your way."

"Sounds good, Dinah."

He went with her into the Club Room and took her to the

best table where Terry Winters was waiting. "Buddy Samson tells me you're going to review the food on Friday," Nick said. "Be nice, Dinah."

"Why shouldn't I? Duke's always been kind to me. 'I've always had to depend on the kindness of strangers.' You know that, Nick."

He nodded to Terry Winters, smiled at Dinah, and moved away, not reassured. They had been to bed once but it had been what Nick called less than a joyous experience. They had both had too much grass mixed with booze and she had been, if not frigid, at least unresponsive to his warmth. He had chalked it up to experience, to the wrong chemistry. Dinah Sheridan had brooded about it for months, even years, blaming herself. Nick had been what Dinah described as "the last of the straight men."

Bess Meyerson and Ed Koch came in and said hello as did Senator Howard Baker. Dinah gave them her professional talk-show smile but she was tired and nervous and it showed. People said it was the price she paid for being the youngest and most important TV personality around. They wondered about the men in her life but they didn't wonder about Terry Winters.

He was a sometimes magazine writer and full-time social climber who had come out of the South when he was a cherubic child of nineteen, had been passed around the homosexual writers' clique in New York until some of the talent rubbed off, and he had published a novel. It received good enough reviews, was optioned by Paramount, and remaindered by Barnes & Noble.

Now in his thirties, he devoted most of his energies to being in the right place at the right time.

"I'm going to Pat Lawford's in Palm Beach for Thanksgiving," he told Dinah. "You want to come along or are you going out to your mother's?"

"God, no."

"Then do come. Pat would love it. Afterward I'm going to run down to Key West. Tom's giving a birthday party for Miss Rose . . ."

"I'm so bored with homosexual escorts and blue-collar lovers."

Terry smiled at her over the rim of his glass. "You mean

black-leather lovers, don't you, pet? That is a bruise under your left eye, is it not? Or has your pancake goop gone rancid?''

''You and that mouth, Terry,'' Dinah said with something like affection. ''One wonders what's going to happen to it and you. You'll probably turn into an unwritten, uninvited Truman Capote, sulking in Brooklyn Heights.''

The busboy, Georgio, reached around Terry to remove a plate. ''I hope, my dear, that I'm sulking with something like that,'' Terry said so that Georgio could hear him. ''Look at his basket, Dinah. He's hung like a bull. He's perfect; he doesn't say a word.'' Georgio moved around the table so that his broad back hid the rest of the restaurant from them and then he very purposely spit into Terry Winters' pretty face.

As Georgio moved off with his tray and as Terry Winters slowly wiped his face with a pale linen handkerchief, he said, ''Now that's exactly the kind of man I could go for tonight. What did you think of him, Dinah dear?''

''The busboy? B minus.''

''Funny,'' Terry Winters said, putting his handkerchief away, ''you have that A plus, kill-me-tonight look in your eyes.''

She looked up and saw Georgio disappear into the doorway which led to the kitchen. ''What about strawberry shortcake?'' she asked, reaching for the menu with one hand, fingering the gold key her father had given her with the other.

Chapter Five

IT WAS a half hour before the theater crowd was due to arrive but William Paley and the de la Rentas hadn't liked their play and were being vociferous about if at table six in the main dining room.

As Lawrence returned from giving them menus, which they hardly needed since they all knew 44's offerings by heart, he gave the nod to Igor Strauss and Marquita, signifying that their table, the best table, was going to be needed shortly.

Igor, who managed to reach five foot one with the addition of lifts in his shoes, snapped his fingers in the air for the check while Marquita powdered her badly aging skin which was red with irritation along the ridges of her still extraordinary cheekbones. At seventy she resembled a starving Russian wolfhound, her hair swept back from her face and tied in the classic prima ballerina bun.

Igor Strauss signed the check with a flourish, pocketing Charles's pen which had the words, "Duke's 44 Club" printed in white letters along its length. Igor collected 44 Club pens. He gave them away to elevator boys and taxi drivers in lieu of tips.

He stood up, bowing low to the once married Nora Ephron and Carl Bernstein as they were being taken by Lawrence to their table. Bernstein wanted to know who the little man in the Toulouse-Lautrec hat was and Nora explained as they watched Igor go through the choreographed movements involved in helping Marquita don her sad sables. Marquita took one last, disgusted look at the dining room, swept the sables around her, and sailed out, acknowledging Nick with the famous enigmatic smile. Igor walked behind her, his hands fumbling for the cigar that wasn't in his pocket.

Nick slipped him one of Duke's, which was made in Jamaica and came in a glass tube with a cork stopper and had Duke's name printed on the interior wrapper. Duke wasn't smoking any more.

It was said that Igor Strauss was responsible for bringing Caruso, Galli-Curci, Maria Callas, and Arthur Rubinstein to prominence in this country. He had made it possible, legend and rumor had it, for Pavlova and Paderewski and Margot Fonteyn to perform here. He was the last of the great impressarios, somewhere in his early eighties, still flamboyant, still speaking with the Russian accent left over from his youth in St. Petersburg but, alas, no longer working. The need for impressarios had died before he had.

He counted his greatest triumph the introduction of the prima ballerina, Marquita, to New York ballet. They were married when he was fifty and she was thirty-five and pregnant and had made her last performance after which she definitely retired from the dance.

They spent money in the grand style of impressarios and prima ballerinas so that by the time impressarios and prima ballerinas were no longer what Igor liked to call "a money-making proposition," they were forced to live on social security, on old friends' largess.

But the old friends were, for the most part, dead. And the new management of Carnegie Hall Studios, where they had lived in one of the larger and grander apartments since 1946, were determined to get them out. They were paying one hundred and thirty-four rent-controlled dollars a month, when they were paying.

Thanks to Duke, they were allowed to dine at 44 once a week—twice on rare occasions—and the bill was always charged to the Duke's personal account. Duke made it understood that the Strausses were always to be seated at the best table, as they had been when they were the mutual toasts of the town. And it was understood—by the Strausses—that they would dine between nine thirty and eleven P.M., between the serious dinner people and the after-theater crowd.

"I don't suppose," Lawrence said to Nick, unusually sympathetic to the Strausses, "that they're going to have many more free meals on Duke, poor things."

"I thought you were all for throwing them out into the streets, hungry and penniless," Nick said, putting his hands in his jacket pockets, a gesture Victor had tried, unsuccessfully, to cure him of.

"That was when I knew Duke would never let that happen. Now, when it's a possibility, my humanity rises to the fore."

"You can let it sink back to its normal rock-bottom level. Carnegie Hall has finally succeeded in ousting them. They're leaving for California at the end of the week. Seems they have a perfectly ordinary, respectable doctor of a son who's going to support them."

"I would give fifty dollars," Lawrence said, turning away, "to see Marquita walk down Hollywood Boulevard in her gold combs and orange sables."

"Nick," Mickey the bar captain asked, leaning over the bar. "You think I can have a word with you?"

"Sure thing." He went to the end of the bar while Lawrence greeted Honey Boyd, Pat Foreman, and Saiad at the door and took them to the best table.

"Nick," Mickey said, "Countess Nickleson's husband is having a few too many at the bar. I want to cut him off but . . ."

"I'll take care of it, Mickey. And Mickey . . ."

"Yes, Nick?"

"Do me a favor. Don't call him Countess Nickleson's husband. The guy's name is Bill. Bill Nickleson."

Mickey nodded. "Sorry, Nick."

"Nothing to be sorry about."

"How are you, Bill," Nick said, moving around the curved bar, putting his hand on the blue-suited shoulder of a man who was blandly handsome enough to appear in yacht ads in boating magazines.

"Terrific, Nick," Bill Nickleson said, looking up, focusing slightly. "Tip top. Couldn't be in better form. What say we have a drink together, toast the coming anniversary, Duke's health? Oh, Mickey . . ."

"Let's have it in my office, Bill."

Bill Nickleson stood up, just, and Nick took his arm. He led him away from the crowded but quiet bar. It was the serious hour when couples were having their last nightcap, deciding whether to go home together or not, whether to go through with the divorce or have the baby, whether to put off buying that estate in Glen Cove.

It was the hour when men got serious about their wives. "I don't need another drink, Nick," Bill Nickleson said as he and Nick walked across the Club Room floor.

"What about coffee?"

"Better take me to the car, Nick. You don't want me passing out in your office, do you?" Nick walked him through the door with its matched pair of bodyguards (Little Mike and Scotty) and down the steps, carefully, to the waiting limousine.

"I have wife problems, Nick," Bill Nickleson said as the chauffeur opened the rear door of the car for him.

"I'm sorry to hear that, Bill."

"I'm sixty-four years old and suddenly, quite unasked for, quite undeserved, I have wife problems." He allowed the chauffeur to help him into the back seat. He leaned forward so he could see Nick. "My wife the beauty queen told me I could have the car tonight. She had work to do. I understand, Nick, that she brought the work here yesterday to give him a meal. Not a very pretty piece of work. You must have seen him. Black hair, muscles, and a surly expression. Kind of man my father used to call a brute.

"Trouble with my wife the beauty queen is that I've always played Chamberlain to her Hitler. We'd sit down for long talks in whatever particular one of her Bechtesgardens we happened to be in and she'd make demands and I'd make appeasements. I think it's time to stop appeasing, to stop shutting one eye and flashing the other cheek. I think Hitler is about to meet her Waterloo, if you don't mind my switching analogies in midstream. I think I am very drunk indeed."

He put his handsome head back against the upholstery—Countess Vera yellow leather—and closed his eyes. "Sorry, Nick," he said when he opened them. "Shan't happen again.

Never again. I'm going to shoot either him or her or myself and then you can bet it won't happen again."

He stopped talking and closed his eyes because he was so tired, because he didn't want Nick Reo to see him cry, because he didn't want to live anymore, not at that particular moment. The yellow Rolls-Royce drove off. Nick stood on the sidewalk in front of Duke's 44 Club for a moment, watching it. And then he went inside where, at the best table, the man named Saiad had his hand covering Honey Boyd's. He was patting it, reassuringly.

"It's just that I never did have a head for languages, Mr. Saiad," Honey Boyd was saying, taking a sip of Amaretto with her free hand. "I was always good enough at English. I mean I always got at least a B on composition but my French and my Latin were hopeless."

"Honey, dear," Pat Foreman said, taking a large gulp of her Brandy Alexander, "no one is suggesting that you become a linguist."

"Well, that girl in the play tonight, the one who played the ambassador's mistress, she sure could speak a lot of languages. Remember how she said no to him in six different foreign ways?"

Pat Foreman and Saiad looked at each other for a moment and then both began to speak. Pat Foreman gave way to Saiad. "She was a plain woman," he said in his low voice. "She needed languages. You, you are very beautiful, if I may say so, Mrs. Boyd. You need no extraneous skills."

"I used to dream of being an actress," Honey said, allowing Charles to refill the glass with the bottle of Amaretto Saiad had asked be brought to the table. "Of course my mother, Ruth, would never listen to a word about that. Politics and actressing, she says, don't mix. Look at Sarah Churchill. And I said look at Phyllis George and Elizabeth Taylor and even Jane Fonda and she snorted in that annoying way Ruth has and went back to whatever she was reading.

"Hutch is the same way. He can't understand why I want something to do with my time. He thinks I should be home all day, or riding that horse he gave me. Do you believe that that horse is pregnant? A four months pregnant horse and he wants me to ride it! I told him I wasn't riding any four months pregnant horse and he told me I should organize a luncheon for the DAR and I said I couldn't understand why because the DAR all hate his guts and then he said I should help Mrs. Anvers fix up the menus for the week. Mrs. Anvers doesn't need me. Truth is, she frightens the heck out of me."

"Your husband's housekeeper has been frightening the heck out of all D.C. since the first Mrs. Roosevelt stalked through the White House with her riding crop looking for mice to kill. Honey, surely Hutch wouldn't mind if you took a job to keep you busy."

"He *says* he wouldn't mind but he also says it has to be 'appropriate.' Hutch and my mother are very big on what's appropriate and what's not appropriate. I can't even buy a dress without one of them telling me whether it's appropriate or not. Las year, right after we were married and I thought I was free of Ruth, I went down to Garfinckel's and came home with this adorable peach satin wraparound and made the mistake of wearing it to the Symingtons' anniversary party. Well, they both hit the roof." Honey paused and took another long sip of the Amaretto and continued again before either Saiad or Pat Foreman could move in. "Showing all of New York,' Ruth said. 'What're you trying to do,' Hutch said, 'get yourself raped?' It was real low cut and clingy and it didn't have much of a back at all but they didn't have to be so mean." Honey Boyd's blue eyes clouded at the memory of her mother's and her husband's meanness.

"Course he made it up to me," she said, looking at the eight-carat aquamarine she wore on her left hand, her drinking hand, she called it. "Still, I have a right to live my own life, don't I, Pat?"

"Certainly, Honey. Now what would you think of going into public relations, Honey? That's what Saiad and I have been talking about. You'd adore it. Playing hostess to visiting VIPs, taking advantage of your writing skills so you could work up little releases, interfacing with the newspapers, television. Honey, you would be marvelous on television as a kind of interested spokeswoman. Ruth and Hutch couldn't object to that, could they?"

"They only said I couldn't be an actress. They didn't say I couldn't appear on news shows even though Hutch thought it was better if I didn't show up that time Barbara Walters interviewed him on the Israeli-Egyptian peace talks."

"What do you think, Saiad?"

He held out his large, dark hands and turned them upward. "Mrs. Boyd would be superb for the position we have been talking about. But she would have to register as a representative of a foreign interest. How would the senator react to that?"

"Oh, Hutch would never, ever . . ."

"How would he know?" Pat Foreman asked. "They don't exactly broadcast the names of all foreign reps, Honey."

"I couldn't lie."

"Not saying anything isn't exactly a lie. And though I've tried not to say this, Honey, I think the time has come when I must: your husband and your mother both treat you abominably. There they are, shouting their hearts out for the Equal Rights Ammendment, telling everyone who asks—and a good many who don't—how women must be liberated. And then they want you to stay home and plan menus. Honestly, Honey, if you had any guts, you would go after this job and, if you get it, just present the fact to them. If they don't like it, you can tell them what they can do and where they can go."

"I'm not sure I could take on both Ruth *and* Hutch, Pat." She took another long pull at her Amaretto glass. "Though I sure as heck would like to give them a little of what they've been giving me."

"Then at least tell Mr. Saiad that you're interested. You know you can count on me when the time comes to break it to them and who knows, you may not even get the job?"

"All right," Honey Boyd said, finishing her Amaretto, reaching for the bottle, pouring herself another. "I apply for the darn job, Mr. Saiad."

"When will she know?" Pat Foreman said, sitting back, following the outline of her throat with her hand.

"I will talk to my superiors. They will let me know in a few days. In the meanwhile let us put it, as you say, on the back burner. Let us talk of other subjects. Have you ever smoked marijuana, Mrs. Boyd?"

Honey Boyd looked around as if someone might be listening. "Once, when I was at junior college in Maryland. I thought I'd never stop giggling. And eating. I was ravenous."

"Perhaps we should all go back to my flat. I have some hemp . . ."

"Not tonight, Saiad," Pat Foreman said with a slight edge to her voice. "Honey's had too much to drink as it is and though I take no moral stand against marijuana, I do know it shouldn't be mixed with alcohol. You're trying to corrupt us, just because we're innocents from D.C. Get the check. It's time this child was in bed. I don't know what Hutch and Ruth would think if they knew we were out so late."

"I know what they would think," Honey said, rambling through her purse, looking for the gold compact she had bought with her birthday money. "And it wouldn't be repeatable in mixed company."

It was after three when Nick decided to leave 44. He resisted the temptation to call up to SayDee, to ask if everything was all right. He knew she would have told him if everything weren't.

He said good night to Mickey who was setting up the bar for the following day and to Georgio who was stacking chairs, cleaning up. He was a strange, silent boy-man, Nick thought, extremely precise in all of his movements. The only table Georgio didn't stack was number eleven where Lawrence had sat himself down to the thick steak Maurice Gotlib had cooked especially for him. He had a napkin fastidiously tucked into his open shirt, a glass of dark red Burgundy in front of him, and the sort of smile on his face lechers, when confronted with their first virgin, wore in old woodcuts.

Of all of the upstairs staff, Nick thought as he walked down the steps of Duke's 44 into the chilly October air, Lawrence genuinely loved food. He laughed at the memory of Lawrence staring adoringly at his pepper steak, his knife and fork poised, ready to pounce, and wondered why Duke had gone into the restaurant business.

He liked food enough but it was far from an obsession. The food served at 44 had to be the best in the way that the cutlery and the glassware and the booze had to be the best. But it wasn't food that had lured Duke into the business. No, Nick thought, it had been the easiest way for Duke to meet the sort of people that interested him. And God knows, Nick thought, he has.

He began to think of all the women he knew Duke had been to bed with when he noticed there was one limousine left at the curb. It wasn't the sort of limousine Nick liked. It was impossible to tell if anyone was inside. The windows had been mirrored. Usually there were half a dozen long black Cadillacs and the occasional Rolls or Lincoln double-parked in front of 44. But rarely at that hour.

This was a Lincoln, a steel-colored Continental, custom-built, with a twisted antenna on its roof, looking like a contemporary swastika. It was the sort of car pimps and rock groups and cocaine dealers hired for an evening. "Definitely Not Our Kind, Dear," he could almost hear Cecil say, when the rear right window went down. "Nick," Brette said, calling out to him, "I thought I might give you a lift."

"I live a block away, Brette."

She looked up at him. Her dark hair had been cut short and waved in the new nostalgic style. In the moonlight she looked like an Art Moderne goddess. "Maybe I can walk you home."

She said something to the chauffeur, opened the door, and put out her hand. After a moment Nick took it and helped her out of the car. She was wearing a long black mink coat that fitted her like a mandarin robe. He had forgotten how cool her touch was, how seductive the scent she wore.

He looked down at the hand he held for a moment. She still wore the same bright red nail polish—Real Ritz Red—that she had worn when she was a girl. "The Dragon Lady returns," he said, rubbing his thumb over one of her nails, letting go of her hand.

"It's been a long time, Nicky."

"Yeah?"

They walked east on the deserted street, the steel gray limousine following them. "You mind if I put my hand on your arm?" she asked.

"A little." He stopped and looked at her. "What did you do with Little Lord Fauntleroy?"

"He was tired. I said I wanted to ride around New York."

"New York via noche. All you need is a paid escort. What was wrong with the driver?"

"Nicky . . ."

"You want to get right to the heart of the matter or you want to be polite old friends for the next block? I can do it either way, Brette, only I may not be all that polite."

"Oh, get to the heart of the matter, Nicky. I can take it."

"You have to choose your role, Brette. You're confusing me. You can't be both the perpetrator and the victim at the same time."

"I wrote to you."

"Fuck you and fuck your letters, Brette."

"I didn't know what to do, Nick. I just didn't know what to do."

"You knew what to do when you were balling me twice a day, when you'd call me during lunch to see if I couldn't stop by the house for a minute and I'd come panting over and there you'd be on the bed with two pillows under your tidy little ass and you were too anxious to even let me get my pants off. You knew what to do when you went to London because, and I quote, 'I just can't write to him, Nick. It wouldn't be fair, Nick. I have to tell him myself, in person.' Goddamn it, it was all right to send *me* a letter."

"It wasn't balling, Nick," she said, putting her hand on his arm, making him stop again. "I wasn't balling you, Nick. I was making love to you."

"We'll put the phrase 'fine distinctions' on your tombstone."

"I honestly did not intend to marry Peter when I went to London. But Duke was there and the bloody archbishop had already agreed to marry us and Peter's mother had gotten a yes from the queen and . . ."

"I understand. It just happened. You had nothing to do with it. Poor little victimized Brette. You went to London to say good-bye to Peter, to explain to him that you had suddenly fallen hopelessly in love and suddenly you woke up, and it was all a beautiful dream. You went on with reality and married Peter Stewart-Greene. The photographs were terrific. You got a very nice play in *Town and Country*. Duke was ever so pleased."

"Duke wanted me to marry Peter. I told him about us and he pointed out the sort of life I would have married to you. You would always love 44 first and me second. And then you never said a word about marriage, about a future of any kind. What was I supposed to do, announce to Peter that I was sleeping with the manager's son, that I wanted to live with him even though he hadn't asked me?"

"I didn't think I had to *ask* you."

"And then there was the Industry. My father and mother left it to me in good faith. You didn't care about the Industry. You only cared for 44. Peter . . ."

"Oh, Peter's managed it beautifully. That agent he hired, Crawford, is running them into the ground with his formula management. Peter's never thought about the Industry until now, when he has the opportunity to sell it. You do know what Peter's doing in New York, don't you, Brette? You couldn't be naïve enough to think that he's here for the anniversary or even to be with his father, could you?

"Peter's here so that he can sell both the Industry and the club for umpty-dumpty million dollars the minute Duke dies. All in one nice, neat package."

She turned away from him.

"I'm not buying tears tonight, Brette. You've become too chic, too smooth and polished. The tears don't go with the diamonds and the perfect complexion. It's like watching Garbo cry. Miraculous but not all that moving."

He left her on the street and went up the steps that led into the empty town house Victor Reo had left him on the wrong side of Forty-fourth Street.

Before he shut the door, he turned to make sure that Brette wasn't being mugged or raped or carted off into the contemporary version of white slavery.

The chauffeur that came with the UNITAS limousine was holding the door open and Brette was getting in and Nick had the thought that she had quite willingly gone into her own brand of slavery, with her violet eyes wide open.

Chapter Six

SHE LET her head rest against the gray leather upholstery. Limousine upholstery was always comforting, she thought. The driver waited patiently in the front seat, his cap squarely sitting on his head, his eyes straight ahead. She knew what he was thinking and it did occur to her that the chauffeur was an attractive man.

But there had been too many attractive men in her life and she didn't want to end up the sort of woman who spent her life getting in and out of bed with chauffeurs. She told him to take her home.

He drove into the underground garage, a man there opened the door, another man took her up to the borrowed penthouse, Peter's valet opened that door. She walked down the carpeted hallway with the Rembrandt drawing underlit on the far wall, noticed a light under Peter's door but went to her own room. Her maid helped her to undress and said good night.

Brette got into the bed and looked at the telephone and wondered if it were too late to call London, to speak to her children, and decided it was. They were so very British, her little girls. Blond and smooth complected and compact, perfectly self-content.

She tried to guess what they would do if they were confronted with the choice of remaining in England with Peter or living in America with their mother.

She knew she wouldn't sleep. She picked up the book she was trying to make her way through. It was a study of communal housing for the poor. Like her mother, Phebe, Brette took an interest in social work. Her dark hair and violet eyes had been increasingly seen in London's poorer districts where the very concept of settlement houses had come to life.

She had a moment's fantasy in which she went to live and work in the settlement house on New York's Lower East Side which her mother's family, the Hamiltons, virtually supported. It wasn't impossible. Social workers and their families often lived within the settlement house.

But she looked across the silent room at a sable rug casually draped over a silk-covered chaise lounge and she knew that though she might give up the sable rugs and the silk chaises, she wasn't the sort of person who could give up more ordinary luxuries. She liked the world, Peter and London notwithstanding, and she wanted to live very much in it.

She closed the book on communal housing studies, pressed the button which extinguished the light, and closed her remarkable eyes.

As it often happened, she immediately visualized Duke. Not a pale and thin and aged Duke, but the virile, youthful man who had been her sole emotional support while she was growing up. The other girls had their parents, their safe, comfortable Fifth Avenue apartments and Newport and Southampton summer houses.

She only had Duke. Aunt Helen had been more like a chaperon, a paid housekeeper. Not wicked, like Mrs. Danvers in *Rebecca* but withdrawn and correct and always very sure of herself, like a character in an Edith Wharton novel.

Aunt Helen, she knew, was rigidly, even admirably, upper class. Phebe and Cecil, though she had only the vaguest memories of them—she associated the words warmth and laughter with her dead parents—were also plainly upper class.

But Duke belonged to no class. He had gone beyond social stratification. He was that archtypical American, the self-made man. Through all of his problems with all of his various women, he had presented a continuously unruffled front to Brette. She had had her own stake in preserving that image.

She knew now she had needed that stability, that ongoing, never changing personality in her life.

It was only when he broke down—that one time—that she realized perhaps it would have been better had he allowed some of the vulnerability to show through. She had grown up thinking that the perfect man for her was one who had, as Aunt Helen would say, no chinks in his armor, no soft spots which could be attacked.

Which was one of the reasons she had married Peter, that perfectly lacquered steel shell of a man. The most important reason she had married him was that Duke had wanted her to. She divined that he had loved her mother; she realized that he felt he was giving both himself and Phebe a second chance by bringing Brette and Peter together. Brette and Peter were to be the surrogate lovers.

It was both a selfish and a romantic fantasy and she meant to play it out until after his death. He had given her so much, she felt he deserved a happy ending: the beautiful Phebe (Brette) living happily ever after with the dashing Duke (Peter).

The fact that she was so obviously not Phebe and that Peter was so obviously not Duke didn't seem to bother him. The fact that she loved the Duke's steward rather than the Duke's son was a problem she would have to deal with.

She remembered when she realized she loved Nick. It was the first time they had been in bed together.

She had been in her junior year at Vassar and very definitely had not belonged to the circle-pin virginal crowd. She wasn't a virgin. Peter had taken care of that when she was a freshman. She wore mini skirts. She went on marches. "You're the only marcher here," Mary Jane had protested during an overnight antiwar demonstration in Washington, "who drove down in a vintage Mercedes convertible and who brought along three changes of silk panties."

"Suppose we go to prison?" Brette had asked. "I'm going to have change my underwear, aren't I?"

But despite all these evidences of being hip, of being very much into the seventies, she still went to deb balls and supper clubs and Princeton weekends.

"You should have been in college in the forties," Mary Jane told her.

"Then I wouldn't have had the inestimable pleasure of knowing you."

"No, I'm serious. You like dating and flirting and cars. You like men and jewels and expensive restaurants. You just go on the marches because, to give you credit, you believe the war is an unjust one; but to be realistic, you'd rather be sitting in the St. Regis's King Cole Bar, drinking a rum and Coke, wrapped in a thousand dollar cocktail dress, surrounded by men with moustaches."

"Well, so would you."

"Yes," Mary Jane admitted. "But I'm not equipped for it. You are."

She hadn't felt very well equipped for anything on that perfect May day when she had decided she had enough of campus protests and mild marijuana parties in off-campus apartments in Poughkeepsie. Aunt Helen was insisting that she come to Bar Harbor for the summer. Peter wanted her to forget about her senior year at Vassar. He needed, he wrote, a wife in London, not a fiancée in college.

Brette had no desire to go to Maine to sit around the big swimming pool at the club or to sail around the chilly waters in Aunt Helen's friends' yachts.

Nor did she want to get married. Not yet. She wanted to finish up at Vassar. She wasn't ready to leave Mary Jane or her art history professor, a woman named Margaret Hunter who brought intellect and taste to primitive Italian art and made it live for Brette.

She wanted to spend the summer in New York, with Duke, going up to Connecticut on weekends to ride, to swim, to luxuriate in his all-approving affection.

She never even got close to the subject. For the first time she could remember, Duke didn't bother to hide the fact that he was pained. Deeply pained.

"Did you drive down?" he asked her, kissing her.

"Yes."

"Where did you park?"

"At the garage where I always park. Duke," she said, not waiting for Robert to leave the room, "what's the matter? Is it SayDee?"

"SayDee? What should be wrong with SayDee? At this very moment she's sitting on the second floor of a Fifty-seventh Street salon having her hair dyed or sprayed or whatever they do to it to achieve exactly that shade of orange-pink.''

Robert came back with tea for Duke, a lemonade for Brette. ''What is it, then?'' she asked, sipping at the lemonade, wishing Robert, who didn't believe in sugar, had used a little. ''I've never seen you look so unhappy.''

He bit the end off a cigar and put it in his mouth and lit it with the gold lighter SayDee had given him for his birthday. ''It's Nick,'' he said.

''Nick? I thought he was in Vietnam, fighting the administration's war, killing Vietnamese to keep Henry Kissinger safe for posterity.''

''He's home.''

''Living with Victor?''

''No.''

''Duke, do I have to drag every single word out of your mouth. Where's he living?''

''In a tenement on St. Mark's Place. Victor only found out he was in New York yesterday. He's been out of the marines two months, back from Vietnam nearly three. He's never told any of us.''

''Maybe he needs a little air,'' Brette said, trying to understand.

''All he needs is a little horse.''

''Horse?''

''H. Heroin. He's hooked. Up to the gills. Victor went to see him last night. We both went to see him this morning. We told him we could get him into a drug rehabilitation program. We told him he could have a job here at 44. We told him we loved him.''

''And what did he say?''

''He told us we were fuck . . . we were messing up his high. He told us to get out.''

She watched Duke smoke his cigar. For once he didn't seem to see her.

''Why are you so turned around?'' she asked after a moment. ''I know you care for Nick and you love Victor but . . .''

''You wouldn't be upset to see a nice kid like that, such a handsome kid, come back from a war all twisted and hooked on heroin? Think of what it's doing to Victor. Think of what Victor's going through."

SayDee came in a few minutes later, a beautiful pink confection, and they went to dinner as if nothing were wrong. They discussed Brette's plans for the summer, they sat at table five and schmoozed with two of the Gabor sisters and their mother, Jolie.

SayDee went upstairs early and Duke began to work the Club Room. Brette cornered Victor in the foyer. He looked as if he had aged twenty years. She got Nick's address from him, told Duke she was meeting friends for a drink, had Little Mike find her a taxi.

It wasn't so much the stink of the narrow stairwell that put her off. It was overwhelming, made up of urine and garbage and the sort of rot and damp that affects any building where the habitually underprivileged live. But it was no worse than the smells of dozens of other Old Law tenements Aunt Helen had taken her through as part of her program to educate Brette as to the realities of New York.

Aunt Helen, in her quiet, faded peaches-and-cream way, was as dedicated a social reformer as her sister had been. She was certain Phebe would have wanted her daughter to be aware that the vast majority of life in New York did not revolve around 44's best table. The problem was that Duke thought it did. It had been up to Helen to prove otherwise.

Brette thought of Aunt Helen as she climbed those foul stairs and reached the landing where she guessed Nick's apartment was supposed to be. Through an open door she looked into a railroad flat where half a dozen young Hispanics sat, salsa music blaring out of an intricate stereo system at them and her. It was very hot. They were obviously stoned on something. The six of them, in their undershirts, with their drugged-dulled eyes, looked at her and she felt for a moment unreal, as if she had wandered into an eighteenth-century Spanish painting: "The Assasins."

"You want grass, lady, you come back tomorrow. We're busy now."

She said she didn't want grass and made her way along the hallway until she came to a door painted a glossy, kitchen enamel blue. It seemed so wrong in that place. It was the sort of door that belonged in a farmhouse.

No, she reflected later, it wasn't the smell or the menacing, drugged boys in the next apartment that put her off.

It was Nick. His eyes were round and sleepless, as if there was never to be any sleep for him. But she wasn't to see that until later.

What she immediately sensed when he opened the door was that in the three years since she had seen him, he had become a man, an adult, that he had lost his adolescence. It was clear to her that she was still holding on to hers. She felt raw and young and embarrassed standing in that fetid hall. He wasn't certain who she was. She told him.

"Oh, yeah. Nancy Drew to the rescue," he said, and then he stepped back so she could come into the narrow kitchen with its tub for a sink and an unshaded forty-watt bulb for illumination.

"Just pretend it's a stage set," he told her. "I do." It was too warm inside the apartment. All he wore was a pair of army-issue shorts. He had developed muscles since the last time she had seen him in a bathing suit, when he was sixteen and she was twelve, and Duke had taken the two of them up to the club in Connecticut to swim. They looked like real muscles, the sort that came from hard work as opposed to the kind that came from athletics. There was a thin line of hair that ran from his chest down his torso and under the shorts.

"Nick," she said, and he stepped backward under the light so that she could see his body was covered with sweat. He turned and lurched sickenly down a narrow corridor into another room. She followed him. Like the kitchen it was long and narrow but it had two windows and a mattress on the floor. The only light came from a neon discotheque sign across the street.

"Are you all right, Nick?" she asked. She could hear him throwing up in the W.C.

"Yeah," he said, coming into the room. "Fit as a fiddle."

They looked at each other across the half-dark room and it was then she saw his used, tired eyes and she became more frightened. "Nick," she said, "come home. Victor, Duke, they want to help you."

"Yeah," he said, lying down on the mattress. "Yeah, they

gave me a lot of help when they came down here. They started shouting at me. I been shouted at enough, you know."

"Nick, this isn't a play. *The Iceman Cometh* is at the other end of the Village."

"This is *Drugman Doesn't Cometh,* baby. And if you think it's ugly now, wait. I am going through what is known as enforced cold turkey. No money, no horse. Simple as that. A lot of guys don't make it through nights like this."

"I'm going to get a doctor."

"The fuck you are."

"I want to help you," she screamed.

"Take off your dress and lie down on this mattress and hold me. Don't worry. I can't do anything. I just need you to hold me, to get me through the night."

The radio in the next apartment was turned off and suddenly the only sounds came from the street, from the kids going into the disco. That somehow made it easier.

She slipped out of the white dress with its sailor blue piping and felt as if she, too, had finally taken off her adolescence. Though she had been to bed with Peter any number of times, in a curious way she had never felt naked with him. As she lay down on the thin, used mattress and took Nick in her arms, she felt very naked and she felt very womanly.

He told her what to do. When to bathe the sweat away, when to get him the bedpan because after awhile he was too weak to get himself to the W.C., and when to feed him water mixed with sugar.

Sometimes he cried and sometimes he laughed but always he sweated and always he talked. It was as if his body were purging itself of not only the addiction, but of the war.

She didn't want to listen but she did. She heard about the whores in Saigon and the company commanders who were shot in the back by their own men in the deltas and about the soldiers who picked up two babies in a mountain village on the tips of their bayonettes and tried to juggle them as the mother begged them to shoot her.

He told her about the first time he shot heroin and how beautiful that first experience was, how it helped him to forget what he had seen, how it helped him to forget that every time he went to the latrine, he ran the risk of getting his body blown to smithereens. And he told her that when he was about to shoot H for the sixth time, he knew he had to make a conscious decision about whether to get hooked or not and after he shot, it didn't seem as if there had been any two ways about it.

Late the next afternoon he finally stopped sweating, and by early evening he had fallen asleep. She put on her white dress with the blue piping and, without thinking, went next door where one of the Hispanic boys said sure, she could use the phone and she called Duke.

"You know I've got the police looking everywhere for you, Brette? You know, your Aunt Helen . . ."

"Listen, Duke, I'm with Nick," she told him. "I think he's going to be all right."

There was a station wagon, a sort of discreet ambulance, downstairs in fifteen minutes. They left Nick's clothes in the railroad flat and carried him out, wrapped in a blanket. She and Victor sat in the back with him. The doctor and Duke sat in front of them, behind the driver and the male nurse.

They went directly to Connecticut, to Silver's, the same drying-out establishment where Duke had once taken Cecil.

Nick agreed to spend the summer at Silver's. Brette managed to spend the summer at Duke's farm, a half hour away, riding, taking care of the horses, visiting Nick.

After they made love for the first time, in Duke's farmhouse bed, Nick lay back and closed his eyes. "I think the cure is complete, nurse," he said.

"Maybe," Brette said, slipping her arm under his head, pushing aside the black curly hair and kissing his forehead. "But we're both going to need a lot more treatment until we're sure."

She went back to Vassar in the fall and he went to work for his father at 44. They spent most of their weekends in bed.

She switched on the light and sat up in the upholstered bed in the borrowed penthouse. She longed for Nick with every particle of her being. At that moment she knew there wasn't anything—even her children—she wouldn't give up to be with him.

The door opened and her maid put her head in. "Is madam all right? Is there anything I can get you? I saw your light."

"No, thank you, Nancy. I'm having a little trouble getting to sleep."

Nancy closed the door and Brette took up the book on communal housing for the poor.

BOOK 3

WEDNESDAY

Chapter One

MONSIGNOR PAUL P. MCGUIGAN replaced the receiver on the telephone. He was surprised. Father Heart had indicated that he was going directly back to Villanova. But the priest with whom he had spoken said that Father Heart wasn't expected for at least a week. Perhaps, after all, Father Heart hadn't said that he was returning immediately to the school, but Paul felt the implication had been there. Usually Father Heart was so direct.

He stood up and walked about the small, exquisite room that Terrence Cardinal Cooke had placed at his disposal while he was, as the Cardinal liked to say, "in between engagements." The mahogany desk, polished and cared for by a long series of dedicated domestics for over a hundred years, took up most of one corner.

It was said that Fulton J. Sheen had sat at it, waiting for Francis Cardinal Spellman's decision in 1966. It was also said that Bishop Sheen had taken his new assignment-demotion to the Rochester diocese without regret, that he had welcomed his first pastoral post in forty years as a new challenge.

Privately Paul doubted it. He had met the bishop on several occasions before he died and he didn't believe Fulton Sheen had been happy in a rustic backwater like Rochester, with few, if any, celebrities to convert.

Paul's own career had followed, at least for a time, Fulton Sheen's. After the years of private tutoring Zoltan had suggested that it was time Paul saw something of the men he would be working with. "The most important alliances," he told Joan Hull, "are often made at university."

There had been talk of sending him off to Rome but Zoltan thought that would be construed as presumptuous. "He's an American. He must begin in America." He was sent to the Catholic University of America in Washington where an athletic sort of religion was practiced and taught. Afterward it was time to go to Europe but, Zoltan and Joan Hull decided, "not as yet to Rome. Rome must wait." He was enrolled in the University of Louvain in Belgium where he obtained his doctorate and later, an *agrege en philosophie* with highest honors.

Only then was he ready for Rome, and it was decided that he should best make his entrance as Cardinal Zoltan's secretary. In his year with Zoltan he had become almost reconciled to the idea of spending his life in the Church. It was peaceful in the Vatican where he and other young men of similar rank glided through the halls with only the purest of thoughts in their minds.

"It was as if we were drugged," he was to say later. "The most heavenly, hallucinatory drug. We were definitely not above arguing, quite brilliantly, as to how many angels could sit on the head of a pin. But if it came to making our way across Rome, then we would have been stymied. As luck would have it, most of the Vatican elite had access to automobiles and drivers."

His red hair and his rugged physique attracted a certain amount of notice, as did his eruditon, his kindliness, and the fact that he was backed by Cardinal Zoltan's considerable influence. He began to be asked to tea by certain members of the upper hierarchy. He began to realize that there were polite but nonetheless deadly battles going on under the serene, mystic facade; that war was a better description of the atmosphere than peace. And he began to enjoy that, too.

"You cannot become a plotter, my dear young Paul," Cardinal Zoltan had said to him. "You must let others intrigue for you. You must remain *sans peur, sans reproche*. I think it is also time that you learned humility. I shouldn't want you to become proud, Paul,'' Zoltan had told him, assigning him to a modest parish in Southern Italy, Bernina, where the people made what living they could from the soil and the sea.

The Berninians demanded that their priest be hardworking as well as a leader, a resourceful judicial authority, a healer, and a man who could sit down with a bottle of the local wine and a group of local men and enjoy the evening. And if he had an occasional woman in the field, that was all to the good. A priest was a man, wasn't he? What he did was between him and his confessor. And of course the woman in the field.

Paul knew no women except for his aunt and his only physical reaction to her was a kind of quiet dismay. He touched her as little as possible. He didn't like the rough wine and he didn't understand the dialect of the village and he hated the dirt and the poverty and the rude ways of the people who were supposed to be his flock.

After two years among them he was less humble than ever. He read mass and heard their confessions but he never achieved any intimacy with his parishioners and was relieved on the occasions when Zoltan and his aunt appeared. They would drive down from Rome in a huge prewar car, hampers in the trunk filled with the delicate sorts of foods that did not exist in his village. The cardinal and the heiress would watch him eat, taking his moral temperature as he attempted to moderate his appetite for the delicacies beautifully packed in the wicker baskets. They had come to see for themselves if he had become humble.

They hadn't realized that it was pride which had kept him in that bleak, unfriendly place. It was pride which had made him stay even after he realized that his only calling was to sit in velvet-lined rooms and discuss arcane theology with other insular men. He stayed even after he knew that he loathed the people, that he despised their roughness and both hated and envied the passion with which they ate and fought and loved and worked.

He realized in those two years that despite his red hair and virile good looks, passion—the sort of passion the villagers displayed in such quantities—was an emotion he knew nothing about.

The villagers, being extremely homogeneous, were difficult to distinguish from one another. When Paul consistently addressed Luigi as Antonio, it did nothing to endear him to their hearts.

They always went around in groups. Never less than five went to the neighboring town each Saturday night for the cinema or the dance and often it was as many as fifty. They worked in the fields together and they came to church together and they fished and hunted and—Paul suspected—even made love together.

Their togetherness, their delight in one another's company gave him an acute sense of his own loneliness. The only human beings he had ever had any intimacy with were Cardinal Zoltan and Joan Hull and that was a very cool intimacy, indeed.

Paul found himself longing for a friend, another priest, perhaps, with whom he could share his feelings, his thoughts, his longings and yes, even his doubts.

Tony Gato was not a priest.

He was an Italian-American of Paul's age who had returned to the place where his parents had been born for inspiration, for what he hoped would be the kind of experience which would help him develop his craft into art.

Though he was very much the opposite of Father Paul Palmer McGuigan, Tony Gato and the lonesome priest shared a trait in common: they were both outcasts. Paul, by circumstance; Tony by choice.

Naturally they were aware of one another. Paul would see the artist coming and going in the village—where he was very popular—for weeks at a time and then he would disappear and Paul would forget about him.

He had rented a shack on a cliff over one of the remoter beaches and it was there that he worked at his painting, like a man determined to finish a cosmic jigsaw puzzle, feverishly trying new ways to fit the pieces, anxiously working to get it right.

Paul had been in Bernina for more than a year before he and Tony Gato did more than nod to each other. And then their friendship developed so quickly, so intensely, that it seemed a sort of miracle to the both of them that they had lived in the same village for so long and not been aware of one another's qualities.

Their friendship began on an early summer's day, late in the afternoon, when Paul had taken a long walk up the coast. Despairing of the people whom he was supposed to be enlightening and leading in spiritual matters, he lay down on the deserted sandy beach under a cliff and watched the sea which, at that point, had created a deep pool.

Suddenly he heard a great whoop of excitement as a nude man jumped off the cliff above him into the pool, without regards for the sharp rocks around its perimeter. The man, a cigarette clamped between his teeth, swam out into the ocean several hundred yards with an aggressive though not especially polished stroke, puffing all the way, emitting clouds of cigarette smoke.

It wasn't until he came back, still smoking, that he realized he had an observer. He didn't seem particularly embarrassed at his natural state.

"Lovely day for a swim, isn't it, Padre?"

Paul said that it was, and smiled. He was not shy about his body and he saw no reason to be taken aback by Tony Gato's.

"I'm celebrating today," Tony Gato said.

"What are you celebrating?"

"I think I've made a breakthrough. Would you like to have a look, Padre?"

Paul realized that he was under the cliff on which stood the artist's house. He said he would very much like to have a look. He was impressed. By the neat and practical aspects of the little house as much as by the strength Tony Gato had managed to embue his painings with.

Paul said as much. Tony Gato, slipping into a pair of shorts, asked him to stay for supper, over which they discussed the museums of Rome, the future of nonrepresentational art, and the charm of the local villagers, the latter of which eluded Paul.

They began to take a great many of their meals together. Though they may have been the same age, Paul felt as if Tony were at least a century more experienced "in life." Tony had grown up on the Lower East Side of New York. An art teacher, a volunteer at the youth program on Tony's block, had taught him to draw and then to paint. By the time his peers were taking drugs and gang raping girls, he was having one-man displays in YMCAs and churches.

"Not that I didn't have my share of drugs and gang rapes," Tony told Paul who tried not to look wide-eyed. "Just that my priorities were in a different place, you understand? I was lucky. I had something else going for me."

He reminded Paul of a more manly Father Heart in that he invariably said what he thought.

He was nearly as tall as Paul but his bulk made him appear shorter. He had a tatoo on his right bicep which was a paradigm of tatoo banality: a red heart with a blue arrow piercing it. There was a blank space where lettering should have been. "I was going to have 'mother' put on it but that bitch didn't deserve to be on my right arm for the rest of my life."

His earthiness, his brusqueness, his incredible zest for living made him a favorite of the villagers when he wasn't locking his door for weeks at a time, seeing no one. They called him "Yankee" and took him, when he let them, into their homes where they fed him enormous dishes of pasta and sausages.

He began to take Paul with him into the villagers' houses, to prove to him that, by and large, they were a generous people. He became the bridge by which Paul felt he was able to reach his parishioners.

Before Tony brought them together, the Berninians had mocked the American priest who spoke such perfect Italian but said nothing they could understand. Now, because the Yankee listened, they did, too, and occasionally allowed that he had something to say.

"Make me a Catholic," Tony liked to shout at him as they swam in the sun-warmed ocean. Paul laughed. He had never met a more pagan spirit and he told Tony so.

It was toward the end of August when a formal letter bearing Cardinal Zoltan's seal was delivered to Paul with much pomp by the local mailman. It informed Paul that he was to report back to the Vatican. It was decided that Paul had learned humility. He was to return in two weeks time when his replacement would arrive.

In separate letters he was congratulated on his progress by both his aunt and the cardinal.

"What's the matter with you?" Tony asked him as they sat on the beach under the cliff that afternoon. The annual heat wave had engulfed the village. It was too hot to talk and too hot to paint. The locals called it devil's weather and made it responsible for the fights and the infidelities that invariably took place during its reign.

Paul told Tony Gato he was leaving Bernina.

"I'm going to miss you, man," Tony said after a moment. "But you got your duty, right? You got to go, right?" He stood up. "Come on, Padre. I'll race you to the island." He took off his shorts and dived into the water, heading for the tiny island that was nearly a mile away.

Paul removed the black trousers and white shirt he wore when he was "off duty" as Tony put it and went in after him. He was used to seeing Tony nude; it seemed very natural. He liked to see Tony's thick muscles; he liked to watch him move with that deliberate, choreographed strut of his.

Paul easily swam past him, beating him to the cove where a deserted monastery sat in ruins. He was lying on the sand, wondering why his fair skin had tanned for the first time in his life when Tony staggered up the beach and lay down next to him. He swam with his entire body—his arms, legs, and even his head—and it always left him exhausted.

"If you give me that sarcastic smile, you son of a bitch, I don't care if you are a priest, I'll knock your block off."

Paul smiled and in a moment Tony was on top of him, pinning his arms back, his powerful body pressing down against Paul's. "Now say something blasphemous. Say damn it. Say shit. Say cocksucker. Say . . ." And then, suddenly, he bent down and kissed Paul full on the mouth. For one moment Paul responded. Then he broke away and lay down with his face in the sand, his knees up.

"Tell me," Tony said, reaching out, grabbing Paul's shoulders, pulling him close to him, "what you're so fuckin' afraid of? Look at that? Man, you got a hard on. So do I. No sin, not in my book. It's not the snake in the Garden, man. It's love. Look at me, goddamn it." Paul looked up. "I love you, you parsimonious, sanctimonious, and whatever other monious there is in this world bastard. I'm going to show you how to make love, man. When you get back to Rome and your confessor, you can tell him I raped you. I'm more than willing to take the rap."

He reached out and pulled Paul to him. They kissed and as his arms went around Tony to bring him even nearer, Paul allowed himself to feel, for the first time ever, the incredible ecstacy, the indelible tenderness another human being could give him.

They had two weeks together. Then Paul returned to Rome. He did not confess. He would in time, when and if he felt genuine contrition. He attempted, unsuccessfully, to put Tony Gato out of his mind; to forget his touch, his particular salty taste, the irreverent way he laughed. He told himself that he had suffered a lapse, one which had proved him to be human.

Oddly enough his superiors felt that his sojourn in the village had done just that, had given the young priest the touch of humanity he had been missing. Great things, he was told, were in store for him.

On that last night before he left the village, he had promised Tony Gato that he would meet with him in a year's time and then he would, if he chose, say good-bye forever. Or, he would leave the Church and go to live with Tony Gato. In the first month of their separation, Paul had thought there was a chance, a possibility, that he would give up everything that he and his aunt, and yes, Zoltan, had worked so hard for for the simple pleasure of sleeping with Tony Gato, of holding that man in his arms. But as time passed, he came to realize that the glories of the church, the real comfort the system gave him, could not be dismissed.

At any rate he had made his decision. He was going to accept the bishopric when it was offered. At the same time the year was up, and Tony Gato was in New York and Paul knew he would have to see him if only to say good-bye.

Chapter Two

NICK USUALLY started his day at eleven but since Duke had returned from the hospital, he found himself arriving at 44 an hour or so early, ringing upstairs, allowing Robert or SayDee to convince him to come up for rolls and coffee.

Duke seemed to be getting thinner by the hour. It was as if death were eating away at him, minute by minute. He liked to sit in the red leather sofa facing the overflow of photographs that had found their way up into his home and tell stories about the people in them: Bob Benchley and Lillian Hellman and Hammett and Max Schmeling and Brenda Frazier and even Billy Carter whom he had developed an affection for. It seemed that anyone who had ever gotten his name into a headline was in the photographs and the stories.

"Remember when Dorothy Killgallen was found dead?" he asked Nick who didn't but knew the story. "I told Abel Green he had a natural headline for *Variety*: 'Drugs, Dope Drop Dot.' But he wasn't buying it."

He sat back and allowed Robert to fill his coffee cup as Hector got himself up onto the sofa and curled himself into a ball at Duke's feet. "I've had a rich life, kid," he told Nick. "So stop with the mournful smiles, already. Everyone has to go sometime, and this is my time. My only worry is 44. Did you get through to Blue Bowen?"

"He's getting back to me."

Duke sighed, reaching for the sugar. SayDee, coming through the room at that moment, pulled it away from him. "At this point, duchess," he said, "I can have the entire bowl." She put three heaping teaspoons into his cup.

At eleven, as Nick was preparing to go down to the club, Duke grabbed his hand. "Give me a hug, first."

"What?"

"You heard me. Give me a hug. Like you used to when you were a little kid."

Feeling uncomfortable, Nick went up to the old man, who had managed to get to his feet, put his arms around the emaciated shoulders, and hugged him. Duke kissed Nick on the cheek. He smelled of medicine and age and Chanel for Men. What was strange, Nick felt, was that Duke, the sick man, was comforting him. When Duke released him, both their eyes were filled with tears.

"When you were a kid, your father didn't like me to hug you. Thought it would make you unmanly. Victor was from the old school, that's what made him such a good father. But Victor's gone and I'm going and I want to tell you something, my boy: I love you. I love you more than I love Peter and that's both a shame and the truth. Peter's his mother's son. You're 44's. You're a good kid, Nick, with a sweet, loving nature and of all those people in all those photographs, I'm glad I know you best. I want you to get that money, Nick. I want you to have 44. Go call Blue Bowen and give the bastard a little goose."

Nick left, drying his eyes, feeling absurdly young and helpless but happy at the same time. What worried him was the interview Blue had given in the morning's *Times* financial section. Blue told the reporter that he saw money markets drying up, new investors getting more nervous, the old pros pulling their resources in.

The writer went on to discuss Blue Bowen's key role among contemporary international entrepreneurs, his mysterious and often incomprehensible ways of doing business. He rehashed all the old rumors of meetings taking place in 44's men's room, of deals concluded in his Lear jet, of the unproven connections with Vesco and Nixon and El Salvador's ex-dictator, General Romero.

"Though a great many of his dealings are impossible to verify," the *Times* reporter summed up, "and rest to some extent on his own account, they place an unusual light on negotiations between such giant international consortiums as Indiana Petrol, Ltd., Shaw Consolidated, and UNITAS, as well as providing insights into international business activities."

"I'd like to know what the hell all that means," Nick said, walking across the Club Room where Mickey was, as usual, polishing the bar. Nick glanced at his watch, was surprised that it was almost noon, and then looked up and over into the main dining room. He didn't like what he saw. Brette was sitting there, a coffee cup in her hands, wearing a thin silk crepe dress in a dazzling heliotrop color. She was smiling the sort of smile women only use on one another. Sitting across from her was Dinah Sheridan in yet another bright red dress, her dark mournful eyes staring at Brette, her father's gold key—number seven—around her neck.

"What are they doing here?" Nick asked Lawrence.

"They met on the street, it seems. They came in and asked for a cup of coffee. What was I to do, I should like to know? I gave it to them on the condition they vacate by twelve forty-five and not a moment later." Lawrence looked aggrieved.

"We're not a coffee shop. In the future, try to remember that." Nick turned and went to his office. Lawrence went down to the kitchen, resolving to write his tenth letter of resignation for the year.

"I told you one day you'd have to beat them off with a stick," Dinah was saying as she stared moodily at Brette. "Of all the men you might have had, of all the men you still could have, one wonders why you're still with that cheap little snob."

"He's an expensive snob, Dinah." She lifted the coffee cup to her lips, then thought better of it and set it down on the best table.

"You hate him, don't you, Brette?"

"Hate Peter? Oh, no, Dinah. It's worse than that. I pity him. When I married him, I thought I was marrying Duke. All evidence to the contrary, I had a fantasy—a rather overwhelming one—of this wild, half-Americanized Jew taking me up to our bedroom on our wedding night and ravishing me until dawn.

"I thought that under Peter's Savile Row suit there beat a man every bit as sexual, as hot-blooded as his father. I was wrong. As Peter says, indubitably wrong."

"Why didn't you go to bed with Duke?" Dinah asked, lighting a Camel.

"It never occurred to me. Not consciously." This time she did sip at her coffee. "Have you ever been to bed with Duke?"

"No," Dinah said and smiled. "Listen," she went on after a moment, putting her hand on Brette's with its Real Ritz Red painted nails, "if you hate your life so much, change it. Leave Peter. Nick Reo's been waiting for you for years."

"How do you know?"

"Darling, Brette. I'm Dinah Sheridan, the food critic par excellence, with her finger on the heartbeat of hot New York. Besides all one has to do is look at Nick looking at you to see how much he wants you. To paraphrase Mae West, that's not a gun in his pocket, honey; he's just glad to see you."

Dinah looked down at Brette's gloves which lay on the table. They were mauve, a few shades lighter than her dress. "Gloves," Dinah said. "You still carry gloves. Do you have any idea how much I envy you, Brette? How much I've always envied you?"

"Me? Dinah, you're famous and young and you have the world . . ."

"Yes, baby. But you had Duke and your auntie and Peter and Nick and tons of other people who cared. You've been spoiled and coddled and loved and you've always gotten everything you've ever wanted and you're still lovely and innocent under that patina of sophisticated lady you put on. You're one of the lucky ones, Brette. You'll always end up on your feet."

"So will you, Dinah," Brette said in an uncertain voice.

"No, baby. I'm the kind of girl who always ends up on her back. I'm the kind of girl who has to fight to get the best table, and even when I'm sitting at it, I don't feel I belong here. When we were kids, I used to watch you and Peter and Nick. You all belonged to 44's world. I would have given anything to have been you."

"Dinah . . ."

"You can pity Peter, Brette. But please, I beg you, don't pity me."

"You seem so desperately unhappy."

"I'm my father's daughter. When the ratings are up, my spirits are down." Dinah laughed, and stood up. "Lawrence is giving me that pained look of his. I have to get to the studio and you've kept Duke waiting long enough."

Brette gathered her gloves and her bag and then looked at Dinah. "If only I could . . ."

"You can't." They embraced, holding on to one another for a moment longer than women at 44 usually did, then Dinah left for the studio and Brette went up to see Duke.

Nick stood in the Club Room, watching them both and then, after they had left, stayed at his accustomed place against the bar under Duke's portrait until Lawrence appeared, evidently over his hurt feelings. There was a crisis in the kitchen.

The second cook, a Frenchman named Delois, was threatening to plunge his pastry knife into the heart of a waitress named Rose Schmidt who had the first four tables in the J. J. Walker Room.

"What did Rose do to deserve Delois's knife?" Nick asked, racing toward the kitchen.

"I didn't stop to ask," Lawrence said, following. "I myself am not a great favorite of Delois and he didn't seem ready to confide in me. Nothing short of dropping a soufflé, I imagine."

Georgio, the busboy at the best table, moved out of their way as they clattered down to the kitchen, as Nick cursed the court ruling that had forced him to hire waitresses, especially one Rose Schmidt. Georgio took Dinah's coffee cup with its lipstick smear and carefully put it on his tray.

Valida Rand studied herself in the mirror in the foyer of her suite at the Plaza. I always do it, she said to herself, adjusting the winter white turban she had decided to wear. Hollywood money stays at the Sherry and I insist on putting up at the Plaza. I might have met someone from the old days; I might have convinced someone to back the film. She pushed the turban to the right side of her head. Somewhere, deep down inside me, there is a self-destructive streak four miles wide.

She twisted the turban to the left and studied the new effect in the mirror. Makes me look like Gale Sondergaard on an off day. She pulled the hat off and fluffed up her black hair with both her hands. I have far too much hair. It needs to be cut, she decided, turning, trying to see the back of her head over her shoulder. Yes, it needs to be cut. And dyed and shaped and pulled and teased and tweezed and all shaved off except for a narrow band at the base of the neck.

She went into the bedroom where her bored maid, Amanda, was sitting, reading a *Life* magazine article about old actresses. "Get me my jewelry case," she snapped.

"Get it yourself, *Miss* Rand." Amanda put her forefinger in her mouth and then, very deliberately, turned the page. "This is a vacation day and well you know it."

"Someday I'm going to fire you, Amanda, and then what will you do?"

"I'll make my fortune writing an exposé of Valida Rand's love life."

"No one will read it."

"I'll make up the good parts."

Valida Rand found the tortoiseshell and jade combs Frank had given her not long before he died. She plunged them into her mass of hair, one on either side, and looked at herself in the bureau mirror.

"Anna May Wrong," Amanda said.

"Well, it's as good as I'm going to get," Valida said, bending down to look at Amanda's watch, deciding that if she walked slowly down Fifth, she would be exactly twenty minutes late which was how long Nick would hold the best table for her.

She was only ten minutes late because she was a fast walker. Of course, there was no sign of Laddy Wister. Even though I know I'm always going to be disappointed by men, why am I always so disappointed when I'm disappointed? she asked herself.

She went to the ladies' room and had a chat with Sophie and then she went to the Club Room and had a chat with Nick and then she went to the best table and Beverly Sills and Pavarotti stopped by to chat some more, about opera, a subject which she knew almost nothing about and then she broke down and ordered a Bombay gin and wondered if she was going to cry.

That would be pretty, she thought. "Valida Rand was seen yesterday crying her eyes out during lunch at 44, drinking gin and cursing her third husband, seven-figure star Laddy Wister."

Laddy Wister. What a perfectly apt name for that overgrown boy. The no-neck monster of a wife was responsible for his no show, she decided. I refuse to call the bastard. I have to decide whether to submit myself to the ultimate indignity of lunching alone—with all eyes on me—or of getting up and out of here, going back to the Plaza, and having a quiet tantrum in that badly wallpapered room. That would also mean reconciling myself to the fact that *Neon Lights* is never going to be made, that Frank is never going to have the posthumous pleasure of knowing his best effort remained just that. I'll give the bastard five more minutes.

She closed her eyes for a moment and when she opened them, Laddy Wister was sitting across the table from her, his face ablaze with the smile that hypnotized American womanhood each time he flashed it on the silver screen.

"I wonder," Valida said, "if chronic unpunctuality can be merely dismissed as neurotic self-involvement or symptomatic of a far more dangerous mental ailment? It appears to me . . ."

"Come off it, Val. You're not playing Miss Jean Brodie now."

"That isn't because I'm no longer in my prime. Do you want to order a drink and get into a lot of delightful small talk about how charming your latest little wife is or do you want to tell me what you—and presumably Harry Monaco's abortion baby—think of it."

"Well, Valida . . ."

"Don't well me, you horse ball. Just tell me what you think of the script and then I'll tell you whether you're going to spend the rest of your life making movies for drive-ins."

"We've only read half of it."

"Laddy, darling. It's all of one hundred and ten pages long with great big wide spaces around the dialogue."

"You know how it is when you play New York, Val. I did the *Today* show yesterday and I'm doing Merv Griffin on Thursday . . ."

"What," she said, finishing her gin, signaling Charles for another, enunciating her words carefully, "did you think of the half of the script you did manage to read?"

"Waiter, do you think I could have a Piña Colada?" Laddy asked, smiling at two women who were sitting at the Rockefeller table, captivated by him.

"Will you cut the shit, Laddy?"

"You always did have a foul mouth, Val."

"Sorry, Daddy wasn't a born-again Christian minister in Chicago, thank God. Like yours."

"You know, Val: I still get a little shot whenever I see you? You aware of that? Damn, you were something else in bed. You know, Val, you're the only woman I ever had that I knew was thinking of just one thing while I was in her? And that was that I was in her."

"I fooled you, Laddy. I used to play a game while you were pumping away, trying to name the capitals of the states in alphabetical order. It got so that I knew that by the time I got to Trenton, you would come and I would have to give a little moan of joy. Trenton's in New Jersey in case you didn't know and that seemed particularly apt at the time."

"I'm getting hot just thinking about it, Val. What do you say?"

"Laddy, pet. You may well nigh be irresistible to every single lady in this room and several of their escorts but for me the idea of going to bed with you is about as tasty as swallowing a diamond-backed rattler, live. I ask for the last time: what did you think of the bloody script?"

"We liked it."

"Dear God, 'we liked it.' The greatest screenplay ever written and Laddy Wister and his wife, the felon's daughter, have the temerity to say they liked it."

"I only read half of it. I told you, Val."

"Scares the shit out of you, doesn't it, Laddy? You're afraid you can't play it, that you'll come off like Van Johnson in *Othello*. Well, Hoffman can do it and so can Pacino for that matter. I don't need you and Daisy Mae and I don't even much want you. Frankenheimer suggested it."

Laddy smiled and then laughed. "I may be dumb, Val, but Daisy isn't. She called Frankenheimer last night right after she finished the screenplay. He's not going near *Neon Lights* unless I'm in it and signed on the dotted line and well you know it. Now let's stop the fooling around, Val."

"By all means, Laddy."

"We're going over the script again, tomorrow, and then we're going to think about it and then we're going to decide who should play in it, opposite me, and on Friday we're going to get back to you. Understood?"

"Perfectly. You and Daisy know you've come upon the one chance you'll ever have to be more than a piece of beefcake playing hot dang Sherrif Asshole roles and you want to savor it. You want to talk to the Coast and get Daddy Monaco's approval and you want to talk to his lawyers and set up a deal. Be my guest. But I do warn you, Laddy: others are reading the script. Others *are* interested, all of them as acceptable as you, if not more so."

"You'll get your answer tomorrow, Val. Right here, over cocktails at 44." He reached across the table and took her hand before she could pull it away. "Remember how the day after our divorce we both showed up only they gave you and that Argentine creep the best table and put me in the bar room?"

"That Argentine creep was president of Brazil."

"I was real upset, Val, seeing you here with that guy. I couldn't imagine how you recovered so quickly."

"Since it has escaped your notice, darling, I feel I have to break it to you: you were not the love of my life. You were a passing interlude, a brief encounter, a speedboat putt-putt-putting by in the night. And as I remember it, the lady you were with was crawling all over you while I was being very much the sport. I even sent you a bottle of Roederer's Cristal as a kind of hail-fellow-well-met gesture."

"Babs drank three fifths of it and spilled the rest."

She disengaged her hand and laughed. "It's going to be a very good movie, Laddy. It's going to give you an entire new career. I promise you that, Laddy, and as you are aware, I keep my promises."

"I'll let you know tomorrow, Val. *I* promise you that. But you got to understand: I have a wife and a father-in-law and a lot of commitments. It's not really up to me, Val. If it were up to me, Val . . ." He smiled his grand piano smile, finished his drink, kissed her on the cheek, and left.

Few women dining at 44 that afternoon were unsophisticated enough to break off their conversation and stare openly as Laddy Wister strode across the foyer in his rawhide jacket. But a surprising number of women did manage to turn and casually glance in his direction.

"You have married some of the worst people, Valida," Saunders, impeccably smooth, said, slipping into Laddy's place.

"Get me another gin, will you, darling? I'm feeling my age."

Chapter Three

"NOTHING COULD be finer than to eat in Dinah's Diner in the morning," Terry Winters sang, walking past Dinah Sheridan's secretary who came running into the office after him.

"If I had a waffle iron for only a day, I'd heat it up and here's what I'd say: nothing could be finer than to eat in Dinah's Diner in the morning."

"I'm sorry, Dinah," Joyce said. "He just barged in . . ."

"Don't worry about it, Joyce. He's an old and awful friend."

Joyce, pushing her glasses against her face with her stubby forefinger, nodded resignedly and went back to her desk. Terry Winters, all smiles, in a green tweed suit and green suede shoes, shut the door after her.

"Why do lascivious women invariably have plain secretaries?"

"What are you got up as, Terry?" Dinah Sheridan asked, swiveling round in the upholstered, pneumatic office chair she had demanded from office services and had received. It cost seven hundred and forty dollars and Dinah considered its possession a minor victory. "Let me guess: a Milanese leprechaun."

"One doesn't wonder that everyone is after your scalp, dear," Terry said, sitting himself in an Eames chair, looking past Dinah and out through the skyline window to the view of Central Park. It seemed pristine and fairy tale-like from that height, Ft. Belvedere a castle, the ornamental bridge over the lake suitable only for gilded coaches.

"Have you asked your current analyst why it is that you have the same view from your apartment as you do from your office? Perhaps you're suffering from the Rapunzel complex. Waiting for the prince to climb up and let you down.

"It is a ravishing vista, isn't it?" He sat back and looked around the room, his eye taking in the Frank Stella painting, the lacquered aubergine walls. "I envy you a little, Dinah, I don't mind saying. You're the youngest woman on the air, earning reportedly the second largest salary on the network, and sitting in the third most luxurious office. How you do it is what fascinates me."

"Terry, I'm busy. What do you want?"

"Have you seen my socks?" He lifted his leg to reveal a sheer silk green sock.

"You go too far, Lady Winters. Terry," she said, reaching for a Camel, lighting it with a gold Dupont desk lighter, "what are you doing here?"

"The Truth?"

"As much of it as your nature will allow you to divulge."

"I'm doing an article for *Esquire* on, and I quote the winsome little editor who assigned me the job, 'The New Breed of Woman Telecaster . . . and What She Can Do for You.' I'm here to interview you, dear."

"Get your feet off my desk. And make it all up. I don't care what you say as long as publicity okays it."

"Oh, Dinah, I need more of a challenge than that." He folded his thin hands and rested them on his thickening waist. "I ran into Albin Krebs at a party at Liz Smith's last night."

"How nice for you, dear."

"He writes the 'People' column for the *Times*."

"No shit."

"He said word was out that you're going to trash 44 in front of twelve million viewers on Friday during your anniversary special. Now I ask you, for my readers: is there any truth at all in that statement and if there is, what effect do you think it will have on the club's business and your career?"

"What do you and Albin think I'm going to be saying?"

"That the food is minus Grade Z, the drinks more water than booze, the service rude if you're John Q. Public and fawning if you're Mrs. Astor. Then it's rumored that you're going to trot out Yul Brenner or Fernando Lamas or one of those and have them discuss, graphically, their ptomaine poisoning."

Dinah laughed but it was a perfunctory sound. "I'll tell you, Terry, what it will do: it will destroy 44's business. Not immediately but that sort of thing is a gradual eroding process. The steak is a little well done, the waiter drops a fork . . . those little things become magnified. People start to respond to them with knowing looks. Dinah Sheridan is right, after all, they'll start to say. It will take maybe a year before it's sold or closed or turned into a disco."

"You are powerful, aren't you, Dinah?"

"As for my career, it can only strengthen my image of pure, undistilled honesty, of uncorruptable, unassailable consumer-oriented reporting. All straight from the hip, all dead on target."

Terry looked at her for a moment, carefully. "Why?" he asked finally. "Your father and Duke Greene were . . ."

"Just like this," she said, holding up her entwined index and forefingers. She swiveled again in her pneumatic chair, turning from him, facing the window that framed Central Park.

"They were the best of friends. When Daddy slit his wrists in the hotel bathtub, Duke borrowed PepsiCo's Lear and was by the body's side in hours. He took care of everything. He chose the coffin (ebony), he called the relatives, he made the Statement to the Press.

"Where, I should like to know, would celebrity suicides be without the Statement to the Press? He sat with my mother and me in the first row and cried genuine tears as such luminaries as Tony Curtis and Yehudi Menuhin said their last good-byes in stirring eulogies.

"He held my hand. He had a long conference with my mother and my then analyst as to how I should be treated. He offered me a summer at his Connecticut farm, a winter with Brette at a fancy private school. He was the first man to treat me as if I were a human being instead of some windup doll.

"The psychiatrists say he's a father substitute, that I've transferred my anger on to him. That's horse manure. Duke is a better, more humane man than my father ever was."

"Well, I can certainly understand why you're out to get him. Nothing like a well-based grudge nursed along for years, festering with old venom, to bring up the ratings. And now that you've got all this power, now that you automatically get shown to the best table, you're going to slip it to Duke and his club because he's such an exemplary human being. Do I have this right?"

"Yes," she said, reaching for another Camel. "And the timing is perfect. Just before Duke dies."

"I seem to be missing a step in your thought process. There's one little eeny-meeny atom of logic I'm not getting. If Duke was so marvelous to you . . ."

"Terry," she said, holding up her hand, swiveling round again to face him, "I have work to do."

"You're not telling me something, Dinah," Terry said, going into his Bette Davis imitation. "Well," he went on, in his own voice, "I have my little article, I think. You don't mind if I quote you, do you, dear heart?"

"I'll deny everything and sue you for your entire one-figure fortune, Terry, if you print one word." She pressed a button on the control panel of her desk.

"What the hell was that? Automatic ejection?"

"A scrambler. It makes gobbledy-gook out of any tape recording being made. I'm told it usually ruins the recorder, as well."

"I paid four hundred dollars for this machine," Terry Winters said, removing a paperback-sized tape recorder from his pocket, examining it.

"Terry," Dinah said, starting to read a script on her desk, "get out."

"Is it fun?" Terry asked, pocketing the recorder, standing up, adjusting the pleats in his green tweed trousers.

"Is what fun?"

"Living life the way you do, one finger always on the scrambler."

"Pigs have fun, Terry," she said. "Fun isn't what I'm after."

She waited for him to leave until she allowed herself to remember.

She had waited a year after her father's death, like a widow in mourning, before she told her mother she wanted to go to New York.

"Sweetie, I can't possibly go to New York now. I have absolutely one million things to do. We're just beginning to probate your father's estate and what an enormous mess that is and I've told you dozens of times I'm redoing the house. I think it's time, don't you? I'm so tired of the salmon wallpaper in the library . . ."

It hadn't been difficult to convince her mother that it would be perfectly all right for her to go to New York alone. She'd stay at the Sherry-Netherland. There'd be tons of people there she knew to look after her. And then there was Brette. She was forever asking her to come and stay.

"Well, why don't you stay with Brette?" her mother asked, not too interested but feeling she should ask the question.

Dinah had said something about wanting her freedom and her mother had said something about a young girl like her not needing all that much freedom but the phone rang at that moment and Dinah's trip to New York was settled.

At first she wasn't going to let him know she was coming, but then she thought she had better, so he'd save a night for her. One night was all she wanted.

He was surprised—even upset—that she was staying in a hotel by herself but she wouldn't discuss it. He was surprised—and again a little upset—at how much she had grown, at how womanly she had suddenly become. That was Duke's word, womanly. She treasured it.

She wore a black dress, cut low in the front and her hair loose and a little disheveled. "One matures quickly in Beverly Hills," she said.

They had dinner, together, at 44, at the best table. It was, providentially, one of SayDee's days in Brooklyn and Brette's time at Aunt Helen's. Lena Horne and David Merrick stopped at the table to say hello to both Dinah and Duke. She had to introduce him to Linda Ronstadt and James Taylor, and explain who they were.

"You know more people than I," Duke said, pleased.

She was pleased, too. After dinner he walked her back to the hotel. She insisted that he come up, that she had something to show him.

She knew he was nervous, but she felt marvelous. It was all going exactly as she planned. She went into the bedroom and took off the black dress and the black panties. She left the patent leather heels on because she thought she would look too young without them.

She walked into the drawing room of the suite. Duke stood up. He looked very serious. "Dinah," he began, but she went to him and put her arms around him and kissed him. He pushed her away. "Go put something on," he said.

She reached for his crotch but he slapped her hand away. "Go put something on," he said, and this time she knew he was serious.

"You don't want me?"

"Dinah," he said, looking away, "go put something on and we'll talk about it."

She went into the bedroom, put on a robe, and came out. She felt numb, as if not only her body had been rejected, but her whole being.

Duke talked to her for over an hour, explaining that he thought she was one of the most attractive females he had ever met but he felt about her the way he felt about Brette. That she was his own daughter. That even forgetting their age difference, he could never make love to her because she was too close to him.

He said other things, about his commitment to SayDee, about how wrong it would be, legally and morally, for him to take advantage of her need for love. He was kind and generous and forgiving. He hugged her and kissed her on the cheek when he left. She could see that it had been a difficult situation for him. She watched him through the suite door's peephole as he waited for the elevator in the corridor. He looked genuinely unhappy for her.

She had never hated anyone more.

Dinah Sheridan sat in her pneumatic desk chair at her electronic desk and thought about Brette and then about Duke and finally about her father. Then she reached for the telephone receiver, switching onto her private line. It took some moments for her to decide to push the correct buttons, and when she did, it was with a sense of resignation. It was as if, from here on in, events were no longer going to be her responsibility.

She had to speak to several people and then she had to wait a few minutes before he came to the phone. She had forgotten what his voice was like, that it had almost a singer's timbre.

"I want you to come tonight."

"Not possible. I'm working tonight."

"Tomorrow night."

"Maybe. If I can swing it. But there's a condition: I bring my equipment."

"Why . . ."

"No questions. I bring me and I bring my equipment or I don't come. All you're going to have to do is what I tell you. Now I got to get back to my work. Yes or no?"

"No," she said after a long moment, replacing the receiver. "No," she screamed so loud that Joyce came in and wanted to know if anything was the matter.

"Nothing is the matter, Joyce," she said.

Chapter Four

"THERE WAS a time, it seems very long ago, when I used to be able to nip down and get Maurice to broil me a brace of double loin chops about this hour," Lawrence was saying as he and Nick stood in the foyer, greeting late luncheon arrivals. "He'd even put those little baby blue skirts on them, and they always looked so festive. It was the part of the day I looked forward to most. Then I'd have a slice of that gorgeous cream cheese pie he'd only make for Lady Bird. And then, to set me up for the evening, I used to take a wee snooze on the cot in that dreary little room back of the kitchen. Why are they doing this to me, Nichlaus? Why is everyone—everyone—suddenly lunching at two instead of one? You don't suppose it's a conspiracy, do you? Oh, dear, look who's turned up? I'll do it, you stay put." Placing a smile on his pouty lips, Lawrence sailed out to greet Iphigenia Sulzberger and Katherine Graham.

Nick retreated into the Club Room where Norman Mailer and an ex-wife, Lady Jean Campbell, were having an argument with their desert. Nick waited a moment to make certain Mailer wasn't going to belt or stab Lady Jean and when he felt that it was safe, turned his attention to the main dining room where Valida Rand and Saunders were drinking coffee at the best table and Peter Stewart-Greene and the week's mystery man were just getting up from table four.

"Nick," Peter called out to him, taking the other man's arm, following Nick to his usual corner at the bar in the Club Room. "I think it's time for you to meet Morgan Brooks. He's senior vice-president in charge of American acquisitions for UNITAS." Peter rolled the man's title off his tongue as if he were introducing Edward the Seventh. "Morgan, this is Nick Reo, 44's manager."

Morgan Brooks was the sort of man who combed his hair across his head in an unsuccessful effort to hide his baldness. He was impeccably slim with thin lips and a long, thin nose. His eyes appeared to be gray but were, in fact, dull brown. Snow-white cuffs extended from his chalk-striped navy blue suit, revealing squares of gold cuff links. He reminded Nick of a letter knife Duke had once owned, dangerous because of its dull edge.

Morgan Brooks held out his hand and Nick took it though he refused to return the other's sympathetic smile. "I've been dining here rather often," Morgan Brooks said. "Quite the little operation. Food's good though service borders on the overconcerned at times."

"Is that going to appear in *Cue*?"

"You could cut down on a lot of the extras if you had a mind too. The fresh flowers are really the most shocking waste, not to mention the expense. I've been in the restaurant business for a good many years, Mr. Reo. Nick. I'm known for making gold purses out of sow's ears. We'll be working together eventually. Perhaps we should have a talk in the meantime, fill me in on the lay of the land. What do you say, Reo? Nick?"

"I say go fuck yourself, Brooks. Morgan. Duke isn't dead yet. Maybe you and the Little Prince Who Wouldn't should wait until the bones are cold before you start picking them."

"Sorry, old boy," Morgan Brooks said as Peter pushed him aside and threw a punch at Nick's head. Nick blocked it with a reflex action of his left arm and came back with a direct connection to Peter's stomach. It made a dull, satisfactory sound. Peter turned and doubled over, falling into the space between the back of the elevator and the end of the bar, throwing up his lunch.

It happened so quickly that only Mickey and two or three regulars actually saw what happened and none of them believed that the smooth, always correct manager of Duke's 44 had so effortlessly, so completely decked the owner's son.

Nick said something to Mickey who, in turn, said something into the speaker at the end of the bar. A moment later a busboy was cleaning up Peter's vomit while Morgan Brooks was dusting off the injured party.

"You'd best go to the gents', old man," Brooks said to him. Peter, white faced, turned to Nick.

"The second after he dies, you're out. The second. I'll have you blackballed in every restaurant in this country. When I get through with your reputation, you won't be able to find a job in a Greek luncheonette."

"Shut up, Peter, before I punch you in the mouth and spoil your pretty face. You'd better get out of here while you can."

Peter looked at Nick as if he wanted to try hitting him again but thought better of it and walked out the door, his chin an inch or so higher than usual. Morgan Brooks stayed behind for a moment. "He's not the kind of man you need for an enemy, Reo. For that matter, neither am I. I have hopes that we can work together later on. You're a good manager. I'm a very good boss."

"Manage a cut-rate 44? No way, Mr. Brooks."

"One last morsel of advice: don't waste your time pursuing the Blue Bowen angle. Take it from me, there's no money for you there."

So he's scared, Nick thought. They both must be scared. They're afraid I just may be able to pull it off.

He went to his office and tried to call Blue Bowen but his secretary said he was in conference all morning, that she would have him get back to Nick as soon as he was free.

Nick went back into the Club Room, looked up at the portrait of Duke, and decided to go upstairs. He felt he needed that man's support at that moment. The fight with Peter had left him unnerved, a little guilty. It was the first time since Duke had made him manager that he had allowed his temper, that hair-trigger temper of his, to go off. He wished he hadn't hit Peter, and even more, he wished that it hadn't happened in 44.

He pushed the elevator button impatiently, looking up at

the noble vision of Duke in white tie and tails, staring forthrightly out at the good table where Honey Boyd and Pat Foreman were just sitting down to what Honey Boyd still liked to refer to as Coke-tails.

"Honey, you've got to stop being such a child. You've simply got to force yourself to make a decision. If you don't accept Saiad's offer—and now it is a genuine offer—you'll end up going back to D.C. and doing what you've always done: playing baby doll to that great big bear of a husband of yours."

"But, Pat, don't you think I should get some advice from Hutch? I mean I never made a decision like this in my entire life. Suppose he doesn't want me to . . ."

"Of course he doesn't want you to take a job. He married you for two reasons: your name and what you got between your shapely legs. He's a very lusty man, our Hutch. You don't think for a moment that he's over there in Bahrain without a little something on the side, do you? You don't think that after a hard day's night working out what he hopes will be a rational agreement with the OPEC people that he doesn't want a little of that poontang. A man like Hutch . . ."

"Hutch wouldn't!" Honey said, and tears began to well up in her eyes. "He wouldn't."

"All right. If you don't want that particular bubble burst, I'll put my safety pin away. But don't do anything foolish like calling his room in the middle of the night. You never know who will answer."

"Mrs. Foreman," Lawrence said, his pudgy hands behind his back. "There's a call for you from Washington. Shall I bring the phone to your table . . . ?"

"It never fails. Soon as I mention the word telephone, one rings. No, don't bother, Lawrence. I'll take it in the booth. Gives me a chance to powder my nose." She stood up. "And get Charles to bring Mrs. Boyd another one of these concoctions she drinks. It will cheer her up."

Pat Foreman said rather less than usual during her telephone conversation, listening intently to the voice on the other end. When she returned to the best table, she found Honey Boyd three quarters through her frozen strawberry daquiri, staring intently at her four-carat engagement ring.

"That was your Mrs. Anvers." Honey looked up blandly. "Your housekeeper, dear."

"Why didn't she call me?"

"I don't pretend to understand the minds of women who keep houses for other women. She had news. Hutch is going to meet you here on Friday in time for the anniversary party. He probably thinks it will be politic if he's here and he's right. And then I spoke to Warren. He's miserable. He has his usual end of fall cold and he's cranky. He wants me home to nurse him and I said I would come. I'm catching the afternoon shuttle flight to D.C."

"Then I am, too," Honey said, finishing her drink, suddenly feeling alone.

"Oh, no you're not. That hotel suite is yours until Saturday morning and Hutch expects to find his bride waiting for him."

"What am I going to do all by myself in New York for the next two days?"

"You can make up your mind about Saiad's offer. It's not fair nor honorable to keep stringing him along. Speaking of the devil."

Saiad came into the dining room, smiling his desert-melancholy smile and Honey Boyd suddenly felt better. It was true that Saiad had the same kind of quiet authority both her mother and Hutch wielded. But he spoke to her patiently, as if she were a thinking human being, which they did not. She was very glad to see him and didn't really mind that Pat Foreman was leaving.

"Good-bye, Honey dear," Pat Forman was saying. "Call me as soon as you get back to D.C. and tell me everything. I must run if I'm going to catch an early shuttle. Saiad, take care of this child and don't let her get into any mischief."

"I'll make her my first duty for the next two days. Where shall we dine tonight, Mrs. Boyd?"

"Tonight I am going to study the contract you gave me, Mr. Saiad, and have room service bring me up a BLT. And then I'm going to make a few phone calls. Tomorrow evening, however, I should love to join you. And that is when I will give you my answer regarding your kindly offer of a job."

Saiad bowed his sleek, dark, handsome head and kissed her

hand. He said he would order a very special champagne to seal their bargain. There was something about his physical presence that seemed to alter her chemistry. It started in her tongue and worked its way right down to places Honey didn't like to give names to. She finally knew what that phrase, her wicked Aunt Lillian constantly used, meant. She was all weak in the knees.

"I haven't said yes yet," Honey did manage to say. "So perhaps you shouldn't order the champagne."

"I can always drink it by myself," Saiad said, contriving to touch Honey's thigh with his own with only the slightest pressure.

Chapter Five

"YOU'RE LOOKING depressed, Nick. Preoccupied. It's not like you," Vera Nickleson said as Nick escorted her to the best table where the pale pink dinner linens had been placed by Georgio with his customary perfection.

"I thought I had a poker face," Nick said, helping her out of her furs. It was cold for late October. Usually the women didn't get their furs out until Thanksgiving.

Vera Nickleson laughed as Nick handed her coat to Georgio to be taken to the special coatroom. "Your father, bless his soul, had a poker face, Nick. I remember coming in once with Rhonda Fleming and Arlene Dahl. We were doing a new promotion called Flame and had given each of them a shocking red rinse and dressed them in shocking red nearly see-through gowns.

"We were in the middle of a shoot for *Vogue*—it was a *quid pro quo*: we took two pages and they gave us a spread. Anyway, I was tired and Arlene and Rhonda were being very good but I knew that they were all in, so I upped and took them here for some of the famous 44 chili. Thought it would buck them up.

"Victor didn't blink an eyelash when those two exceptionally good-looking women strode in here with their hair and their gowns in Flame. He even sat us at the best table.

"But Duke's jaw dropped, quite literally. He's such a snob. Not that I'm not but not in the same royal way Duke is. I suppose people who were once poor and have made their way up in society have to be snobs or they would have never tried. Anyway, Duke thought I had brought in two ladies of the evening and he came over all set to toss them out when he realized who they were. He did an immediate switch, going into cool and gallant and sat with us for hours, charming us completely. He said later that he didn't care what particular aristocracy one was a member of—Hollywood or Hapsburg—as long as one was aristocratic.

"You're much more like him, you know, than you are Victor. Quieter sort of charm but still genuine for all its worth."

"Thank you, Countess," Nick said, smiling down at her. He moved off when Ivan Kotuk sat down without saying hello.

"I see you're indulging in your usual blend of airy good manners and polite high spirits," Vera said, looking at him. "You look as if you just this moment woke up. Your suit's rumpled and your hair needs brushing. I'm afraid you're not a very good advertisement for Countess Vera's mens' line."

"You and the maître d'hôtel are on good terms," Ivan said, putting his hand up to attempt to smooth his unruly black hair.

"I thought it was the older woman who was supposed to be jealous."

"I don't like living this way, Vera. It is not good for my mentality to make love and then to go to sleep and then to wake up and find you are not there. You know I like to make love in the mornings, too. It is very frustrating for me."

"Poor thing."

"I want to know, Vera, when you are going to get your divorce. I want to know when we can live together and sleep together. When are you going to marry me, Vera?"

"I've been putting off speaking to Bill," she said, looking down at her hands which had aged faster than any other part of her body. She had stopped wearing rings because they called attention to the dry skin, the puffy veins.

She folded her hands, placing them primly in her lap, out

of sight. "I want to get the new moisturizer launched before I cause havoc in my personal life."

He made a sound that was supposed to be a laugh but was more of a bark. "Work. That is your secret, Vera, the one you never share with the women who buy your potions. Work keeps you young. Look at you. Your facial skin has the tone and texture of a woman of thirty. I do not know how many lifts you have had but you could not get that skin with surgery. It is the work that feeds you. My love feeds you. Your husband's idolatry feeds you. You are Jack Spratt's wife, Vera, eating up life from every fatty source."

"Did anyone ever tell you, Ivan, that analogy is not your strong suit? Now do order a drink and be a good boy."

"A good boy. Why do you always treat me . . ." She lost interest in what he was saying. She wondered why she was so enamored of him. That was the word, enamored. She didn't love him. Who could love that coarse animal with the lithe body and the heavy, plodding mind of a first-rate chemist? Marriage to him? A great many people would laugh and that wouldn't matter if it were worth it, but after a very short time she didn't think it would be.

She suddenly felt empathy for the aging millionaires she had known and the young women they had married much too late in life. She thought that she might be able to avoid that trap. She thought that in time Ivan would blow over, like an uncomfortable summer storm. That she would recover from the Slavic flu that afflicted her. She hoped so.

She looked up and her thoughts took another turn as a group of young people were being led by Lawrence through the main dining room to a table in the rear. They were rich young people with blond hair and blue eyes and that awesome poise only a moneyed background can give.

The last member of the party was a portly young man in a vested Brooks Brothers suit. He seemed well pleased with himself, radiating the sort of goodwill based on a belief that all of life's problems can and will be solved. Vera realized, with a mild jolt, that he was her son, Donald, senior vice-president in charge of product development and perhaps, she wasn't certain, marketing, for Contess Vera, Inc.

Vera liked her son in the way she liked great art. She wasn't about to go out of her way to see a Rembrandt but, if she were confronted with one, she would sit down and take the time to try and understand. Usually she found that she had enjoyed the experience though not enough to seek it out again on her own steam.

"Will you be joining your mother, Mr. Nickleson?" Lawrence—who was confused as to which party Donald belonged to—asked.

"No, I hadn't planned on it," the fair young man said. "But I expect I shall say hello." He bent down and kissed his mother low on the cheek where he had been taught, as a child, so that her makeup wouldn't be disturbed. "How be you, Mother?"

"Marvelous. As you seem to be. I didn't realize you would be dining at 44 tonight." Implicit in that statement was the idea that she usually knew where her son took his meals. She didn't. She had sent him to Exeter and to Yale and he had turned out very much what she wanted him to be. But they had such different frames of reference now, they had such different interests, that Vera found it difficult to talk to her son. "Allow me to introduce you to our young genius, the man responsible for the new moisturizer, Ivan Kotuk."

The two men shook hands. "You look terribly familiar," Donald Nickleson said. "I thought so the other day when I caught a glimpse of you at the factory. You weren't, by any chance, at the London School of Economics in 1965, were you?"

"For one semester," Ivan allowed, unmoved by the coincidence. "It was a beastly time for me. Economics! A fool's game. I switched to Brussels and chemistry."

"Small world. I distinctly remember you in one of my earliest classes winning an argument with the instructor. No one," Donald said to his mother, "won arguments with the instructors."

"Ivan can be very persuasive."

"Well," Donald said, not knowing how to respond to his mother's remark. "I expect my friends will be wondering what's become of me. Been a pleasure, Mr. Kotuk. I imagine I'll be seeing more of you at the plant. Good night, Mother. *Bon appetit.*"

"He won't be seeing me at the plant. The work is finished." Ivan looked down to find his appetizer—smoked white fish—in front of him. He took up his fork and began t eat, devoting all of his attention to that necessity.

She looked at the far end of the room and saw her so laugh at something an incredibly young, dark-haired girl wa saying. It hadn't occurred to her that Donald dined at 44 wit his own friends, that Lawrence would know who he was b name. She suddenly felt old and she refused to feel old.

"When will you marry me, Vera?" Ivan asked, puttin down his fork, loosening his tie, looking like a passenger i coach on a long night flight.

"I'm going to talk to Bill tomorrow," she decided and sai at the same time. She couldn't identify the exact reason, bu she knew she absolutely hated the idea of Donald and Iva having been in the same class together.

"And Friday we shall celebrate. I will give you a ring Vera."

"No rings," Vera Nickleson said, not looking at her hands

"You seem fatigued, Nicklaus," Lawrence said as the afte theater patrons came in, looking expectantly at the two me in the foyer.

"I am," Nick said. *"Très fatigué."*

"Your French doesn't improve with age. I gather yo haven't heard from Blue Bowen."

"No. Not a word."

"There's still time, Nick."

"Yeah." Nick put his hands in his pockets. "Who's at th best table? I thought Honey Boyd . . ."

"She canceled. Behind all those sunglasses and veils is th shah's sister and that other personage is best described as h woman friend." Their conversation was interrupted whe Fritz Mondale and his wife came in and clearly indicated the wanted Nick to take them to their table. The Kennedys we at their usual table in the main dining room so Nick, wisel escorted the former Vice-President and his wife to the table i the Club Room under the autographed photo of Hubert ar Muriel Humphrey and Duke Greene.

At that moment Honey Boyd was pushing aside the r mains of the steak sandwich the Plaza's kitchen had sent u and took a long sip of her favorite drink in the world, Di Pepsi. She was half sorry she hadn't gone with Saiad. Sh missed 44 and the attention she got there. If she had her drothers, she thought, she would order Diet Pepsi at 44, but Pat Foreman would have a cow if she did.

There is no Pat Foreman, she reminded herself. And there is no Senator High and Mighty Hutchinson Boyd. I'm all alone in the world. Except for Mr. Saiad.

She stood up and went to the long mirror in the dressing room, untying the belt that held her pink peignoir together, admiring her long, blond body. There is no Pat Foreman, she repeated and felt a delicious sense of freedom which settled somewhere below her solar plexus. "And there is no Ruth and there is no Hutch. There's only Mr. Saiad."

Her hand caressed her full, high breasts, massaging the suddenly taut nipple. She allowed her hand to descend until she found the soft flesh between her legs.

Abruptly she pulled her hand away and closed the peignoir. I'm not going to allow myself to think of Mr. Saiad in that way. I'm Honey Boyd, Hutch Boyd's wife and that is that.

She had made love to only one man in her entire twenty-three years, and she wasn't going to start fooling around now with some dark-skinned Arab, or whatever he was, even if the thought of him—the sound of that low voice and the cool touch of his long fingers—made her get all hot and bothered and maybe even a little moist "down there."

She switched off the volume of the big color television set but left the picture on. Dinah Sheridan was interviewing Danny Kaye in his kitchen and though it looked as if it were live, Honey knew it must be taped because she had seen Dinah Sheridan on Central Park South that very afternoon.

I wish I had a job like that, she said. So interesting, meeting all those people and eating in all those places. She reached for the white telephone, attempting to calculate what time it was in Bahrain but she was hopeless at that sort of thing and always had been. She guessed it was some time the following morning because she wanted it to be. Hutch would be missing her in the morning. He was always especially easy to get around in the morning, especially before he "socked it" to her as Honey privately described their lovemaking.

She didn't care what she had promised Pat Foreman, she thought, as she waited for the Plaza operator to make the necessary connections and as Dinah Sheridan and Danny

Kaye were tasting some Chinese concoction on the TV. I'm not going to sign all those papers and take a job without Hutch saying it's okay. It just wouldn't be fair. He married me expecting I would be his wife and here I am ready to embark on this glamorous public relations career and I just want to make sure Hutch says yes.

She knew he would but she had learned it was best to give him the option of saying no, like the time she went out and bought that yellow Porsche . . . The operator interrupted her thoughts to inform her that her call was being put through. She listened to the avant-garde music sounds of the overseas connections going to work and then she heard a man answering quite clearly in whatever language they spoke out there (Bahrainese?) and, after a moment when it turned out the man spoke English, and was the hotel operator (a man!), she heard the telephone ringing in Hutch's room and for no reason at all her heart skipped a beat.

And then it nearly stopped. She swore later that the shock of hearing that particular voice—one she knew too well—was responsible for all that followed.

The voice, which was as clear as gin even at that distance, belonged to April Gold who was Hutch's redheaded thirty-eight-year-old secretary who had supposedly been fired or rather let go the week before they were married because Honey's mother, Ruth, had insisted. Even Honey had insisted.

Hutch had said it had all been over for years but everyone in D.C. knew otherwise; everyone knew that April Gold had been his mistress up until the time Hutch suddenly began courting Honey Boyd and so April had had to go.

Where April had gone had been a mystery Honey hadn't been all that interested in probing. But now she knew that April with the green eyes and the red hair and the thick white skin hadn't gone very far at all, even if she was in Bahrain answering Hutch's telephone in Hutch's bedroom.

Honey put the receiver back on its cradle, gingerly, as if it were alive. When the operator called back to ask if she didn't want to speak to her party, Honey said no, it had been a mistake and that the party wasn't to be told who had done the calling.

She switched on the volume on the TV, using the control gun as if it were real, aiming it at Roger Mudd as if he were

Hutch. She shot her way around the channels, threw the control gun on the bed, and searched out the Manhattan directory which she found in one of the bottom drawers of the mock French bureau.

Mr. Saiad was not listed. She went to the dressing room, found her lizard purse, the one Hutch had given her (April Gold must have picked it out), upended it until she found the ivory-colored card on which Mr. Saiad had written his telephone number.

She called it, was disappointed to find he wasn't home but informed his answering service that she would be delighted to have dinner with Mr. Saiad on the following night. "And tell him the answer is yes."

"To what?" the woman at the service wanted to know.

"To everything," Honey Boyd said, allowing her peignoir to fall open, allowing her hand to move up and down her body, caressing its fine baby skin.

BOOK 4

THURSDAY

Chapter One

ON THURSDAY morning a very proper Lawrence, in a double-breasted black suit that made him look like a cross between Robert Morley and Charles Laughton, sat poised on the tip of one of Duke's red leather sofas, reporting on the progress of the fiftieth anniversary party.

"Lawrence knows how to spend money on food," the Duke had said when he had insisted that Lawrence be in charge of the party's buffet. "Nick's sensuality is in his dork. Lawrence's is in his tongue."

The two men carried on an amiable conversation, one they had had for the several months preceding the anniversary date. The restaurant was to be closed on Friday and yes, Lawrence had made those arrangements. The staff was to work late on Thursday so that little would have to be done on Friday. There were to be extra guards so that Scotty and Little Mike could circulate, if they so desired. No one would be allowed in without a gold key. Each gold key was numbered so that it would be a simple matter to get out the book and see if anyone claiming a lost key really had received one in the first place.

"It's going to be a marvelous party, Duke," Lawrence said, closing his leather notebook. "Everything is very much in order."

"I can see that, Lawrence. I have great confidence in you. Would you like a shot of something to start the day?"

Lawrence, looking up at Robert who wore his usual glower, contented himself with patting Hector, and saying no, that he had best get himself downstairs. He really wouldn't have minded a cup of jasmine tea, he decided as he took the elevator down to the restaurant.

He was surprised to find a bowler-hatted Peter waiting at the elevator doors. "The street door was locked," Peter explained as he took Lawrence's place and ascended into his father's private domain.

Robert was serving Duke his breakfast. SayDee, in a dressing gown which looked as if it came from a Frederick's of Hollywood's catalogue, was sitting on the arm of the sofa, buttering pieces of croissant, alternately feeding Duke and the dog, Hector.

Peter thought he had never seen a more slovenly woman, a more loathsome scene. The ridiculous dog and the insanely morose valet and that slut of a woman in that caricature of a great English room made him nauseous.

He said hello, shook his father's hand, declined a cup of anything and, after a moment, asked if he might speak to his father alone.

"You find my life distasteful, don't you, Peter?" Duke asked after Robert and SayDee and even Hector had left the room.

"It really has nothing to do with me, Father. We all live our lives as we choose."

"And you choose to be a cheap snob, trying to win a title in a country whose aristocracy and economy died thirty years ago."

Peter took from his case one of his Egyptian cigarettes, tapped it thoughtfully, and lit it. "Don't you understand, yet, Duke, that I am a creation of yours? I am very much like you. Only you made your own false little duchy here on Forty-fourth Street. You have your castle, your mistress, and your court. You're the original little king, the self-titled duke. Can you blame me, as your son, if I went off to another realm to earn my title? Can you blame me if my life is a mirror of yours, except that I choose a larger arena?"

"But I created something."

"The creation is the part of your life that I find so vulgar. What did you create? A restuarant that's not a club, a club that's not a restaurant? And who will care ten years from now, except for all those people who have managed to hang on to their gold keys?"

He stood at the baronial mantel, smoking, looking down at his father who wouldn't or couldn't look at him. "I'm your son, Duke. You'd best face it while you can."

"What do you want from me today, Peter?"

It was a half hour later, while SayDee was watching a Miriam Hopkins film in the television room that she sensed a tension she didn't like. She teetered down the long mirrored hall in the platform heels she only felt comfortable in and decided she didn't care that Peter had wanted to see his father alone. She burst into the drawing room. Duke was sitting where she left him, a cashmere afghan covering his knees, his face suffused with more color than it had been in weeks. He was obviously furious.

His son, Peter Stewart-Greene, stood by the door which led to the elevator, a red welt across his face, Duke's ivory-headed cane at his feet.

"I won't go so far as to promise that you'll live to regret this, Duke," Peter said. "But I can promise you one thing: Duke's 44 is going to be destroyed, one way or another. If Nick comes up with the money, I'll put him in the law courts for the next five years. If he doesn't, and I assume he won't, I'll sell to it to UNITAS the moment I can." He picked up his topcoat from where it had fallen and put it over his arm. "I don't expect we shall be seeing each other again. Good-bye, Father."

The paneled door shut after him with a decisive sound.

"You hit him, Duke?" SayDee asked, going to him, putting her arms around his sad, thin shoulders.

Duke laughed, not happily. "Nick punched him in the gut yesterday. Best I could do was cane the little bastard. You know what he wants? For me to leave him 44 outright. He's scared Nick will come up with the dough-re-me." He took SayDee's big and not very soft hand and kissed it, then held it to his cheek. "I'm just as scared Nick won't."

"Duke, I have an idea: let's have lunch in bed. Let's get Maurice to send up a huge steak and a bottle of something rare and old and awful tasting and we'll get Robert to serve it and then we'll kick him out and we'll hold on to each other for the rest of the day. You know how I love bed, Duke."

He allowed her to help him into the bedroom where she got him undressed and back into that majestic, ridiculous bed that *Life* had once featured on its cover, headlining a series called "American Royalty and How They Sleep."

"American Royalty and How They Die," should be the title of this feature, SayDee thought as she looked down at that face that even now, with its skin stretched too tightly across its bones, seemed genuinely aristocratic.

"Peter's right, you know" he said, looking up into her eyes. "I don't like it but the bastard's right. He is my son. I gave him his mother and between us we gave him our values. He wants to be a lord. He wants to have a title. He thinks that will solve everything."

"Your son Peter's looking for nobility in the wrong places," SayDee said. And then she climbed into the bed with her own personal sovereign, dismayed that he was so unhappy, but glad that he was human enough to admit it.

"You try and sleep," she told him, holding him tightly. "You got to look gorgeous for tomorrow night, right, Duke?"

Paul McGuigan knew something was wrong, askew, from the moment he took the phone call.

"Hey, man," Tony Gato had said. "I been trying to get you for days. They either got you locked up or you're hiding from me."

"I meant to call but so much is happening . . ."

"Yeah?"

"Tony, I don't think . . ."

"You owe me, you bastard. You owe me the courtesy of telling me face to face. You owe me for the two weeks and the past year I've given you. I'm not letting you hang me and the phone up at the same time, Padre. I'll meet you anywhere you say. I want to hear it from you. In person. You want to come down to my place?"

"No," Paul said, too quickly. "It wouldn't be convenient. I . . . what about lunch?"

"Anything you say."

"Lunch. Today."

"Where, Padre? Where we going to have this lunch?"

Paul couldn't think. He felt suffocated, trapped, nauseous. "Duke's 44," he said because he could think of nowhere else. "Duke's 44 Club at one o'clock."

"Duke's 44, huh? Ah, the poverty of the Church, me lads," Tony said, doing an Irish accent. "I guess I have to wrap a tie around my neck, huh?"

"Yes. You'll need a tie, Tony," Paul said, finally saying his name. "And a jacket."

"I'll dig one up. See you later, Padre."

He had gone into the chapel and tried to pray but all he could do was feel a terrible weakness. He wondered, as he was on his knees in front of the huge gold cross, whether or not he was getting ill. He tried with all of his being to pray, to block the images that were filling his mind but he couldn't.

He purposely wore clerical garb. White collar, black suit. Everything is arranged, he told himself as he walked to the restaurant, wondering why he hadn't been able to think of a less celebrated place, somewhere quieter where he wouldn't be known. "I am going to get the offer, the new assignment, tomorrow. Zoltan promised. I will confess this afternoon, when I return, about my transgressions in Bernina. I was born for the Church. I have a true calling. I . . ."

"Right this way, Father," Lawrence said, surprised that he was in uniform, so to speak, slightly disapproving. "Will your aunt be joining you?"

"No," Paul managed to say as he was taken to the best table, realizing he had neglected to make a reservation. Lawrence must have thought Joan Hull was going to be there, otherwise he would never have been given that table, with or without advance booking. Apprehensively he followed Lawrence. Tony Gato was already there.

He wore a double-breasted, well-cut blue suit and a white shirt and a simple tie and the appropriate shoes. He had shaved. His hair was recently cut and in place. Still he looked like he worked for a Mafia capo.

He was talking to Nick who said hello and moved away when Paul was seated. "You know Nick Reo?" Paul said, because he couldn't think of anything else to say and his hands were sweating and he didn't want to touch Tony's hand.

"Hey, man. Don't you read anything except the *Vatican Times*? I'm a famous painter. Two of my works were bought by the Whitney Museum this year. You want to be a famous painter, you got to get around New York. Even to 44."

He looked at Paul who sat bolt upright, one hand on a glass of water, the other in the pocket of his jacket. "What's the matter with you, man?"

"I'm just surprised we're at this table. They must have thought my aunt . . ."

"Bull shit, man. We're at this table because I made a reservation and I'm hot stuff, Padre." He put his hand on Paul's arm and Paul felt as if he had been burned. "What the fuck is the matter with you, huh? I been waiting a solid year to see you, man. I love you. Or I think I do. And you're sitting there like you have the D.T.'s."

Charles hovered about them.

"Shall we order?" Paul asked, sounding, he knew, like his aunt.

"Hey, Paul," Tony said, sending Charles away with a wave of his ham-fisted hand, putting his leg against Paul's. "I'm going to take you out of here, man. Any way I can. You don't realize it but you're having a little breakdown. I've seen it before. Guys get it from drugs, from killing people. Now I want you to stand up. If you need my arm, tell me."

"I'm going to pass out."

"No you're not. Just stand up." Somehow, Paul stood up but everything had turned into a hazy, mindless sort of dream. He heard Tony explain that the monsignor wasn't feeling well, that he would see him home, that it wasn't serious. Perhaps a flu. Paul wanted to giggle but he didn't.

He kept his mouth closed. Even in the filthy cab, during the interminable ride to SoHo, he didn't speak. He didn't feel he had to. He just held on to the big hand that had grabbed his.

Later, in the loft, Tony had undressed him and put him to bed. And then he had undressed himself and got in and the last thing Paul saw, before he started crying, was Tony's unfinished heart-shaped tatoo with the arrow piercing it and the empty space for the word, mother.

"What're you crying about, man?" Tony asked after what seemed like hours. "Talk about it."

"I'm not crying," Paul said crying. And then after a moment: "I'm crying because I almost became a bishop and not too many people become bishops and part of me wants it so badly, I can taste it. But the terrible thing is I don't want it for me or for the glory of God but because I want my Aunt Joan to come and pat me on the head and tell me she loves me. She never will. Even when I become Pope, she'll want me to go on and become Christ.

"And I'm crying because for the last year I've been denying the only person in my life I can honestly thank God for letting me know. That's you, 'man.' But if you think I can give up all the years of comfort and solace the Church has given me, to leave all that behind me and take the risk of starting an entire new life with you, you're going to be disappointed, Tony. I'm a priest, Tony."

"Yeah?" Tony ripped the blanket and sheet away. "That's a man's equipment, pal." He started to become erect as Tony held him and he knew he was blushing.

"Do something, Tony," he said as Tony kneeled over him, holding him.

"Not this time, man. This time, you do something."

Paul reached up and brought Tony's head close to his and while they made love—the incredible love he had denied for the past year—he knew the definitive answer though he never was absolutely certain what the question had been.

Chapter Two

IT WAS close to three P.M. The last of the luncheon crowd was leaving or ordering another pot of coffee, perhaps a second bottle of wine, preparing to spend the afternoon.

Nick went to his office and gave in to the temptation to try Blue Bowen once more. The *Times* had run a concluding piece on Blue in the financial section, detailing his South American and African dealings, describing his relationship with Libya and Tunisia and Morocco. It didn't inspire confidence.

He tried Bowen Frère's public line, first. It gave off the sort of busy signal that indicated either Ma Bell was in trouble or the switchboard had been turned off.

He called the private number Blue had once given him when he was in the process of his first divorce, rendezvousing with his soon-to-be second wife in the remotest corners of the J. J. Walker Room. Nick allowed the telephone to ring half a dozen times and was about to give up when it was answered.

For perhaps the first time in his adult life, Blue Bowen had answered the phone himself.

"Blue? Nick Reo. I'm calling . . ."

"Nick. How are you? Sorry. Thought it was someone else. I can't talk right now. I'll get back to you one way or another tomorrow. Promise. For the moment simply can't talk. You understand.''

Nick sat on the edge of his desk for a few seconds, holding the receiver, allowing the empty sound of a dead line to reverberate in his ear like a sophisticated torture device.

His first thought was that he'd have to tell his secretary to quit wearing Countess Vera's Fontanna di Jeunesse cologne. She invariably left traces of it when she used his phone and it made him queasy.

He wondered if Lawrence had ordered enough Roederer's Cristal for the anniversary party and then he caught himself, caught that trick of his of concentrating on small stuff when there was big stuff that needed attending to. Very big stuff.

He wondered what Blue Bowen was going through, if he were planning on leaving the country, if his financial pyramid were falling down, if he were just being eccentric and nervy because some key deal was in the works. It had been known to happen before. Occasionally that rare vintage known as Blue Bowen became uncorked and he engaged in what was kindly put as peculiar behavior.

He would trust in Blue's promise, he decided. He didn't have much choice. Perhaps it was the two million dollars for 44 that Blue was sweating out. Though Blue's sweating out two million bucks was like another man sweating out two hundred Kennedy half-dollars. Still he would have to wait.

He went into the Club Room, waved at Valida Rand who was just being seated at the best table with her ex-husband, Laddy Wister, and started to reach for the elevator button when he felt a hand on his arm.

Buddy Samson, the TV executive, was standing there in a gray pin-striped suit and a silk tie, his fat face a mass of crinkly false bonhomie smiles. ''Don't forget to tune in your Betamax to Dinah Sheridan tomorrow night when she covers the anniversary. But keep your Pepto-Bismol handy, Nick. What she's going to do to 44 shouldn't happen to Joe's Grease-A-Teria. I sat in on the dress rehearsal this morning . . .''

Nick took the fat man's sausage fingers from his arm and moved away, intending to talk to Little Mike. But as he turned, he saw an unfamiliar figure in the hallway which led around the elevator shaft and down to the kitchen.

''Georgio, what are you doing here?'' Nick asked.

"The other stairs were blocked. Sometimes I come this way. It's faster."

Nick understood the logic of that statement and started to signal Little Mike when Georgio said, "You know, Mr. Reo, this is the best job I ever had. I love it in this place."

It was the most conversation Nick had had with the best table's busboy. The other kitchen workers called him Silent Georgio. He was an odd boy. Well, an odd man. It was difficult to say how old he was.

"I hope what that guy said ain't true. I wouldn't want that Sheridan lady to kill off the trade, you know what I mean, Mr. Reo?"

"She can't, Georgio. Nice of you to worry, though," Nick said, realizing that Georgio had heard his conversation with Buddy Samson. "Don't you think it's time you got back to the table or the kitchen or wherever you're headed?"

"Sure thing, Mr. Reo," Georgio said, nodding his head. "Nice talking to you."

It was also the first time Nick had ever seen Georgio smile. He was glad that he had never seen that particular tiny-toothed grimace before. There was something anthropomorphic about it, as if Georgio had an animal's mouth.

He filed that idea under Lunatic Fancies and signaled Little Mike to come into the Club Room.

"I thought I told you that Buddy Samson was barred."

"Sorry, Nick. He came in here sandwiched between Baroness Rothschild and Mrs. Edward Murrow. I thought he was with them but by the time I realized he wasn't, he was at the bar and Mickey was serving him."

"Let him finish the drink and get him out of here."

"Strong arm?"

"Not so anyone will notice."

Nick took the elevator up to Duke's apartment. SayDee met him in the foyer. "He's a little better, Nick. He's trying to save his strength for the party." She was wearing what she called her Lana Turner coat. It was a white cashmere wrap-around. Hector, straining at his rhinestone leash, was dressed similarly. "He's even got himself some visitors. Don't go way, Nick. Go get Robert to give you a cup of tea. I'll be back in a few minutes. Hector has to do his duty." Her endearing rasp was nervous. Whenever SayDee came on like

Queen Mary, offering cups of tea, Nick knew she was uncomfortable.

He held the elevator for her and the dog and then he went into the drawing room. Duke was reclining on his red leather sofa, dressed in a midnight blue smoking jacket, a red silk ascot, gray striped trousers. The fur rug covered his feet. He looked frail but wily, like a blue-gray fox in an Aesop's fables illustration.

Sitting opposite him, holding a teacup in her hand, wearing a pale pink suit, looking expensive and lovely, was Brette.

"Come on in, Nick," Duke called out as if he were hosting a riotous party and a favored guest, long overdue, had just appeared. "Robert, get Nick a drink."

Robert, dressed in the scarlet uniform Irene had designed for him, but as serious as ever, looked inquiringly at Nick, who shook his head. "SayDee said something about a cup of tea," he said, coming into the room, wondering why everyone, from the dog on up, was in high drag.

And then he saw the third guest who had been sitting on the sofa facing the leaded paned windows. It was Morgan Brooks, the man from UNITAS. He stood up and offered his hand. "Mr. Reo and I have met," he said, cutting smoothly across Brette's attempt at introduction.

Nick took the outstretched hand. "Yes. When I lost my temper with Mrs. Stewart Greene's husband. I apologize again." Nick chose a wing-backed chair that stood with its back to the fireplace. "I gather Brette brought you here to meet Duke?" Nick asked.

"Wrong, Nick. I asked Brette to bring him," Duke said, waving an unlit cigar around. "I thought we might as well come face to face. I wanted to know if there was any way we—you—could hold off the wolf if Blue doesn't come through." He allowed Robert to light the cigar and took a puff, the rich tobacco scent immediately filling the room.

"And is there?" Nick asked, pouring his own tea.

"No way. UNITAS is determined to own 44, to turn it into an airport restaurant with plastic steaks and American caviar. Aren't you, Mr. Brooks?"

"We are determined to do no such thing, Duke," Morgan Brooks, unassailably affable, said. "We want to incorporate the spirit of Duke's 44 Club into the UNITAS family, that's all. And this might interest you, Mr. Reo: we are prepared, today, to give the Duke three million dollars, cash, for his interest in 44. He could stay on as long as he chose, of course, and the management, the running of the club would be his until . . ."

"Until," Duke said, regretfully putting the cigar aside because it made him cough, "I float up to that big restaurant in the sky." Robert came and handed him a cup filled with coffee and cream and sugar.

"They're smart, Nick. Goddamned smart. Two million would go to meet the divorce agreement, my obligation to Peter. The other to leave to people I love. They know I'm more or less broke."

"Now, Duke," Morgan Brook began, "UNITAS only wants . . ."

"UNITAS only wants what UNITAS wants. You're perfectly willing to undercut my son, Peter, to get it. What gives me heart, what fills me with a quiet joy, is that you're running scared. It's a good sign, Nick. They think you're going to come up with the money. Or he wouldn't be here."

"They're right," Nick said, allowing Robert to fill his teacup. "I've just spoken to Blue. It looks good."

Morgan Brooks sprang up from the sofa as if an ejection button had been pressed. "My best wishes, Mr. Reo, for success, then. You must realize, of course, that my company's sympathies do not lie with your cause. And I'm afraid Mr. Stewart-Greene"—he bowed at Brette—"will be fearfully disappointed. The board has decided that if UNITAS cannot have 44, UNITAS does not want 44 Industry. One suspects he might take you to court. Providing Mr. Bowen comes up with the money. His promises, it has come to light only recently, have not always been based on the ability to bring them about."

He bowed again, to the company at large, and allowed Robert to take him to the door which led to the street stairwell.

Duke laughed as the door shut behind him. "Is that true about Blue Bowen coming through, Nick?"

"More or less."

"Poor Peter. He's really up against it, isn't he, Brette? He may have to be content with two million dollars." He relit the cigar as SayDee and Hector came in. She handed the dog to

Robert, who held him at arms' length and moved across the room like a scared rabbit, snatching the cigar out of Duke's mouth.

"Are you off your nut, Duke Greene? Smoking a cigar in your condition?"

"Darling SayDee, I ask you again: in my condition, what does it matter?"

"You want to be at the party tomorrow night, don't you? I intend to get you there."

Duke looked up and smiled. "You're right, my dear. You're right. And I think it's time for my nap. Too much excitement." He motioned to SayDee and Robert to help him up, at the same time signaling Brette and Nick to stay seated. "I'll see you two later." At the door to the hallway he turned back. "That's great news about Blue, isn't it, Nick?"

"Yeah, Duke."

They watched him walk with difficulty into the hall leading to his bedroom, one arm around SayDee, the other around Robert, Hector—for once not yipping—at their heels.

They looked at each other for a moment, Brette turning away first. "What was that supposed to be?" Nick asked, getting up, moving to the window where he could see the limousines lined up in front of 44's canopy. "Hastening the death of your father-in-law by bringing the enemy onto the scene?"

She played with a cigarette box made of fluted gold and set it carefully back on the smoking table. "I thought Duke would like to know that UNITAS is on the defensive. After all, he asked me to bring Brooks here."

"You had the option of saying no. It hasn't helped . . ."

"Benevolent lies. You believe in that for the dying, don't you, Nick?"

"Up to a point."

"Blue Bowen isn't coming up with the money, is he?"

"Probably not," Nick admitted, sitting on the window seat, facing her. "But it won't help Duke to die knowing that UNITAS is about to turn 44 into, and I quote, 'the luxury flagship of our fine fleet of international three-star restaurants.' "

"I'm sorry, Nick."

"No you're not. You don't care about 44, you never have."

"Not in the shining, dewy-eyed way you do, Nick, no. It is not my holy grail. But I don't want to see UNITAS get it. Duke's 44 was my father's life and it certainly is Duke's. For them it was more than an enterprise, it was, is, symbolic of the way those two very different men approached life. As an approach, full of amenities and pleasures, I agree with it, Nick." She looked at him with her violet eyes. "I would do anything I could to save it, Nick." She stood up, placing a pink suede clutch purse under her arm. "If you can think of any way I can help, let me know."

He didn't say anything as she left. He moved to the red leather sofa, and sat there, looking at the central-casting fire Robert had created in the fireplace, listening to the sounds of the apartment, to the traffic noise from the street.

Chapter Three

VALIDA RAND enjoyed the unseasonably cold weather. If it had been unseasonably warm, she would have had to wear light silk dresses that clung, and she knew that her figure wasn't clingable any longer. It was one of those difficult facts of life one had to face: if she lost too much weight, her cheeks caved in and her throat began to look stringy. If she kept an extra five or even eight pounds on her body, her face looked full and young. Frank had called her a face whore, one of his less charming epithets.

She thanked the gods for the cool weather, putting Frank out of her mind, putting on the long, oversized white fox coat, wrapping a white fox scarf around her neck, placing the white fox Russian officer's hat firmly on her head.

It's a bit much, she thought, studying herself in the mirror, wondering how many women all over the world were, at that moment, studying themselves in their mirrors, thinking they were a bit too much or a bit too little and what did it mean, after all?

It means my life, my future, my creativity, she answered herself, going to the safe the Plaza had installed in her room, taking out the cabochon ruby earrings and attaching them to her ears. "Nothing like gilding the lily," she said aloud, taking stock of herself once again. ''But they can't fool me. Everyone loves a gilded lily.''

She let herself out of her suite and tried to smile at herself in the hallway mirror, pleased that she had avoided waking her maid from her afternoon nap, pleased that she had avoided the caustic comments her outfit would certainly have drawn from that annoying woman.

She decided that if she didn't appear as showroom new and shiny as the young blonde standing next to her, also waiting for the elevator, she certainly was tons more glamorous. Well, she said to herself, as the young blonde made opening conversation noises, I always adored the vindictive roles.

''Excuse me, I just can't help but asking: are you, by any chance, Valida Rand?''

''I am,'' Valida said, thinking that this blonde was far more attractive than Laddy Wister's blonde.

''I'm Honey Boyd—Senator Hutch Boyd's wife—and I know this is awfully rude but I just can't help but say you've always been my very favorite actress and *That Wentworth Woman* is, and always has been, my very favorite film. I've seen it dozens of times,'' Honey said in that soft Southern drawl that somehow, on her, wasn't as annoying as it usually was. ''You are lovely, Miss Rand.''

''So are you, my dear. Hutch Boyd is a very lucky man.''

''He was,'' Honey said, half under her breath and then launched into half a dozen questions to which Valida gave the automatic answers she reserved for such queries.

She and Honey walked down Fifth Avenue together until Honey went to keep her appointment at Elizabeth Arden's (where she belongs, Valida thought, not altogether kindly). Valida gave herself up to the luxury of thinking of Frank as she walked downtown, trying not to gasp at the prices in the windows of the new Italian shops.

He had been an inch shorter than she and possessed a face that looked as if he had battered around in waterfront bars for most of his life. He was chronically thin and tough and romantic so that he continued smoking his ''coffin nails'' long after the doctor said he couldn't, long after he had stopped enjoying them.

He drank his gin straight, and when he was drunk, he was

awful, worse hung over, and they had fought like cat and dog for the ten years they had managed to stay together.

But he had understood her artistry, just as he understood her womanhood, and the four films they had made together—even though the studios had cut two of them to shreds—were the only films she had ever been genuinely proud of.

She had schooled herself, forced herself not to think of Frank, not to let that aching need for him surface while she was trying to "wrap up the package."

The package was the current *sine qua non* for movie-making. Without it, no money would be given or lent, no film would be made. All one needed to get eight million or so dollars out of a studio—or a group of tax-loss-happy Canadian backers—was a package: the script, the director, the stars.

Sometimes it was easier to get a package together than rolling out of bed and sometimes it was harder than rolling up Everest but always it was painful and debasing and, depending upon one's temperament, exhilarating, all at the same time.

Valida Rand had always been part of the package. Now, at fifty, she had been turned into a package maker. "Dear Frank," she said, closing her eyes for a moment as she stopped for the light at Forty-eighth and Fifth, "if they let me make this damned film, it's going to be a great movie. I promise you that, Frank."

"Valida Rand," a stout lady in a plaid wool coat with a fur collar that looked as if it were a cat curled around her neck, said to another whose hair had been ill-advisedly done up in hundreds of tiny curls. "Still gorgeous, isn't she, Lil?"

If you think it's easy, Valida wanted to say to her fat admirer. If you think I enjoy walking around locked into this iron maiden of a girdle, on heels two inches too high, with earrings that weigh three pounds apiece . . .

But she didn't. She smiled and drew the fox scarf around her neck for security because no matter how often she was recognized, it always scared her a little, made her feel a little too vulnerable. They knew who she was. But who the hell were they?

She remembered a terrible moment on Broadway when *That Wentworth Woman* opened and an enormous mob bore down on her, to congratulate her, to touch her. She had fainted, luckily. Otherwise she would have screamed.

She walked up the brownstone steps of 44 and felt nostalgic, secure, as if she were coming home. Duke's 44 was not a place where she might be mobbed. They frowned on autograph seekers in Duke's club.

Little Mike and Scotty held the door for her, genuinely pleased to see her. They had always been a little wary of Frank. They had had to throw him out on his keester one night after he punched his first wife in the mouth in the Club Room. He had been barred from 44 until Valida came on the scene and then she had called Duke and asked nicely and Duke had said sure, certainly, if Frank can behave himself. And then she had worked on Frank and finally the two of them had gone for dinner on the Tuesday night after they were married. Duke had greeted them and kissed them and sat with them at the best table. Their marriage hadn't been popular. They had needed a friend, and Duke had been a friend.

She told Little Mike that she wanted to keep her furs, that she had a slight chill but the real reason was that she felt she needed all the props she could use.

Lawrence greeted her in that way of his that she adored but had made Frank want to kick him in the balls ("to see if he has any"). He took her with his endearing, mincing pomp to the first table on the left, the best table, where Laddy Wister was sitting, his hands wrapped around the extra large Baccarat glass 44 had used for its Scotch since she could remember.

He stood up, actually jumped up, to help Lawrence help her into her seat. She caught sight of Nick in the Club Room, waved to him, ordered a glass of white wine because she didn't want to get drunk and then decided that it didn't matter and changed it to Bombay gin.

Finally she turned her attention to Laddy. "You'd better get me the two little white pills in my purse, darling," she said, smiling. "I think I'm going to have an attack. The surprise of it all. Imagine, Laddy Wister waiting for me."

"You're thirty minutes late," Laddy said, consulting his Rolex, a gold and chrome affair his father-in-law had given him.

She suddenly felt sorry for Laddy Wister. He was as much victimized by the system as he benefited from it. He would have been a divine supermarket manager, she thought. Cheating on his wife with the check-out girls, being as athletic as all get out with his kids. They should outlaw certain roving talent agents, she decided as she asked him if he wanted another Scotch.

"Definitely," he said, and his square-jawed face broke into that dimpled, devoutly self-believing smile as he ordered from Charles with an ersatz goodwill. Laddy had never known how to treat waiters or servants or doorman or car hops or anyone, for that matter, who waited upon him.

"Cut to action," Valida said after he had gotten his drink and was a little ways into his how-marvelous-you-look routine.

"All right. Harry's read the script, Vali."

"Darling, who you trying to fool? Everyone east of Pecos Boulevard knows Harry Monaco doesn't read."

"He likes it, Val. He thinks it's great. He's got one or two little reservations . . ."

"Such as?"

"He's not sure you're right for Eleanor, Val. Daisy thought it would be better for Ali. We'd have to . . ."

"Lop two decades off the heroine or make a May/December movie about a thirty-year-old woman and a ten-year-old boy." She finished her gin. Charles went to bring her another. "I gather they still want you to play the boy?"

"Listen, Val. I told Harry you owned the property and Harry said . . ."

" 'Find out how much she wants. If she won't deal, bottom line is we'll make it with Ali and give her a production credit, two points. But she don't get no script approval, no final cut approval, and no foreign rights.' Little Laddy, I have been playing this game with Harry and Jacky and Bobby Evans for a lot longer than you, and though I know the rules, I hate, fear, and loathe the game. I intend to keep control over *Neon Lights*, Laddy. I intend to play Eleanor."

"Harry won't make it, Val. He won't let me make it. I'm telling you. Daisy's against it."

"Has it ever occurred to you that Laddy, Daisy, and Harry may very well have been the names of Dagwood Bumstead's dogs? Strike that." She finished her second gin. Charles went for another. "Do I understand this correctly, Laddy: Harry Monaco will make *Neon Lights* but without me. I will get some producer credit but I will probably be barred from the set and will certainly not appear in the film."

"That's Harry's bottom line, Val."

"Laddy, why are you looking like your drawers are down when it is I who am being raped? All right. I understand it, now. If I want Frank's film to be made, I have to bow out. Let Harry Monaco make it. Well, worse people I suppose have made good films. He'll use Frankenheimer?"

"He doesn't want to commit to anything, Val."

"How long have I got, Doctor?"

"I have to let him know on Saturday. Daisy and I . . ."

"Then I'll let you know tomorrow night. Here. Why don't you and Daisy come to the anniversary as my guests? I'm sure Daisy would enjoy it. As you know, the answer is, barring miracles from heaven, most likely yes. I haven't much choice if I want *Neon Lights* made. Now go away. I want to get drunk and pass out and cause a scene."

He stood up and kissed her. "It will be a good movie, Val."

"But I won't be in it. Till tomorrow, Laddy."

He left and Saunders, immaculate, perfectly dressed, took his place.

"Just as you thought," she answered his silent question.

"Give it up, Valida. Let them make the film. Let them . . ."

"I told Laddy I would tell him yes or no tomorrow night. I want you to keep working on it, Saunders."

"All right. Though not much will happen in the next twenty-four hours."

"You can't be sure."

He took her hand. "Do you want to sleep with me, Valida?"

"Not even a little."

"Do you want to marry me?

"Find someone who will make that movie with me, some male movie star who's bankrollable, whose movies have legs, and I will sleep with you and marry you and any other damn thing you want. But it has to be by tomorrow night."

Chapter Four

"WHERE'S HONEY BOYD and the Ayatollah?"

"I was forced to inform Mrs. Boyd that 44 didn't carry Diet Pepsi though of course we were prepared to send someone out to find some. She said she preferred it in the can which was not a particularly adroit way of putting it. She said Diet Pepsi in the bottle was awful, that she had had it with bottles, that she had to have it in the can. Her escort said not to bother sending anyone out, they weren't hungry anyway and he knew a place where there were several cans of Diet Pepsi on ice. Then they left. I'm giving the best table to Countess Vera and her husband unless you have some objection? Governor Carey, his latest wife, and some minor dignitary—perhaps it's the president—from Pakistan are here but I thought they would prefer the relative anonymity of table eleven. You don't think, Nick, that we should add a Moslem entrée to the menu, do you?"

Honey Boyd sat on the edge of the quilted mattress which was the only piece of furniture in the room. She sipped at a Diet Pepsi through a straw and watched Saiad. He stood at the counter which partially hid the kitchen, rolling a cigarette with marijuana and hashish.

"Are you ever going to get any furniture?" Honey asked, switching her attention to the white carpet that covered the floor and the bed's platform, to the mirror suspended over the bed. The lighting, indirect, came from above the mirror and was soft and flattering.

"I do not think so, Mrs. Boyd. I only need one piece of furniture."

Honey looked at him doubtfully. It was very quiet in Mr. Saiad's small but luxurious studio in the Olympic Towers. There was one window that framed Fifth Avenue as if it were a trick picture, its lights blinking on and off, the Empire State Building in the near distance, its tower all pink and white.

Mr. Saiad moved across the room silently. He held an ashtray in one hand, the lit marijuana cigarette in the other. In the rheostated light, he seemed almost sinister standing over her.

"I always wanted to try pot again," Honey said, whispering for some reason. "I just never did get back to it. All the girls at junior college . . ." She let the thought run out as Saiad sat down beside her, placing the round white china ashtray between them.

"It is the way we celebrate certain business agreements in my country." He inhaled deeply. Honey wasn't at all certain she liked the smell of it. She wasn't at all certain she liked the smell of Mr. Saiad. There was something musty and foreign and not clean about the smell he and the cigarette gave off. Still she did as he told her to do, with that quiet insistent authority of his, inhaling the sweet, sticky smoke, holding it deep down in her lungs, miraculously not coughing.

"You have signed the papers. You now represent Pan-Arabian Interests, Inc., in the United States. Now we smoke a 'peace pipe.' Afterwards we make love." He traced a line down her arm with his beautiful forefinger. Honey broke out in goose bumps.

"I don't know about the making love part," Honey began but Saiad shook that same thick, dark finger at her, warning her not to let the smoke escape from her lungs.

"I'm feeling so dizzy suddenly, Mr. Saiad."

"It is a sign that we must stop smoking." He took the remainder of the cigarette and put it out carefully in the ashtray which he placed on the floor. "Put your head back," he told her, and she lay full length on the quilted mattress and stared up at her reflection in the mirror above. She was happy she had worn the peach satin dress even if Hutch always complained about its neckline. She tugged at it so that it revealed a little more and looked up to see if Mr. Saiad had noticed. Honey gasped.

Mr. Saiad had taken off all his clothes. He was a beautifully made man. No excess anywhere. Except between his legs, Honey thought and giggled aloud. "I never saw anything that big in my life," she said as Mr. Saiad knelt beside her and undid the belt that held her peach satin dress together. He helped her out of it, his finger on her lips so that she wouldn't speak and then he helped her to lie back down on the mattress. He knelt over her and kissed her, his tongue going into her mouth, his hands caressing her thick white breasts, his fingers searching for and finding the pink, erect nipples.

He pulled back and then his mouth closed around her right nipple and he began to massage it with his tongue as Honey watched fascinated in the mirror above them. He traveled downward, taking her legs, placing them against his shoulders and slowly making his way between her legs so that his tongue was reaching into her, deep into her, so that Honey was grasping his sleek, black head and pulling him closer, and begging him to stop at the same time as she had an orgasm.

He pulled away then, leaving Honey exhausted. She watched, helplessly, as he reached into a drawer in the platform and came up with a small white jar of salve. "Cocaine and ointment," he explained, applying some to her swollen breasts, massaging it in, and all of a sudden she felt deliciously cool.

Then he applied some to the place between her legs and suddenly she wanted him back there, with his tongue in her. She reached for his head and tried to pull him down but he kissed her instead and swung himself around so that his enormous erection was over her face. Slowly he let himself down into her mouth. But just before he entered, he painted a rim around her lips with the salve. And as he went into her, as he worked himself in and out of her mouth, his head went down between her legs and his tongue was back in her. Honey had her second orgasm soon after, as Mr. Saiad responded by coming in her mouth. For the first time in her life, Honey Boyd swallowed semen and she actually, at the time, enjoyed it.

Saiad's knife-hard body lay on top of her soft, ripe one for a moment and Honey could see herself in the mirror, her face between Saiad's lightly haired legs, his balls under her chin. Eventually he extricated himself and lay down next to her.

"I never," Honey Boyd began to say but Mr. Saiad had a finger over her lips again and not too many minutes later, Honey Boyd was on her knees with her head in the mattress and her back seat in the air and Mr. Saiad was entering her again, this time with his huge penis and he was telling her, in that soft voice of his, the progress he was making. "The head is in now. Can you feel it? Can you feel it in you? And now, slowly, the shaft; now the trunk is in you, can you feel that, Mrs. Boyd? And now I am all the way inside you. Can you feel *that*, Mrs. Boyd?"

Honey Boyd felt, though she was too far beyond speech to say so, as if the very core of herself had been penetrated and was being massaged in a way that the Elizabeth Arden masseuse would never be able to figure out.

Later Honey Boyd was on her back and later she was on top of Mr. Saiad and still later Mr. Saiad taught her how to sit on him—"the fat man's position," he said—and Honey Boyd laughed out loud with pleasure. She wondered what Hutch and his April Gold would think if they could see Mr. Saiad's enormous member going all the way into her and then pulling all the way out for what was hours of ecstacy.

And he didn't shut off the lights, either, she reminded herself when she compared Mr. Saiad's performance to Hutch's the following morning. She knew she would never forget the mirror's image of her legs over Mr. Saiad's shoulders, her hands pulling his thighs toward her, as he fucked her on the only piece of furniture he needed.

Countess Vera hadn't had a good day. She had woken up feeling stiff and used and her maid had pointed out a bruise on her thigh which was gray blue and ugly and the way she felt.

She had gone up to the greenhouse which took up most of the roof of her Sixty-fourth Street town house and received her hairdresser there. Usually he amused her, prattling on about his love affairs with what passed for brutal honesty, about the discothques and the after-hours bars and the clothes and cosmetics and "the girls," the models that he knew, as he fussed over her hair.

This morning he had seemed stale and silly and she had asked him if he could hurry because she had an appointment and that had thrown him off and now her hair looked more than usually set in cement.

As she dressed, selecting a gray winter Galanos suit, her secretary came up with a penciled request from her husband. He wanted to talk. She had her secretary call him back and tell him she would talk to him at dinner, if he was free and it turned out he was.

Then she called Ivan herself and broke their date and almost hung up on one of his predictable tirades. "I'll see you tomorrow night at 44," she had told him, knowing that his being at the anniversary party would shut him up for a while.

She selected a large green emerald pin which reputedly had once belonged to the Empress Eugénie and affixed it to the lapel of her suit, wondering how men in her position treated their young mistresses. Probably in the same way I handle Ivan, she thought, leaving the house, getting into the car, having the chauffeur take her to her office.

Countess Vera Cosmetics, Inc., takes up fifteen floors of the International Building on Fifth Avenue. The space is expensive and not altogether necessary but Vera liked being part of Rockefeller Center and she liked the statue of Atlas holding up the world that stands in front of the building.

The offices were occupied by the marketing and creative groups, all of which depended for their final okay on Countess Vera. Strategies and promotions were planned, packages and point-of-sale displays were created on Fifth Avenue in the Vera yellow-painted rooms. The fragrances and cosmetics were manufactured at the gray-white factory in Long Island City, just over the Fifty-ninth Street Bridge.

She went to her offices, smiling at everyone smiling at her, saying hello to a half-dozen people whose names she happened to remember, and sat down on a yellow leather sofa. She was tired and that wasn't like her. She looked out at

Rockefeller Center and thought about Ivan's young body for a moment and wondered what on earth she was going to do. It was clear that she was going to have to do something.

There was a knock on the door and she saw her husband standing there.

"May I come in, darling?"

"Please." She didn't like to see Bill in the office. He was as out of place in the pale yellow room as Ivan would have been. Countess Vera liked her men in the factory in Long Island City. "I received your message and I thought we might meet at dinner . . ."

"Yes, but I wanted to know what you thought about the Christmas packaging . . ." He went on to talk about the next Christmas, still over a year away, and the packaging for their products. The new and young designers wanted to get away from Countess Vera yellow but the more seasoned hands in the design department knew they were stuck with it and did their best to minimize it with narrow strips of silver and clever graphics.

As Bill showed her the proposed packages, she watched him, only one part of her brain taking in what he said. She always liked his legs. Unlike Ivan's muscular, hairy ones, Bill's were long and thin and elegant and his four-hundred-dollar lizard shoes looked perfectly appropriate at the end of them.

Though they were the same age, he hadn't stood up to the years as well as she. Perhaps cosmetics do work, she thought, looking at his skin which was dry and lined and nothing like the pink and white skin she had admired when she first met him, and, almost on the spot, decided to marry him.

He had been a good husband and she had been more than a good wife. She had given him a son and a steady salary and a style of life which he could never have enjoyed had he been on his own.

He was, it turned out, good at public relations, at filling in at dinner parties, at taking people to lunch, at mediating between the marketing, design, and packaging factions as they warred between themselves and with the people at the plant.

She knew she still loved him a little and that he still loved her a great deal, but she had built her life on taking risks, on making changes. During their thirty years together he had not remonstrated with her once; he had never argued, he had never fought, he had never slapped her. Life with Ivan would be filled with remonstrances, arguments, slaps. It might be hell, she thought, but it certainly would be exciting.

She told him which packaging she liked and which she hated and she said she would meet him at 44 at seven thirty when it was quiet and they could talk and he had kissed her on the cheek and said he was looking forward to it.

She would have liked to have stayed on at the office, making blitzkrieg visits to her various department heads, those nervous senior vice-presidents, and perhaps even step in on her son. Perhaps we can spend Thanksgiving together, she thought, thinking about opening the Palm Beach house, about having an old-fashioned Thanksgiving. Well, as old-fashioned as one could get in a pink stucco palazzo surrounded by palm trees and aging lounge lizards.

Then she remembered Ivan and thought that he would probably want to spend Thanksgiving at Régine's.

As she hurried home to the town house, for her next appointment, she thought that not least among Ivan's unhappy predilections was disco music and the dances that went with it.

She changed into a silk dress, a creamy daytime Balenciaga with a high neck and an old-fashioned air, inspected the dining room and had the yellow roses, which seemed a little used, replaced and was upstairs in the drawing room when Princess Grace was announced.

She was making an unpublicized trip to New York to see what, if anything, she could do about Caroline and, of course, to attend 44's anniversary. When she had been a bachelor girl in New York, she had virtually lived at the best table.

They discussed Caroline over shad roe on Tiffany plates and Vera thought that the princess was looking, if not old, at least stout and tired. She needs a lover, Vera said to herself. A young lover. As the sorbet was served, she looked over the princess's blond head and surveyed herself in the mirror over the mantle. I may be in the midst of upheaval, she thought, but decided she hadn't looked better in years. There was color in her skin—natural color—and a bright light in her eyes. Even Grace commented on it.

"You look too well," the princess said as Vera went with her to the car.

"You know that old joke," Vera had said. "I'm having an affair."

"Yes," the princess had answered, "who's your caterer?"

As she watched the car go off, Vera wondered if the princess would still lunch with her after she was married to Ivan. Probably not, she decided, going inside, going upstairs for her bath, a massage, and a light nap.

Young lovers were all very well but other precautions had to be taken against the inroads of time.

He's nervous, Vera thought as her husband sat across from her, drinking too much wine, eating too little food. And he's a little drunk. He's fortified himself for this conversation. It didn't increase her respect for him, the two or three martinis he must have had before he had come to 44.

"I love this table," Vera said, wondering how long it was going to take him to come out with it. "I'm always disappointed when I don't get it. It's supposed to be for visiting royalty and for years I pretended to Duke that I didn't live in New York. Of course he knew all the time. But that's Duke."

"Vera, darling," Bill Nickleson said, putting his fork and knife down in the manner proscribed by etiquette. "There's been a great deal of talk."

"About?"

"About you and that young chemist, Ivan Kotuk."

"Yes. Well, I'm going to put an end to the talk tomorrow," she said.

He accepted that as meaning she was going to rid herself of Ivan, that she was going to become his wife once again. She could see how he congratulated himself on the adroit way in which he had handled the matter. He had never been one for confrontations. Even in business he had sidestepped arguments, displays of power.

Thanksgiving was on his mind, too, and he suggested what Vera had been thinking, that they open the Palm Beach house for the holiday, that they ask their son—and who knew, perhaps a date—to join them. She let him go on because there was a piece of her that wanted to believe in their little family, that longed for the comfort and solace that the familiar can bring.

"We can firm up plans over the weekend," he said, and he suddenly looked very happy as Vera called for the check.

Chapter Five

DINAH SHERIDAN was tired and depressed and the joint she smoked, laced with angel dust, only made her feel more disjointed, more removed. She had worked all day at the studio, rehearsing for Friday night's special, working with the editors to integrate the taped and filmed segments with her own live comments.

She had told the survey team, the producers, to go on without her, to make their own inspection of 44's electrical system to insure enough juice for the umbrella lights. They would be shown around by Scotty and they could make their own decisions where the camera would go, where people would be interviewed.

She had told them that she knew 44 well enough. She didn't have to go back there to decide where she would stand.

The program was scheduled to begin with a history of 44. Photographs of the then young Cecil Townsend and Duke Greene, their arms around the requisite celebrities were to be flashed on the screen, interspersed with film clips of the two men welcoming visiting royalty, politicians, movie stars. It was going to be a social history of the past fifty years. Her father appeared in one of the clips. The sight of him, on the wall of the screening room, clowning, pretending to be

Fred Astaire, dancing up the steps of 44 into the foyer, around the bar room, and right up onto the top of the best table, had brought tears to her eyes.

Dear Clown. Dear Suicide. Dear Lover.

She had left the studio, no longer feeling it necessary to do her number on 44, to end her special with a detailed critique of the cuisine's downfall. The food had never counted at 44. It had always been the people. People like Duke, like her father.

Dinah Sheridan told her maid and Joyce, who had followed her home because there had been the thought of dictating her final on-camera speech, to leave, that she would see them both in the morning when she was fresh.

Fresh, she thought. I feel about as fresh as yesterday's mashed potatoes.

She picked up the telephone with the exaggerated languor deep depression and drugs always lent to her movements and, after a moment, called her mother in California.

"Oh, Dinah," her mother said after the butler had called her to the telephone, an operation which took some ten minutes by the clicking numbers of Dinah's digital clock. "I was just this minute thinking of you. It's scary." Dinah's mother always said she was just thinking of her, that it was scary. "Some people stopped by and are insisting I go to a drinks party and I keep telling them it's too early in the day for a drinks party and they keep on insisting.

"But how are you? I want to know everything. What are you doing about Thanksgiving? Petey Schriber and this adorable girl have invited me to Palm Springs. I said no, no, no, and they said yes, yes, yes, and so I finally gave in. Petey said he saw your last special on the television in England. Can you imagine that they'd be interested in American restaurants in England? Well, their own food is so desperately dreary. Oh, Dinah! Darling, I must hang. They're all talking so loud—we're out by the pool—that I can't hear a word you're saying. I will try to be better about calling, Dinah, but really, I don't know where the time goes . . ."

Dinah let the receiver slip back into its cradle. She looked out of the window at the long stretch of Central Park. It spread out before her in the dark like a huge black flag, surrounded by the toy towers and minarets of a miniature town.

She lit another joint and let the blinds fall on the winking lights and then she took up the telephone once again, this time holding it in her arms as if it were a warm child needing succor. She punched out a number on its control panel, spoke into its mouthpiece slowly, carefully enunciating her words, telling the person on the other end that it was a sort of emergency, that she was prepared to wait.

And after several moments she heard his unfamiliar voice. "Can you come over now?" she asked.

"Are you out of your ass? I'm in the middle of . . ."

"I told them it was an emergency. Say your best friend's ill."

"Listen, you dumb bitch . . ."

"I'm willing to do whatever you want. You name it, I will do it. You bring your equipment. No questions asked. I'm all alone. Use the service elevator. I'll buzz you in. I have some money for you. I'm ready to go all the way. I'm waiting for you."

There was a long pause. She could hear the sounds in the background. "I'll see what I can do," he said, his voice an octave lower, and then he hung up.

She stood up, carefully, and began taking off her clothes. She fingered the gold key her father had given her, the one with the number seven inscribed on it. She relit the joint which had gone out and wondered how long it would take him to get to her. She pretended to wonder, to herself, just how far he was willing to go. But she knew.

It took him a good two hours. He had had some work to finish up, work he wanted to finish, before he used Dinah's excuse, the sick friend. "This friend of mine is sick," he told his immediate superior. "Real sick. Going to die any minute. You think I could . . ."

"Of course. Go ahead. But we do need you tomorrow . . ."

"No sweat. I'll be here bright and early."

He had gone home first, to the one-room apartment on West Twenty-third Street, where he changed into jeans and a motorcycle jacket. He tried not to think because he knew if he thought, he'd get excited and maybe spoil it for himself.

Carrying a nylon knapsack, he took a cab up to Sixth Avenue and Fifty-eighth Street. Then he walked to the middle of the block between Sixth and Seventh avenues and waited at the service entrance to Dinah's building. Through the lobby he could see the doorman and the two elevator men talking at the Central Park South entrance. He buzzed Dinah's apartment. The door clicked open almost immediately. He put on a knitted cap, pulled up the collar of his jacket, and stepped into the aluminum-paneled service elevator, his head down, hoping the doorman and the elevator assholes weren't watching the TV surveillance monitor.

"Where you been?" she asked as she opened the door.

He didn't answer. He shut and locked the door behind him and looked at her. She was nude and her tits were erect but her eyes were glassy and obscure. He slapped her, open-handed but with some force, across the face. She fell backward, as if in a slow-motion film.

"You're wacked out of your mind, you stupid cunt. I wanted you to feel everything." He put his heavy black engineer's boot on her right breast, forcing the hard leather toe into her nipple. She tried to push it off. "We're going all the way tonight. Right? That's what you want, isn't it? Answer me," he said, applying more pressure.

"Yes."

"Yes, what?" he asked, now putting all of his weight onto his foot.

"Yes," she said, closing her eyes, her two hands on the relentless boot. "Yes, master."

He took his boot away from her breast and placed it between her legs, taking her hands, pulling her to her knees, pressing her face against the worn denim of his jeans. "Suck me," he said, undoing the black leather belt and the brass buckle which was shaped like a cowboy's lasso. "Start with the balls. You like that, don't you, Miss Sheridan? You like the sweat and the crud, don't you? You're just a piece of shit, aren't you?" He took her head between his hands and fucked her as hard as he could in the mouth, fucked her until he came and held himself against her until she swallowed it all, until she stopped choking. And then he pulled himself out of her and slapped her, leaving red welts across her cheeks.

"Go to the bathroom and get down on your knees in the shower, facing the wall. I'll be right there."

"Hey," she said, and he could tell she was scared. "Maybe . . ."

He slapped her again, this time with his closed fist along the side of her head. "We're going all the way tonight. Too late for maybe. Get into the bathroom." She went to the bathroom. He crossed the foyer and pulled the phone cord out of the wall and then he picked up his nylon duffel bag and followed her.

"Don't turn around," he told her as he took off his leather jacket and hung it on the hook where her robe was. "Trust me." She was kneeling on the white tile shower floor, facing the white tile wall, as if she were about to pray.

She could sense him standing over her and then, suddenly, her eyes were blindfolded. "Hey," she said.

"Hey is for horses," he said, taking her arms, slipping something cold around them, something that embraced her chest but left her breasts curiously free. "Hey," she said again and this time he didn't answer but slipped something down around her head, also cold and binding, like a ski mask only without an opening for the mouth because she found she couldn't speak.

And then she was lying full length on the tile and he was pulling something cold and hard that hurt her skin up over her legs.

"Now stand up, Miss Sheridan," he said, binding her hands behind her, pulling her up so she faced the full wall of mirror, pulling the blindfold out from the steel mask.

She tried to scream but she couldn't. She moved as far from the mirror as she could, back up against the tile wall of that cocoon of a shower stall. She looked like a girl she had once seen in an underground film, a "snuff" flick, in which the girl was dismembered by the two men raping her.

The steel mask had cutouts for the eyes but otherwise was of solid construction. The steel vest had round cutouts so that her breasts were pushed up and out from her body and seemed like disembodied, Magritte sort of breasts, suspended without support. The girdle had one cutout and that was between her legs.

He was smiling at her. He didn't take his eyes from her as

he dropped his trousers to his knees. He was erect again. She could smell his ripe animal scent as he came to her and pushed himself into her and rode in and out of her in a hard, steady gesture, like a man riding a horse.

When he came, he rested his head on the wall behind her for a moment.

"That was just the beginning," he said, pulling himself out of her, standing back. Suddenly she started to hobble across the tiled floor, to escape. He caught her by the hair and pulled her back into the shower stall, punching her in the stomach, in the space left between the girdle and the bra. She fell and he kicked her in the face, the tip of his boot smashing against the mask and the mask pushing in so that she felt her nose break with a sharp crack, like a twig being broken in water.

When she opened her eyes, he had taken off his shirt. He helped her back into a kneeling position. She could see the strained muscles of his chest and his neck but she tried not to look at his face. His torso was covered with a fine film of sweat, as if he had been oiled for the sun.

He took a long black knife from his back pocket. It had a button on it which he pressed, and the blade flicked out. He knelt down in front of her, forcing her to look up at him.

His eyes were big and of no particular color. She could see her own reflection in them. She could see her father in him. She wanted to beg him to stop. She wanted to beg him to leave her, to not do what he was going to do.

He opened the fly of his jeans and forced her head down to see that he was erect again. Still holding her head down, he forced her to watch as he slipped the knife into the slit in the metal girdle and began to twist it.

He pushed her head back up against the wall so he could see the fear, the exquisite pain and terror in her eyes. It was the only time she had ever seen him smile.

Later, after he was finished, he washed himself and his knife in the shower. Then he took his nylon bag and his leather jacket and walked through the apartment, thinking that he must leave. He found the service door but stopped, remembering.

He went back into the bathroom. Dinah Sheridan lay in a bloody, crumpled heap by the far wall. He wondered if she were still alive as he bent over her and decided it didn't matter, to her or to him.

He removed the gold chain and the gold key from her neck with some trouble, washed it under the tap, and placed it around his own neck.

Then he made his way down the service stairs and out onto Fifty-eighth Street without anyone seeing him. He walked to Broadway, got into a big Checker taxi—he liked Checkers best because they were so roomy—and told the driver to take him down to Twenty-third Street.

He was going to need his rest, he told himself. He had to go to work. He paid the driver and went up to his room where he lay down on the carefully made bed and fell asleep, fingering Dinah Sheridan's gold key.

BOOK 5

FRIDAY

Chapter One

DUKE GREENE woke up suddenly and, as usual with him, was totally clearheaded, ready to start the day. Actually that was before the drugs. Since the drugs, the shots, the little white, yellow, and blue pills, he usually woke up groggy, not knowing who he was or where he was.

But this morning, this fiftieth-anniversary morning, he was as he had once been. Alert. He gently pushed the sleeping SayDee to her side of the mammoth bed, folded his hands, placed them on his stomach, and waited for the pain.

When it didn't come, when he realized that it wasn't coming, that today he would not have to resort to the mind-clouding pills, he offered up a small prayer to the god he didn't believe in.

"Everyone believes in God on their deathbed," Cecil had once told him.

Well I don't, he decided. Oh, perhaps a little more than usual but not so anyone could tell.

He got out of bed as quietly as he could and—surprise—managed to put on his dressing gown without any help from SayDee or Robert. He found Hector waiting outside his door, ssshed him, and conspiratorially, the two of them walked down the long corridor which led to the drawing room.

He sat on the red leather sofa that flanked the baronial fireplace and surveyed the room in the dawning light with the same pleasure he had felt when Elsie de Wolfe, Lady Mendl, designed it for him in 1938, when he and Cecil were first starting to make real money.

"It's fit for a duke," Elsie had declared, surveying the twenty-five-foot-high ceiling, the huge leaded-paned glass windows, the fireplace which demanded and received two cords of wood each winter.

"I am pleased, Duke," she had announced when she had finished, when the upholsterers and the painters and the carpenters and the mirror men had finally left. "I hope you are."

She had never sent him a bill for her services. She and her husband, Sir Charles, had always gotten the best table.

He fingered the stack of thick white envelopes Robert had placed on the table at the side of the sofa. Everyone was in town—from Lynda Bird Robb to the Ali Kahn—and they all wanted to see him.

He had, finally, agreed with SayDee and the damned doctors that he would see no one, that he would save himself for the evening, for the great open house he and Lawrence and Nick and Maurice Gotlib had planned to celebrate a half century of Duke's 44 Club.

He stood up and looked at the rows of leather-bound books that filled the floor-to-ceiling bookcases. He hadn't been much of a reader, he had to admit. He had been too busy living. He wondered if anyone, besides Cecil, had ever read any of those books. He smiled when he thought of Cecil and Phebe's town house next door. It had always looked as if it were inhabited by people suffering from genteel poverty, by a family just able to keep up appearances. This, long after Cecil had become a multimillionaire.

"Gentile bad taste," Cecil had said when Duke asked him why he didn't "fix up the joint." "It's endemic in my family." After they had all become respectable, after Prohibition had been repealed, Cecil liked to escape from Phebe's concerned young matrons' committee parties and camp out in the drawing room over 44, finding pleasure in what he called "the Dook's library."

He wondered if Cecil, had he been given the time, would

have gone through this intense period of remembering just before his death. He decided he was glad that he knew he was going to die, that they hadn't withheld the information from him in some excess of sensitivity and sentimentality. It was important for him to have the time to remember, to sum up, and yes, to make certain amends. There was one amend, if that was the word for it, that as painful as it might be, he felt he was going to have to make.

And suddenly, sitting there in his drawing room at an hour when once he was just preparing to go to sleep, he was aware that he wasn't frightened anymore. He felt so liberated. Death held only mystery for him now, a mystery which, he decided, he wanted to explore.

He looked at the clock above the mantel—an ornate whimsical gilt boat of a clock—and wondered if it were too early to call. He thought of Irene, who had insisted on telephoning people at all hours of the day and night, in that aristocratic way of hers. "Suppose I die," she had said, "and don't have the opportunity to say what I want to say? Better they suffer a little middle-of-the-night discomfit than lifelong curiosity."

He reached for the white telephone. If he was no longer afraid of death, he could no longer be afraid of truth. It was time—it was way past time—for him to face this particular truth.

Nick sounded sleepy and anxious at the same time. He wanted to know if Duke was all right. Duke reassured him and Nick said yes, he would be right over, that no, it was perfectly all right.

He began to stand up, to go to the photographs. There was one of Garbo and that fraudulent dietician of hers he wanted to see close up. But the pain, deep in his being, flared up. He let himself back down onto the sofa and lay still for a moment, hoping it would subside. Miraculously it did, though it didn't altogether go away which, in its own way, was comforting. He had lived with pain for so long, it would be more frightening than not to find it had suddenly abandoned him.

He closed his eyes. He never thought that he would die of cancer. He had hoped that he would meet his maker in a fast car with a fast woman in an exotic locale. Isadora, a Silver Phantom, the Grand Corniche.

That was his trouble, he knew. He was a romantic. "Only

a romantic could live in a room like this for all that your Lady Mendl did to disguise it,'' Irene had said. She had so emphatically not been a romantic. She was a realist, a pragmatist, a survivor.

Unlike their son. Peter seemed to have inherited the worst of their traits. He had Duke's romanticism but he applied it, pragmatically, to his own not altogether unrealistic cause. It made Peter ruthless. Duke didn't like his son; he admitted it to himself. But there was an atavistic strain of love he felt for Peter he couldn't deny. He wanted him to win more than he wanted him to lose and he hoped he got his knighthood, that his theater was a success, that he found he could like life.

At the same time he was still fascinated with Irene, even now, long after the acrimony and the alimony.

''What will she think of my death?'' he asked aloud. ''What will her immediate reaction be? Tears? Perhaps a few. Certainly nothing like a full-scale, sobbing breakdown. She's too concerned about her skin and the whiteness of her eyes. Gray eyes. The sort that see right through things.''

She had been able to see through everything but him. I have the singular distinction of being Irene's only mistake. But what a mistake. For an earl's daughter to marry an American Jew boy in the restaurant game! A great mistake.

''Mama,'' he called out, conjuring up a vision of that diminutive, durable lady. ''Look at me, Ma. I married an earl's daughter. So what do you think of that?''

''What do I think?'' he could hear his mother say in her thickly accented English. ''It's like Menasha Skulnik marrying Queen Mary. That and a nickel could get you on the subway.''

Oddly enough, he thought, looking up at the carved coat of arms Elsie Mendl had been so against (''It looks as if you raided Metro's prop department.''), Irene and his mother had been very much alike. No-nonsense ladies.

The others had been different, full of nonsense and pretense and what the movie posters used to promise as soul-searing adventure.

We've all had our adventures, he thought as Nick suddenly appeared above him. ''Duke, you all right?'' He had let himself in. In the early morning light, with his tousled black hair and that absurdly earnest expression of concern on his handsome, manly face, Duke felt a nearly overwhelming love for Nick Reo.

"How you doing?" Nick asked, relieved to see Duke open his eyes, sit up.

"I'm perfect. You?"

"Poifect," Nick said, smiling, sitting opposite him.

"No, sit here, next to me. I want to tell you something and I don't want you to be too far away when I do." Nick moved to the seat next to Duke. "First, as always, business. What do you hear from Blue Bowen?"

"He told me it looks good," Nick lied. "I'll know a lot more today."

"Well, that's something." He put his white, thin hand on Nick's big tan one. "You know something, Nicky?" he said and looked away, "I'm a terrible coward."

"Come on. I've seen you walk straight into more hot situations . . . remember when Murray Fein wanted his 'percentage' and you told him what he could do with his percentage right in front of . . ."

"I was never a physical coward, Nick. I was a social one. I cared what people thought. I cared what Society thought."

"SayDee isn't exactly a delicate blue blood."

"I came to her late in life and I never married her. One of my regrets. I didn't think she was good enough to carry the Greene name." He paused and took a breath.

"You okay? You want me to call SayDee or Robert?"

"No. I'm fine. I'm just breathing. All I want you to do is sit still for a moment. I've got something to say. About the hardest thing I've ever had to say." He took another deep breath.

"There was another woman I never married and should have, Nick. I got involved with her immediately after Irene and I were divorced.

"I was lonesome and a little scared that I might wind up with another Irene, or even worse, someone like my first wife, Laura, so I was watching myself carefully, keeping away from the society broads.

"There was this soft-touch hatcheck girl working for us at the time. She was just eighteen and this was her first job and she had that black hair that turns almost blue in certain lights. She was funny, always ready with a snappy line and seemed a lot more hip than she was. She even had a little reputation, so one night I asked her upstairs.

"It turned out I was her first man, that the snappy one liners were an act, her reputation undeserved."

"So SayDee wasn't your first hatcheck girl," Nick said, looking at Duke who was finding it hard to look at him. "Listen, Duke, you don't have to . . ."

"Yeah, I do. Let me go on, Nick. So when this eighteen-year-old girl found out she was pregnant, I told her I'd fix her up. But she nixed that. She didn't want an abortion and I didn't want another bride. We were at quite a little impasse, as Cecil called it in that dry was of his.

"She wanted a baby. A bambino. She wanted a husband. Cecil knew, somehow—he knew everything, that guy—that Victor Reo liked her. More than liked her.

"Victor had been a bachelor for longer than anyone could remember, visiting Polly's place two or three times a week to take care of his needs. But he was forty and he was tired of Polly's perfect girls and Cecil had seen the way he eyed Rose, the courteous, too gentle way he looked after her.

"So one night Cecil and I cornered Victor and asked him if he would marry little Rose. He looked at us as if he hated us when we said there would be something in it for him.

"When she died, giving birth to you, I wanted you, Nick. I swear it. Victor told me to go fuck myself. That you were his son, goddamn it, and he was going to bring you up because he knew I'd be a lousy father and he could already see which way Peter was going.

"The picture of that clumsy, oversized bastard in that house he bought on the wrong side of Forty-fourth Street diapering you is one I treasure more than any of the photographs I ever had taken. Talk about tough. Victor once took on four of the boys and walked away without a scratch on him. But when it came to Rose, and when it came to you, Nick, he was so goddamned gentle."

There were tears in Duke's eyes as he turned to look at Nick, as he reached out for him. "He made a much better father than I ever would have, Nick."

"So what do you want from me, Duke?" Nick said, pushing the older man's hand away, standing up.

"Forgiveness."

"You always want everything, Duke. It's the last reel, father confesses paternity, royal bastard takes father in arms and comforts him. Not likely, Duke."

Nick's face had gone a dead white. He went to the door and then he turned. "You know, you're right, though, Duke. Victor Reo *was* a much better father than you ever could have been. He could give. All you could do was serve.

"The four hundred. *Tout Paris* and *tout* New York. The blue bloods. Any pimp or whore who got their picture in the paper, any Astor who adored life with a pinch of spice.

"For Victor, 44 was a career, a job he was dedicated to. For Cecil it was a rich man's hobby, an avocation, fun. For you, Duke, it's been everything: marriage, family, life. I hope, I guess, it's been worth it. Happy anniversary, Duke."

"Nick," Duke called out. "Forgive me. I want you to call me 'father.' "

"I don't know what there is to forgive, Duke? You did what you had to do, right? But I tell you this: I'll never call you anything but Duke. Victor Reo was my father."

He watched Nick close the door and wondered which of the two pains attacking him was more intense: the cancer in his gut or the one lodged in his consciousness.

Chapter Two

"ARE YOU ILL?" Lawrence asked as Nick came out of the elevator into the Club Room.

"No. Are you?"

The staff had worked late the night before, taking the tables out of the Club Room, preparing for the fiftieth anniversary.

"There are two men in your office," Lawrence said, taking Georgio by the arm, pointing to a chair sitting by itself in the far corner. "Get that upstairs, will you?"

Georgio complied as Nick asked where the television crew was. "I thought Dinah was going to be here this morning, chalking up the carpet, making marks on the marble floor."

"You'd better go into your office, Nick. And I think I'd better come with you. You're not looking yourself."

"I'm not myself," Nick said, leading the way. "Duke just told me I was someone else."

"I adore it when you're being cryptic, Nick, but I think you'd better stow the ironic chitchat for a while. Bad news awaits."

Buddy Samson, the television executive, was standing by the window in the office, staring at the building three feet away, looking lean and hungry for a fat man. A man in his forties with blond-white hair and the kind of hat Nick always envisioned Raymond Chandler wearing was sitting in the visitor's chair.

"Hey, Nick," Buddy Samson said, turning around as Nick and Lawrence came into the room.

Nick nodded but didn't say anything. "Nick," Buddy Samson went on, "this is Bob Walker." Bob Walker removed his hat, made a stab at a smile and didn't say anything.

"Don't worry, Nick, about the special. We still got the tape portion scheduled. Naturally," Buddy Samson said with a sickly grin, "we had to cancel the live."

"Why?"

"Dinah Sheridan was killed last night," Bob Walker said, standing up, taking control. He removed a set of photographs from a manila envelope, handing them to Nick. They were glossy and black and white but still, Nick had to turn away after he looked at them. Though he hadn't liked Dinah Sheridan, he felt devastated; angry and sad at the same time.

Lawrence, who had been looking over his shoulder, made a sound and then left the room quickly, without excusing himself.

Nick handed the photos back to Bob Walker. "Are these supposed to shock me into making a full confession?"

"You're not a suspect," Bob Walker said, though it didn't come out reassuring; not the way he said it. "But it's fairly common knowledge that the late Miss Sheridan was going to do a number on Duke's 44 on national hook-up and that's not the worst reason I ever heard for killing someone.

"No," he said, holding up a big blond hand, "let me finish. I'm not saying it's you or your fat friend who ran out to vomit. But it could be. It could be someone involved with 44, someone who heard she was going to do the dirty on the food or the sanitary conditions or whatever food critics find to criticize. It could be someone from 44 who went up to her apartment with a knife and an incurable psychosis. I don't know. What I do know is that the only item removed from her person or her place of residence was a gold key, the one which fits the lock of this particular restaurant. Her secretary said it had belonged to her father.

"What I want to know is what's going to happen at tonight's um, celebration, when the guests turn up. Are they going to have to produce a gold key?"

"That's the general idea," Nick said. "But obviously

people are going to show up who don't need to show a key, special friends of the house."

"Yeah?"

"And then they're going to be those who lost their keys and those who never got one but supposed or wished they had. We're going to let them all in."

Bob Walker looked at Nick for a moment, as if he were weighing his chances in a fight with him. Nick looked back without blinking. He had dealt with the police before and he wasn't intimidated. "Would it be possible," Bob Walker said after a moment, "to have someone at the door checking the keys against a master list so that if number seven does turn up, we can make a very quiet, discreet arrest?"

"It might be possible," Nick allowed. "Who would be doing the checking?"

"Me," Bob Walker said, smiling a full smile for the first time in their encounter. "I'll put on a tuxedo so I won't stick out too much."

"Just your run-of-the-mill sore thumb," Nick said.

"I'll see you at seven," Bob Walker told him, starting to leave.

"Listen, Walker," Nick said, pointing to the envelope. "Nobody did *that* to crash this party."

"Whoever did *that* didn't need a reason," Bob Walker said, leaving.

"He asked me to introduce him," Buddy Samson said after the door had closed. "Sorry to involve 44 with this but he insisted . . ." Nick let him talk on as he studied a photograph of Victor Reo that was on his desk.

"I look like him," Nick said after Buddy Samson had left. "Goddamn it, I look like him." He wondered if Duke were lying, if Duke were having delusions of parenthood. But without looking at any photographs of Duke, he knew that Duke hadn't lied, that Duke was his father.

"Jesus," Nick said, slamming his hand down against the old wooden desk. "Jesus." He put his arms down on the surface of the desk and his head in his arms and then he let himself cry. He cried for Dinah Sheridan and he cried for Victor Reo and he cried for the mother he hadn't known and he cried for Duke because Nick finally realized that so much of that man's strength stemmed from weakness. And he cried for himself because a part of him had always known that as loving as Victor Reo had been, he had always played a part, a role based on movies and tradition: the stern but kindly father. While the Duke, having engaged in his own version of *droit du seigneur*, had been the generous family friend, allowing little Nick to eat at his table once a month . . .

The door to his office opened and he looked up. Brette was standing there. Even through the hurt and the pain, he was aware of her perfume, of that expensive gardenia scent.

"I just heard about Dinah," she said, walking across the room, taking Buddy Samson's place at the window.

"I'm not thinking about her now," Nick said. "I can't afford to. I'm putting it away, filing Dinah's death for future feeling."

"I can't stop thinking about it," Brette said. "All of the stock phrases seem to keep running through my mind."

"Which one seems most appropriate?" Nick asked, and she saw that he was too pale for the objective, removed attitude he was taking.

"The waste. 'What a waste.' I liked her but I didn't really know her well. Occasionally, when we were little girls, her father would bring her to New York. We'd all sit at the best table: Cecil, Phebe, Duke, Dinah, her father, myself. I was always dressed in something plain from Best and Company. Dinah was always outfitted in gorgeously expensive frocks that looked as if they had been whipped up by Don Loper.

"God, when I think of what she must have gone through." She shuddered. Nick looked up at her and thought about putting his arms around her.

She came to him first, putting her arms around his shoulder, kissing his cheek, making him feel young and small and not like the big, tough Nick Reo he had been a little while before.

"He told me," Brette said. "Duke told me."

"He should have taken a page in *Variety*." He moved to the far side of the desk, facing her.

"He asked me to plead with you, Nick."

"Duke is usually adept at chosing the right emissaries. But maybe he's used you once too often. First he had you schlep down to St. Mark's Place to save me from 'hopeless drug addiction.' Now he wants you to help me see the light, accept my repentant father, be a good boy."

"Nick, Duke is dying. Nick, he's . . ."

"Give me some time, for Christ's sake. A lady I knew intimately was just found all sliced up and a man I thought I knew intimately just told me he's my father. Let it sink in."

He put his hands in his pockets and tried to smile at her. "All my life I've been so grateful to that bastard for patting me on the head on odd Thursdays, for slipping me a buck here, a few dollars there. All my life I've idolized the royal duke for allowing me to stand on the edge of his circle—the outer edge—and letting me be witness to the glories of his magical mystery kingdom.

"I jumped at the chance to take Victor's place, to be Duke Greene's palace steward. Man, this guy's doing me the kind of favor I can never repay, I thought to myself. You got to remember, Brette, that despite you and Silver's, I was all strung out for a long time on Nam and drugs and then Victor's stroke. Not to mention your marriage.

"But the Duke, he doesn't forget his loyal soldiers. He paid for my rehabilitation. He sat me down and made me see that it was only right that you married Peter."

"He saved your life, Nick. He gave you . . ."

"Fuck that shit," Nick shouted at her. "He's my goddamned father. Who the hell else should save my life? And now, when he's playing his deathbed scene, he tells me—just out of the blue—that I'm his bastard, his royal bastard. He lets me know, when it's too goddamned late, that all my life I've been cut off from what I deserve and want. Even now I'm supposed to bite the bullet, to go out and scrounge to keep the empire going, the flag of 44 flying."

"Nick, he's given you a lot."

"He hasn't given me that much. Not enough so that he could take Victor away from me. Duke's dying, his conscience is now clear. It's me who has to live with the fact that my father didn't want me until it didn't matter any more. Not such an easy fact to live with, Brette."

"I know, Nicky," she said, and she walked around the desk and put her silk-covered arms around him, pulling his head next to hers. "He wanted you every minute," she said.

"Every second. That was his hell, Nick." She held him as tightly as she could. "He loves you, Nick."

They stood that way for several moments until Nick's secretary buzzed through that Lawrence wanted to talk to him. "Tell him I'll get back to him in a minute," Nick said. He looked at Brette who had moved to the door. "If you ever want to divorce your husband, Mrs. Stewart-Greene, I won't be corespondent but I'll be waiting for you."

"I know that, Nick," she said. She opened the door. "Go see Duke, Nick."

"Not now. I've got to call a man about a two-million-dollar loan."

"Please, Nick. You'll be sorry if . . ."

"I'm already sorry, Brette."

He called Blue Bowen but couldn't get through, and then he wandered out into the Club Room. They had removed the tables and the stools from around the bar so that there would be room to stand. Extra tables had been set up in the main dining room and upstairs but there was to be no regular seating. Tonight everyone was special. The buffet featuring 44's hot chili was upstairs and waiters would circulate carrying hors d'oeuvres, but it wasn't to be a full-scale dinner party. More of a club cocktail party in the Prohibition spirit in which the club had been founded.

Nick looked up once again at the grinning portrait of Duke in his prime, Duke in his white tie and tails, Duke looking ineffably elegant and a little rough at the same time. He remembered a remark Valida Rand once made when she and Bette Davis were comparing Hollywood and New York men.

"Astaire had class," Bette Davis had said in her final-judgment voice.

"Yes," Valida had added, "but Duke had sex."

Too much sex, Nick thought as he moved into the main dining room. He couldn't remember the last time he had seen 44 empty during lunch hour. It wasn't exactly empty. Florists were decorating tables, cleaning men were removing the spots from the soft gray carpet, the electrician was playing with newly installed rheostats. But the regular staff, having worked late the night before, was off and the usual noise from the kitchen was limited to Maurice Gotlib swearing in French at his much maligned chief sous chef.

Nick sat down at the best table. He had lied to Brette, implying that he would be busy all day. He had nothing to do but wait for Blue Bowen's phone call. Nick had no doubts that it would come. Blue Bowen might equivocate but he never told an outright lie. Nick wondered if there was any chance he might come through and wondered how much he really cared.

"I care," he said aloud, not being able to fool himself. "I love this place quite apart from the question of who my father was or wasn't." He loved the noise when it was filled with people and he loved it now, with its almost eerie quiet, with its ghosts of famous people haunting the Club Room walls with their photographs.

Most of all he loved the expensive restaurant smell of butter and rich women's perfumes and sporting men's cigars.

"I thought you never sat at the best table," Lawrence said, coming from the kitchen, mopping his high domed forehead with a silk handkerchief. "Wasn't that display particularly unnecessary? Dear Lord, that poor young woman. Why on earth do you suppose they showed us those pictures. Every time I let myself think of that last one—in color, yet—I get *mal de mer*."

"What's Georgio doing here?" Nick asked, seeing the best table's busboy hold the ladder for a man intent on cleaning the domed light fixtures.

"He insisted on coming in. He had to leave early last night and he's feeling all guilty. The poor boy thinks he's found a home."

Nick stood up and grinned, looking at Lawrence look at Georgio, his muscles straining to hold the heavy ladder straight. "And a mother."

"You're not a nice man, Nick Reo," Lawrence shouted after him. "You can fool a great many people but you cannot fool me. You are not a nice man."

The Wall Street Journal was on his secretary's desk. She played the stock market with disastrous results. He picked it up. There was yet another article about Bowen Frères. "Some of the city's leading businessmen," it read, "are forming a coalition to give public support to the many fragmented concerns of Bowen Frères. Rumors in recent weeks have the keystone financial house moving in troubled circles, teetering on the brink of, if not bankruptcy, at least large-scale reorganization.

"David Rockefeller, chairman of Chase Manhattan Bank, is heading the drive to give investors renewed confidence in Bowen Frères' dynamic but sometimes elusive president, Blue Bowen. Others in the new supportive coalition include Richard R. Shinn, president and chief executive of the Metropolitan Life Insurance Company and William M. Ellinghaus, president of the American Telephone and Telegraph Company."

"Strong supports," Nick thought, deciding that Blue Bowen would manage to pull himself out of whatever he had gotten himself into this time, certainly with men like Rockefeller and Shinn backing him.

There was a knock on the door. It was SayDee in one of her flame-red day dresses which, for any other woman, would have been suitable only after midnight. She wore a huge hat and carried a white mink coat, but no makeup. The diamond, ruby, emerald pin and the pearls and the rings were all in their place, however. She looks, Nick thought, like a call girl from another era.

"You mind, Nick?"

"Come on in, SayDee."

She put one ample hip on the side of the desk and dropped the white leather gloves casually across her knee. "He wants to talk to you, Nick."

"You forgot your makeup, SayDee. Not that you need it."

"Ha, ha. The Duke insisted that I go for broke at the beauty salon. He told me this morning, after he spoke to you, that I looked one hundred and five and tonight was only a fiftieth anniversary. He said I'd better do something about it.

"He wanted to get rid of me, Nick. But Ronnie at Magador's couldn't take me until now so I was there when Peter arrived and I was standing in the hall when the Duke talked to him. He tried to get Peter to give up 44, Nick. He offered him whatever he could. As Peter pointed out, Duke doesn't have much to bargain with. I saw Peter when he left. He had that vindictive pussy smile on his face. I bet he always wears it when he beats up on the old and the helpless." She stood up, put on the mink coat and the white leather gloves. "I'd better move my little feet or Ronnie will give me the punk rock look he keeps threatening. Can you picture me with a blue crew cut, Nick?''

''Your true beauty would still come shining through.''

''Yeah.'' She opened the door. ''Talk to him, Nick.''

''I will, SayDee. Promise.''

Duke and his ladies, he thought. He stood up and tried not to look at the telephone. I feel like a spinster on her last date, he thought, and then he said what-the-hell, I am a spinster on her last date, and picked up the telephone and dialed Blue's private number.

A woman with a low, slightly hysterical European voice answered after half a dozen rings. ''Who?'' she asked and he knew that she had either been crying or was about to.

''Nick Reo for Blue Bowen.''

She made a sound that was a combination sob and laugh. ''Nick Reo for Blue Bowen, yes? I have to tell you this, Mr. Nick Reo. There is no more Blue Bowen. There is no more money and there is no more Bowen Frères. Bowen Frères and Blue Bowen just fell out of a window on the fifty-second floor. They took a dive, is that how you say it?''

Nick thought of the neat, self-contained, brilliant Blue Bowen as he had appeared with the giants of international finance at his Wednesday luncheons at 44 and then he thought of all the people who had invested with Blue Bowen and then he remembered to hang up the receiver.

He had put off talking to Duke until he was able to reassure him that there would be a 44, that Blue Bowen had come through after all. Nick had always felt that he would.

Now, there didn't seem all that much to say to Duke.

And though he wasn't superstitious, he didn't like the fact that two people he knew had died that day.

Chapter Three

IGOR STRAUSS moved in and out of the rooms of the cavernous apartment in the Carnegie Hall studios he and Marquita had shared since their marriage in 1947.

There was a wrought-iron staircase which led to a second story where their bedrooms were located and from which Marquita could make a lovely, indeed memorable entrance. Other women found the steps difficult to negotiate which was why Marquita often asked them to do so.

The rooms, which had once had creamy white walls and gold-leaf moldings, now showed their age, the plaster peeling, the gold leaf tarnished a dark and uninviting green. The producers of the film *Rosemary's Baby* had made inquiries as to the possibility of filming in the Igor Strauss apartment. They received no reply and were forced to take their cameras elsewhere.

"It is a little spooky," Igor had said, privately, at the time.

"It is our home," Marquita told him, ending the discussion.

Most of their furniture had long since disappeared. The carved mahagony sideboards; the Biedermeyer clock; the laquered Chinese opium bed; Marie of Rumania's bleached and painted writing desk had finally been sent to Parke-Bernet's auction house. The few odds and ends of furniture, eloquent witnesses to their life together ("the springs in the sofa creak fearfully," Igor informed Marquita at least once a week) had been packed and shipped.

The new tenants were in the record business. They could afford the twenty-six hundred dollars per month the management would be charging once the difficult Strausses were finally out.

And on this Friday, October 31, that was only a matter of hours.

Igor was relieved, now that the worst had come. And the new tenants, young people in designer jeans and quilted, furred vests, had infested their lives for months, coming into their home-to-be with bevies of decorators and interior designers and wallpaper hangers, with yardsticks and measuring tapes and reams of paint and fabric samples.

Marquita, who had a brooding Russian temperament, grieved. "I have lived in this dump for too many years. I have become part of it."

The management and progress had finally won their two-decade fight to oust Igor and Marquita. In the morning they were off to southern California; "that strange, diseased place" was the way in which Marquita referred to it. Their son, an earnest, conventional man who treated his parents as if they were his children, was a successful orthopedic surgeon. He had found a small cottage for them in Laguna. He was prepared to pay for its upkeep, to give them a small allowance; to allow them to live in what Marquita described as "middle-class squalor."

Their son had refused to support them in any style in New York, much less the one Marquita insisted upon. He distrusted Manhattan nearly as much as they distrusted "L.A.," two initials into which Marquita managed to pack an enormous amount of venom. She tended to say "L.A." rather as if she were biting off the head of a poisonous viper.

"You've been very good to me," Marquita was saying to the sable coat on that final evening in their home. She put it over her shoulders, carefully. "Very dear and very kind and very good. This is our last appointment together, my dear, warm coat." She put her lined face, powdered dead white with rice cake makeup, against the faded furs, and closed her eyes, which were outlined in kohl.

"You should take your sables with you," Igor called out as

he struggled into his greatcoat, lined and collared in astrakhan, which had worn rather better than his wife's furs. "You never know what the climate in that place is going to be like. The last time we visited Albert, we nearly froze our *tuchashes* off."

Marquita laughed, avoiding the image in the blue-mirrored wall, holding the coat up to the light which came through its seams in several places. "She will not make the trip," Marquita said. "I wonder if I will."

Igor went to her and, reaching up a bit, put his arm awkwardly around her still graceful shoulder. "So what difference does it make? You'll no longer have the sables and I, I'll no longer have to have dollar shines on my shoes. We'll be wearing hippy clothes, sandals and scarves. We'll live a simple life. We have our health, no?"

"Igor," she said, putting her hand to his cheek. "You know how much I hate it when you start counting our blessings."

"And," he continued, undaunted, "we have each other. Remember that, Marquita: we still have each other." He kissed her with a passion that the years hadn't diminished.

"As always," she said, surfacing, "you are right, maestro. But you have forgotten one last blessing: we still have our final dinner at 44. Personally I intend to eat myself into a stupor. Let us hope that the buffet contains those luscious baked potatoes stuffed with caviar and that divine black and white bread . . ."

When Igor Strauss and Marquite arrived at 44, it was just seven o'clock and Lawrence was at the top of the steps, attempting to calm four minor tourists who were demanding to be allowed in.

"But you must call in advance, monsieur," Lawrence was saying in his least convincing French accent.

"I called a week ago," a plaid-coated man said indignantly.

"Oh, monsieur, next time you must call two weeks in advance."

Igor and Marquita walked around the irate tourists and entered 44. Igor showed his gold key, number fifty-one, to Little Mike and a white-haired man he didn't know as Marquita asked where the food was.

"Upstairs," Lawrence said, "Mrs. Strauss."

Marquita led Igor through the main dining room to the stairway which led to the J. J. Walker Room as Nick, in a dinner jacket, his hands in his pocket, came out of his office.

"Wouldn't you know they would be the first to arrive?" Lawrence said to him. "I hope she leaves some food for the others. Are you feeling better? I thought not. You look sleepy and dangerous, rather like George Raft, and that's always a sign you're upset about something."

"Make certain Igor and his bride get a bottle of Cristal."

"Ah, *oui, monsieur.*"

"It's their last night."

"What a pity," Lawrence said, telling Charles to send a bottle of Roederer's Cristal to whatever table the Strausses plopped themselves at. "It's certain not to be too far from the food." He turned to look speculatively at his friend and employer. "When is Duke coing down?"

"Around eleven. I'm going up to see him now."

As Nick entered the elevator, he noticed that half a dozen Whitneys and a score of Warburgs were flashing their gold keys at Little Mike and the detective, Bob Walker, who duely noted each number on his master list.

Behind them, looming over Nan Kempner's artfully coiffed head, he could see Hutch Boyd and a secret service man.

The doors closed as Nick wondered where Honey Boyd was, whether there was going to be enough food or too many people or too little staff. And then he decided he would let Lawrence worry about those possibilities. He had other cares.

SayDee had returned that afternoon from her session with Ronnie at Magador's to find Duke in his great bed, sitting up, looking both pensive and elated at the same time.

"Dukey," SayDee said, sitting on the edge of the bed, turning her white mink coat into a ball and throwing it on the baronial chair where Duke liked to sit when he was deciding what to wear each morning. That was when he was well, SayDee had to remind herself. That was when he wasn't dying.

"I like your hair," Duke said, though she knew he didn't. Ronnie had gone all elaborate on her, creating an enormous puff of pink clouds that seemed to have a life all their own, drifting above her head as if in a perpetual light windstorm. She had vowed to have it done simply but, as usual, she had been seduced by Ronnie's magic teasing comb.

"Dukey," she began again. "I've come to a decision."

"You're going to run off with Robert and Hector and set up light housekeeping in the south of France."

"Dukey, I don't want to go downstairs tonight. No, let me finish. Shut up for a minute, let me talk for once. Listen, this is your night, your highfalutin' friends, your anniversary. I don't belong down there with all those fancy people. I never did. I'm the hatcheck girl, remember? If you don't, they will. Duke, I'm going to feel uncomfortable down there. You'll be much happier without me, believe me, saying hello to all your old pals, rubbing noses with C. Z. Guest and Gloria Vanderbilt . . ."

"Now you shut up and listen to me, SayDee: you don't come down to the club with me tonight, you don't stay with me every minute, I'm not going down. I don't care if you're uncomfortable. *I* want to be comfortable and I won't be unless you're with me. Why, where would I be without my duchess? Now go get dressed. I want to have a cocktail in the drawing room before we go down. I've told Robert to set up the bar, to have a fire, to steal a tin of caviar from 44's kitchen. I want this night to be like old times, SayDee."

"You really do want me with you, Duke, don't you? Okay, you twisted my arm. I'll wear something quiet. Very little color. No jewelry to speak of. I'll tone down my makeup . . ."

When Nick found Duke in his drawing room, he was already dressed in his tails and white tie, his Lobb black patent-leather dancing shoes on his feet, Hector on the leather sofa, Robert standing at attention at the door in his gold-braided livery.

"Nicky," Duke said and for a moment Nick shared SayDee's hopes: there had been a miracle. The doctors had been wrong. The Duke had color in his face. He even seemed to have put on a few pounds. He was smiling and there wasn't a hint of pain or drugs in his eyes. As he stood up and walked across the room to embrace Nick, he didn't seem too many years older than the man in the portrait in the Club Room, than the man in all those photographs with all those *Time* magazine personalities. "Nicky," Duke said again.

The two men held onto one another for several moments, and then Nick took Duke's arm and led him to the sofa. "Get my young friend a drink," Duke ordered Robert. "Get my son a drink."

It was almost an hour later when SayDee came into the drawing room. She had been in her own dressing room, putting on and taking off the bright red peau de soie gown with the daring backline, the eight-inch heels, the diamond and jade clip, the emerald earrings. When the buzzer rang, signifying that someone had come up in the elevator, she started all over again, putting on the red dress, the high-heeled shoes, the clanking jewelry. "So I don't look like a rich lady," she said, surveying what several hours of fevered dressing had done to Ronnie's efforts, jabbing away at it for a second or two, giving up. "So I look like a rich hooker. If the Duke doesn't care, neither do I."

She stopped at the door to the drawing room, wonderfully pleased to hear Nick's voice. "I got the two million bucks," Nick was saying. "Blue came through."

"I knew that sonofabitch would," Duke said.

"Tomorrow we can make the arrangements," Nick said, standing up. "Now there'll be a Duke's 44 Club for a long time to come."

"You know something, Nicky," Duke said as SayDee came into the room. "That's nice but suddenly it doesn't seem to mean so much to me anymore. Not nearly as much as my love for you. I love you, Nick. I love you, kid."

"I love you, Duke." Nick bent over, kissed him, and left.

SayDee took his place next to Duke, putting her arm around his shoulder.

"What are you blubbering about?" Duke asked as she rummaged through her purse for a handkerchief.

"Same thing you are," she answered, finding a square of red rayon and dabbing at her eyes.

Duke laughed and kissed her. "What I love about you, SayDee, is that you never let me get away with being anything less than one hundred percent honest."

"And isn't it great," she said, putting the handkerchief

away, "that Blue came up with the dough-re-me? Now, Nick . . ."

"Now nothing. Blue Bowen jumped off One Chase Manhattan Plaza this afternoon, taking a lot of Wall Street reputations with him. Nick forgot we've got a little invention called television. Jim Jensen and the six o'clock news practically replayed the entire suicide.

"But if that kid wants to think he's protecting me, comforting me, let him. He's comforted me in more ways than anyone will ever know."

SayDee stood up. "You don't really care about 44 any more?"

Duke looked up, surprised. "You know, I don't think I do. I mean I care about what's been, but I'm not so interested in what it's going to be. I think from now on I'll let Nick be my gift to posterity."

"Oh, Duke."

"Now what're you crying about? And where you going?"

"I'm crying because you're such a *mensch* and I'm going to the bathroom to repair my war paint." She caught sight of herself in the mirror over the mantel. "My face looks like a melted cheese sandwich."

Duke watched her go. He thought of her and then of Nick and then he looked at the wall on which were hung the overflow of photographs from the Club Room. And, as always when he felt mellow and a little bittersweet, he thought of Cecil. And Phebe. He remembered the last time he had seen them.

It had been a sunny winter's day, early in February. Phebe hadn't wanted to go to Palm Springs but Cecil, who loathed the cold, had insisted.

"We're going to see all sorts of famous people, my dear," he had reassured her in the back of the limousine he had borrowed from one of her aunts. "Bob Hope and Charlie Farrel and Lord knows who else. Duke will be absolutely green with envy, won't you, Dukey?"

"Purple," Duke said, looking past Phebe's clean, perfect profile at his friend who was bundled up in a camel's hair polo coat.

Brette, in a navy blue coat with gold buttons and black

patent-leather Mary Jane shoes, sat on Duke's lap, perfectly content to peer out of the curtains which hid the windows at the rows of red brick apartment houses which lined Queens Boulevard.

Duke and Brette had volunteered to accompany her parents to the airport, to see them off on their first winter vacation without her. She was going to be a good girl. Aunt Helen was going to stay with her and Duke had promised to take as many meals with her as he could. Still she knew she would miss her mother.

She got off Duke's lap and got onto her mother's.

''You're going to mess Mommy's clothes,'' Duke had said.

''It doesn't matter, Duke,'' Phebe had told him, hugging her child. ''Can you imagine what I'm going to look like after I get off that plane?''

''Absolutely glorious,'' Cecil said. ''A sort of dream.''

''Cecil,'' Duke told him, ''you've got some mouthpiece.''

''I'm lucky, dear boy. I'm married to my inspiration. Look at her. She gets more beautiful every day. Look at Mummy, Brette. You lucky little rapscallion. Mummy is what you're going to look like when you grow up and take the world by storm.''

''Did you take the world by storm, Mommy?'' Brette wanted to know.

''No, I took your father by storm and that was quite enough. Let's stop talking about mummy and look at the scenery.''

''We'd need a good sharp scissors to get through the curtains your Aunt Iona has seen fit to drape the windows of this car in. You don't suppose she and Uncle Winslow do it in the back seat, do you, each Friday afternoon as they make their stately way up to Rhinebeck?''

''Cecil,'' Duke said, ''that woman's in her late seventies.''

''Duke,'' Cecil said, ''I hope very much that when we're in our late seventies, we'll all still be doing it.''

''Doing what?'' Brette wanted to know.

The car drove onto a private road which ended at the terminal building. A man in a TWA uniform was waiting for them. ''Everyone's on board,'' he said.

"Do you think I have time to make one phone call?" Cecil asked. "It won't take but a moment."

"Oh, Cecil," Phebe said.

"I forgot to tell Barbara Gendell about that new shipment from Inverness. You don't want Duke to pour anything less than 44 Scotch down his customers' gullets, do you? I'll be right back," he said, flashing his famous smile at the patient TWA purser, taking Brette's hand and running into the terminal.

The purser said something about telling the pilot and walked off, leaving Duke and Phebe alone on the tarmac. It was windy and cold but the sun was shining and there was a certain exhilaration they both felt, standing out there by themselves. Over the years they had spent very little time alone together. There had always been Cecil and later, Brette, and that one secret they had together.

For no reason she could think of, Phebe took off her glove and reached over and touched Duke's cheek.

"Your hand is cold," he said, taking it in his own.

"Warm heart," she answered.

"Phebe . . ." he began.

"Don't say it, Duke. Just hold my hand for a moment. And let me tell you something. I made the right decision, Duke. For everyone concerned. You do believe that, don't you, Duke?"

"Yes," he said, looking into her violet eyes. "Though I've never stopped wanting you. Not for a moment."

"And there have been times, mostly late at night, when I wondered what it might have been like if I hadn't married Cecil."

"Dear me," Cecil said, carrying Brette in his arms, "leave them alone for a split second and they're holding hands, making assignations. It's a good thing I'm taking her away or who knows what might not have happened." He deposited Brette in Duke's arms. "Now you take care of your uncle the Duke of Forty-fourth Street," Cecil said, hugging the both of them, kissing them on each of their cheeks. "Make sure he stays away from college boys when he's on a spree." He turned to go and then looked back. "I love you both."

Phebe didn't say anything. She kissed her daughter and then she kissed Duke and then she took Cecil's hand. The last Duke and Brette saw of them, they were running across the tarmac to the waiting plane, hand in hand. The TWA purser ran after them, like a nurse following high-spirited children.

"Are you crying, Duke?" Brette asked him as the plane took off and circled above them.

"Nope. It's the wind."

"Same here," said Brette, putting her arms around him, burying her face in his neck.

SayDee came back into the drawing room, her makeup repaired. "You dreaming again?" she asked Duke.

"A little." He smiled at her. "What time is it?"

She consulted the diamond and ruby cocktail watch nearly lost amidst the bracelets on her wrist. "Nearly nine o'clock. You want to go downstairs?"

"The Duke never makes his entrance before eleven."

"Pardon me, Your Majesty. What are we going to do for the next two hours? Want to play a little gin rummy?"

The Duke smiled at her again and then told Robert to get the cards.

Chapter Four

HONEY BOYD did not like going out, unescorted, in New York at night. I wasn't brought up that way, she told herself. What's more, she hadn't liked Hutch's telegram. I sure would like to know who that man thinks he is, ordering me around, she thought as she sat in the back of the taxi the Plaza's doorman had gotten for her. She had only pretended not to see the attention she was getting from the Texans in their polyester cowboy shirts standing in the lobby.

They probably think I'm a loose woman, dressed like this and all alone. Well, I am a loose woman, Honey thought, thinking of the night before, of Mr. Saiad and his incredible prowess. A little thrill went through her, and she resettled her body in its white sequinned gown—one she was certain Hutch was going to find fault with, if only for the price. She had bought it at Martha's on Park Avenue that afternoon, feeling she deserved a present. She couldn't wait to tell Hutch she had a job, and again she wondered why the heck he hadn't just met her at the hotel instead of forcing her to come to 44's anniversary party all by herself.

She felt in her purse for her key, found it, presented it to Little Mike as Lawrence said hello and a white-haired man made a check mark in his book.

"The senator is upstairs, Mrs. Boyd," Lawrence told her.

"Upstairs?"

"Yes, Mrs. Boyd. You'll find him at the last table but one. He asked me to request that you go straight there, without making any stops."

He treats me like a child, Honey thought, following one of the maître d's across the main dining room, resisting the temptation to say hellow to Tip O'Neil and Dolly Parton and a whole lot of other people she knew and liked.

There weren't too many people in the J. J. Walker Room despite the fact that a fourteen-foot-long table piled high with marvelous food had been set up there. It was dark at the far end of the room and it occurred to Honey, as she followed her escort, that she had never, in her life, been in the J. J. Walker Room and really it wasn't bad at all. In fact she rather liked it. Then she spotted Hutch, sitting by himself in a banquette at a half round table, a triple bourbon in front of him.

Despite his nearly sixty years, he looked big and strong, sort of like a cross between an American Indian and a bison, his leathery skin more tanned than usual, his brown hair combed back in the Victor Mature style he had worn since he had first become a congressman three decades before.

Seeing him looking so all alone, Honey felt a sudden surge of affection for him. Mr. Saiad, she thought, might know a lot of fancy tricks but Hutch was so solid, so dependable, so full of that quiet authority Honey adored. Mr. Saiad seemed very thin, in more ways than one, when compared to Hutch Boyd.

Hutch Boyd looked up and saw his wife. He didn't give her that crinkly sincere smile of his, the one that still turned on hundreds of thousands of voters in the home state where he hadn't lived in years. No, he looked very serious.

"Hello, Honey," he said.

"Hi, Hutch." She slid into the banquette right up against him and kissed his cheek. "I sure have missed you, Hutch," she said and she knew something was wrong but she couldn't quite decide what it was. "I sure didn't understand, though, why you didn't want to meet at the hotel, Hutch. Honestly I been to 44 almost every day this week and we could have come to the party after . . ."

He allowed her to talk while his stubby fingers undid a carefully done-up manila envelope. "And I know, Hutch, that this dress cost a little bit more than I was supposed to spend, but prices up here are simply outrageous and I know you wanted me to look nice . . ."

"Where's Pat Forman?"

"In the middle of the whole shebang Warren went and got sick and Pat felt she had to be in D.C. and of course I said I would go with her, but she insisted I stay. I should have gone with her. I've been so lonesome up here by myself, Hutch . . ."

His fingers pried open two cardboard rectangles and he looked at several glossy photographs. Honey leaned over to see them but he put them face down on the table.

"I understand you got yourself a little job, Honey," he said, not looking at his wife.

"Well, yes, sort of. I mean I know you won't like the idea. But I've decided to be my own person from now on, Hutch. I'm too old to still be treated like you and Ruth . . ."

"Honey, don't you want to know how I know?"

"I suppose you spoke to Pat Foreman."

"I don't talk to Pat Foreman any more, Honey."

"All right." She pushed her lower lip out just a little, letting him know she was displeased. "All right, then. How do you know?"

"I know because the man I was dealing with in Bahrain—he's a sheik, only they pronounce it shake over there—he got this special courier's package from New York. You know what was in it? A copy of your contract with Pan-Arabian Oil and a copy of your application to represent a foreign national company."

"I don't see what's wrong with that? I mean hundreds of . . ."

"Honey, you do know that I've been working on a separate non-OPEC oil agreement with Arab moderates for the last six months, don't you? That's why I was in Bahrain, talking to this sheik, this moderate, liberal sheik who has no axes to grind against Israel or the U.S. but who still doesn't altogether trust us that much. This sheik—pronounced shake—controls a lot of oil, Honey. Maybe enough to keep us independent for another five years, for as long as it takes to develop alternative sources of fuel.

"So you do understand, Honey, why my negotiations with this fellow have been very fragile, very tough, very important. Right, Honey?"

"Whatever you say, Hutch."

"He thought I was acting as a more-or-less disinterested but partisan American. Just for my country. Any hint of another involvement and that would smash all the long months of tedious, aggravating work. You still with me, Honey?"

"Yes, Hutch."

"Now's the time when we come to your friend, Mr. Saiad. He's no longer in New York, you know. He's no longer in this country. He's back in Libya or Syria or wherever they hatched that guy. Do you know who his employer is, Honey?"

"The Pan-Arab . . ."

"No, Honey. His employer is the Palestine Liberation Organization, the radical branch. That would be your employer, too. Now, Honey, how do you think my little sheik—pronounced shake—out there in Bahrain is going to feel when he finds my wife is working for the PLO? How do you think my constituency is going to feel about me when they find out you are working for the PLO?"

"Hutch! I had no idea. Why Pat Foreman . . ."

"Pat Foreman does whatever she's paid the most money to do."

"Well, I can deny it, can't I? I can say I was tricked."

Hutch looked at his fluffy, beautiful blond wife and shook his heavy head. He almost found it difficult to be angry with her. "They'd never believe you were that dumb, Honey. Not Ruth Tyor's daughter. Not Hutch Boyd's wife. When the story breaks—and that will probably be tomorrow—it's going to look as if you knew what you were doing and didn't care. It's going to look as if you were doing it for the money."

"But Hutch . . ."

"And then there's something that won't be printed but that can never be denied, Honey."

"What's that, Hutch?" She didn't know whether to be hurt or ashamed but she did know to be scared.

"The photographs."

He turned them over and fanned them across the table. She wanted to look away but she couldn't. There was one of Mr. Saiad entering her mouth. Her eyes were looking up with dazed joy, as if she were eating an enormous lollipop. There was another of him fucking her up the ass and there was one of Mr. Saiad on his back while Honey, her eyes closed for this one, her head held back in an ecstacy of sexual abandon, was sliding herself down onto his enormous erection. There had been someone watching, Honey realized. Above the mirror. Taking pictures.

"I was drugged," Honey heard herself say as if from far away, as if from inside a distant echo chamber.

The final picture, the one Hutch said the press would undoubtedly use, showed Honey and Mr. Saiad, fully dressed, their arms around one another, kissing like a honeymoon couple. It had been taken in the empty, carpeted apartment with the bed looming significantly in the background.

"I got one shot to save my seat in the Senate, Honey."

"I'll make a denial, Hutch. I'll tell them . . ."

"Oh, you sure will do that, Honey. Your mother's sitting in D.C. right now with her best speech writer at the typewriter, going over your denial.

"But that's not going to be enough, Honey."

"What are you going to have to do, Hutch?"

"Much as I hate it, I think you and I are going to have to get a divorce, Honey. Either that or I'm going to have to retire and I don't want to retire."

"I don't want a divorce," Honey said but Hutch had already stood up and so had the secret service man and she had no choice but to follow them down the stairs and then down another set of stairs into the kitchen where that woman, April Gold, was waiting.

"You were right, of course, Hutch," she said in her hard, northern voice. "The paparazzi are out there in full strength, waiting for you. At first I thought it was just the usual crowd celebrities always bring out, but all the networks have sent their heavy politico johnnies. We'd better go out this way."

They exited through the back door into an alley where a limousine was waiting. Honey got into the back with the secret service men. Hutch and April Gold got into the front with the chauffeur. They had business to discuss, Hutch said, patting Honey's shoulder as he closed the door after her.

And I never really got to the party, Honey Boyd thought as the limousine took a circuitous route to LaGuardia and the Lear jet that was waiting for them.

Chapter Five

IT WAS nearly ten o'clock when the two men in dark clothes stopped a little ways from the crowd that had gathered to watch celebrities enter 44.

"I do love Diana Ross," Father Heart said as that women went up the steps of 44. "Who's that with her?"

"Isabelle Huppert," Paul answered. "She's better known in France than here."

A Rolls-Royce filled with fashionable Europeans pulled up and Father Heart turned away. He was really only interested in the movie stars. "Do you want me to come in with you, my son?" he asked.

Paul was seeing his old teacher in a new light. The weakness he had made fun of as a youth now turned out to be a rigid modesty, an unwavering sense of purpose: to protect the sanctity of the priesthood and through the priesthood, the Church.

"No, Father," Paul said. "I think I can brave this one by myself."

"You mustn't be angry with me," the older priest said. "Or with them." The sun of the Italian coast had reddened Father Heart's pale skin. Paul could imagine the Irish-American priest with his wholesome, discontented smile trudging from house to house in Bernina, interviewing the pupils Paul had once taught, slowly searching, waiting, methodically plodding, until someone turned up, someone who had seen the young priest and the artist on the beach together.

"I'm not angry. Why should I be? I expect it will be very much the other way round."

"But you will be angry soon; you will be angry about the life they—we—caused you to live. You will regret it."

"Have you always known I was homosexual, Father?"

"Always. Though I thought the spirit of Our Savior had conquered it."

"As He conquered your homosexuality?"

"As He conquered mine." The older priest put his two hands on Paul's shoulders. "Is there any way I can convince you not to leave the Church, to come back this very moment and confess to me? You will not be a bishop, now, it is true, but the life of a simple priest . . ."

"There is no way, Father Heart."

"I love you, Paul. Our Savior loves you."

"And luckily," the younger man said, allowing himself a smile that made his face more relaxed and vulnerable, "so does Tony."

He turned and made his way through the crowd and up the steps that led to 44. Father Heart had been right. He was angry. He had trusted Father Heart and Father Heart had turned out to be one more Vatican spy, one more priest he couldn't trust.

Little Mike greeted him at the door and explained to the detective that Paul was a guest of Joan Hull's and directed him to the table in the main dining room where she and Cardinal Zoltan were sitting. It was not the best table, Paul noted. That was empty, a rope across its chairs.

He walked past a table filled with Rothschild women—Olympia in a half-black, half-white Yves Saint Laurent suit, Marie-Hélène and Liliane de Rothschild in dark Dior dresses—and found an unsmiling Joan Hull smoking cigarettes while a silent Cardinal Zoltan drank from a small liqueur glass.

"Already in mufti, Paul," Zoltan said, shifting his thin frame around in the chair, looking so flat as to be one-dimensional in his black cleric's suit. "Your new clothes fit you admirably but aren't you being just a trifle premature?"

"You've read the Vatican's report?" Paul asked, sitting down, directing the question to his aunt.

"I've heard the substance from someone who was privy to it," Cardinal Zoltan said. "Father Heart shall not go unrewarded for his, uhm, loyalty to the Church."

"What did you want him to do with that piece of news?" Joan Hull said to Zoltan, biting each word as if they were bullets and she were an automatic rifle. "He couldn't very well pretend he hadn't found anything. He had the local priest with him."

"He could have come to me first," Zoltan said.

Paul realized that once again, as they had done for so long, they were arguing about him as if he weren't there, as if he didn't have his own voice.

"That he," Zoltan was going on, "that sniveling little backwater schemer, should have been sent to investigate . . ."

"I wasn't going to wait for his report," Paul said, and Zoltan looked at him. "It came at a propitious time. I have written a letter to the archbishop . . ."

"My dear nephew," Joan Hull asked, rotating the end of her cigarette in the ashtray for some seconds after it was clearly out, sitting back, folding her arms across her chest in the way she had when something displeased her. "What exactly do you believe Father Heart's report says?"

"I would guess that it says that I am a practicing, unrepentent, unconfessed homosexual, engaged in a love affair with another man."

"You always did have a facility for hitting the nail on the head," she said, still not looking at him, still staring at a point somewhere beyond him. "Would you care to tell me if that is all true?"

"Every single word."

"I gather you are going to leave the priesthood. You have little choice. What are you going to do to earn your daily bread? You needn't imagine I would support you. The money you inherited from my father is in trust until I die and I intend to live a very long time. Will your lover, this man, support you?"

"I should like to teach."

"Teach?" And now she looked at him and he could see the

fury in her eyes and it scared him. "They're not going to let a self-confessed pederast teach, Paul."

"And I shall write, Aunt Joan," he said, not wanting her to see his fear. "I shall write, I think, on Church matters."

Joan Hull stood up, abruptly, put her thin, expensive coat around her shoulders, and looked down at her nephew. "I wonder what I've done," she asked, "to deserve this particular hell on earth." She brushed past the cardinal.

"If you're leaving," Zoltan called after her, "how shall I get home."

"Crawl," she said over her shoulder as she made her way out. "It will be good for your sins."

"Perhaps your aunt will get her just reward in heaven," Cardinal Zoltan said, allowing himself another glass of brandy and a defeated smile.

"You hate her very much, don't you?" Paul asked.

"I am ashamed to say that I do. She is my particular devil, one who has tempted me with false pride and even falser prizes. She has won, in her battles with me, at any rate." The cardinal stood up and put out his hand. "I wish you luck, Paul. I wish you happiness. And I beg for your forgiveness."

Cardinal Zoltan bowed his head and was gone.

After a moment Paul stood up and the table was immediately occupied by Betsy Bloomingdale and her husband, Alfred, and Princess Feryal, whose brother was the King of Jordan.

He made his way to the Club Room and up to the bar where Mickey asked him what he wanted and he said a beer. Then he felt a casual hand on his shoulder and he looked next to him to find a stocky, black-haired man who looked as if he might have trouble, on any ordinary day, getting past Little Mike, and said, "You'd better make that two beers."

"How'd you get in here?" Paul asked him.

"I told you, man," Tony said, strengthening his grip on Paul's shoulder, "I got the key." He opened his broad hand to reveal the gold key Nick had given to him some months before, one of the last issued. Paul put his hand on it.

"Now I do, too," Paul said.

At the last moment she had told the chauffeur to wait, that she had forgotten something. He offered to get whatever it was, but she said no, he wouldn't be able to find it.

As the elevator took her swiftly and silently to the penthouse suite UNITAS had given them in Olympic Towers, she wondered why it was that Peter had found the chauffeur "insufferable" and she had found him courteous, eager to please.

"Short evening," Peter said, looking up, putting down the manuscript of a play he wanted Olivier to star in.

"Peter, I came back because I hoped you'd reconsider."

"Ever noble, our Brette."

"Goddamn it, Peter, he's your father and he's dying and this is the most important night of his life, in this decade at any rate, and why, for once, can't you put aside the old shit and do something for him? Why, for once, can't you step out of character and play the devoted son?"

"Duke made me what I am today, dear heart. The truth of the matter is, I don't want to give him pleasure. The truth of the matter is, Brette, I fear and hate and loathe the bastard and will, long after he's dead. I didn't choose Duke for a father. The fact that you would have doesn't affect me in the least."

"Isn't it time you . . ."

"Isn't it time you left for the party? Believe me, he wouldn't thank you for dragging me, kicking and screaming, into 44. I'm the living symbol of the fact that the moment he's dead, Duke's 44 Club, as he knew and loved it, will have vanished up UNITAS's chimney." He picked up the leather-bound manuscript and the gold pencil. "I shan't wait up for you, love. There wouldn't be much point, would there?"

Brette Townsend Stewart-Greene had no difficulty in entering 44 by herself, manless. She allowed Lawrence to take her mandarin-style black mink coat, she paid a visit to Sophie in the ladies' room, she chatted with Dina Merrill and Cliff Robertson in the bar.

"Quite a party," she said to Nick, when she spotted him, standing alone next to the portrait of Duke, his hands in his pockets, his dark eyes half closed as protection against the smoke.

"Where's Peter?"

"He decided not to come."

"You're by yourself?"

"Yes. Peter felt he shouldn't be here tonight. Where's the Duke?"

"There's still a half hour or so until he's scheduled to make his entrance." He looked down into her face. "Brette, let's stop doing this to each other, okay?"

She searched his face. "I want you so badly, Nicky."

He bent down and kissed her on the lips. "You can have me in half a second, Brette. All you have to do is give up Peter and the flat and the limo and come live with me in Victor's house down the block. I want to wake up with you next to me every morning, Brette. Not just tomorrow morning. We've done our one-night stands. Now, as we used to say when we were kids, it's for keeps. Or it's nothing."

"Nicky," she said, putting her arms around him, putting her face next to his. "Nicky."

"I hate to interrupt," Lawrence said into Nick's free ear, "but Rose Kennedy with Ethel and her entourage have just stolled in and I think, to use understatement, that it might be politic if you greeted them. Or would you rather retire to the privacy of your office?"

Lawrence swept on and Nick let go of Brette. "Think about it," he said, going off to greet Mrs. Kennedy.

"I have thought about it," she said, but he was already lost in the crowd. She turned to go to the ladies' room, to cry in Sophie's lap, but Lord Cavendish was bearing down on her.

"My dear Brette, what a lovely surprise. Margaret and I decided, at the last moment, to come Stateside. One couldn't, in good concience, miss this celebration, could one? Come," he said, taking her arm. "You must say hello. Dickie Perkins is here with tons of people. We've cornered a table in the main dining room and someone's fetched us a few bottles of bubbly. It's just as if we never left London. It is pleasant to travel two thousand miles to another continent and still be among one's own, isn't it?" He steered her through the crowd, talking all of the time. "You know Duke and I were very tight during the war. We met at Burma House . . ."

She tried to catch sight of Nick but all she saw was his back as he helped Rose Kennedy into a chair at a table Georgio had just that moment finished clearing.

Countess Vera had decided on ermine because, after all, it

was a regal night and she was going to arrive at 44 with Princess Grace. But the princess had worn a cloth coat—albeit a cloth coat costing a great deal more than most fur coats—and made her feel vulgar and a little stale.

Grace, immediately upon entering 44, had gone to talk to Cary Grant and Audrey Hepburn and Bacall and the Hollywood set. Vera, feeling not terribly certain of herself, had gone to the ladies' room where she chatted with Brette Stewart-Greene for a few minutes and then, when Brette had left, had addressed the pinkish mirrors to reassure herself.

She had asked Sophie to get rid of the ermine, to park it in some private coatroom, wondering if the dark blue satin Balenciaga was too regal, too much a symbol of the poor girl who had clawed her way out of The Bronx, out of her father's drugstore.

She asked Sophie for an aspirin. This was exactly the sort of event that always made her feel more insecure. Yes, she had been accepted by Princess Grace and yes, she was invited to scores of New York and Palm Beach charity affairs, always one of the more publicized guests.

But she was rarely invited to the little dinners given beforehand, and never invited to the simple dinner parties for eight given by Mrs. Robert Wagner and Marietta Tree and Thomas Hoving. They were the people—old New York—that were never going to accept her. Not because she was Jewish or because she ran a business but because she pretended she was someone she was not and social pretense was the last bar New York, old New York, kept in place.

She swallowed the aspirin and the water, tipped Sophie, and went out into the Club Room, her stomach rumbling. There was always someone who managed to frighten her.

Barbara Lee Diamondsteen smiled hello but she didn't invite Vera to join her table and Sophia Loren and Mastroianni had just strolled in and were embracing Grace, and Vera never did have much interest in Italians or their movies.

She didn't quite know what to do with herself.

It was with relief that she saw Ivan at the bar. He had turned up too early but this once she would forgive him. "Darling," she said, and he looked up, scowling, getting off the barstool, allowing her to perch on it. She felt a little ridiculous in her gown on the barstool but at least she was off the floor. "You're a tiny bit early," she said, accepting a glass of champagne from Mickey. "Cheers." She clinked her glass against the shot glass full of vodka Ivan was holding.

He upended his and stood staring at her, scowling. "Are we going to get married or not?" he asked, much too loudly and the thought occured to her that he was drunk. "Yes or no, I want to know now. I am tired of these games, of this foolishness, of you coming at one hour and me coming at another and pretending, always pretending. What is your decision, your choice, Countess Vera?"

There was a noticeable silence around them. "If you lower your voice, Ivan, I will tell you." She was definitely frightened now. He was acting like a child, irrational, offering threats, an ultimatum. He was not above, she knew, a scene.

Brooke Astor chose that moment to say hello, to introduce her new foundation person, to ask if Countess Vera was interested in cohosting a charity ball for Odyssey House the following spring.

"Madam," Ivan said, and now Vera knew he was definitely drunk, "we are talking about a serious subject. You have interrupted. You continue to interrupt. Madam," he said to Brooke Astor of all people, "please go away. And take your 'foundation person'—whatever it is—with you."

Brooke Astor looked Ivan Kotuk up and down, from his rumpled shirt to his scuffed boots, nodded at Vera and sailed off, her foundation person in tow.

Now there was a profound silence about them, the sort of silence in a theater while the audience waits for the star's turn.

But Ivan had timing. He held out his shot glass for Mickey to fill it while everyone—including Vera—waited to see what he would do, what he would say next.

She had known, all along, that if she married Ivan, she would have to give up all the pretense of having been "accepted," that no one would accept Ivan. No one who counted. There might be more confidential chats with Princess Grace. *She* could hardly afford to be choosy. But New York, old New York, wouldn't even take her on sufferance as they had for the past two decades. Ivan would not be a hit at even such a plebian sort of money-maker as the April in Paris ball.

"Ivan," Vera said, wanting to sleep, to quietly curl up

under the barstool where no one would see her. "Please take me home now. We can discuss it in the car."

He moved very close to her and whispered in her ear, a gesture which caused the onlookers to lose a certain amount of interest. "Shit, Vera," he said and just for a moment, as his strong, young body touched hers, as his breath—never sweet but certainly manly and again, young—brushed her ear, she felt that incredibly potent attraction of his. Had they been alone, she would have put her arms around him and placed her face in his neck.

But they weren't alone. Everyone who had ever counted—in Vera's public life—was there.

"Shit, Vera," he whispered, a bit louder, in her ear. And then he pulled away and said, at the top of his voice, so that virtually everyone in the Club Room could hear him, so that Little Mike turned, his antennae up, sensing trouble, "when are we going to be married, Vera?"

"We are not going to be married, Ivan, dear," she returned, coolly, low, as if she were wooing a boardroom filled with recalcitrant stockholders. "I am prepared to keep you on as my lover," she whispered so that he had to draw near to hear her. "If you sober up this minute and be quiet. If you take me out of here, with as little fuss as possible. You will get an allowance. You will live in a style to which someday you will become accustomed. And when our love is over, as it surely must someday be, you will get a very generous stipend. Now that is my offer to you," she said, still whispering.

Ivan stood back and Little Mike and the crowd in the Club Room, reassured during Vera's low conversation, once again drew to attention. In the English tweed suit she had made him buy, he still managed to look like a member of the first wave of the Russian revolution: lean, mean, and irredeemably uncouth.

He slapped her across the face once and then twice again and not a person, not even Little Mike or Scotty or the detective at the door, moved. "You think you can buy me like a whore," Ivan shouted at her, and even in the main dining room there was silence. "You bought your husband and your title and your fake youth, yes. But you cannot buy me, Ivan Kotuk. You are an old woman," he shouted at the top of his voice so that not even Brooke Astor could pretend she hadn't heard. "An old Jewish peasant woman got up like a middle-aged tart. I leave you to your memories, to your past."

He lifted his hand as if to slap her once again, and before Scotty or Little Mike could get to him, a nice-looking man in a dinner jacket blocked the slap and punched Ivan, with a satisfying, resounding sound, squarely in the mouth, so that he fell backward into Little Mike's arms and was then taken to a side exit where he was revived and warned and dismissed.

Lawrence and Scotty and Nick formed a shield around the man in the dinner jacket and Countess Vera, until she recovered, and then Nick escorted them to his office where he offered her a variety of patent reliefs, none of which she accepted.

"Will you leave me alone with my husband, Nick? And have my car pull up to the back exit? I don't think I could face that crowd again. Thanks, Nick. My regrets to Duke that I wasn't able to wish him a happy fiftieth."

Nick shut the door and Vera went up to Bill Nickleson and put her aging hand against his lips. "Don't say a word, I beg you. Whatever you want for the future—divorce, separation, marriage of convenience—I promise I will go along with it. But just for the moment, Bill, even if it's only from pity, hold me close."

He took her in his arms. "I think we should open the Palm Beach house for Thanksgiving, Vera. Just you and I and our son. Family. We'll get a goose which I always think is far more appetizing than a turkey and . . ."

"Stop, Bill," Countess Vera said, for once not caring about her makeup. "You're making me cry so dreadfully."

Chapter Six

LAWRENCE JOINED Nick at the door. "The carriage trade seems to prefer the back door tonight. There's more limousines in the alley than on Madison Avenue. When's Duke making his entrance?"

"Any second," Nick said, watching Brette in the main dining room accept a glass of champagne from Nelson Doubleday.

"Then I'd better get downstairs. You'll buzz me?" Nick said that he would. "Any luck with The Missing Gold Key?" Lawrence asked Bob Walker.

"Nope," Bob Walker said, looking up from his master list. "But the night's still young."

"And you're so beautiful," Lawrence said, leaving for the kitchen.

A few moments later Robert called downstairs and told Nick that Duke was on his way. Nick signaled Lawrence in the kitchen, the lights were lowered and the piano player engaged for the occasion began to play on the old white upright that had originally stood in the Club Room, "A Room With a View," which had been suggested as Duke's favorite song.

The restaurant suddenly became very still, much stiller,

Nick thought, than it had any right to be considering the number and style of the people in it. The brass elevator doors opened and a beaming, aged Duke Greene came into the room, SayDee on his arm.

Everyone stood up and clapped as Duke led the way to the first table where Nick was waiting to seat him and his duchess. "I've always wanted to sit at the best table," Duke said, putting one arm around Nick's shoulder and Nick could feel him trembling both with illness and exhilaration.

Then the lights went even farther down and a pontifical Lawrence led a cart from the kitchen, across the main dining room, to Duke's table, to the best table. On the cart, piloted by Maurice Gotlib, with Charles and Georgio in hushed attendance, was a fifty-tier cake and on the center of the top layer stood a man in tails and white tie.

"If Cecil could've only been here today," Duke said, and then he embraced Maurice Gotlib, who had been with them almost since the beginning and then he shook hands with all the members of the staff, saving a special hug for Lawrence who, Duke said, "never gets any work done because he's always having parties. Wonderful parties."

"Step on my toe," SayDee said to Nick as the staff went back to their places, the lights went up, the piano player segued into a Noel Coward/Cole Porter medley and Lawrence began to cut the cake.

"Why?"

"I think I'm going to cry and I don't want to embarrass Duke."

"That's all right, SayDee," Nick said, handing her his handkerchief. "You won't be alone. There's not a dry eye in the house."

They watched as the richest, most famous, most glamorous, most powerful people in the world lined up to shake Duke's hand, to kiss his cheek, to thank him for giving them the perfect setting in which they pursued their pleasure.

Valida Rand had been one of the first in line.

"I've been looking for you for hours," Laddy Wister said. "Where have you been?"

"Upstairs. Loading up on caviar. Look at that man," she said, pointing to Duke being kissed by Bo Derek. "Look at him! Doesn't he make you want to live? *Look at him, Laddy, look!* He's dying, riddled with cancer and pain and yet he's still pinching Bo Derek's behind, if he can find it under that gypsy creation she's got herself into. There is a man, Laddy, who can still wheel and deal in a commodity most people never touch: joy. Pure, unadulterated pleasure. I'm going to miss Duke Greene, Laddy, in much the same way I miss Frank."

"Are you drunk, Val?"

"Blotto. Look, Jackie Onassis and, is that Kissinger? Yes, it is—are getting up. Come on, Laddy, we'll have a nice little corner table to play on."

She was wearing black but it was a lively black with a scarf and sequins and it moved against her body in a way that made her seem infinitely attractive, mysterious. Laddy, following her, inadvertently walked into Georgio who had been carrying a drink which spilled down the front of his white jacket.

"Sorry," Laddy said as Georgio picked up the glass, which hadn't broken, and Lawrence told him to change his jacket.

"Daisy sends her regrets," Laddy said when he was seated, his earnest blue eyes looking confused, as if he were a boy who knew he knew the correct answers but had failed the exam nonetheless.

"Send her mine."

"She said she had a headache. Truth is, she gets nervous at big parties. Feels she can't hold her own."

"No one can say Daisy Monaco doesn't know her limitations."

"Val," Laddy said, taking one of her hands in his. "I spoke to Harry myself this morning. Val, he won't make *Neon Lights* with you in it. That's his last word."

"Laddy, I wouldn't let Harry Monaco make *Neon Lights* with me in it. I don't trust Harry Monaco. Not simply because he's a thief or because he spawned that goldfish you're currently mated to. But because Harry Monaco is just another of those child-men Hollywood seems to produce in such numbers. He, like they, have no conscience, no artistic judgment, no moral values. He, like they, is an overgrown pimp, pandering to the lowest common denominator of taste." She lifted her champagne glass. "I say to hell with Harry Monaco, Laddy."

"Harry will never let me make it if he's not producing, Val. Believe me."

"Fasten your seat belt, darling, and hold on tight. Mama has a jolt in store for you: I don't need you, now, Laddy, darling. While you and Harry and Daisy were playing with each other, pretending to read the script, Dustin Hoffman was trying very hard to break his commitment to *Moon Man*. I am delighted to say that he has done just that.

"He and Frankenheimer were signed this morning at the big oval table in Saunders's office high up in the Chrysler Building. Metro is to be the home studio. I am the exec producer as well as the leading lady. Cameras will roll within the month."

"But, Val . . ."

"What I'm telling you, and Harry and Daisy, Laddy, is thank you very much and we'll be in touch."

Laddy Wister stared at her, not knowing what to do.

"That was your exit line, darling. Let's take it from the top: thank you very, very much, Mr. Wister. I shall be in touch.

"Oh, God, please don't look like that, Laddy. It was that puppy-dog look—well, that and certain other physical attributes—that got me to marry you in the first place.

"But it doesn't play anymore, Laddy, sweet. Not much at any rate. Listen, you've got hundreds, thousands of movies to make. I have just this one. I've got to be as ruthless and as terrible as Harry Monaco if it's going to be the film Frank intended it to be.

"Yes, I used you and Harry and Daisy. As soon as word went out that you were interested, *Neon Lights* became a very hot property, indeed. All we needed was for you—you and Harry and Daisy—to be interested.

"Go home to Daisy, Laddy. Go make your hot damn movies. You do them better than anyone else and I virtually guarantee you that years from now, we'll all be standing in line—well, I shan't be standing but we won't think of that—patiently waiting to get into Laddy Wister Festivals at the New Yorker."

Suddenly he pulled her close. "I love you, Val. I always

have. I'm always going to. Stay with me tonight, just this one night."

"No, Laddy, darling. It wouldn't be one night. Our chemistry is too good. It would be six loathsome months. Laddy," she pushed him away, "I'm one hundred and five years old and you're thirty going on eighteen. Please go away before I bite your biceps and ravish you right here on the floor of 44. Not another word. We'll see each other in Hollywood at Sue Mengers's parties and we'll be all bright and clever with one another."

He stood up and looked down at her. "And just for the record, Laddy," she said before he turned to go, "I'll always love you, too."

Even in that crowd there was the usual turning of heads as Laddy Wister made his way across the room.

Saunders, immaculate in his custom-made double-breasted dinner jacket, took his place. "Why are you crying, my dear?" he asked, signaling for a Scotch. "You've had the most triumphant day, Valida. You're going to make Frank's film Frank's way and you beat that secondhand snake, Harry Monaco, at his own pasttime. But those aren't tears of victory, are they, Valida?"

"I don't feel very much as if I've beaten a snake, Saunders. More as if I've stepped on a very beautiful, very muscular butterfly. But I'll get over it," she said, loosening the silk scarf around her neck, taking off one of her ruby earrings because it pinched, throwing it into her purse. "Did you bring the contracts? I want to take another look at them."

He took her hand. "Do you want to sleep with me, Valida?" he asked again.

"At the moment? I don't think so."

"Do you want to marry me, Valida?"

"That's a possibility, Saunders. A distinct possibility. We'll talk about it as soon as *Neon Lights* is wrapped. I'll come back to civilization and you can treat me to lunch at Duke's 44 Club and propose to me and I'm very certain I will say yes. Just make sure you book the best table."

Brette had joined Duke and SayDee at the best table as had Igor Strauss and Marquita. To Marquita's unaided eyes—she made it a point not to wear glasses in public—Duke seemed the same as he always had as he reminisced about times past. Cointreau was ordered, the bottle brought, and Duke talked of the time Chevalier brought a fifteen-year-old girl for dinner; of Caruso and Lanza and Ava Gardner; of Jimmy Donahue pouring a Pernod over the Duchess of Windsor's lap, quite on purpose, while her husband worried about his cigar. The three of them—Duke, Marquita, Igor—raked up scandals and anecdotes and stories—real and imagined, and told them to Brette and SayDee as if they had happened yesterday.

Only Nick, and perhaps SayDee, knew what effort lay behind the Duke's charm. There were only a couple of dozen or so guests left, the others having gone home or to Régine's.

"Nick," Lawrence said, coming up to where Nick stood with Bob Walker, the detective who had already closed the book which contained the master list of issued gold keys. "Something's wrong."

"What is it?"

Lawrence mopped his egg-shaped face with his handkerchief and looked as if he were going to faint. "Do you want something?" Nick asked. "Scotty, get him a whiskey."

"I was down in the kitchen," Lawrence said after he had sipped at the glass Scotty had brought him. "I was talking to Maurice about the cake and we were arguing about which dessert wine should have been served with it when Georgio came out of the waiters' dressing room without his shirt on.

"I had sent him down to change after someone spilled a glass of something or other on him. He said there weren't any clean shirts. I couldn't help staring at him. He was wearing a gold chain around his neck. You know what was hanging from it, Nick? Dinah Sheridan's key, number seven . . ."

Bob Walker, pushing Lawrence out of his way, talking furiously into a hand-sized walkie-talkie, sped across the Club Room, down the stairs into the kitchen. Several men in dinner jackets followed him.

". . . and then it suddenly occurred to me," Lawrence said as Nick led him to a chair, signaling Mickey to get him another whiskey, "that Georgio didn't work on Thursday night, that he had been called away. 'A friend is dying,' he told me. I took the call myself. It was a woman, a woman with a distinct and familiar voice. I know now, finally—dear

Lord, I'm slow, like some old lady in a Miss Marple thriller—who killed Dinah Sheridan. Nick, where you going?''

''You sit still. I'm going down to the kitchen.''

''No.'' He handed the whiskey glass to Little Mike. ''No. I am going with you.''

The two of them went down the stairs to where Bob Walker and his men stood in front of the waiters' dressing room, a long and low-ceilinged space, filled with lockers and the presence of Georgio. He was at the far end of the dressing room, his back against a barred window. He wore no shirt. The gold key hung like a religious symbol between his massive chest muscles. He was smiling his small-toothed smile and he was sweating and he held his knife in front of him.

''I don't want to shoot him,'' Bob Walker said. ''I sent for tear gas.''

''That won't be necessary,'' Lawrence told him, moving into the dressing room.

''Hey,'' Bob Walker tried to stop him but Nick held him back.

''He knows what he's doing,'' Nick said.

''You'd better hope so.''

Lawrence walked up to within a foot of Georgio. ''I want that knife, Georgio.''

''You sure, Mr. Lawrence? You positive you want this knife?'' He had begun to sweat and his hand was shaking.

''Yes, Georgio. I'm quite certain. I'm ashamed of you. Carrying on like this when you've always been so exemplary a busboy. I had great hopes for you, Georgio. And now this. Please give me that weapon, Georgio, before you cause a greater disturbance. Tonight, of all nights.''

Georgio suddenly, alarmingly, advanced and brandished the knife over Lawrence's chest. Just as suddenly, he flipped the knife around and handed it, handle first, to Lawrence. ''Sorry I caused such a ruckus, Mr. Lawrence,'' he said as Bob Walker and another detective shoved Lawrence out of the way and grabbed onto Georgio's arms, handcuffing them behind his back.

Georgio seemed to be unaware of what was happening to him. ''Was the Duke's fiftieth anniversary a success, Mr. Lawrence?'' he asked as they took him out of the waiters' dressing room to the patrol car in the alley.

"It was a great success, Georgio," Lawrence told him.

"I'm real glad," Georgio said. He got into the patrol car as if he were relieved, not unlike a child finally going on a long promised adventure. Bob Walker sat in the back with him.

As the rest of the staff returned to the kitchen, Nick and Lawrence went up the narrow stairs to the dining room. Lawrence wiped his forehead with a large, white silk handkerchief. "You don't suppose," he said to Nick, "that I could break all the rules and have a third whiskey, do you?"

"I'll pour it myself."

It was time to go, Marquita decided. An entire herd of Auchinclosses had finally left and she and Igor and Brette were the final guests. Duke looked tired. Marquita could see that, even without her glasses.

Brette offered them a ride home in the limousine and Marquita thought and said that was a wonderfully fitting way for them to end their last night in Manhattan.

She kissed Duke good night. He didn't stand but he put his arms around her and held her for a moment. His cheeks felt cold. Igor went to shake his hand but his Russian blood got the best of him. He embraced Duke and kissed him on both cheeks and came away with his eyes more watery than usual. Marquita slipped her thin arm out of her frayed sable coat and put it around her husband and led him down to the car. Brette joined them a moment later and directed the chauffeur with her usual polite firmness.

After a moment Marquita put her free arm around Brette's shoulders and suddenly the girl was crying as if her heart would break. There was no need to ask her why.

"I never thought," Marquita said to herself as she held the crying old man and the crying young woman in her arms, as the car drove through the silent and somehow secure Manhattan streets, "that I was very maternal and yet here I am." And then tears formed in her own eyes as she thought of Duke and 44 and such never-to-be-regained glories as a seat at the best table.

"Do you want to go upstairs, Duke?" Nick said, standing over Duke at the best table, not liking the color of his skin or the way his hand shook when he brought the glass to his lips.

He had switched back to Roederer's Cristal champagne, served in the Baccarat tulip glass he loved because it was fragile and perfectly shaped and very expensive.

"What did you say?" he asked Nick.

"I wanted to know if you're okay."

"I'm fine. I just want to sit here for a while. Here at the best table. Sit next to me. Hold my right hand. SayDee has my left, don't you, Duchess?" She said she did as Nick sat down and took hold of his father's hand.

"Cheap irony, as Noel used to like to say. You're the two people I should have recognized above all others but all I did was hide you in the bedrooms of my life. That's my biggest regret. That's what I would change if I had my life to live over."

He looked around the main dining room, at the empty tables, and then across the foyer, into the Club Room, at his portrait in white tie and tails. Beyond that was the wall of celebrity photographs. With sure eyes he picked out one of Cecil and Phebe. Though it was a serious, society photograph, taken just after their honeymoon, he was certain they were smiling at him.

"They've turned the lights down," Duke said, though they hadn't. "I do wish Cecil and Phebe had been here tonight. I miss them so much."

"Duke," SayDee began, but he couldn't hear her.

He was grasping their hands as tightly as he could; his eyes were closing. But suddenly he opened them and he half stood and said, defiantly, to the young man in the portrait on the far wall: "I don't care what anyone says. I've had one hell of a good time."

EPILOGUE

Chapter One

IT'S all been very neat, Nick thought as he sat himself down on the banquette behind the best table and looked around him. Duke's 44 Club was more than temporarily closed. It was deserted.

The funeral, discreetly Jewish, but not so anyone would notice, had been held on the Sunday following Duke's death. The only mourners invited were Lawrence and Maurice Gotlib and the staff. SayDee, Nick, Peter, and Brette represented "family." The notice Peter had placed in the *Times* had requested, in lieu of flowers, that donations be sent to the Memorial Sloan-Kettering Cancer Center. It had also stated that the funeral would be private.

Duke would have hated it, Nick thought. He'd have wanted to go out in a custom Silver Cloud, at midnight, kleig lights illuminating Fifth Avenue, Roederer's served to the sobbing, cheering mob.

The Duke is dead. Long live the Duke.

But his son, Peter, was having none of it. "We want to call as little attention to his passing as possible," Peter had said, looking at Nick, waiting for an argument, lighting one of his sweet Egyptian cigarettes.

Why, would it be bad for business? Nick wanted to ask but

didn't. There was no argument. Peter was right. Peter was legal. Peter was the heir.

And that's what it said in the full-length biography the *Times* gave Duke on Saturday. It had begun on page one with the lead: "Noted Restaurateur/Society Figure, Jacob 'Duke' Greene died yesterday in the restaurant he and his college roommate founded fifty years ago to the day, the world-famous Duke's 44 Club."

There had been pictures of Duke with Tallulah Bankhead, with Eisenhower, with John F. Kennedy. There had been inset photos of his first wife, Laura van der Velde, of Irene, and their son, Peter. It had been the full, first-class treatment. That, Nick thought, Duke would have enjoyed.

The funeral itself, at Campbell's, was another story. Too quiet by half. Even the cemetery in Metuchen, New Jersey, a "perpetually cared for" monumentless golf course of a cemetery, seemed like a set for a second-rate production.

Nick stood far back, a respectful distance from the chief mourners. He didn't cry. He didn't feel much of anything, just a sort of yawning emptiness in his gut, a sort of neutral numbness in his mind. Only SayDee had displayed emotion, enormous tears dripping down her full cheeks, destroying the carefully applied layers of pancake makeup.

Peter and Brette had stood straight and nobly British, the pea-soup November day lending authenticity to their postures. Peter hadn't said a word to Nick. But he had extended his hand when Nick entered the chapel at Campbell's and gave a melancholy, Hamlet smile when Nick took it.

So we're to be pals, Nick had thought as the rabbi in mufti spoke of Duke in heavenly terms (". . . never a more generous, openhanded . . ."). Death has robbed us of our grounds for enmity. The rightful son has come into his inheritance. I'm to be the good sport.

And he was. At the cemetery he had stood back and watched Brette and Peter, just as he had when he had been a child, hiding on the kitchen stairs, watching them in their dark blue children's serge greeting guests along with Duke.

He was feeling, he knew, as lonesome as he ever had.

On Monday the will had been read in Duke's drawing room. Nick was sitting at the best table waiting for Peter to come downstairs, because Peter had asked him to wait while he had a few words with the lawyer.

The will had been read by the lawyer, a thin, tobacco-colored man named Sarno who took great pleasure in reading the legalistic phrases, enunciating each one—letting his tongue taste each word—as if he had invented them. For all Nick knew, he had.

''Can I ask a question?'' SayDee said after he had finished. She was distraught but had made an effort to pull herself together for the will reading, wearing one of her more subtle black dressing gowns which might have served as a costume for the merry widow. Though she hadn't looked at all merry.

''Yes, of course,'' Sarno said, smiling.

''Do I have this right? I get a quarter of a million bucks?''

The lawyer had said, patiently, patronizingly, that that wasn't exactly what he had read. SayDee had been left a trust fund of two hundred and fifty thousand dollars, the interest from which would be hers for life. After her demise, the capital would go to Duke's two grandchildren.''

''I thought he was broke,'' SayDee said.

''His fortune was considerably diminished in recent years,'' Sarno told her as if he were rebuking her for a lesson poorly learned. But he had had the wisdom to set aside certain money. SayDee also received, he told her, the use of 44's duplex for life, maintenance free.

''That Duke,'' SayDee said, beginning to cry again, holding a huge, floral handkerchief to her red nose, ''he thought of everything.''

Nick had been left fifty thousand dollars and the portrait by Chamberlain which decorated the Club Room.

Peter, in lieu of the two million dollars agreed upon in the divorce settlement between his father and mother, was left all of Duke's shares of the restaurant which included the building in which it existed.

Nick sat at the best table and waited for the elevator door to open, for Peter and Brette and the little lawyer to come out. He was anxious to get away. He was impatient to begin his own period of mourning.

When they finally descended, he found a newcomer had been added to the party. Morgan Brooks had joined the others by going up to the duplex via the street entrance.

"How are you, Nick?" Brooks asked, coming toward him with his manicured hand outstretched, shaking Nick's hand, sitting next to him on the banquette as if they were old acquaintances. "Awfully sorry about Duke. But he did die in style. Chose his moment, what?"

Morgan Brooks looked around the room, his tiny eyes and earnest face contracting slightly. "First step is to get rid of all these little tables. We can get twice as many people in this room with a little planning."

He looked up, surprised, as Nick stood up. "Naturally we want to keep you on, Reo. Want you to help guide the old ship through it new incarnation. You can virtually name your own price."

"My best wishes for a successful launch," Nick said. "But I'm afraid I'm not going to be on board, Mr. Brooks."

He called down into the kitchen and a rather restrained Lawrence came up the stairs. He nodded his egg-shaped head at Brette and ignored the others. He followed Nick into the Club Room and helped him undo the portrait of Duke.

"You need a hand with that?" Brooks asked. Peter, a thin smile on his face, watched as Nick and Lawrence carried Duke's portrait through the foyer to the door. "We can have it sent, you know," Brooks continued. "There's no need . . ."

"We don't have that far to go," Nick said. He looked at Peter, who was standing, one hand on Brette's shoulder. Then he looked into Brette's violet eyes and thought they seemed less bright than usual. She turned away, busying herself with her furs.

He had his answer without having to ask the question again. "Good-bye, Peter," Nick said. "Good-bye, Brette."

And in the next moment Nick and Lawrence and the painting of Duke were gone.

Chapter Two

"MY LORD," Lawrence said, coming up the stairs from the kitchen into the drawing room, "what in God's name is that?" He pointed a white, plump finger at a crate which stood in the middle of the empty room in the town house Victor Reo had left to his son, Nick.

"Do I know?" Nick asked. He put down the ledger he had been studying and joined Lawrence who was experimentally tapping at the wooden crate. "The delivery men just brought it."

"I hate to think what it might be," Lawrence went on, circling the offensive object. "You don't suppose," he asked, stepping back in what seemed like genuine horror, "that it's yet one more Maurice Gotlib extravagance, a three-thousand-dollar juicer or a contraption for turning out perfect *quenelles de brochet*, do you? Does it have any French labels on it?"

"No," Nick assured him.

"Then perhaps we should look on the bright side of the coin. Perhaps Mrs. Guest took pity on us, two impecunious though well-seasoned restaurateurs beginning a new venture with a minimum of money and a maximum of élan, and sent us a present. Let us open this gift, Nicklaus, and see what we shall see, shall we?"

"By all means," Nick said, looking with a mixture of fondness and exasperation at Lawrence, who had already borrowed a hammer and a crowbar from the carpenters working in the other room and was attacking the crate with the gusto he usually reserved for caviar.

"Dear Lord," Lawrence said, stepping back, kicking some stray excelsior out of the way. He stared at the uncrated object that stood in the middle of the room, for once at a lost for words.

It was the table Cecil Townsend's stepfather had left him. It was the table that for fifty years was known as the best table at Duke's 44 Club.

"Who, do you think, sent it?" Lawrence asked, brushing its top with his sleeve.

"Morgan Brooks, probably, as a goodwill gesture," Nick said, staring down at his reflection in the beautifully polished mahogany top.

"I shouldn't think so, unless it's booby-trapped. Word is that 44, under its new management, is slipping rather badly. One wishes," Lawrence said, clasping his hands together, "one could say one was sorry. However, I for one cannot. I can only say . . ."

What Lawrence could only say was lost when he realized, belatedly, that there was another presence in the room; a gardenia-scented presence. He turned to find Brette in the doorway.

"My dear," Lawrence said, moving around the table, allowing that young woman to kiss his cheek and even going so far as to peck at hers. "My dear. I should have known. What a delightful double present. The best table and you. What are you doing in New York? Shall I nip down and have Maurice do one of his little omelets I seem to remember your savoring? Or shall I . . . Dear me, I seem to be the only person in this room capable of talking." He looked at Brette looking at Nick and he smiled. "I think that I had better go have a talk with Maurice Gotlib. He's getting entirely above himself lately."

"What *are* you doing in New York, Brette?" Nick asked after Lawrence had left.

She undid the catch of the fur coat she wore and removed it along with the matching hat. In the dim light from the fireplace, she looked—Nick thought—like the two million dollars he hadn't been able to raise.

"I came to give you your present," she said, reaching across the table, placing her thin, elegant hands on his shoulders. He pulled her to him and kissed her.

"The answer to the question is yes, Nick." He kissed her again and then moved around the table and held her to him.

"I've missed you so much," he said. "You have no idea."

"I've left him, Nick. He has his theater and all the money he'll ever need now." She waited for him to kiss her again and after he did, she said, "I've left him for you, Nick."

"Yeah?" he asked, looking into those violet eyes for a moment. Then he took her hand and led her upstairs to his bedroom.

Much later, after they had made love and shared take-in Chinese food with Lawrence and Maurice Gotlib who hadn't been able, after all, to get the new stove to work, he took her on a tour of the town house.

He showed her the newly outfitted kitchen, dominated by the recalcitrant stove; he explained where the tables and the bar were going to go; he ended the tour in front of the fireplace over which Duke's portrait smiled down at them.

"He looks as if he belongs here," Brette said. "He seems very comfortable."

Nick looked at her for a moment. "I have one more question," he said. "What about your children?"

She wouldn't look at him. She continued to stare up at Duke. "They didn't want to come to America. Not yet. They said perhaps in the summer. They talked about their school and their friends and a tea Princess Alexandra is giving to which they're invited."

He put his arms around her and held her close. "If I thought for a moment they cared, I would have never left, Nick. Never. But they have so much life, so many engagements, pursuits, plans. I only fit into their schedule for Sunday breakfasts and I'm certain Peter will find a replacement soon enough, one the girls will approve of.

"They've never approved of me. They're much happier that I left. They think it's glamorous, having a divorced mother and father, especially with the mother—who never quite fits in—off in America. They're Peter's children, Nick.

"Certainly I might have stayed and Peter and I could have worked something out. He was willing. It would have been nice and secure and I would have had a far from terrible life.

"But there was one thorn in the rosebush."

"What was that?"

"My need for you, Nick. It makes everything else—money, houses, a title—insignificant. I love you so very much, Nick."

He went to her and they held onto one another for a moment until there was a discreet cough in the room, announcing Lawrence's presence.

"Is there any way you can let go of her, Nick, while *I* ask a question?"

"No," Nick said. "I'm afraid she'll disappear."

"Then I'll ask it anyway: now that we've got it," he said, pursing his lips, pointing to the table, "what are we going to do with it?"

"We're going to find the most inconvenient spot in this impractical, ridiculous excuse for a restaurant and we're going to put it right there and everyone in New York, in the world, is going to fight to sit at it. We'll call it the best table."

Chapter Three

AGAIN IT was a sweltering Saturday in August. It was nearly two P.M. and every table was taken except for the best table. Grand Duchess Rose-Marie of Rumania's secretary had called at the last moment and said the duchess was suffering from heat prostation, that the doctors had positively ordered her to the ocean for the weekend.

She didn't say which ocean, Lawrence thought as he studied his reservation list and decided he would give Mrs. Carlos de Kalb the inestimable honor of being seated at the best table.

He didn't know her personally but he knew that her husband was one of the three richest men in Mexico City and, as more and more rich people seemed to be coming from remote places south of the border, Lawrence thought it would be a wise public relations move. The best table wouldn't go empty for want of a suitable luminary and La de Kalb would return to her hacienda, singing the praises of New York's newest, chicest, and best restaurant, Nick's.

Lawrence later reflected that it might not have happened had Nick been there, had he not let Brette convince him to spend the weekend in Connecticut, at her Aunt Helen's, riding horses and sailing boats and engaging in other pastimes no serious restaurateur should ever engage in.

Still, ultimate responsibility had to rest on his shoulders. He should have recognized her. But again, there were mitigating circumstances. She had had her nose bobbed, her hair bleached, her face lifted, and three inches of unsightly fat removed from her waist. Also she wore an enormous black straw hat with an attention-getting rose on its brim and those huge sunglasses popular that season.

She came in with a great deal of fuss, followed by the lawyers Cohen. Lawrence gave her his half bow, pretended to study the reservation list, turned and smiled, and led her and her bevy of lawyers to the first table on the left.

"I think you must be mistaken," she said, halting in front of that table, immediately noting that it was in the most inconvenient spot, right near the entrance. Everyone who had to leave—or enter—would have to pass by. Gusts of hot air would assail her across the foyer. She would be continually jostled by waiters.

"I'm Mrs. Carlos de Kalb," she said. "And this table won't do at all. Not at all."

Lawrence executed a quarter bow, apologized in a few words, and led Mrs. de Kalb and her party to the back dining room which was upholstered in dark, cool leather and where no one could be seen. "This is more like it," she said, allowing the senior Cohen to help her into her chair.

Sweating lightly, Lawrence returned to his post, cursing himself and the glass of white wine he had allowed Maurice to press upon him at noon.

For he had finally recognized Mrs. Carlos de Kalb. Not too long before, she had been Mrs. Henry de Petrie and not too long before that she had been known as Mrs. Morton Landau. Soon it was evident from her lawyer luncheon guests, she would be known by yet another name.

Lawrence made a careful notation on a pale green card in his file. From that moment on Marion de Kalb would only be known as *persona non grata* on his premises.

For she had once again given up the one item in the world—well, in her world—that only a subtle and perfectly balanced combination of money, power, social understanding, background, blue blood, and beauty can buy: the best table.